A DELICATE BETRAYAL

JESSACA WILLIS

A Delicate Betrayal.

Hardcover ISBN: 978-1-953072-09-2
Paperback: 978-1-953072-08-5
eBook ASIN: B0BBM1SX7Z

Front cover art by Fay Lane Cover Design.
Editing by Kate Anderson with *Red Ink Ninja*.
Proofreading by Colby Bettley with *Novel & Noted*.

❀ Created with Vellum

A DELICATE BETRAYAL

JESSACA WILLIS

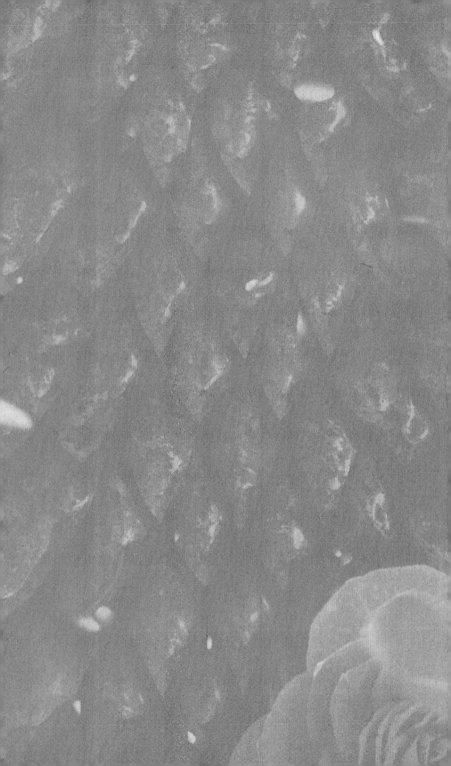

A DELICATE BETRAYAL

JESSACA WILLIS

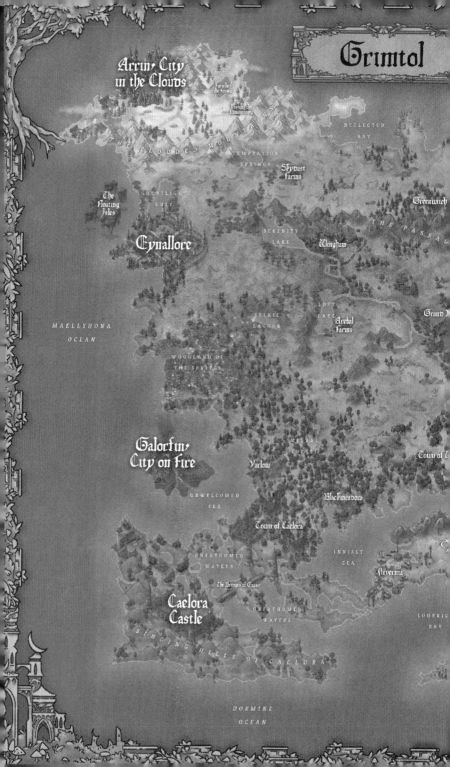

ISAZ
OCEAN

ISAZ
OCEAN

Fortress of Vaught Back

NOFASKI
SEA

SNOW MOUNTAINS

SpirisFogar
(North)

Kingdom of
Irongate

KINGSOL
LAKE

Silent Crossing

HAILSTONE
SEA

SeFogar

SFogar

Thornwood

The Hollows

RepsFogar
(South)

LAKE OF
SHADOWS

The Secret Barrow
Zeush Grimeshane

DORMINE
OCEAN

Shavemoor

Rayong

MISTMOOR
FENS

Hanvor

DESOLATE PLAINS
OF SADRE

The Great City
of Vallonde

Fortress of
Thunder

BAY OF
LOST SOULS

Vallonde
Temple

Vallonde
Ruins

The Isle of
Lost Souls

The Spears
of Barpa

The Cursed
Prison

DORMINE
OCEAN

MAW OF
DEATH

Mutiny
Bay

Hidden
Oasis

CARMAERN
BAY

MORE BOOKS BY JESSACA WILLIS

THE CURSED KINGDOMS OF GRIMTOL

A Delicate Betrayal, Book 0

A Reign of Ashes, Book 1

TBA

REAPERS OF VELTUUR

Assassin Reaper, Book 0

Soul of the Crow, Book 1

Heart of the Sungem, Book 2

Fate of the Vulture, Book 3

PRIMORDIALS OF SHADOWTHORN

Shadow Crusade, Book 1

Blighted Heart, Book 2

Immortal Return, Book 3

BLOOD & MAGIC ETERNAL

Hunger & Cursed Shadows, Book 0

Blood & Magic Eternal, Book 1

Death & Wicked Monsters, Book 2

ACADEMY OF THE FORSAKEN

The Demon in the Mirror, Book 0

TBA

THE AWAKENED

For the broken, the beaten, and the betrayed.

And for Penelope Windell.

1

QUEEN'S TEARS

AENWYN

Marrying a king was not the joyous event that Aenwyn had imagined it would be.

Where she came from weddings involved music, laughter, food, and enough mead to keep the Skogar folk singing, dancing, and warming each other's furs well into first-hours of the following day.

Weddings in Caelora seemed to take a different approach.

It seemed she would die of boredom by the time she reached her betrothed at the end of the aisle, the entire court gathered around her. She had been instructed to step in time with the melody, but that was proving difficult since the song gave her no sense of invigoration or joy. It was utterly lifeless by comparison to the bone-chilling drumming of her people. It lacked the impassioned harmonizing she was used to, the wailing choruses that could bring one to tears or raise a roaring army to battle.

With a pained smile, she passed the troubadours where they had gathered at the edge of the throne room with their pipes, flutes, and strings, doing her best to appear grateful for the dull

1

and repetitive tune, when in reality it made her want to rip right out of the breezy, silken gown she had been forced to wear.

That would really get the people talking. As if they weren't doing enough of that already. Everywhere she looked in the gilded, gleaming throne room, people were whispering to each other at her expense.

"She doesn't deserve to be queen."

"The savage witch should burn!"

"She'll destroy the kingdom from the inside out."

Aenwyn heard them all. She felt their ire like a hot iron poker pressed against the freckled flesh of her face.

"Careful now," cautioned the grizzled man walking arm-in-arm beside her. His heavy elbow nudged the tender place between her ribs. "Or that frown will cause a war."

Aenwyn's chest tightened. War was the exact opposite of what she wanted. It was the whole reason she'd gotten herself into this arranged marriage mess.

She glanced to the man keeping her steady. Baug the Bear he was called, the fearsome leader of the distrusting, isolated Skogar people. But to her, he was more than that. There was a gentleness in his heart that he kept hidden, but she had witnessed it from the very first day they met, nearly three years ago now. The day he rescued her from the deserted island where she had lost everyone she'd ever known.

Baug the Bear had given her a choice: stay with the dead and decayed or join him as his daughter.

He'd been her savior then as he was her savior now.

Through his presence, she found the strength she needed to keep walking with her head held high—until her envious gaze noticed the famed bear pelt and battle axes he'd been allowed to wear. Meanwhile, she hadn't even been granted the courtesy of donning something more suitable like one of her own furs or even the elk skull crown that would've been expected for the daughter of a Skogar chieftain to wear on the day of her wedding.

The Caelorans didn't respect her people. Her culture. And they definitely didn't respect *her*. In time, she hoped to earn that respect.

When her father noticed her eyes lingering on him too long, he gave her arm a comforting squeeze. "If you've changed your mind, it's not too late to—"

"No," Aenwyn said, fixing her attention forward. This was what she wanted, what she needed to do for her people. She plastered on a thin smile and beheld the crowd of judgmental lords and ladies who'd gathered around the pine runner. "This marriage is what Skogar needs."

"Skogar needs nothing," he growled, somehow holding onto the pleasant look he'd donned since their arrival in Caelora. "We have survived this long without an alliance. We don't need one now."

Aenwyn barely refrained from rolling her eyes, and only because of their rapt audience. This was not the first time she and her father had broached this conversation, and she wasn't about to delve into it again. Especially not here, now, on today of all days. It was not only risky but increasingly futile.

For the life of her, she would never understand how he could be so sure that Skogar was safe without a Caeloran alliance any longer. Not after what she'd done to their previous king and queen...

"I have to do this," she whispered, and he nodded. He understood, even if he didn't agree.

Her noble smile didn't falter again as they made their way across the rest of the throne room, though it never seemed to quite have the effect she wanted it to have. Of the hundreds of lords and ladies gathered to witness this momentous day in history, every single one they'd passed possessed the judgmental gaze of someone who had never seen a member of the Skogar before. They watched the two of them the way a mother fox stood between her young and a circling wolf, ready to defend what they loved to the death.

Aenwyn was used to judgment.

When Baug the Bear had taken her into his own home, and for the better part of a year the Skogar people were weary of her, hesitant to accept her as one of their own. In the end, she had earned their loyalty. Their trust. Their love.

She could do it again. Be an outsider for a time until she'd proven herself.

She had to.

But as Aenwyn strode down the aisle, the lightweight wedding gown making her feel exposed and fragile without the heavy pelts of fur she was accustomed to, she somehow knew this endeavor would be far more challenging than winning the hearts of the Skogar. Perhaps it was the air, taut with tension, or perhaps it was her inclination for the sight, but something told her that she wouldn't be able to impress the people of Caelora with her useful abilities like setting bear traps, skinning deer, and navigating the lands by starlight.

No, she feared that Baug had been right. The people here—especially the ladies, whom Baug told her would be the people she would interact with the most after her wedding day—were far more interested in gossip, fashion, and religion. Topics she knew nothing about and cared even less for.

Fortunately, she wasn't marrying *all* of Caelora.

Aenwyn only truly needed to make one person fall in love with her. And he just so happened to be the most powerful man in not only the Caelora Kingdom, but all of Grimtol.

As Aenwyn took the final step and Baug gave her arm to the regal King Everard, she beheld her betrothed for the first time. It was true what they said about him.

King Everard had a striking beauty that reminded her of freshly forged, gleaming steel. He was all sharp angles and fierce edges. The way he looked down upon her, his cold, grey eyes piercing straight through her, she could feel the power radiating off of him. Feel his possessiveness. His dominance.

Before today, she had found comfort in knowing that many people who found themselves in arranged marriages grew into the relationship, how some of them even eventually found love. But as King Everard's cold hands clutched her arm and hoisted her up the steps, Aenwyn understood that she would find neither. This marriage would be just as glacial as his eyes, as his touch. And she had willingly walked herself into it.

Oblivious to the tears forming in her eyes, King Everard shoved a ring onto her middle finger. It wasn't *the* ring. They hadn't even spoken their vows yet. So the gesture took her by surprise.

Aenwyn glanced over her shoulder, back to her father, before returning her confused gaze to the black band topped with a sky-blue stone. It was the same shade as the dragon that haunted her dreams. The dragon that she'd hatched from an egg on her sixteenth birthday with a mere touch of her hand. The same dragon that had killed King Everard's parents.

"What's this?" Aenwyn stammered, daring to look up at the king. She'd be damned if she would be in a loveless marriage *and* cower to her husband's authority. "I wasn't aware it was your custom to exchange gifts the day of the wedding."

King Everard shifted his attention to the priest, but he answered his soon-to-be wife. "It isn't. But I am aware of your...condition. The visions that plague you."

The way he said *condition*, like it was a disease to be feared and contained, rather than the blessing she'd been raised to see it as. Baug had warned her about this too. As the Skogar had once coexisted with the Sky-Blessed demigods in the northern regions of Grimtol, their people were not afraid of magic, but rather embraced it. That sentiment was not shared in other regions of the realm, however. Especially not in Caelora.

Still, she hadn't expected *this*. She hadn't even known the king would know about her power of sight.

"This will suppress the magic that's been ailing you," King Everard said dismissively.

He gestured for the priest to begin the ceremony, but Aenwyn interrupted again.

"I appreciate the sentiment, but I assure you, it's no ailment," she said, beginning to twist the ring free. "The visions can be quite useful. I imagined they could be of use to you, even. In time, should you so choose—"

Fingers that felt like talons clamped around her hands.

"Don't," he said in warning, a hush befalling the room behind them. "The ring will remain on your finger for as long as we are wed. Do you understand?"

Aenwyn's confusion was quick to burn with ire.

She wasn't some helpless, senseless girl for him to dictate. She was the daughter of a chieftain. She was a seeress and sorceress, a woman who had slain a wild boar with her bare hands by the young age of fourteen and could very likely bury an axe into this king's skull should she ever need to.

But her father's words echoed in her mind. *"Careful now, or that frown will cause a war."*

Aenwyn did not convince her father to strike a marital alliance with Caelora just for her to ruin it the day of the wedding. She came to repent, to right the wrongs she'd made.

Gritting her teeth, Aenwyn twisted the ring back into place. When she smiled at her betrothed, she could've sworn that something inside her was already beginning to wither and die. "Of course, my love."

King Everard waved her off. "There's no need for false pretenses." Then turning to the priest, he ordered, "Please, let us get this over with so that the rest of the Skogar filth may leave my halls."

It made her fingers bite into her palms to hear him speak of her people so caustically. But it was also precisely why she was here today.

For Skogar, Aenwyn reminded herself as the rest of the dismal day unfolded. She would do this for Skogar.

2

WAKING IN DARKNESS

AENWYN

Bloodred flames roared so close to Queen Aenwyn's face that she finally awoke from her nightmare. The fire disintegrated and the king's pitch-black bedchamber filled her vision. The agonizing screams, however, still rang in her ears. Chilling. Horrific.

But it was the assault on her stiff body that caused her the most alarm.

The queen couldn't move. Not so much as wiggle a toe or a finger. Her body was as rigid as death where it rested atop the plush, royal bed that now felt more like a pyre than a place of comfort.

She strained to regain control of herself, of the limbs that had been so easy to move just a few hours before. But no matter her efforts, they wouldn't obey.

With fear so close to her heart from having just narrowly evaded a blast of dragon fire, it was quick to gnaw at her now as unhelpful thoughts whispered into her ear of their dark promises.

What if she never moved again?

What if she was frozen like this, helplessly trapped and forever petrified?

What if it lasted for so long that the nurses finally gave up on her? Or worse, what if the king grew weary of allowing such a frozen, dead existence that he finally had her burned for the wicked magic that he believed to have seized her?

Aenwyn could feel the scream forming at the base of her throat, like the talons of a dozen frantic crows shredding her vocal cords as they clawed out of her.

But her lips wouldn't so much as part. No cry took flight from her.

The queen was stuck and alone as she always was when the demon-sleep claimed her. A prisoner trapped inside her own mind and body, as if a dark force was trying to bind her there, keep her restrained.

Hot tears seared her vision.

There was nothing more terrifying than being so powerless and helpless to the world.

But this was not her first encounter with the demon-sleep, as her late mother had called it. The debilitated inability to move, the frightfully cynical thoughts, they always passed. And this would too. After all, she was a queen. More than that, she was of the Skogar. She had the willpower of a mountain that had endured a hundred avalanches and somehow stood taller, stronger, for it.

As a girl, her mother had schooled her on how to free herself from the debilitating hold that her nightmares sometimes had. All she had to do was show them no fear.

And so, Aenwyn did just that.

She took a deep, shuddering breath, let the cool night air prick her throat and creep into her lungs, then released it. She inhaled again, this time following the breath all the way from her nose down into the pit of her belly, allowing her awareness to unfold around her until she could feel the warm, silken bedsheets against her skin, hear the deep breathing of her husband next to her, taste the dryness in her mouth.

Whatever darkness had seized her began to relax its grip, and soon the queen could move her toes, her ankles, her knees, hips, elbows, and shoulders. Finally, her body was her own again.

Queen Aenwyn heaved a heavy sigh, and let her head fall to the side, auburn curls cradling her like a soft pillow. The fire in the hearth had almost died, but she could just make out the details of the striking man lying beside her.

King Everard was on his back, blond hair as soft as the feathers of baby birds splayed atop his pillow. His hands were folded neatly atop the smooth plane of his stomach, making him look as majestic and poised in his sleep as he was in wakefulness.

Even with his mouth slightly agape, a snore rumbling softly from his throat, he was still as devastatingly beautiful as he had been on the day of their wedding nearly a year ago.

There had been a time when that realization had saddened her. To know that their connection and attraction would develop no deeper than a surface-level appreciation of each other's physical traits. And although she told herself that her time of grieving their loveless union had long since passed, on nights like these, she knew she was lying to herself.

In the early months of their marriage, Queen Aenwyn had woken him after her nightmares, seeking comfort and warmth after her body had been so utterly violated. To her great dismay, King Everard had waved her off with annoyance, telling her to bother the nursemaids if she needed a stronger sleeping tincture.

She had not bothered him about her nightmares since.

Before melancholy could plummet her further into self-pity, Aenwyn rolled her head back the way it had come and returned to staring up into the gauzy canopy of the king's bed.

The horrific inferno of her nightmare singed the edges of her thoughts, dragging her back down into the burning town from which she'd awoken.

It had been a Caeloran town. Of that much, she was certain. The trees that had surrounded the area were a clear indicator, but ultimately it was the people she saw fleeing in all directions that settled any doubt she might've had about where the dream had taken place. It wasn't that she recognized any of them personally. After all, in the year she'd been queen, she'd only visited Bayeux the one time, and only at the king's request to have her properly anointed in the Xiran Sea.

But Queen Aenwyn didn't need to recognize any of the commoners fleeing around her. She knew they were Caeloran the same way a mother knew when a babe's cry meant it was hungry versus bored. Some truths were simply known through her demon-sleep. Others, she had to work for.

When Aenwyn had touched that strange egg all those years ago, she hadn't known a dragon would emerge from it and lay waste to Grimtol. But something had changed that day. That moment was the first in many threads of fate casting a web around her, and every so often, she could see it weaving into place.

This dream glinted with those ominous threads.

Her connection to the dragon. Her connection to Caelora. All of it was weaving into place around her, not in any way that she could pretend to explain, but she understood it at a visceral level.

Aenwyn remembered watching the people flee, some clinging onto to their wares; some clutching wounded children, wives, and brothers; some engulfed in flames.

Though she couldn't see the dragon, she knew it was just overhead, its mighty wings flapping, another cyclone of fire whirring from deep within its belly.

This was no mere nightmare.

On more nights than not when Queen Aenwyn was invited to share a room with her husband, she found herself startling from sleep in the middle of the night. Sometimes she'd pace the room until her heart would stop racing or take a seat on the chaise near the window and glance out over the quiet kingdom that she was now sworn to represent and protect, or simply lay in bed and wonder how her family and her people were fairing without her, how her sisters were growing into themselves.

In all that time though, since the year she had come to Caelora, the horrors that had invaded her slumber had never felt so real. Not like this.

The web forming around her had finally been disturbed.

Tentatively, Queen Aenwyn put a hand to her cheek, to the heat that she could still feel radiating from her pale, freckled skin. This dream had been different. It had felt like the visions she had been blessed with before King Everard had gifted her the magical ring.

Her confusion was only temporary as Queen Aenwyn fumbled for her middle finger, for the place where that binding ring had lived every day since her wedding.

The flesh was bare now. The ring, gone.

Now, it was often accustomed that a wife would remove her jewelry before bedding her husband. However, that was never the case for this queen and her king.

King Everard, much like many of the denizens of Grimtol, had a deep seeded fear of magic. The ring was an ancient relic that a Caeloran King of old had confiscated from the Sky-Blessed during the Battle for Freedom many generations ago. Or at least, that was what the king had told her about it. It had been presented to her as a gift, a means to soothe an ailment— her demon-sleep and the visions that sometimes overtook her.

But she knew the truth. She knew how he'd lost his family to dragon's fire, two years ago now. How ever since the Ashen rose from the dead, people had become even more wary of magic than they had been back when they merely thought it was a gift from the Sky-Blessed. How the ring was no mere gift. It was a prison. It kept her powers of foresight subdued, and she'd sworn to wear it until her dying breath—or his—all for the sake of an alliance between Caelora and her people.

At the time, it had seemed an easy sacrifice to make.

Now a year into her cold, barren marriage, she sometimes wondered. And it had been that wondering, that inkling of doubt, that had led Queen Aenwyn to remove her ring last night after her husband had spent himself and lay fast asleep beside her. It was that doubt and regret that had her peering into the shimmering, light-blue stone crested atop the black band, wondering who else had stared into its beauty before, and had kept her staring until her eyes had finally slipped shut.

Wearing the ring had been written into their vows. It had been written on the very certificate of which they'd both signed. It had been an oath to the most powerful man in Grimtol, and she'd broken it.

With a start, the queen fumbled through the bedsheets, frantic but as quiet as she could, so as not to arouse her husband. If he awoke and found her without her ring, without her magic in check, she wasn't sure how he'd react.

She *had* to find it.

Jostling the bedsheets at her sides, Queen Aenwyn felt around until her hand skimmed atop something small and circular. Hastily, she shoved the ring back into place and snuck a cautionary glance at the king to make sure he was still sound asleep. Of course, he was. For all the political tension of Grimtol, and the stress of governing the realms' largest country, King Everard somehow managed to sleep as sound as a milk-drunk baby every night.

She wished she could do the same.

But even after pulling herself from the hold of the demonsleep, discovering the missing token of her marriage and finding it again, Aenwyn was still unable to resume anything resembling rest.

The searing heat of the dragon's fire had been too real for her to simply fall back asleep. The threat of danger too poignant; the threads of fate too personal.

If dragons were assaulting her dreams, it was for one reason, and one reason alone.

This was the sign she'd been waiting for.

She might've inadvertently killed King Everard's parents. She might not have been able to bear him an heir in the year they'd been trying to conceive. But *this*. Atonement. *That* she could give him.

The blue dragon was coming for Caelora. And Queen Aenwyn believed she could stop it.

3

INTO THE NIGHT

AENWYN

The demon-sleep might've shown Queen Aenwyn the fiery demise that awaited them, but it hadn't told her how to stop it. For that information, she'd need to use magic, the kind that required blood.

She needed an animal sacrifice.

Any animal would do, but she wasn't used to procuring one for herself. If she were back at home, Baug the Bear would command his people to present his daughter with the heartiest oxen in their herd so that she could prepare it for the ritual. Their people would've celebrated the creature's life, the sacrifice it was making. They would've sung it soothing hymns, fed it a hearty feast, and decorated it with beautiful flower-chain necklaces. The precious creature would've been revered as a hero for the part it was going to play in aiding Aenwyn in finally stopping the dragon she'd brought to life.

But here in Caelora, there would be no such celebration. No veneration.

Whatever creature Queen Aenwyn procured wouldn't have the honored death it deserved. It would be slaughtered, its

15

bloodied corpse discarded, its death a kept secret that no one could ever know.

Unless she succeeded in her mission. Then the whole kingdom would hear the tale of how Queen Aenwyn, daughter of the Chieftain of the Skogar, saved the continent from the dragon's fiery reign.

And she would succeed. She had to. This was Aenwyn's purpose, after all.

For four years, dragons had wreaked havoc on Grimtol. And now she could put an end to it. Or at least put an end to the blue dragon.

First, the matter of her sacrifice.

If Queen Aenwyn were to seek wisdom from the entrails of an animal, she'd need to do so without anyone discovering her, otherwise she'd risk punishment. After all, the use of magic on Caeloran lands remained outlawed.

Fortunately, as far as she could tell, given the throbbing weariness of her bones, they hadn't been resting for long and her husband and the rest of Caelora would remain sound asleep for at least a few hours more. Maybe longer if the moon decided to grace their skies for one of its extended stays. One could never truly tell. The sun and moon were erratic things—dawn, day, dusk, and night fluctuating of their own accord ever since The Day the Land, Sky, and Sea Shook, the bizarre moment in history when the Sky-Blessed had fallen from the clouds all those generations ago and graced the realm with their permanent presence. Sometimes the moon would return after only a few short hours, other times it would vanish for what felt like days, even weeks.

Now the people recounted their days by calling them first-hours, mid-hours, and late-hours, regardless of what the sun and moon were doing.

There was no way of knowing when nightfall would end, or

daylight begin. Nor was there any way for her to tell when the first-hours would begin, and the palace would reawaken.

But until either of those things happened, Aenwyn would use the obscureness of the dark to her advantage.

Slowly, she inched out of bed, careful not to disturb the partition of blankets tucked snugly around King Everard's body like a shield that she could not penetrate.

As she slid one foot and then the other into her slippers, Aenwyn considered her options. She'd need something small. A rat or a mouse. Something that could be easily discarded without anyone noticing.

The kitchen—and perhaps, even more so, the larder—were oftentimes crawling with rodents that no one would mind if one were to go missing. But she didn't want to waste what precious little nightfall she had left chasing down evasive rodents. Not to mention, it was always harder to read the intestines of an animal that was so disease-ridden.

There was another option. A place where they kept an assortment of gray and white birds caged together but only vaguely monitored considering it was so common for them to go missing and the messenger's counts to be off.

The pigeons in the dovecote.

They were small animals which would make the reading more difficult and less nuanced. But at least it would save her some time having to hunt something down.

Throwing on a verdant, velvet robe that matched the deepest shade of her emerald eyes and made her hair look like fire sparking in the middle of a forest, Aenwyn cracked the king's bed chamber door open and slunk out into the chilly hallway.

She turned her back to the room, ready to embark on her stealthy mission to the high tower where the pigeons were kept, but instead of darting into an empty corridor, Aenwyn spun directly into a knight instead.

She gasped.

A rush of air hefted from his lungs, as well.

"Dragon's fire!" the man grumbled, two strong hands clasping around her arms to steady them both. "Watch where you're—"

Their eyes met. Aenwyn dreaded the recognition that flooded his gaze, only because it was always followed by fear.

"M-my queen," the man stammered. As if she was made of fire, he released his hold of her and stooped into a low bow as he staggered backward.

Aenwyn never could tell what they feared more: her being Skogar, and therefore seen as a feral outsider capable of carnage, or if it was the rumors of her powerful magic that kept them at bay, afraid to touch her, afraid to so much as look her in the eyes.

Mostly, she suspected it had to do with her being the king's wife. Her husband might not have shown much interest in her beyond the nights they attempted and failed for an heir, but he was a possessive man by nature. Queen Aenwyn knew as well as any of the guards in his employ that she was not to be touched by anyone. Especially another man.

Little did her husband know that ship had sailed long before they were wed. It was simply the way of her people: be ferocious in battle, be fierce in life, and don't forget to have a good fuck every now and again. It was a simple creed to live by, but she knew the concepts of it evaded the king entirely.

Collecting himself, the knight before her finally straightened. The umber locks that had fallen in front of his face flung back with a quick jerk of his head, revealing a subtle scar that cut across one of his dark eyes.

Aenwyn knew she recognized him—the scar alone was quite memorable, quite intriguing—but she couldn't quite place his name. There were likely thousands of knights under King Everard's command, but he kept a select few of those he trusted most close by. They handled his more sensitive, or dangerous tasks. The ones he couldn't trust to the hands of anyone less than impeccable.

This knight was one of them. She was sure of it.

A hardness settled into his expression, one that seemed quite at home there.

Queen Aenwyn fell under his scrutinizing gaze as the cogs of his mind twisted, beginning to piece together the information available to him: a restless queen wandering into the quiet halls on her own? It wasn't exactly *normal,* and that was precisely why she'd wanted to remain unseen. She didn't need to arouse suspicions. And she didn't need some trusted, astute, loyal knight reporting her strangeness back to the king.

"Are you alright, Queen Aenwyn?" the knight asked, his voice like a brewing storm.

She could tell him about the nightmare. There was enough sincerity in his tone to convince her that he might actually show her some modicum of understanding.

But that's what the king's righthand guards were trained to do. To gain trust. To gain intel. But their loyalties lay exclusively with King Everard.

Besides, she wasn't about to share information of her demon-sleep with a stranger. It was bad enough the whole kingdom knew of her magic and despised her for it. What would they do if they knew she had terrible visions of their kingdom's demise?

When Aenwyn didn't answer him, the knight's worried gaze flicked to the door behind her. "Is the king—"

Now she was drawing far too much suspicion.

Remembering her role, Aenwyn held her head high. Idle conversation was a game for the people of Caelora, one of strategy and oftentimes even flattery. A game that Aenwyn had quickly learned how to play.

"The king is resting," she replied, side-stepping the knight to put some distance between her and the door. Sound traveled easily in a slumbering castle. "And I'd like to keep it that way. He works too hard and takes too few breaks. He deserves to sleep soundly, even if his wife cannot. Surely, a loyal knight such as yourself would agree?"

It wasn't a truth she believed herself, but it was one she'd often heard the king's advisors telling him as they urged him to leave the stressful and sometimes cumbersome decision-making to them. It was true that her only experience of men in power was with Baug the Bear and King Everard, so it was possible she simply didn't comprehend the full weight of the crown. But she could say with certainty that in the past year her husband had taken far more leisurely strolls, naps, and participated in more idle past times than Baug had in the entire three years she'd been living with him.

Granted, King Everard was still in mourning. And grief, Aenwyn knew, required time, solitude, reflection.

"Indeed he does," replied the knight, drawing her away from the darkness of her thoughts that always seemed to be lurking nearby.

Refocusing on the present instead of the gloomy past, she thought she might've detected a hint of wryness in his tone, but she couldn't say for certain. She was too distracted trying to think of an escape plan. She needed an excuse to depart so that she could be on her merry way to the dovecote.

But the knight's fixation on her seemed too heightened already. If she left now, she was almost sure he would follow.

Perhaps she could tell him she was going for a stroll in the garden, to get some fresh air. But that would lead her to the opposite side of the castle. Not to mention, he'd be a terrible guard if he just left her alone outside, no matter how safe the castle walls were meant to be.

"Shall I accompany you to your bed chamber?"

Aenwyn choked on the frigid air in these breezy castle corridors. "Excuse me?"

It wasn't often that someone could make a Skogar woman blush, but here this knight was, making Queen Aenwyn's cheeks burn as fiercely as when they'd been branded by the dragon's flames in her vision.

She didn't think it possible for a queen to be propositioned so...so blatantly. But, if she were being entirely honest with herself, she could hardly say she minded. The art of flirtation was one of the things she missed about her people. Where the Caelorans considered idle conversations a game of strategy, for the Skogar the game to play was the art of seduction. That and battle. But Aenwyn had learned how to wield every weapon possible by the time she was fourteen, but she hadn't taken an interest in flirtation until after she was rescued by Baug and brought to the Skogar Mountains. Any conversation was enjoyable after spending a few years in complete isolation with nothing but her horrific memories to keep her company, but especially the conversations that involved subtle innuendos, a smoldering wink of an eye, and a sensual bite of the lower lip that really piqued her interest. She enjoyed the way flirtation would start out small—a simple graze of the hand or leg—and how the flutter in her chest would sink lower and lower as each caress lasted longer, each word play becoming more overt with desire and need. It was like rolling a snowball down the mighty slopes of the Skogar Mountains and watching it amass, the once small thing taking a shape of its own until it was too unruly to stop.

Sometimes it wasn't even that the interaction would lead anywhere, it just felt nice to be wanted. Needed. To not feel so alone.

Conversations and tristes with the king were nothing so entertaining.

Earlier tonight, he'd held her hand as he guided her to his

bed chamber—a gesture that she'd mistaken for sweetness the first few times they'd shared a bed, only later noticing the strange positioning of his hand and how astute his thumb was in caressing the ring he'd given her on their wedding day. Making sure it was in place. Making sure his dog was leashed.

Once they'd arrived at his bed chamber, he'd shut the door behind him and the two of them undressed themselves. There had been no intimacy between them. No desire. His touch had been as abrasive as the hot desert sands of Vallonde. King Everard had crashed atop her, fumbled with their bodies until the key found its keyhole, and in a matter of moments, the deed had been finished.

There was no romance. No excitement. No tenderness or fierceness.

It was just a joyless, dutiful act, as it always had been between them. As it always would be.

As enticing as the fantasy was to feel something akin to joy again, to experience the longing and lust of two forbidden lovers in the dead of night, it was just that. A frivolous fantasy.

Aenwyn had a duty to uphold.

"I don't know what you're insinuating, Ser...?"

Beneath the groomed facial hair that he kept shaven close to the skin, the corner of the knight's lips tugged upward.

"Graeme," he answered. "Ser Darius Graeme. And I believe I owe you another apology, my queen. I only meant that it seemed like you might like an escort through the dark corridors to the comfort of your own chamber."

Suddenly, Queen Aenwyn found herself blushing all over again. Of course that had been what he'd meant. No one in their right mind would've suggested anything else, especially from right outside the king's bed chamber.

"Of course," she said, chuckling to herself. "Which would mean it would be *me* who owes *you* the apology, Ser Darius Graeme. Not the other way around." She brushed a stray lock of hair behind her ear, but the calluses she'd worked so hard to create in Skogar had softened. Sometimes, it made her own touch unrecognizable, and after such an unsettling nightmare and vision, she didn't like how foreign they felt. She dropped her hand and focused her attention on straightening the wrinkles in her robe as she mustered the courage to smile harder. "Although, you did just insult me."

"Insult you?" Darius cocked his head. "How so?"

"Me and half of Skogar," she embellished. At his confused expression, another chuckle escaped her. "You aren't *really* implying that a Skogar woman would be afraid of the dark, are you?"

Finally, his confusion subsided, giving way to a clever glint in his eyes. "You aren't really implying that Skogar women are above fear, are you?"

Oh, he was clever. Far cleverer than any of the other dull knights she'd spoken to.

"No, not above it—" Her smile broadened. And it wasn't the perfect, dainty slit she'd been told was acceptable for a graceful, obedient queen to wear either. This was a genuine smile full of untethered enjoyment. "But we like to think that we've convinced the rest of the realm we are." She clucked her teeth, another thought occurring to her. "You're telling me that when you think of Skogar women, you don't imagine fearless warriors?"

"Mmm, you're assuming I think of Skogar women at all."

The way he said it, a headiness to his tone that suggested he did, in fact, think of Skogar women. Maybe even often.

The very air in the corridor bucked. This conversation had just turned acutely dangerous. What's worse, Queen Aenwyn didn't want it to end.

The last time she could remember feeling so light and carefree was when she and her family had reached the Passage of Tomorrow, headed south for Caelora for her wedding. It had been a long stretch of dusk that seemed like it would never end, but the weather had at least stayed relatively cool, pleasant.

As they began the ascent through the tight passage, young Snow-Bird Katla had innocently asked, "Is it called that because it'll be tomorrow after we climb the big mountains?"

Of course, it hadn't. The journey had taken the better part of a week, but it had been faster than traversing the dangerous, snowy peaks of the Skogar Mountains.

She missed light conversations like those. Missed the laughter that had seemed so natural to her people but so foreign to those in Caelora. She missed smiling.

Walk with me. If she was still the bold young woman she'd been when she first arrived to Caelora, that's exactly what she would've said to him. Without love for her husband, there would've been no respect, no amount of loyalty that would've kept her from taking this handsome man to her bed chamber and giving into uninhibited ecstasy.

But guilt, as it turned out, was a powerful controller, one that was increasingly magnified by King Everard's power.

Instead, Aenwyn said, "Thank you for offering, but surely you have more pressing matters to attend to. I'm sure I can manage finding my way to my quarters on my own."

Queen Aenwyn promptly spun on her heels, moving in the direction of her bed chamber and wondering what corridor she might be able to turn down once Ser Darius was long gone so that she might still make her way to the dovecote.

"That might be so," he said, appearing beside her and making her jump. "But it would seem that I'm heading that direction anyway."

He left no room for debate, and she feared that if she tried to argue otherwise, it might rouse his suspicions. The king's guards were trained to find even the slightest misstep or anomaly suspect, but this one in particular seemed to have an astute eye.

So did she.

"And where might that be?" she asked, her own suspicions rising. "You never did say where you were headed at this late hour, and in such a hurry, no less."

He smirked at her as if he was watching one of the novice soldiers he was responsible for training out-spar him for the first time. "No, I did not."

Their stroll down the corridor lasted only a few more steps before Aenwyn realized he wasn't going to answer her, not without more prompting.

She stopped abruptly, the green robe falling from one of her shoulders to reveal the delicate cotton chemise beneath. She'd been around enough men to know that most wouldn't have resisted the urge to sneak a peek of the flesh that was surely visible beneath the thin fabric. But Ser Darius Graeme was living up to his role as one of the king's most trusted knights, as his eyes remained fixed on hers as he turned around to face her.

"Something wrong?" he asked wryly.

"Just waiting for an answer." She folded her arms, mostly to show her irritation, but also to protect against the chill that was creeping in. "I am your queen, after all."

"And yet, you are not my master."

"I beg to differ."

He shifted on his feet, an amused look creeping into his expression. "Oh, I don't doubt you do. But I answer to King Everard, and him alone."

She was losing her patience. Not just with him, but with this life. What use was it being queen without any power? What use was magic without the option of utilizing it? What use was her coming here if she couldn't complete her task?

"That might be true, Ser Darius," she said at long last, the cogs of her mind quick at work. Navigating the egos of men was her specialty. She'd learned long before being King Everard's wife just how little most men thought of the women of Grimtol. All but Baug the Bear. But even he had his moments where he'd forget that she had as much conviction and determination as he did. "However, as I'm sure you're aware, it is very late, and you have insisted on accompanying me to my bed chamber. Who's to say your motives are pure? How am I expected to believe that a man so secretive and evasive has anything but nefarious plans waiting for me, should I continue to follow him."

His eyes thinned to slits as he considered his options.

To deny her would leave her no choice but to awaken the castle, and whether he was up to no good or not, it would not end well for him if that were to happen. No matter if Queen Aenwyn pleaded for him, if the king found them alone in the dead of night, Ser Darius would be punished.

Finally, the knight sighed and continued strolling toward her bed chamber. Aenwyn only followed because she knew she'd won.

"I was heading to the dungeons," he said when she caught up to him.

"What's down there?" Before he could provide her with some sarcastic remark, she added hastily, "And don't just say *prisoners*."

Out of the corner of his eye, he watched her with something close to amusement. Finally he sighed. "Not just any prisoner. Better?"

Queen Aenwyn scoffed. She was prepared to give him an earful of what she would do if he didn't tell her right that instant what she wanted to hear, but his expression turned knowing, empathetic. To make her demands would do nothing. He knew as well as she that the only person he had to answer to was the king.

It was one thing to allow her husband to make her feel so small, but she'd be scorched if she allowed this knight to do the same.

"Fine. Don't tell me who it is. Just tell me why you're going down there in the middle of the night."

Planting her feet and crossing her arms, Queen Aenwyn prepared not to move another step until he complied. It made her appear more like a petulant child than a queen, of that she was aware. But she didn't care. She was so tired of letting men hold all the power over her, when it was she who should be exerting her power over them.

She was the seeress.

The one with magic.

The one who had awoken a dragon.

But as she stood her ground, she sensed that Ser Darius Graeme was the sort of stubborn man who would do the same. The hard set of his gaze and his nerves of steel made her wonder if they'd be stuck in this hallway for hours, staring each other down, waiting for one of them to finally cave in.

It would be him, Queen Aenwyn assured herself. He would be the one to budge. Not her.

At long last, he sighed and continued walking once more. Sensing her victory but unsure how it would play out, she followed after him.

They walked in silence for a while, with only the soft patter of her slippers and the heavy thuds of his boots to fill the void. Every now and then, they'd pass a window, and Queen Aenwyn noted the pink hues lightening the sky. Nightfall was coming to an end. And truth be told, she was becoming sleepy again. Perhaps it could wait until tomorrow's bedtime for her to complete her task. Then she'd have the entirety of the late-hours to complete her sacrifice and remove all evidence of it.

By the time they reached the door to her bed chamber, Queen Aenwyn had grown accustomed to his silence. In truth, it had become her new norm ever since her wedding day, since she spent so much of her time alone now.

There was a comfort to his peaceful presence though, comfort in knowing that even if they weren't speaking, at least she wasn't alone.

She *hated* being alone. Even now, the mere thought spurred in her a dark swirl of fear that made her heart race.

By the time Aenwyn entered the room, she'd already forgotten that she'd asked him a question until he finally responded.

"A few years ago, my village was attacked."

Queen Aenwyn froze in the doorway, a cool coastal breeze blowing in from the opened window in her bed chamber and caressing her practically bare skin. She missed her pelts. But she suspected it was more than that. The bones in her body felt like they'd been replaced with spears of ice and a sinking dread overcame her.

She already knew what he was about to say. She could sense fate's hands binding her to yet another tragedy. And though fear was quaking through her entire body now, she needed to hear him say it. Needed to ask the obvious question.

Holding her breath, she turned around to face him. "W-was it...the dragons?"

The gold-rimmed armor of Ser Darius' suit clanked as he reached up to run a hand through his dark hair.

Aenwyn couldn't tear her gaze away from that white line of a scar that dragged over the arch of his brow to the crest of his cheek bones, somehow narrowly missing causing any damage to the eye itself.

Darkness flooded Ser Darius' gaze. A vortex of misery swallowed him deep into a cruel maw of memories that Aenwyn knew quite intimately, even if their memories differed from each other's. After all, she had a darkness like that of her own. A place where nothing but her greatest torments and grief remained. A place that often haunted her when the demon-sleep wasn't consuming her instead. A place where the eerie silence drove her to insanity and a wall of noxious fog threatened to suffocate her.

"Yes," he answered, voice still drifting farther and farther away. "Dragons."

"Which one?" she heard herself ask, already knowing the answer. "If you don't mind me asking."

It must've been the specificity of the question that it drew him from his stupor because he fixed her in that hardened gaze of his in a way that made her feel like she'd said the wrong thing. Poked and prodded too much.

But on second inspection, she noted him softening, and wondered if anyone had ever bothered to ask him.

"The blue dragon," he said, and the very tiles beneath Aenwyn's feet seemed to buck. She had to catch herself on the doorframe to keep from falling.

When would it stop? Her role in so much suffering, so much sorrow and pain, when would it end? There was of course only one answer. She had to slay the blue dragon.

"I'm so sorry," she told him. Though he nodded as if he understood, she knew he didn't. He couldn't. No one but her and Baug knew how her magic had awoken that dragon all those years ago. They wondered who might've awoken the other two. "What village?"

"Rayong."

She remembered hearing about that attack. Baug the Bear had spies everywhere. But Rayong was closer than most of the other Caeloran towns, so he kept close tabs on their goings-on in particular. Not to mention it was a hub for trade, one that Baug utilized frequently, making the news of its destruction all the more harrowing.

The obliteration of Rayong was unlike any other dragon attack Grimtol had ever seen, before or since. Rayong had once stretched from the Xiran Sea all the way to the eastern Dormine Ocean. It had covered more land than many of the kingdoms, including Irongate and Skogar, even though it was just one of the many territories under Caeloran rule. Not anymore though. Not after the dragon's fire had laid waste to everything in between the two seas. Now there was hardly a village left.

Prior to the attack, the population had been sizeable already, but what made their death toll even worse was the number of refugees they'd been sheltering. For more than a year prior, people had been fleeing north from the Great City of Vallonde, the desert capital that had been the target of numerous dragon attacks.

But Vallonde only ever saw a few hundred deaths. The scourge in Rayong killed thousands.

It was a miracle that Ser Darius had been one of the few to survive. Then again, Aenwyn knew better than to believe in miracles. Fate always had its fingers tangled in everything.

What she couldn't figure out was what any of this had to do with Ser Darius' visit to the dungeons tonight.

Seeming to sense her lingering uncertainty, he straightened. "I joined the Caeloran Guard after the attack. I served under King Aldous briefly, until the same dragon that destroyed Rayong and took my mother killed him and the queen as well. And now I serve their son, King Everard. And this might come as a shock to you, but when the king assigns me to be on duty in the dungeons, I obey him."

It took her a moment to realize what he had just done.

It was all a trick. A rouse. He'd never intended on telling her anything.

Or perhaps he'd told her everything that actually mattered. This futile conversation served as a good reminder of who he was. One of King Everard's most trusted knights. Loyal to the bone. Subservient. And, although Queen Aenwyn had never understood how any of King Everard's guardsmen were able to stand by his side despite his blatantly selfish and misaligned morals, this was at least one reason that made sense to her.

She understood all too well what it was like to feel responsible for putting the blue dragon to rest.

It didn't mean she appreciated him jerking her around though.

"All you knights are the same," Queen Aenwyn growled. "Giving your mindless allegiance to a king you're too blind to ever truly know."

"Blind?" His laugh was a bitter thing. "I've seen more hardship, suffering, and bloodshed in my short twenty-six years than you'll see in your entire life tucked away here in this castle."

Red flashed in Queen Aenwyn's vision. "You have no idea what I've seen!"

"Nor you, I," Ser Darius countered.

The statement cleaved their conversation short.

His obsidian eyes hurled into her like mighty boulders threatening to bury her. She'd never seen eyes so dark before. But these were not the chilling darkness of a quiet forest. There was a warmth to them, a stoked flame that made their weight searing. They were nothing like the king's cold gaze. Ser Darius' possessed a dark heat that promised vengeance.

Aenwyn stood firm beneath the weight of his black gaze as he stepped closer, seething.

"You're just another bored, disappointed wife whose life lacks meaning because you chose to marry for wealth and power instead of anything remotely resembling love."

No one had ever spoken to her in such a way. Not here in Caelora, anyway.

Before she had time to respond, he kept going.

"If you're looking to spread your misery, go back to the other bitter, noble wives you spend your time with."

Aenwyn's fingernails bit into the tender flesh of her palms.

He had her all wrong. She was *nothing* like the petulant women of court who had no sense of the world or care for anyone else inhabiting it but themselves. They were incapable of seeing any truth that lay beyond the reach of their husbands' pockets. They spent their days occupied with frivolities like deciding which balls to attend, what gowns to wear, and which areas of study their children would master.

Queen Aenwyn might spend some of her time with them, but only as a means of attempting to fit in. Not by choice, but as a means of survival. It was just the way it was for an outsider, to learn the culture, to blend in, to adapt. It was all just an act.

Ser Darius had been right about one thing though. Aenwyn *was* bored. And every day she grew increasingly bitter about it. This was the life she'd foolishly chosen for herself, the life she'd begged Baug to allow her to commit to. And now, she was growing restless and frustrated trying and failing to make meaning of it.

Until tonight.

The dream of the dragon meant something, and soon she'd prove all of them wrong. Including this know-it-all knight.

There was nothing left for her to say except, "How dare you—"

"Right." He sounded so condescending, eyes rolling in that way that men did when women spoke in their presence about things they believed themselves to know more about. "How dare *I* insult a queen by speaking truths."

"You don't speak truth though!" she squeaked, a dainty sound that only served to aggravate her more for how it seemed to reinforce his misguided and unfair perspective of her. Tugging her robe tighter around herself, Queen Aenwyn took a moment to fortify herself. "I am *nothing* like those conceited brats that I'm forced to spend my days entertaining.

You do know who I am right? Where I came from? You think my life was all about delicate dresses and meaningless gossip when I was in Skogar?"

He gave an unsympathetic shrug. "Maybe not. But you seem to have learned how to blend in quite nicely."

With a jerk of his head, he indicated to the lavish, velvet robe she had draped over her. But the gesture meant more than that. Something about it made Queen Aenwyn recall *all* the things she'd done to survive since coming here. How promptly she'd allowed her husband to silence her. How easily she'd fallen in line with the other ladies and learned to convey an interest in their stitchwork and chatter. How she no longer cried after her husband had spent himself inside her before she closed her eyes for bed.

"You're either quite the liar or you're as unpredictable as wildfire." Ser Darius scoffed before adding, "And in my experience, neither are the trustworthy sort."

The way he said it set her skin aflame. Like it was something to be ashamed of. Like she had dishonored herself, and in so doing brought humiliation to her entire family, and all of Skogar.

But Aenwyn had only done what she had needed to do to survive. Just as she always had.

When everyone in her village died, she had adapted.

When Baug brought her to Skogar, she learned to become like them.

When she came to Caelora, she feigned smiles and put on pretty dresses.

Aenwyn would always choose survival over stubborn pride. Always. And she'd be damned if she was going to let some arrogant, judgmental knight make her feel bad about it.

"I'd choose the unpredictability of wildfire over being a mindless, obedient puppet like you any day."

He raised an eyebrow. "Mindless puppet?"

"Yes. You and all the knights, just blindly following your king's every whim without a single thought for yourself."

Darius' arms folded across his broad chest. "Is that what you think we do?"

His cocky tone made Aenwyn grit her teeth. It felt like he thought he had the upper hand, even though she knew she did, so rather than playing into where he was attempting to lead her, she veered the conversation back to the idea of wildfire. "At least I have the freedom of changing with the wind and burning everything in my path, should I ever see fit."

"Are you threatening to burn down your own kingdom? In front of one of the very knights who's sworn to protect it?"

He looked at her like she was the greatest fool in all the lands, and she supposed she was, the way he put it. In the wrong company, to even hint at *burning everything* in her path could get her bound to a boulder and tossed out at sea. But she didn't care. Not tonight. Not with more important things to focus her attention on like an impending dragon attack that could kill dozens, if not hundreds.

"Keep your secrets, Ser Darius," Aenwyn said, deflecting back to the original matter of where he was going and why. "I'm sure your king values your silence just as much as he does anyone's. It's time I head for bed."

There was a mocking slant to his smile as Ser Darius bowed, but Aenwyn paid it little mind and spun on her heels.

"Right," he teased. "I almost forgot. You need to get your beauty sleep. Wouldn't want you unrested and looking unkempt for your royal visitor."

Her fingers clenched around the golden doorknob. He was baiting her; she was sure of it.

She didn't want to fall for it. She wanted to storm into her room, slam the door in his face, and be done with him.

But if they were having visitors, she needed to know. It

could impact her ability to sneak off and complete the sacrifice later.

Begrudgingly, Queen Aenwyn pivoted around again and leveled him with a look. "What do you mean, *my royal visitor*?"

To his credit, he actually seemed surprised by her naivety. "Didn't you hear? Your sister will be arriving soon."

The breath caught in Aenwyn's chest. "Signe's coming?"

Suddenly, the tense banter they'd been volleying all night was a distant memory and Aenwyn beamed up at the knight. This was the most elated she'd ever felt behind Caeloran walls.

Even with the short distance between them, Aenwyn rushed Ser Darius, colliding into him until her hands were splayed across his broad chest, his metal armor somehow warm to the touch.

"Is it Signe? Or do you mean Katla—" she reached up to play with her bottom lip— "You couldn't mean Katla. She's still much too young for travel. It was difficult enough to come here with her the first time, and our father swore he would never travel with her again after her incessant nagging and whining. Oh, it must be Signe! How wonderful! How utterly—"

Aenwyn's heart wrenched when she noticed Darius' grim expression.

The events caught up to her then.

The ominous vision.

Darius' strangely secretive task of heading to the dungeons when the rest of the castle was sound asleep.

The unannounced arrival of her sister.

None of it was adding up, but all of it seemed to forebode something dreadful.

Something like sizzling coals seared the inside of her throat when she asked, "Why has Signe come for a visit?"

The knight looked uncomfortable. "I...am not sure I should be the one to tell you—"

"Nor I," Aenwyn agreed, remembering the power he'd channeled into those very words himself just moments earlier. "But here you are, the only person available to tell me, and so you must. Unless this is another tedious secret you've been sworn to keep for your king?"

He snorted. "Shouldn't you already know? She is *your* sister, after all, coming to make a request of *you*."

"And what is this request?" Aenwyn was losing her patience.

Perhaps he could tell because he finally obliged her.

"She—Signe, is it?" When he looked to her for confirmation, Aenwyn nodded, trying to speed him along. Ser Darius exhaled, dragging a hand through those lush locks of his. Even with the armor, Aenwyn could practically imagine the muscles that flexed beneath. "King Everard received word that, after all these years, an alliance has finally been struck between Irongate and Skogar."

It was like the world suddenly came to a stop.

Aenwyn understood his words—she knew their individual meaning, as well as their collective—and yet, her mind still couldn't quite grasp what he was saying. She failed to see how any of this could be connected to Signe.

Irongate had enslaved the Skogar for generations. Her people had only recently regained their freedom and sovereignty, and so the tension between the two people was still raw and palpable. Hatred for Irongate bled into many of the Skogar customs. They had legends of the *monsters* that dwelled on the other side of the mountains; holidays to remember their rebellion, honor the lives of their fallen, and celebrate their independence; and spiritual practices and offering ceremonies dedicated to the Sky-Blessed so that they might protect them from ever being enslaved by Irongate again.

Although some hoped an alliance would someday be possible, Aenwyn couldn't fathom it happening within her lifetime.

But then she thought of Caelora.

How she'd convinced Baug the Bear into agreeing to an alliance with the most powerful nation in all of Grimtol.

It should've been obvious from the start. Signe was now the eldest heir to the Skogar throne. There could be only one way to make such an alliance so quickly. Aenwyn of all people should know that.

Ser Darius cleared his throat, but he looked sympathetic when he said, "Signe comes to ask that you accompany her to Irongate for her wedding. She is to marry King Ulfaskr."

4

A STRANGER IN THE DARKNESS

DARIUS

Darius Graeme wasn't sure how to handle the situation before him. The queen was pressed against his chest. Those big, green, hopeful eyes were just gazing up at him, begging him for answers, begging him to fix a problem that was beyond anyone's scope. Especially his.

In his experience, once a king had made a decision, it was final.

Signe's fate as the future queen of Irongate was inevitable. If anyone understood that he would've guessed that Queen Aenwyn would.

But whether or not he could intervene on a royal marriage on behalf of his upset queen was not the issue.

The real problem was that if anyone were to walk around the corner and stumble onto them, they'd catch Darius in such close proximity to Queen Aenwyn—alone and standing in her doorway with her robes askew—that rumors would abound faster than he would be able to get a handle on them.

It'd be his head on a spike before the moon could even dare to change course.

38

Darius was rather fond of where his head rested upon his shoulders. And so, gently, he grabbed Queen Aenwyn's arms and guided her a step backward into her room.

"You should get some rest," he said in between glances down the hall. "And—"

Queen Aenwyn waved him off, her eyes vacant in that dreamy, distant way that she often became when she and the king were holding court in the throne room. Admittedly, Darius had watched her for months now and had seen that look more times than he could count. He'd been given a direct order by his king to monitor her every move, for fear that Baug the Bear might've had nefarious plans following their betrothal.

Darius had never quite understood why King Everard would've agreed to the arrangement if he had suspected ill will, but he didn't pretend to be prolific in the ways of court and politics. And an order was an order.

Besides, he was an excellent spy. The proof of which could be verified by the fact that Queen Aenwyn had not seemed to have noticed him before, because when they'd run into each other just moments earlier, she hadn't known him—at least no more than she knew any member of the Caeloran Guard. But he'd been there, this past year. Since even before their wedding, he'd kept a close eye on her, had scouted the area as Baug the Bear and the bride-to-be approached the Caeloran border, had eavesdropped from outside her bed chamber as she prepared for their wedding ceremony, and had continued to lurk in her shadows everywhere she went since arriving to their kingdom. He had even read the letters she'd sent home to her family in Skogar.

Not once had she caught him. Nor had he caught her doing anything suspicious. Until tonight.

Finding her sneaking out of the king's room was troubling, but he felt better already knowing that she was back in her room. Still, he'd have to send someone to double check the king's quarters and guard her door. Just to be safe.

"Yes," Aenwyn said, lost somewhere far away. "And you have somewhere you need to be." She blinked, bringing herself back with a pleasant, cordial smile fit for a queen. The same hollow one he'd seen her brandish in court. "Thank you for ensuring my safe arrival, Ser Darius Graeme."

Yep. He'd definitely be sending someone over to watch her tonight. Something felt amiss here. He would've done it himself, if he didn't have other, more pressing matters to attend to.

Darius bowed and took a hearty step backward, giving her space to close the door. "Rest well, my queen."

And then he was alone again. Just the way he preferred it.

Not always, of course. Sometimes he enjoyed the company of others. Mainly the few friends from his childhood whom he still kept in touch with. But they all lived in Rayong still, and since he'd been promoted to the king's special guard, he'd had less and less time to travel back home to visit them.

On most nights, that was maybe a blessing. Being far away from home and from the friends whom he considered family, it made the dark parts of his job a lot easier. He could be someone else when he donned his Caeloran Guard armor. He *was* someone else. All that mattered when he was in this metal suit was that he did his king's bidding, and that he helped bring his kingdom closer to peace.

Tonight, that meant talking to *her*.

When he was preparing to go down into the dungeons, yeah, he preferred the solitude of his own mind. He needed it. Needed the time it took him to sink into the depths of the castle to become the very shadows that dwelled down there. It was part of his process. He would tuck himself into the crevices of his mind as he chiseled himself to cold stone, becoming the punisher, terrorizer, enforcer. Like he did every time he visited this particular prisoner, he used the quiet time to mull over the perfect plan that just might prove fruitful this time, a line of questioning that might finally get her to talk, to tell them anything.

For two years they'd been trying to get information from her.

For two years, she'd not told them a word.

He doubted tonight would be any different.

Darius waved to the knights guarding the bolted door that led into the dungeon and torture chambers. He dismissed one of them from their post so that they could alleviate his worry by seeing to the queen and king, and he already felt a little more at ease.

As he entered the dark underbelly of the castle, Darius braced himself against the acrid stench that crashed into him like a brick wall, the sweat and blood of the thousand prisoners who'd been kept down there before permeating the walls and stinging his nostrils.

Sometimes the dungeon was overflowing with criminals—murderers and rapists, people who had lost their minds and could no longer be trusted out in the world.

These days, the dungeons were fairly empty. A time of relative peace was upon the Caeloran kingdom. And he preferred it that way. It seemed that *she* did too. And if she was at ease then maybe—just *maybe*—they could get somewhere today without bloodshed.

Darius stopped at the iron door, cold gaze cutting through the bars. He had to squint, but finally he made out her dark figure inside.

The Ashen Princess was curled in the back corner.

For all the adages his mother had taught him about fearing the Sky-Blessed who could smite him for stepping into a sunbeam incorrectly, whenever he found himself in the company of the Ashen Princess or her people, he wondered why none of the cautionary tales were about them. They were the true threats, after all. Far more dangerous, it would seem, than the Sky-Blessed, now that they'd been knocked down from their thrones.

Darius knew better than to believe the façade before him. Though she was cradled in the darkness, she was not some frightened child, skittish to the sound of his footsteps as he had drawn nearer. Nor was she quivering in anticipation of the pain that usually accompanied his visits.

The Ashen Princess was a hibernating bear who'd been disturbed from her slumber and was now realizing just how hungry she was.

Shadows spilled around her, radiated from her. Her silver eyes slid open. It was the only thing he could see clearly down here in the darkness, that razor-sharp, moonlight glow of her gaze.

It always reminded him of the night he'd lost his mother, the moon full and heavy where it hung in the black sky before death and carnage struck. If he had been home with her rather than trying to woo one of the many beautiful women in a long list of Animali who had deserved far better than him, maybe things would have been different. Maybe his mother would still be alive. Or maybe they'd both be dead.

It wasn't just his fault though. Not a day passed when he didn't curse the Skogar for not coming to their defense, even though they clearly had figured out a way to keep themselves protected from dragon attacks. To this day, not a single fire had burned through their villages, unlike the rest of Grimtol.

But mostly, he blamed the Ashen.

After all, it was their dark magic that brought the beasts to life. It had to be. For there weren't dragons before the Ashen rose from the dead.

Darius' blood boiled at the thought of it all, so he took it out on their prisoner and rapped against the iron bars.

"Rise and shine, princess. It's that time again."

Through the darkness, her silver gaze pierced him like twin daggers. There was no need for her to utter a word; he could read her wicked intent regardless: there would be no cooperation tonight.

Just once he wished it didn't have to be difficult.

Just once he wished she'd give them the answers they sought without forcing him to obey the king's orders of obtaining it *through any means necessary.*

Fortunately, tonight would be different though. He had special news, a change in their regular weekly routine.

"You're to be transported tomorrow." Darius pressed an arm against the door, the cool iron biting into his flesh as he leaned against it. "Did you know that?"

It was difficult to say for certain, but he thought he saw her twitch at the words. Already that was more than he'd seen from her in months.

"They're taking you to Irongate," he continued, hoping to gain momentum. "Do you know what happens there?"

Silence. But a different kind than she normally showed him. Rather than ignoring him, the Ashen Princess was hanging on his every word. Rightfully so, considering what lay ahead of her.

It knotted his gut to think about the horrors they'd inflict upon her in Irongate, even though he supposed what he'd done to her wasn't much better. Over the months—dragon's fire, maybe it had been approaching years now—Darius had convinced himself his actions had been merciful. At least whenever he'd been given an order to torture her, he'd made it quick, never dragging it out too long, and always making sure to send a healer to tend to her afterward.

His experience inside the torture chambers at Irongate was limited, but considering their brutal history, he imagined they rarely showed their prisoners such compassion.

Of course, that remorse was his to bear alone. Never would he allow her or any prisoner to see it. He had a job to do. A duty to his kingdom to uphold.

He bore down on his callous regard, grateful that no one from home could see this side of him.

"You know what happens at Irongate right? What they do to folk like you?" He released a breathy laugh. "Right. I forgot; you were alive during the Battle for Freedom. You lived the horrors of what happens to prisoners in Irongate."

Darius paused, thinking—hoping—that maybe that reminder of the war and what she and her kind had endured would be enough.

But he should've known better.

When she continued to remain speechless, Darius had no choice but to press her even harder. To provoke her. Because just maybe this conversation might be the one to finally get him the answers he needed.

For a splinter of a second, he doubted himself. He worried what it might cost him if she didn't talk. What it would mean for him if he failed his king again.

He pushed every worrying part of himself aside, for tonight, he just needed to do what needed to be done.

Instead, he harnessed his anger, threw himself back into his memories of Rayong and let the screams of his people wash over him like cold blood, let the rage of their unjust deaths fuel him into becoming the monster he needed to be when he was down here.

"Tell me—" he said, voice as dark and cold as a starless night — "Did they tear off your wings before slitting your throat, or after? Do you think they'll find something else to take from you this time, since your wings never grew back?"

Like a bolt of lightning splitting a stormy sky, the Ashen Princess was crashing into the cell door. It rattled on collision and Darius was startled for a moment, if only because he hadn't been entirely sure he'd get a rise out of her. He so rarely ever had. The deceptively young-looking woman—despite being centuries old—had an ironclad willpower and never let anything slip.

Until now.

But Ser Darius Graeme was one of the king's most trusted knights for a reason. His instincts and reflexes were as sharp as hers, and he had his dagger drawn and pressed to her bellybutton before her grey fingers could reach through the bars.

"Back. Up."

It was the only warning he would give her. If she so much as blinked wrong, he'd have no choice but to thrust the steel into her flesh. It wouldn't be the first time, though her charcoal complexion showed no signs of the torture she'd endured over the last year or more, by his hand or another's.

It's not like she had any power down here anyway. Not with the light-blue bands clasped around her ankles and wrists that kept her death magic at bay.

The look in her dimming eyes told him what he already knew. The fight had left her.

Teeth bared, the Ashen Princess shoved herself back, but not before giving the iron bars a mighty whack.

"So you do remember." Only once she was a safe distance away again did Darius lower his blade, but he didn't dare sheath it.

She bit down on her snarl and already he could see her impervious exterior falling back into place. That cold, unfeeling cloak of nothingness that she wielded like a shield.

He was losing her. And that was a problem because she was the only one he had access to who knew about the dragons and therefore was the only one who could give him the answers he'd been searching for since the day his mother died. He needed her to tell her why the Ashen had created such vile beasts? Why they were letting them destroy the lands and murdering so many innocents along the way? It couldn't just be for petty vengeance, not when the ones truly responsible for their predicament—the Sky-Blessed and the Skogar—were the very people who had seemed to go unscathed by their fiery blazes.

But most importantly, what he and everyone in Grimtol truly wanted—no, *needed* to know, was at what point would it stop? What did the Ashen want, and how could he or anyone else put an end to their suffering?

Once the princess left the Caeloran Castle, that would it. He'd have no other link to an Ashen, no way of learning the secrets of the dragons so that he might slay them. No way of avenging his mother and laying her memory to rest.

This was his last chance. Tonight. Now.

"Look," Darius said, and it was perhaps the first time he'd ever spoken to her with any ounce of kindness, the first time he'd ever allowed for her to see the truth of him. He couldn't afford it before, but now it seemed that he had no other choice. She was right to be wary of it. "If you don't want to go to Irongate, just tell the king what he wants to know. Confess what your people have done. Tell him how you made the dragons and how to stop them. Show him you're willing to work with us, and I'm sure he'd keep you here. It's that simple."

They called themselves the Ashen, presumably because of the grey pigment of their skin that had lost its luster upon death and never quite returned once they had revived.

But there was another name for them too. A hushed moniker that some would utter into the darkness whenever they felt a dreadful omen pressing down upon them.

Death's Revenge.

Darius had never personally called them by that name, but when he saw the princess' flat affect twist into a hideous sneer, the dark moniker was called forth in his mind.

Her demented countenance was incongruous with her graceful, velvety tone. "You will never defeat the dragons."

Darius' fingers curled tight, and it was all he could do to keep his composure. He didn't want her to see how much those words had impacted him, even though he was certain she'd chosen them specifically to rile him.

Before he could do something brash, Darius spun on his heels. Their meeting was over. He had lost, and he hoped she knew that she had too.

He called over his shoulder as he stormed for the entrance, "Enjoy your time in Irongate, Princess Elora."

* * *

Red blazed his vision. His irritation was fire and flames, and that always made him think of one, dreadful thing. By the time Darius had exited the dungeons, his fists were bound so tightly that nothing would bring them release except the hearty pounding of knuckles upon flesh. Since his brawling days were over though, and since he didn't want to take his rage out on anyone undeserving, he stormed his way to the training grounds, head down and mind a vicious storm, refusing to leave the fire blazing in his thoughts, burning huts in Rayong. He carried his past with him like the horrifyingly behemoth shadow of the dragon was still high overhead, the screams of the dying—and those of the survivors, some of whom had jumped into the lagoon rather than be singed—rattled through him until his entire body was abuzz.

Darius tore off his armor, chucking it to the ground with a clank. He didn't care about having to polish the scuffs out later. Nothing mattered but air and freedom and violence.

Normally he sparred with a broadsword. Tonight he used nothing but his fists.

The first blow to the dummy made his knuckles sting and

shook his bones. He jabbed again, the exhilaration of it building. As his fists pumped into the straw figure, he imagined it was the dragon's body instead, its vicious face, its precious heart. He imagined it was any number of the Ashen, though it was too real to envision the princess herself—he was already too familiar with what it felt like to pummel her flesh. But the Hand of Death, Aethic Venlar, the ruler of the Ashen? Their face was a welcome imagining as he tore through one dummy and then another.

Darius pounded and pounded. Even after his knuckles began to bleed, and long after his fists numbed to the pain of every blasting jolt. He kept hitting until his naked torso was coated in sweat, despite the chill air of the late-hours.

He kept beating the dummy until reason kicked in again. Until he was able to remind himself that it wasn't really the dragon before him. Nor Princess Elora. Nor the Hand of Death.

This wasn't solving anything, but it did help to get all of that rage out of him. It felt like it had been pent up for weeks now, and he could finally think clearly again now that it had imploded.

Chest heaving, Darius shoved away from the dummy and started pacing the training grounds instead. He *would* defeat the dragons. Even if it was the last thing he did. Even if none of the Ashen would help him.

Hands clasped atop his head, Darius tilted his gaze skyward as he tried catching his breath. The full moon beamed down upon him, and he had to turn away. He wondered if he would ever be able to gaze upon it with awe again, or if the sight of it would always make him sick to his stomach with guilt and regret.

It was only when his attention had fallen back to his discarded armor that Darius realized there was someone else there with him.

A figure stood in the shadows just beyond the perimeter.

Darius drew his dagger for the second time that night. "Who goes there?"

Whoever it was chuckled, a sound that was decidedly unsettling and made Darius grip the hilt of his blade all the tighter.

Slowly, the figure approached, footsteps thudding in the soft dirt. A man appeared from the shadows, his face shrouded behind a large, ominous hat, the brim squeezed together in the front.

"Is that any way to greet an old friend?" The man tilted the broad-brim back, a familiar, cocky grin coming into view from beneath it.

"Emile?" Darius shoved his dagger back into its sheath and heaved a sigh of relief, though his irritation still bubbled. A good brawl would've done him well tonight, and he was admittedly disappointed there wouldn't be one. "What in the Hollows dragged you all the way out here?"

Emile laughed, a sound as mischievous as the seas for which he used to sail. "Why, I came to see you, of course. Not much else could persuade me to grace this place with my presence."

Darius rolled his eyes. Emile's visits were rarely *just* of the social sort anymore.

"Well," Emile shrugged sheepishly, the corner of his sly grin ticking up. "Not *just* to see you."

With a knowing grunt, Darius stomped over to his pile of armor and began the arduous task of plucking each piece off the ground, dusting it off so as not to scuff the metal, and putting himself back together again. Emile came over to help him, tightening the leather straps and fastening the buckles that were difficult for just one man to reach.

Though Darius knew he should be grateful, part of him loathed receiving help from Emile D'Entremont of all people.

It wasn't that he disliked the man—far from it. The moment

Darius had met the former-pirate-turned-family-man he'd been inspired by him, much like anyone who crossed Emile's path. Emile was a *good* man. The kind of man Darius' mother had always hoped he'd become, and subsequently the exact kind of man who Darius had put off becoming in his youth. Emile made it look easy too, the way he'd turned his back on a life of wild freedom, of hedonistic desires and impulses. Then again, Darius supposed that losing a wife and having to raise a child alone could do that to a person. Losing his own mother definitely had given him a change of heart, after all.

After his mother's death, Darius had joined the Caeloran Guard, and he began to understand firsthand just how difficult it was to change. Every day felt like a constant struggle. But every day, he reassured himself that it would be worth it.

"It's been a while since I've found you in such a state." Emile gestured to the disheveled dummies, a knowing look in his eye. Though he was a few years younger than Darius, in moments like these, it was easy to forget. "What's eating at you, Dare-Bear?"

Shadows darkened the grooves of Darius' face. "Don't."

"Sorry. Sorry." Emile held up his hands in mock defense. "Just trying to make you smile. It seems you've forgotten how to, ey?"

His friend wasn't wrong. It had been a long time since Darius had felt so much as a tickle of a smile. Until he'd run into the queen earlier. She'd stirred from him more pleasantries than he'd shown anyone in the past two years—before the conversation had turned sour, that is.

Before tonight though, no other instance of joy or laughter came to mind. Duty had become his focus. That and learning to defend himself and anyone else who needed it. There wasn't much room for anything else.

When Darius didn't reply, his friend patted his shoulder with a sort of apologetic look that said he wasn't going to press the matter any further. At least not now. "What do you say we grab a pint over at the—"

"I don't drink."

Emile's eyebrows shot up.

Darius hadn't touched a single drop since his mother had died. A lot of his old habits had died that day with her. It had been torture, constantly refraining from his every impulse, turning a cold shoulder to every possibility for fun. But it was what he deserved. What *she* deserved.

"Don't have an ale then," Emile said. "Have a—" With one arm draped over Darius' back, Emile twirled his other hand in the air as he sought a more compelling option— "Have a warm glass of milk."

The scoff broke Darius' cold façade, and with it, a grin broke free.

"Ah, there it is!" Emile rejoiced, whacking Darius' back one last time before shoving off of him. "I knew I could get through to you. Carmen said it wasn't possible. But I knew."

Darius' heart dropped to his stomach at the mention of that name. His wide eyes locked onto Emile's. "Carmen? Is she...is she here then?"

He swallowed, hoping he didn't sound as panicked as he was and knowing he was failing miserably.

Emile nodded. "Of course! She's waiting for us at the Drunken Owl."

"For *us*?" Darius clarified. "Who said anything about me going to the Drunken Owl? I'm on duty."

"Oh really?" Emile's laugh came breathy. He walked over to the straw dummy and flicked the fake head with one calloused hand badly in need of a washing. "Is that what you call this? *Being on duty*? Stripping down to skin just to blow off some steam?"

That anger was starting to rise again. Not at Emile, but at himself.

As always, his friend was right. He couldn't very well perform his duties when he was out here acting like a frustrated child throwing a tantrum.

"Now, don't be doing that either," Emile said, frowning and pointing at Darius accusatorily. "It's nothing to be ashamed of. You need a break, Dare. That's all." Darius started to shake his head, but Emile would hear none of it. "Just one drink—one *non-alcoholic* beverage. Surely if you have time enough to be out here, hacking away at straw, then you can spare a few minutes with some old friends. She just wants to talk to you before tomorrow."

Tomorrow.

There it was again. The day that should be so meaningless and for some reason everyone kept planning such momentous events around it.

It couldn't be a coincidence, and he knew Carmen well enough that it raised his suspicions. He leaned in conspiratorially and asked, "Why tomorrow? What's she planning?"

Emile sucked in a breath, resituating his hat. "I'm afraid she wants to be the one to tell you." There was no shame in his voice when he prompted Darius again, "So? Are you intrigued enough for that drink yet?"

If it hadn't been everything else that had happened earlier, he might've been able to hold his ground. But he was exhausted by his failure of not being able to get the Ashen Princess to talk, he was on edge by his queen's erratic behavior, and honestly just plain tired. Tired of doing nothing day in and day out but guarding the castle, spying on the queen, torturing their prisoners, and making his rounds across the grounds over and over again.

But mostly, he was curious.

"One drink," Darius grumbled. He didn't wait to see if Emile was following him as he headed out of the training grounds. "And I need to be back by first-hours."

"What a coincidence. That's our timeframe as well."

In the amount of time it took for them to reach the Drunken Owl, Emile had nearly finished singing his third sea shanty, apparently not wanting to risk holding a conversation and accidentally revealing Carmen's mysterious secret before arriving. That, or he didn't want to risk saying anything that might make Darius change his mind about accompanying him.

They arrived to find the tavern packed with patrons like hens in crates. Darius nodded to the familiar faces of the off-duty Caeloran Guards smoking cigars outside. He knew he risked being spotted by coming here. He knew also that some of the guards had been tasked as spies and sent around the town to gain intel and report what they learned back to the king. If any of them were here tonight, the king would have his head for coming to the Drunken Owl while on duty.

But once he was inside, he realized just how unlikely it was for him to be spotted among the dozens of knights already enjoying the atmosphere of the tavern. The Drunken Owl wasn't the only place of relaxation and entertainment within the Keep, but to was by far the favored locale of the locals. It was where all of their worries faded away.

Darius remembered those days fondly.

He might've been wrong about just how much he would stand out though, seeing as everyone here was unwinding and he was still in armor.

The patrons inside tried to clear a path once they noticed Darius in his knight garb, but they weren't quick enough for Emile who was dragging him through the crowd to a dark corner in the far side of the tavern.

Even with her back turned toward them, Darius recognized Carmen in an instant and it sent his heart a flutter—or perhaps it was the fluttering of his heart that had alerted him of her presence. Either way, unease and anticipation swirled within him, and he no longer knew if he could keep walking.

Carmen Louviere stood out like the last bloom before a winter storm. Everything about her reminded him of summer and heat and dancing, from her tawny complexion to the golden hoops and beads looping through her thick braids, down to the tangerine and poppy-patterned skirt he could just barely make out from under the table.

She was a much-needed splash of color in such a drab establishment, and a much-needed sight for his sore eyes.

The world seemed to slow as they approached her. As Emile bent to plant a kiss on her forehead, Darius halted, his palms slick with sweat. He had the sudden unfathomable and humiliating urge to run. Just like he had in Rayong. He wouldn't be so cowardly now.

Darius sat across from her and when their eyes met—hers dazzling with that reptilian glow they always seemed to carry —all his worries dissipated.

"Carmen—" her name was a breath of air caught in his throat. "You look—"

She waved him off, smirking as she so often was. "Horrendous, I'm sure. The journey here was not kind and we have not yet rested."

Carmen's gaze rose to meet Emile's who was still standing beside her, one hand gently caressing her shoulder. A memory of Darius' own touch upon her skin had him resituating in his chair, folding his arms, and doing his best to look away from them. He knew they were together now. He was happy for them. But it was still difficult to get used to, her not being his, even after all these years.

She had said something to Emile that Darius missed, caught up in his own memories of late-night strolls through the sunken swampland of Rayong, walking hand-in-hand as the fireflies illuminated a path for them and made her glow with a positively radiant shine.

"Of course," Emile responded, before disappearing to the bar.

And then, they were alone.

Conversation had always come easy for the two of them. Carmen was one of the first people—aside from his mother—whom Darius could actually talk to, in depth. Before her, he'd mostly been bored by the mindless prattling of others. It was always the same idle chat: the weather, the crops, homes in need of repairs, and being too impoverished to afford them. But with Carmen, their conversations had been lively, electrified. They spoke of ideals and how they wished the world would work, of their plans for any number of futures—and that was the thing with her; she understood that their futures were not fixed, but what they created, and Darius had always appreciated that about her. He hated feeling stuck, like his life was already determined. With Carmen, he got to dream. They both did.

But words did not flow easily between the two of them tonight.

There was too much left unsaid, years of catching up to be had, years of questions that they'd left unanswered too long to even dare to bring them up now. It clogged the space between them, making the air as dry and hot as freshly grinded sawdust.

Behind the shimmer of her golden-brown gaze, Darius thought he knew the question she would ask first: *why did you leave me?*

Instead, she wasted no time on personal matters. Carmen cut straight to the point.

"Tomorrow we'll be petitioning the king for our sovereignty."

If Darius had been drinking, he would've spewed it across the table. "Come again?" Darius roared so loudly that it drew the attention of the drunk patrons nearby. He placated them quickly enough with a cordial, gleaming smile. Once he was sure they had resumed their respective social affairs he leaned over the table, voice quieting. "Have you gone absolutely mad?"

Across from him, Carmen rolled her eyes and leaned back in her chair, crossing her arms. "It's a pleasure to see you too, old friend."

Not a moment later, Emile returned with three mugs in hand. He slammed them down before sliding one to Darius, Carmen, and taking the third for himself, all the while keeping a wary eye between the two of them.

"Ah—" He sat down, took a swig, and smacked his lips— "I see you gave her the same rude welcome you gave me. And here I thought I was special."

"Not special," Carmen replied, a sly lilt in her smoky voice. "I don't believe it's his fault. His armor is so tight it's cutting off his circulation and making him act like a bastard."

Darius glowered at her, but part of him was warmed by her brazen humor. He'd missed her immensely this past year. Missed them both. But they still felt so distant, impossible to reconnect with. So much had happened. So much had changed.

Emile turned to Carmen. "I take it you told him?"

It was Darius who replied thought. "Yeah. She told me your foolish plan."

The words came out clipped and it was all he could do to keep the anger from rising again, to keep his voice down lest someone catch wind of the wrong word and it be the death of them all.

"That wasn't a *plan*," Carmen replied. "More of an update. I'm still waiting to tell you the rest of it."

Darius grabbed his mug, wishing there was something stronger than milk inside. "Why? What you're talking about is treason. I'm a Caeloran Guard. I should have you both arrested if what you're saying is true."

It stung to say it aloud. But any dutiful knight would've

acted without hesitation were someone to tell them they were absconding from the crown.

Yet here he was, stalling. Hesitating. Waiting to hear more.

No matter what Queen Aenwyn had said about him earlier, even after all this time as a knight, Darius still couldn't muster what it took to be anything remotely resembling loyalty, duty, and least of all obedient.

He didn't want to arrest his friends. No matter the consequences. When he had been knighted, when he'd accepted a position to defend the Caeloran crown, never in his wildest dreams had he imagined being put in the position of having to risk his own neck by turning a blind eye to his dimwitted friends or having to imprison them.

Knowing Carmen Louviere though, it shouldn't have come as a surprise.

She arched an eyebrow at him. "It isn't treason to want a better life for our people. Or have you forgotten how they suffer? Have you already forgotten where it is you came from?"

If she had said that just minutes before, it would've been exactly the kind of barb that would've struck a frayed nerve. But he was already becoming comfortable in her presence. It had always come natural to her to bring down his walls and put him at ease.

At the same time, she also always had a way of winding him in trouble.

"I would never." Darius said, gentler than anything he'd said all night. "But the truth of the matter remains: Rayong belongs to Caelora. It is treason to suggest that it could be anything different. If King Everard hears of this—this fantasy of yours, he'll send the Caeloran Guard to Rayong and make an example of you."

"Oh, he knows what we plan to do already," Carmen said, seeming rather proud of herself. Boastful, even. "And it's not just Rayong. We have all the Xiran territories to back us. They want out. They want better for their people, for the Animali."

The table fell silent for a long, painful moment while the rest of the tavern bumbled and slurred about. It had been ages since Darius had been in such a boisterous, grimy place such as the Drunken Owl. Even longer since he'd been one of the ones among the inebriated. He longed to be that carefree again. And at the same time, he knew he couldn't afford it. It was that untroubled nature that had cost him everything. And it was precisely the kind of mentality that would get Carmen and Emile killed. Although, admittedly, he was surprised to hear they had others following them.

"Please," Carmen said before he could think of a way to talk her out of it. The pleading tone of her voice beckoned his gaze away from the drunken patrons and back to hers. She was vexing to behold. Always had been. It was one of the many reasons they'd been drawn to one another initially. That heated spark of infatuation. On sleepless night, he'd often wondered what it could've grown into, even though he knew she was better off now. "We've tried requesting an audience with the king, but he keeps denying us. We've been turned away at the door too many times to count. Meanwhile, the Animali continue to be harassed and arrested for no other crimes than being true to their own natures. Even I've been arrested."

Darius' knuckles tightened around the handle of his mug. He wanted to hear more about that story, but with little more than a knowing look, Carmen told him now wasn't the time.

"I was one of the lucky ones," she said. "The guard on duty knew me and released me the next day. But it isn't always the case, Darius. People have lost their lands, lost time. Families have struggled to eat while their fathers and mothers rot away in cells awaiting unjust trials that all too often result in execution."

"Execution? The king wouldn't," Darius managed to grit

out, but each word was more difficult to muster, his conviction waning with every syllable. "Execution is a last resort, one we reserve for the worst criminals."

"For those with magic," Emile amended. "And anything resembling it, yeah?"

Darius ground his teeth together, afraid to utter another word. On the one hand, he wanted to believe in the crown he represented—it was why he'd become a knight, to have something even close to resembling honor, a cause to fight for. On the other hand, he'd learned a lot about the king since coming to the Caeloran capitol; he knew exactly the kind of dishonorable, despicable man he could be, knew just how far his disdain for magic could go.

"We can't remain a part of a kingdom that wants to see us eradicated." Carmen's soft words were sharper than a blade's edge.

Darius hung his head. "I know."

"We just need a moment of the king's time," she continued. "That's all we ask of you, to bring us to him. Let us tell him that a decision has been made for the Xiran territories. It is the best way to avoid a war."

A war seemed to rage within Darius now, fire seeming to burst from beneath his chest, his belly heavy with rot. He couldn't do what they were asking of him. To take them to the king so that they could proclaim sovereignty from him? They'd be beheaded on the spot.

"He won't allow it. And the war you're wanting to avoid? You'll just be bringing it to your doorsteps. The king, he—" Darius glanced around to make sure no one was looking. Even though no one was, he still lowered his voice— "He is an unsteady man. His ego is frail. He'll take this as a show of disrespect and have no choice but to retaliate."

"He does have a choice," Carmen argued. "He's had one all

---

along and he's chosen to ignore it. We can't keep living like this, Darius. Our people are frightened for their lives."

Emile offered her a comforting caress before addressing Darius. "We know what he's like. We know what the course he's likely to take. But our people have entrusted us to be just leaders, and we can't be afraid of standing up to tyrants like him any longer."

Leaders? Darius had wanted to ask, but Carmen was faster.

"Letting him know our decision *is* the respectful thing to do. Even if the boy-king is too big-headed to realize it. All we need is access."

Darius felt as if the ground beneath him was giving way. He hadn't felt this unsteady since…well, since Rayong, of course.

He felt untethered. These were the friends he'd grown up with—or Carmen was, at least. But from the day they'd met, Emile had been the closest thing to a brother that Darius still had left. If anything happened to them—to the last two people he cared about in the entire realm—Darius wouldn't be able to forgive himself.

But he recognized the glint in Carmen's eye. That spark had illuminated many of their bold dreams about how they would change the world.

There would be no stopping her.

The question was, would he stand in her way or step aside and watch the world they'd always dreamed of unfold?

Any other night and he might've been stronger. Might've held firmer to his new morals and convictions.

But the Ashen Princess was leaving tomorrow, and he was beginning to lose hope in just about everything. Besides, this was Carmen Louviere. There wasn't anything he wouldn't do for her, and he knew the same to be true for her.

"Dragon's fire!" Darius exclaimed, dragging a rough hand over his face and through the scruff of his beard. "I'm going to need that drink after all, and for you to tell me *everything* you're hoping to achieve tomorrow."

Emile sprung to his feet and was at the bar before Darius could even finish talking.

The corner of Carmen's lips quirked up in that mischievous way it did in their youth. "Oh, we just want to lead a revolution."

5

ALLIANCES & ENEMIES

AENWYN

There was a lot of tedium to being queen, but the most boring of all was sitting through court.

It wasn't that Queen Aenwyn disliked listening to the grievances of the Caelorans. In fact, for her it was the opposite. Hearing from the commoners, learning of their struggles, their needs, it was one of the reasons she had begun to feel connected to them, to see them as her own people, to truly step into the role as their queen.

In the last year, she'd come to care for every single person in Caelora and was truly committed to aiding them in whatever ways she could to ensure that they led the most fulfilling lives possible.

The problem was that her futile desire to help was as far as her aid went. Her opinions, her thoughts and solutions, they were not welcome in court. Only the king's voice mattered. Not hers. It made court excruciating.

It was difficult to keep her ideas to herself every time a problem was brought to her attention. For as long as she could remember, Aenwyn had been someone with strong convictions. She had an agile mind, and a knack for solving problems in a way that left everyone satisfied in the end. It was a skill she'd honed even more once becoming a big sister and having to navigate squabbles between her and Signe, Signe and Katla, or Signe and the other children they played with—essentially, the queen had her middle sister Signe to thank for how well she had learned to navigate conflict resolution, a skill that was woefully underappreciated and underutilized in her new life.

"I mean no disrespect," the king would say. "But my people venture all this way to seek the counsel and aid of their king, not some outsider from a faraway land."

That had been King Everard's position on the matter since the very first day she'd joined him, and he'd maintained that stance ever since.

At the time, it had seemed reasonable enough that Aenwyn had simply accepted it. There was a certain inherent truth to it that she could apply to her own experiences of Skogar and their distrust of outsiders. People were either inherently cautious or they had grown up in a world that had forced them to be. It wasn't something to be faulted for, but rather seen as a method of survival, and she understood that all too keenly.

King Everard had even convinced her that the best way she could show she cared for the Caeloran people was simply by being present, smiling, and supporting every decision he made.

"They'll take comfort in knowing we're a united front," he'd said.

That was the scary thing about her husband though. Some semblance of truth was always lurking deep within the nefarious bowels of his motives. It took a keen eye to detect it, but it hadn't taken her long to see the dark innerworkings of his mind, less time still for her to understand his true intent for her and her presence in the throne room.

No matter how much she smiled, how agreeable and

friendly she made herself appear, her presence rarely ever put their visitors at ease. More often than not, the opposite. Sometimes they'd flee the throne room the moment they'd arrive. The moment they laid eyes upon her.

No, Queen Aenwyn believed it far more likely that King Everard rather enjoyed the fear it struck in their hearts to see a Skogar woman at his side, someone they perceived as ruthless and feral. And for him to stoke fear, he didn't need her to speak. He didn't want her to. As long as she kept silent, the people wouldn't come to know the real her, and she would remain the terrifying savage from the north.

Her crown might as well have been made from sand that scattered in the oceanside winds for all the power it possessed.

She hated feeling so powerless.

She hated court.

She hated being his queen.

However, today, whenever Queen Aenwyn felt herself lamenting too much over her uselessness as a ruler, all she needed to do was consider what her life might've been like had she been wed to King Ulfaskr instead, and suddenly she would feel a little better.

Only a little though.

After all, it wasn't a fate she wanted for her sister Signe either.

To put it delicately, King Ulfaskr seemed practically ancient compared to either sister. He was at least a decade older than their own father, but his cobwebby hair and dry, cracked skin made him seem even older still; a ghost of a person whose youth had abandoned him long ago while his soul loitered about in a body that was ready for the earth.

Queen Aenwyn had been fortunate that at least King Everard and her were only a few years apart. But Signe was still only seventeen, still a girl in many ways, and it didn't seem right that she would be wed to some decrepit tippler.

Aenwyn couldn't bear the thought of their wedding night, nor any of the nights that would follow. At the rate that King Ulfaskr produced male heirs, she doubted Signe would be allowed to leave the bed chamber until she was ripe with child, much less permitted to join him in court—which was a whole other matter entirely. As the daughter of a former slave nation, a nation that had been kept in slavery by the very kingdom that King Ulfaskr ruled over, Aenwyn couldn't imagine a world in which Signe would be welcomed with open arms, let alone anything less than hostility and vitriolic judgment.

But many a young woman had learned to endure much more, and Signe was as fierce and resilient as any of them.

What worried Aenwyn more than anything though, more than how he was old enough to be their grandfather, and more than the infuriating potency of his seed, was the fate of King Ulfaskr's last two wives.

To the best of Aenwyn's knowledge, there was outright no indication of foul play, so she knew better than to start up the rumors herself, but part of her found it suspicious that his first two wives had met such early demises. Women died frequently enough during childbirth—the fate met by his second wife— but for his first to have mysteriously vanished? There was something about a queen disappearing without anyone being able to find a trace of her that Aenwyn simply couldn't believe.

For that reason alone she would've been eager to accompany Signe to Irongate.

Unfortunately, fate was calling her elsewhere.

It would not be easy to decline her sister's invitation, but Signe would understand. She knew that the blue dragon was the only reason why Aenwyn came to Caelora. She knew this was her destiny. And Aenwyn was growing impatient waiting to tell her that everything was finally falling into place, that all of her guilt and torture would finally be for a purpose.

But for all the people who entered the throne room, Signe was nowhere among them.

"Thank you. Oh, thank you, my king." The farmer at their feet bowed graciously, the bland, baggy tunic hanging limply from his hairy chest. "My family is forever in your debt."

Beside her, the king's smile was pleasant enough, but Aenwyn knew the hatred in his heart too well to be deceived.

"It is more than an honor to serve," King Everard told the farmer and his wife. "My father saw the great Kingdom of Caelora into an era of peace and prosperity, and I will do everything in my power to ensure his legacy continues."

A saccharine smile pulled taut against his lips as his gaze veered to Aenwyn. It was all part of the show, part of their *united* front, but to her, it was a reminder of her cage. A warning stitched through his lips. *Smile and nod or risk my wrath.*

In one year, she had learned to become quite the obedient thing.

The king returned to his audience. "The spring drought has affected us all. I only hope that our offering will be enough until you are able to get your crops back in time for the summer harvest."

"The grain is more than enough," said the woman, her arm looped lovingly with her husband's. "Thank you—thank the both of you."

When she looked to the queen, Aenwyn upheld her duty. She smiled the delicate thing she'd spent days practicing at her vanity to perfect. "Of course. Anything you need."

She knew the smile didn't quite reach her green eyes, but she hoped that they could at least sense her sincerity. It was difficult to be fully convincing when she was so distracted by her sister's delayed presence, the impending threat of the blue dragon, and also by the king's cloying gallantry.

This was how he played the game. When there was an audience, he put forth every effort to appear kind, chivalrous, dutiful. He wore the mask of the king he believed the people needed and wanted, and he did so quite convincingly.

But behind closed doors, the king spoke of his irritations freely.

Their neediness irked him. Any time he had to draw from his own resources to provide for them, he'd spend the next few days counting his spoils over and over, grumbling about every silver or grain lost to the tiresome needs of people who should just provide for themselves.

Martyr, malice, and manipulation. Those were the tenets her husband lived by.

"Safe travels," King Everard said.

He waved for the nearest guard to escort their guests out and bring in whoever else was waiting in the halls.

When he was sure they were alone, he leaned over to his queen, his smile a sharp, thin thing that could cut.

"Tell me, dear wife, when they return for aid because you've promised them *anything*, will it be from your treasury or mine that we pillage?"

Small and fragile. That's how he made her feel.

For someone who had once felt so strong, so indestructible, so powerful, Aenwyn didn't know how she'd ever reached this place where she was forever shrinking in this man's shadow. This puny man who had likely never even held a sword.

If she didn't find a way to hold onto some semblance of power—of *self*—she feared that someday there would be nothing left of her.

But he was her husband. The most powerful man not only in her life, but in all of Grimtol. And even though he was no swordsman, he knew how to wield his authority with lethality.

Aenwyn was getting better at learning how to dodge, to

duck, to protect from his blows. As much as she wanted to argue with him, to assure him that it was a nicety that no commoner would ever dare take them up on because they knew as well as anyone that the crown's charity only went so far, she knew the consequences of quarreling with a king. Knew that there would be no benefit to vocalizing her disagreement, only further chastisement.

Besides, today was not the day to ruffle his feathers.

Today, Aenwyn needed to be the docile creature he wanted her to be. She needed him to trust her, so that in the late-hours he would allow her some independence to do what needed to be done.

"Yours," she admitted, knowing it was the only answer he would accept.

King Everard hummed his approval. "Then I suggest you remain silent, or I'll have no choice but to have you escorted to your boudoir to rest for the remainder of the day. Do I make myself clear?"

It was a test, but one Aenwyn was determined to pass. So she didn't utter a word, only nodded.

"Good," the king said, resettling into his bold throne just as the double doors opened wide. "Perfectly timed for our next guests."

Just outside the doors stood a knight, a man, and a woman. Even from this distance, Aenwyn caught the smiles that faded from their faces, heard their casual conversation dying the moment they were exposed to the king's scrutiny.

Aenwyn straightened, her curiosity piqued. It wasn't often that they were visited by anyone who seemed to know of the king's darker side; he'd put forth tremendous effort to ensure that side of him was reserved for his queen, his advisors, and a select few of his most trusted guards.

But they were still too far away for her to tell if they

belonged to any of those categories. She wanted to lean closer, to get a better look at the trio disbanding from their intimate circle and entering the room. But she was all too keenly aware of the air constricting around the king. Sometimes he made it look so easy, the masks he donned. But there were other times when he could change the very essence of the world around him into darkness and danger, turn the polished marble tiles into shards of broken glass beneath her tiptoeing feet, make the very air feel as if it was crackling with lightning.

She feared that any subtle change in her own body might cause him to combust, and Aenwyn was far too close to him that she would surely be engulfed in his flames.

Instead, she remained transfixed as the group approached, the two commoners falling in line behind a knight who marched in silence like he already knew the mistake he'd made by slipping into such a casual state with these people before entering. Or at least, that's what Aenwyn assumed the king's ire was about.

Especially as the knight drew nearer and she recognized him as one of the king's trusted few: Ser Darius Graeme.

It was funny how that could happen. She'd been in Caelora for an entire year and had only ever seen him a handful of times in passing. Yet now, here they were, running into each other two days in a row.

Once the trio reached the place where no commoner was permitted to cross, Ser Darius bowed, one hand clasped over his heart.

"My king," he said, the fervor in his voice impressive to Aenwyn; she couldn't for the life of her ever muster such undying loyalty for her husband. As Ser Darius came up from his bow, he shifted his dark gaze to hers, something like unease wavering behind those eyes. "My queen."

An unspoken question hung in the air between them. Two

strangers with a shared secret, one that neither knew if they could entrust to the other.

If he'd thought for one second that she had told the king about their encounter in the halls last night, he had severely underestimated the value she placed on her own well-being. As far as she was concerned, it was in their shared interest for their run-in to remain a secret. The king needn't ever find out, just as he needn't ever find out about the haruspicy she'd be conducting later that day.

She could keep a secret.

The real question was, could Ser Darius?

"Ser Graeme," the king greeted his guard, but the words lacked any warmth or respect.

There was an edge in his voice that Aenwyn was all too familiar with. Normally, it was directed at her, but something told her this was more than just leftover irritation from her misstep earlier. It had something to do with this visit, or perhaps it was just that the king was displeased with the casual way one of his most dependable guards had seemed to be conducting himself while on duty. Or, she had to consider, perhaps this was something else entirely.

The king examined the two guests before addressing Ser Darius. "I don't recall hearing that we'd have visitors from Rayong today."

"It was news to me as well, Your Majesty." With a sweeping arm, Ser Darius gestured to the people behind him. "If it's alright with you, I'll let them explain their sudden arrival."

It was so unlike the king to show signs of his annoyance so openly that Aenwyn felt her entire body going into full alert. She flinched when he waved Ser Darius away, grimaced as he took his place among the other knights standing dutifully on the outskirts of the throne room.

Everyone standing watch seemed to hold their breath as the Rayong man bowed. It was perhaps the only thing saving them from collectively gasping when the Rayong woman curtseyed, for Aenwyn knew—like everyone else in that room—that she didn't dip nearly as low as was the custom.

"Welcome to Caelora Castle. I hope the journey was kind to you both," King Everard said, a venomous bite in his voice. He'd noticed the slight too. Still, he managed to incline his head by way of greeting with what modicum of respect he could muster. "Madame Louviere, if memory serves. I'm afraid I forget the name of your pirate husband."

"*Former* pirate," corrected the man. If the insult offended him, he made no show of it. If anything the quirked edges of his mouth seemed to deepen as he tipped an invisible hat. "Emile D'Entremont," he reminded the king. "We've met before."

"Of course, of course." King Everard's charming disposition was coming more easily for him now, his smile less forced. "It is quite the journey from Rayong, and I imagine it wasn't made lightly. Tell me, what troubles led you here and how might *your king* be of support?"

There was that bite again. That undertone of warning.

Aenwyn couldn't decipher it. It was not unusual for King Everard to flaunt his title about like a peacock in heat, but most of the time he seemed to do it out of pride and arrogance.

This was different.

There was something about the way he proclaimed his title like a conqueror staking a flag in unclaimed territory that made her think this was an attempt to assert dominance. But she didn't know why. He was the King of Caelora, and Rayong was within his territory. He already held power over them.

Or so she believed.

Emile gave a contemptuous snort that Aenwyn was sure echoed throughout the entire throne room. She had never seen someone be so blatantly disrespectful and flippant with King

Everard, and she was equal parts worried and intrigued by how this meeting would end.

Madame Louviere adjusted the bundle of hair wrapped in a turquoise and gold silk atop her head before resting the same hand on her popped hip out. Though it was clear that she held the same level of contempt for the Caeloran King, her features remained kind and inviting. "Now, King Everard, don't go making me have to treat you like an imbecile. Sky-Blessed knows you are already aware of why we've come here."

Her accent was familiar. In fact, *she* was familiar.

She reminded Aenwyn of dense, drowned woods where the greenery surrounding the trunks was just as likely to be grass as it was to be moss floating atop murky lakes of danger. She reminded her of late summer when the heat refused to relent, and her skin was left dewy for days. Of insects buzzing, their bodies aglow like fallen stars that had drifted down to Grimtol simply to dance to the music twanging and humming from the guitars and harmonicas played by the locals.

Queen Aenwyn was certain that Baug the Bear had done trade with the Rayong people at some point in time, and that when he had, she'd met the woman before her. She was certain that the melodic lilt of her voice had entranced her then just as it was now. There was a confidence within it that Aenwyn appreciated, one she might've even aspired to when they'd first met, and one she yearned to repossess now.

As Aenwyn stared at Madame Louviere with something akin to awe, she saw something golden flash behind her eyes.

Something wild.

Something...reptilian.

But it was the king's reaction that caught Queen Aenwyn off guard.

Never before had she seen him lose his composure faster. Not in front of guests, anyway.

King Everard shot to his feet, fists clenched at his sides.

"You come to *my* castle, accept *my* hospitality, and then exhibit such blatant disrespect and disobedience!"

The throne room seemed to rumble. If Aenwyn blinked, she swore she would see the very floor tear open and swallow their guests into the fiery belly beneath.

Emile—who either hadn't notice his impending demise or didn't care—folded his arms. "Only a king would call fighting for freedom disrespectful."

Madame Louviere held up a hand, silencing him before he could make the situation even worse. "It is not out of disrespect that we seek independence from Caelora, but out of necessity. Our needs are different than that of the rest of the country, needs that are often forgotten because those in power do not consider them when decisions are made."

"This is why we hold court." King Everard's voice was a midsummer storm, powerful and thunderous. It was a single strike of lightning cutting through the night sky, leaving a trail of quivering silence in its wake. "To listen to our people, hear of their plights and struggles, and respond accordingly. If there is something that you require—"

"It goes beyond petty grievances and complaints, Your Majesty," Madame Louviere said. "We have never needed your aid because you do not understand our needs or our people. You refuse to see us. And so we have been left to fend for ourselves, something we have done well enough."

Aenwyn marveled at the woman who possessed so much confidence and had such a hold over the king who was struggling to collect himself.

Caught somewhere between pleasantries and tearing into the prey at his doorstep, King Everard's teeth flashed. "Then what is the problem?"

"The problem is we have no voice. We manage ourselves independently, but we have no genuine say in the laws that govern us, our trade, our customs, our people. The time has come for us to manage ourselves."

"Xirans deserve a say," Emile added.

Aenwyn dared a slow, cautious glance to her king, finding him seething beyond control. He was a writhing den of poisonous snakes, a kill strike in his menacing eyes.

But whatever reply he was conjuring, Madame Louviere was quicker.

"You outlawed magic in Caelora after your parents died—and it is understandable for you to grieve and want to prevent such tragedies from happening within your borders again. But to outlaw magic is a violation of Xiran culture. Most of the Xiran people have animal blood in them, and they have been that way ever since The Day the Land, Sky, and Sea Shook. To outlaw magic is to outlaw them. To make people illegal. To make *me* illegal."

There it was again. That golden flicker of carnal instinct. That purely animalistic glint in her eyes. And now Aenwyn understood why.

Many of the Skogar were animal-blooded—or as Aenwyn knew them, Animali. It was a power different from her own and one that granted a person the beautifully tortuous ability to become a singular animal at their will.

Baug the Bear had taught her that during the Battle for Freedom—or the War of Destruction, depending on which side you were on—when humankind rebelled against the Sky-Blessed demigods that had ruled over them for centuries, many of the Animali had chosen to stand with the Sky-Blessed. Some humans did too. But the Sky-Blessed were forced to yield, their numbers suffering too greatly in death and worse, and then the Animali took their animal forms and fled back to their homes, leaving the human traitors to suffer punishment and enslavement to Irongate.

Those human traitors later created the Skogar nation, and

many of the Animali who had fled returned to help their families and friends fight for their freedom, making their homes in the Skogar Mountains once the battles were won.

"For all we know," King Everard said, gazing at one of his many jewel-encrusted rings. "It's those vermin who have been terrorizing Grimtol these last few years. Who's to say they have not taken the forms of dragons themselves, to retaliate against the peace we've created."

"You will not insult my people!" The echo of Madame Louviere's voice carried like a crack of a whip, silencing even the king. Blinking, she took a moment, collected herself. "Forgive me, King Everard, but you are not one of us. You do not know the way our magic works. I can assure you, we are not capable of becoming dragons. Each of us is united with but one creature. No more. And none of us are aligned with the dragons."

Aenwyn could put this conversation to rest right now. All she had to do was tell the king the truth: that it was her magic, her touch that had awoken the blue dragon, and that it was likely the touch of others like her that had awoken the other two.

Uttering such a thing now would be foolish though. The king could have her locked away or beheaded for being a traitor.

Soon, she'd be able to come clean. But only once she'd slain the dragon she was responsible for unleashing.

With a haughty laugh, King Everard waved Madame Louviere off. "You can provide no such assurances. I've seen your kind transform into beasts of the vilest natures. Sharks, snakes, wolves, bears. Even you have a killer residing just beneath your flesh, always waiting to strike, and yet you mean to stand there and try to convince me that you are purely docile?"

Madame Louviere's wide nostrils flared. "We have been living peaceably for generations—"

"Or so you claim." The king leaned forward, clasping his hands. "But the truth remains that dragons didn't come from nowhere. Magic brought them to our lands and whether it's a magic your kind practices, or the Skogar, or anyone else, I will not permit it if it puts the safety of our realm at risk."

The yellow gleam to her reptilian eyes was all warning, a declaration of war. "And I will not allow you to deem living beings illegal and to blame us for a crime you have no proof we committed."

"Do not speak to me—your *king*—of what you will or will not allow in *my* kingdom." King Everard all but spat at their feet as he motioned for the Caeloran Guard. "Get them out of my sight."

Ser Darius was the first to move forward, and if Aenwyn thought the king might stop him, she either misjudged his ire earlier or he was too distracted now to remember.

Instead, King Everard's attention remained fixed upon Madame Louviere as he added, "Do not return to me about such nonsense again. Rayong and all of Xiran will remain under my control for as long as I shall reign. Do I make myself clear?"

To her credit, the woman did not bow, did not look away. She simply glared at the king like a force to be reckoned with, a tornado shredding through a storm.

Only Emile could pull her away from her standoff, Ser Darius ushering them out of the throne room as quickly as he could.

Aenwyn was left sitting stiffly beside her tense and primed king.

There had been a time when she would've attempted to offer her wisdom, some kind words to ease his stress. But she'd learned by now that there was nothing she could say to him that would ever earn his favor. He hated her as much as he hated the dragons themselves, purely because of what she was, what she could do.

When the double doors at the end of the room opened again, and a new knight poked his head in, Aenwyn nearly deflated with relief.

"Your Highnesses," the knight addressed them. "The Lady Signe has arrived."

6

SISTERS SPEAK SILENTLY

AENWYN

"**B**ring her in."

With a forefinger and the thumb that displayed his signet ring, the young king rubbed the weariness away from his brow. Aenwyn marveled at how easily that hand rid him of his woes, or at least all traces of them. It was like watching rain wash away the blood from a felled deer, the deed all but erased from existence, and anyone who happened by would be none the wiser of the devastation that had occurred there.

It was as marvelous as it was bone-chilling the way her husband could remove all signs of his emotions just as easily as he removed the crown from atop his head before laying down for bed every night.

And he thought *her* abilities were unsettling.

As King Everard massaged, bright beams of sunlight drifted in through the skylights that pierced the ceiling from one end of the throne room to the other, and warmth bled into the room. It dazzled the high archways in gold before making its way down to cast the king in a radiant, rejuvenating glow.

Through the warmth and vibrancy of their rays, the last remnants of his foul mood were washed away.

Now, sitting beside Aenwyn was the same collected, enchanting man she'd met the day of their wedding. The same casual elegance. Confidence. It was the mask he wore for everyone but her, so she was not surprised to see him donning it now as their company finally entered the room.

She was surprised, however, by the sight of her sister.

Aenwyn saw no bones stitched into or hanging from Signe's attire. There were no knives fastened in belts at her hips. No feathers braided into her flaxen hair. No signs of the Skogar home that Aenwyn had missed so immensely over the last year.

Signe entered the room the way an innocent doe grazed in a peaceful meadow. Head down, every now and then her alert eyes skittered to the shadows, searching for signs of danger, and naïvely finding none.

Her sister was the definition of bashful beauty, a model of effulgent elegance. A true Caeloran lady, or at least she fit the part.

If Signe had been ambling through a crowd of other Caeloran ladies, not a single person would've been able to point her out as Skogar, let alone as the Chieftain's natural born heir. Signe looked as though she belonged here, aside from the red velvet gown that draped over her every curve; it was a far bolder shade than any dress a Caeloran lady would wear. But that was only because the people of Caelora wore earthen tones. Mossy greens and muddy browns. Their attire represented the *growth* and *vitality* of their kingdom—which was of course all just a rouse to help everyone forget the truth of the bloody foundation that Caelora was built upon.

The Kingdom of Irongate, however, the kingdom where Signe would soon reside over as queen, made no such attempt to hide their brutal history. Their banner was as red as the blood-soaked battlefield the day they sawed wings from the backs of their Sky-Blessed prisoners. Their banner—three swords piercing through a set of dimly glowing wings—was a warning to everyone who walked through their gate. It was a promise of the cutthroat way that people were treated beyond their border, a reminder to never turn one's back on an Ironblood.

Even if the way she carried herself was contrary to Irongate's ruthlessness, Signe's gown reflected it all.

The fierceness.

The power.

The sheer brutality.

Every step her sister took made the red fabric ripple, a current of blood dripping down her slender form. Two streams of sheer, golden silk trailed behind her like wilted wings made from thousands of stars, the world glistening in her wake.

But Queen Aenwyn's eyes were particularly drawn to the slate gray hem banded around her sister's wrists. Manacles. Not *real* manacles. The soft velvet likely wouldn't chafe her sister's tender flesh beneath, but the message behind them was loud and clear. If Aenwyn had wondered before about what Signe's marriage to King Ulfaskr would be like, now she understood.

It would be a prison.

Then again, Aenwyn wasn't sure she knew marriage to be anything but.

Signe sauntered toward them, pale hands clasped together like a true lady, like someone who'd already been beaten into obedience.

"Lady Signe," King Everard greeted, his voice as rich and as dark as honey melting in the summer sun. It coated the room in its syrupy sweetness, and Aenwyn hoped her sister could sense the danger it posed to anyone who drifted too close to its sticky trap.

Signe curtsied; a smile adorned her pink lips. "Your Grace."

Formalities be burned. It had been a full year since they'd last seen each other, maybe longer. She wouldn't wait another second for this reunion.

Aenwyn hurled herself from her chair, nearly tumbling down the few steps that separated her from her family, before flinging her arms around Signe's slender neck.

"Sister!"

Despite her best efforts to refrain from squeezing too hard, Aenwyn still managed to squeeze the wind from Signe's lungs.

Just like when they were younger, Signe squeezed back. She never was one to simply allow someone else to triumph, even when a competition had never been declared. To Signe, everything was a fight worth winning.

When they were younger, Signe's competitiveness had often been a sore spot of contention between the two girls. Sometimes Aenwyn grew frustrated constantly finding herself in contests she wasn't prepared for or in rivalries she had no interest in being involved with—who could snare a rabbit quickest, who could return with firewood the fastest, who would entrance a young man before the night was over. For Aenwyn, none of those things required competition. Oftentimes, rushing them caused her to make mistakes—to tie her snare wrong and injure the poor rabbit unnecessarily; to trip with her bundle of firewood and fall onto a piece of kindling, spearing her shoulder; to bed a young man she actually had no interest in bedding.

Their petty rivalries almost always ended with Signe becoming enraged by jealousy when her eldest sister won, or with Aenwyn losing and her becoming enraged with Signe for convincing her to participate in such childish games to begin with.

Today, the queen felt no such irritation, and even less desire to compete.

With a huff of laughter, Aenwyn released her tight grip and buried her face deeper into Signe's silken hair. Signe, too, loosened her hold with a belly full of laughter, the two of them folding deeper into one another until they could hardly breathe.

Finally, they separated. As Aenwyn drew back, taking another look at her sister and how much she'd grown in just one—albeit rather long—year, she noticed that the intricate braids resting against Signe's exposed collarbone were the only remaining relics of Skogar her sister possessed. She tried not to think about how soon it would be until King Ulfaskr erased even that small part of her as well.

Shaking away her worries, Aenwyn's smile grew wider. "I am so happy to see you! What a blessing it is to have you here." Remembering they had an audience who detested not being the center of the world, she gestured anxiously up at her husband. "Signe, you remember my husband, King Everard?"

"Of course." Respectfully, Signe's eyes fluttered to the floor when she dipped her head again. "It is difficult to forget a king, let alone one—and forgive me for being so bold for saying as such, but—one as handsome as your husband."

Aenwyn had to actively rebel against her own eyes for fear that they might roll right out of her skull. It made it easier that she knew what her sister was doing, and she knew how beneficial these small compliments would be. In the year she'd been away, Aenwyn had written home to her sisters dozens of times, telling them all about her new life as queen. She wrote to them about everything she was learning about Caeloran culture, the food, the weather, the way the sun shone differently in this west than it did in Skogar.

It was too risky to ever overtly share with them anything that would besmirch her husband's name, but she could speak in generalities and share some personal accounts. Like when one of the royal painters depicted her husband with a slightly weaker jaw, his nose too prominent for his liking, and the king had not only banished the artist for life from Caelora, but also his children and children's children as well. She told them how her husband was a proud and cleanly man, and that one day when he had noticed a seam torn from his surcoat, she didn't see him leave his room until the royal tailor could tend to it—which had taken a full week due to an illness that had left the tailor bedridden.

Every time King Everard acted in theatrically childish ways, Aenwyn did her best to retell the tale to her sisters in a way that made her seem like she was on his side—complaining about the servants' inadequate performances or feigning a level of appall that mimicked his own—while simultaneously painting a crisp image for her sisters of the king's fragile ego and short, if not sometimes covert, temper.

Signe was using that knowledge now to her benefit. And it seemed to be working. The king all but beamed with pride at her sweet words, sitting taller in his throne as he considered his response.

"Boldness, I have learned, is only the mark of a strong Skogar woman." He spoke as if he meant to flatter her, but Aenwyn knew better. He'd never said a single kind word about her people, let alone actually meant it. This was all part of his usual act. "In the name of being bold, dare I say you, Signe, will make a beautiful bride."

"Thank you," her sister said with a bright smile, but Aenwyn noticed the slight bob of her throat. Fear swept through her, wide eyes meeting Aenwyn's with a silent plea: *save me*. "So you've heard the news then?"

The conversation caught up to her then. This was the cue she'd been waiting for.

"A bride?" Aenwyn asked. Forcing a furrow into her brow, she addressed her husband. "To whom?"

She'd practiced this reaction all first-hours. If Ser Darius had known of Signe's arrival today, that meant the king had too. It also meant that for whatever reason he'd kept it from her.

Unless Aenwyn wanted her husband to find out about her wandering the castle with Ser Darius last night, she needed to act convincingly surprised.

Glancing between the two of them, she feigned impatience. "What news?"

The king rose from his throne and strode to his wife's side. He placed a cool hand against Aenwyn's lower back, and she stiffened. "Calm yourself, my dear. You have nothing to fear. Your sister shares with you pleasant news. I only didn't tell you because I thought it best you hear it from her directly."

Lies.

Information was power and King Everard liked to hoard it the way the sea hoarded sand.

The question was, *why* hadn't he told her? What power could she have possibly obtained from knowing of her sister's arrival? Aenwyn wasn't sure she'd ever find out, so she tried not dwelling on it.

"I am calm."

Aenwyn jerked from her husband's grasp. It wasn't part of her usual placated façade, and she worried what he might do the moment she did it, but she couldn't stop herself. Being in Signe's presence had invigorated her. Signe who had never seemed so docile, so broken, so *wrong* a day in her life.

Aenwyn took her sister's gentle hands into her own. "Then tell me. What news brings you to Caelora?"

"Oh, it is happy news, Aenwyn. Our father has forged another alliance." Though her words were full of merriment, her tone was anything but.

"With whom?"

Signe swallowed, releasing Aenwyn's hold. "With the great Kingdom of Irongate."

There it was. A truth that Aenwyn had already known thanks to Ser Darius, and yet it still swept the floor out from under her and swallowed the room into darkness.

Aenwyn couldn't find the words to convey what she was feeling. Even if she could, she wouldn't dare say them in front of her husband.

Finally she settled on a meager, "Then I suppose congratulations are due."

Absentmindedly, her thumb found the black, metal band around her finger and began spinning the ring that kept her powers trapped.

Oblivious to the small, anxious act, the king smiled broadly at Signe. He reached out and stroked her pale shoulder with a presumed friendliness that didn't belong between two people who'd only met once before, nearly a year ago. "It is wonderful news indeed. Has a date been set?"

Aenwyn's stomach revolted at that gentle caress. She wasn't even sure why. Though he'd never shown her—his own wife—anything remotely resembling romance, let alone something as simple as basic kindness, it wasn't like she wanted affection from him anyway. She'd known the day they married that this man would never be worthy of her heart. And on most days, she could even accept it.

So it wasn't jealousy carving into her, but more the blatant show of disrespect. It was one thing for a king to flirt aimlessly with young, pretty women in the privacy of his own chambers or secret outings. But to do it in front of her? With her own sister, nonetheless?

Her throat tingled, and she couldn't tell if she was about to scream, lunge for his throat, or throw up all over him.

Fortunately, Signe responded before Aenwyn could do anything. "We plan to wed as soon as I reach Irongate. King Ulfaskr is eager, as am I. So, I expect about two months' time. However long the journey is from here to there."

Signe played the part of a blushing bride well. To any stranger—to the king—she likely seemed excited. But Aenwyn knew better. She could read the small signs.

As Signe and King Everard made small talk about the wedding and what a celebrated occasion it would be, Aenwyn watched the way her sister's hands trembled ever so slightly, saw the repeated lumps in her throat that she had to swallow down, either full of tears or stomach bile, Aenwyn wasn't sure.

And all the time she watched—too distracted to truly listen —Aenwyn just kept thinking about the grey cuffs of fabric around Signe's wrists. She didn't know King Ulfaskr personally herself, only met him once, and very briefly. The pores of her skin had puckered in his unsettling presence. The rumors that abounded about his indecencies toward women rang true. She understood the kind of man he was and what misery awaited her middle sister. And for all the ways that King Everard belittled, begrudged, and chastised Aenwyn, she was certain that it would be nothing like the wretched marital existence that awaited Signe.

"But why?" Aenwyn blurted when she could contain herself no longer. "Dragon's fire! You're only seventeen. You're still a child!"

"A child?" King Everard's chest puffed. "Are you suggesting that your king was a child when you wed him then?"

Aenwyn couldn't answer him. She wouldn't. For the truth was that they had both been children when they'd wed at seventeen for him and nineteen for her. Naïve, unsure children parading about as near-adults. But saying as much now would do her no good.

Fortunately, by some divine intervention, Signe had found the resolve Aenwyn could not seem to muster, and she smiled at the king, a soft and gentle thing that would've charmed even a den of hungry wolves.

"My king, I have traveled far, and I fear this unexpected news might have made my sister weary as well. With your permission, might we be excused and permitted time to rest and discuss matters more privately?" She glanced around the room before stepping in closer, whispering to him like they were co-conspirators. "Aenwyn needs time to adjust. She always has. Let her do so in private where she might not embarrass your house, or mine. Please?"

If anyone else had spoken about her in such a manner, Aenwyn would've had no choice but to bite.

But it wasn't anyone else. It was Signe. Signe, who'd always had a tongue dripping with venom. Signe, who'd never possessed a single diplomatic bone in her body.

If Aenwyn was wildfire, it was because Signe was a strike of lightning that had set her ablaze. Aenwyn hadn't known how to be herself—how to be truly free of fear and doubt—until she'd met her middle sister. She had been forced to learn the basics of survival, but it was Signe who had turned it into an artform. She'd tested survival's limits, set new boundaries, and had understood far younger than any of them that existence had just as much to do with desires as it did eating.

Signe had been born and raised Skogar. She could be as brutal as the mountains themselves, as feral as the churning sea, and as wild as an arctic fox dashing across an endless tundra.

It seemed her sister had been busy this past year, and Aenwyn couldn't wait to hear all about the ways she'd grown and matured.

As the king considered her plea, the corner of his mouth ticked up with deviant pleasure. "How could I deny such a reasonable request from such a lovely lady?" He snapped his fingers for one of his knights, and Ser Darius stepped forward. "Accompany the Lady Signe and my wife to the queen's chambers. See to it that they are not disturbed while they rest." Turning back to Signe, he inclined his head. "I do hope that you'll be able to join us for supper."

"It would be my honor, King Everard."

7

BOUDOIR SECRETS

AENWYN

A thousand questions bounded around Aenwyn's skull as she, Signe, and Ser Darius maneuvered through the bright halls of Caelora Castle. She didn't dare break the silence though.

Not one of them had uttered a single word since Ser Darius had said, "Follow me," and guided them out of the throne room.

The absurdity of her being escorted to her own bed chamber was almost laughable, but if the others thought so, she couldn't tell. Signe's elegant façade wouldn't be broken, her graceful expression trained forward for the entirety of the silent, informal tour through the castle. And for Ser Darius, there was too much tension in his shoulders to suggest he thought anything about the day was worth chuckling about.

When they reached the queen's bed chamber, he opened the door and checked inside before returning to them. "I'll just be out here then, should you need anything."

"Thank you, Ser Darius," Aenwyn said with a little more sincerity than she might've normally directed at one of the king's knights. But he had messed up today, at least in the eyes of her husband. And Aenwyn had no doubt that giving him such a trivial task of guarding her door while she and her sister prattled on inside was only the start of the punishment that awaited him. There was no need to pour salt into his wounds.

Besides, her sister and what would surely be an enthralling story awaited her inside.

Aenwyn closed the door and scuttled to the opposite end of the room to where her middle sister was wrestling with the laces of her corset.

"Get this suffocating bone trap off me!"

A smile broke through Aenwyn's worried expression. There was the spirited sister she knew and loved.

"Don't just stand there gawking at me like some lovestruck dope," Signe snapped. "Help me."

Aenwyn did her best, but the task did not come easy. The corsets were one custom she herself had still not yet been able to bring herself to adopt. Of all the Caeloran customs, it was the one thing she'd refused. Her body had not been made for such restrictions, and any time she'd tried to squeeze herself into one of those contraptions, it just made her feel like an overstuffed meat pie that had sat in the sun far too long.

Her voluptuous figure was one of the many ways she differed from the slim women of the Caeloran court, and she knew it displeased her king more than he would ever vocalize. But Aenwyn had worked hard for the weight she'd gained after Baug had rescued her from that abandoned island. She'd earned every dimple in her thick thighs, every pound of flesh. And though the people of Caelora seemed to equate tight-fitting corsets and petiteness with beauty, Aenwyn would rather be burned at the stake than shed a single inch of her proud waistline.

When they finally freed Signe of the crimson corset, she heaved a great sigh that made Aenwyn wonder if she'd even been able to breathe for the hours predating her freedom.

Signe slumped onto the edge of Aenwyn's bed. Tossing her braids over her shoulder, she let her head loll back and sank into her arms where she kept herself propped up. "What a fool I am, allowing Katla to pick my outfit for today. She said this attire was the custom, but you're not even wearing one."

"It is the custom," Aenwyn assured her. "But I am a queen. I do have some modicum of power to determine what I wear."

Eyes as black as pitch roved over Aenwyn's body, the stifling length of her green gown, the heavy bodice embroidered with stones of gold. "And you're telling me you chose *that?*"

Aenwyn flushed. "I said *some* modicum of power. Not a lot."

Signe's laugh was isolated to her nose, a single, short burst of air. "More than I'm guessing I'll have." She resettled then, tilting her head back to gaze up at the ceiling as if she were watching the clouds like they used to do. "I stand by my former statement: Katla is forbidden from ever dressing me again."

"Well, she is only five. It's not like she's a trustworthy judge of the customs of all the kingdoms yet." Gently, Aenwyn lowered herself to sit beside her sister. Even this close, it still felt as if they were miles apart. Aenwyn couldn't fight the solemn way she felt. "It sounds like soon you won't have to worry about Katla meddling with your personal life though."

Her sister tensed, every muscle in her body winding tight like a cobra coiling before a strike. It was her usual *leave-me-alone* posture, but Aenwyn was one of few who was allowed to ignore it.

"A wedding? Signe, how did this happen?"

Still gazing up into the gauzy fabric hanging over Aenwyn's bed, Signe shook her head. "How do any political alliances happen? Fear. Power. Money. Take your pick."

Aenwyn's forehead bunched. "Baug hardly had any interest in an alliance with Caelora. I had to beg him for months before he would allow me to follow this path. I can't imagine he would so readily bind you to Irongate. I mean, it wasn't very long ago when our people were still enslaved to them. Our father was only a child, but even he still remembers it. Why would he—"

"I don't know, Aenwyn! Maybe after your wedding, he realized that the best thing he could do for Skogar, the only way he could strengthen our developing nation, was to solidify more alliances, especially with the most powerful kingdoms of the realm. For as much as our people boast, we are a small nation. Baug likely realized that he had very few prospects, leaving him no choice but to marry us off, one-by-one."

Biting the inside of her lower lip, Aenwyn tried not to think about what this would mean for Katla, and instead considered what her sister was saying. But what was there to consider? Signe was right. The Skogar had few prospects, and when it came to strong marital alliances, they had even fewer still.

Given the volcanic climate of Galorfin, they weren't a suitable option, even if Signe could withstand the same levels of heat that the Molten could. They likely wouldn't have accepted a proposal anyway, considering they'd all but extricated themselves from Grimtol when the dragons came.

Vallonde was a dying kingdom, their lands scorched to the point that the majority of their inhabitants had fled north, seeking refuge. It was no place for the daughter of a chieftain.

Although the Skogar had always been strong allies to Arrin, City in the Clouds, home to the divine Sky-Blessed, they didn't marry outside of their own kind, and therefore would've turned Baug down if he had even attempted to preposition them.

And he most certainly couldn't marry her to an Ashen in Eynallore. Unless he meant for her certain death.

That left Caelora, where he'd already established an alliance, and Irongate.

"It doesn't matter." Signe sighed, sitting up straighter and turning toward her sister. "I didn't come here to plot a way out of this. As the chieftain's daughter, I've known what fate might await me my entire life. I've only come to see if you will be at my side the day of the wedding."

Aenwyn sucked in a breath, but Signe didn't let her answer just yet.

She turned her gaze toward the tangle of her hands. "Baug won't let Katla come. If things turn for the worst, he doesn't want her in danger."

There was bitterness in her tone that twisted Aenwyn's stomach. It was not unlike Signe to be wrought with jealousy, especially that which was directed toward her sisters and the small ways in which Baug had expressed his love for them.

For once though, Aenwyn understood why Signe would feel so slighted. The way she told the story, Baug might as well be throwing her into the Maw of Death just to see if she would survive like some of the Vallondeans had when the earth had cracked open The Day the Land, Sky, and Sea Shook.

He was risking her life on a whim. Signe, more than most, was bound to feel slighted.

It made breaking the news to her that Aenwyn wouldn't be able to attend all the more difficult.

"What about Ingrid?" Aenwyn asked, remembering some of the other children whom they'd grown up with. Ingrid's father was Baug's right-hand-man, so they'd been fairly close, the lot of them. "Or if she's protecting the women, what about her brother, Hrolf?"

Signe shook her head. "He says anyone who has never seen battle won't be allowed to come. It'll just be me, walked down the aisle by Ingrid's father as some of his warriors stand watch."

This made Aenwyn start. "Baug won't be there?"

Signe tensed. "No, he won't."

Deflating, Aenwyn averted her gaze to the floor. She couldn't imagine walking down the aisle to be wed to a stranger without her father at her side. It was because of him that she'd remained fortified to her cause. It was because of him that she didn't start a war that day.

How would her sister fare without a single member of her family there?

Signe reached for and took Aenwyn's hands into her own. She flinched at their smoothness, caught off by the lack of callouses on them. Aenwyn might've jerked them away and saved herself the shame if Signe hadn't been clutching them so tightly, the look in her eyes so desperate.

"So?" Signe asked, blue eyes shimmering. "What do you say? Can I count on you to be there?"

"Oh, Signe." Aenwyn's fingers tightened, and remorse twisted her gut. She braced herself for the beast she was about to evoke from her sister. "I wish that I could be. But you've only just arrived in time for my own departure."

Signe's eyes turned as sharp as steel.

She jerked her hands back, nearly tearing the flesh from their palms. "Departure? Where are you going?"

She was losing her. Aenwyn heard the strain in Signe's voice and knew that depending on what she said next, Signe would either storm out the doors or perhaps decide to listen for a little longer.

"It's happening," Aenwyn said, her voice tightly wound. "The blue dragon is going to strike Caelora again."

Signe sat back, arms folding. "All the more reason for you to come to Irongate with me then."

"You know I can't. The whole reason I came here was to stop that dragon from killing more innocent people."

"*Innocent?*" In an instant, Signe was on her feet, a gust of wind trailing in her wake and leaving Aenwyn chilled without her sister by her side. "Has it been so easy for you to forget the Skogar histories since you've been away?"

"No!" Aenwyn tried matching her sister's fierceness, but her voice wavered. She had to correct it. "I came here *for* Skogar."

"Right, to slay a dragon that has evaded every army in Grimtol." Pacing the room, Signe kicked at the discarded corset on the ground. "It's not going to be like felling a deer, Aenwyn. Have you even thought about that? Have you thought about how you're going to kill it?"

"Yes and no," Aenwyn muttered. But at her sister's irritated scoff, she amended, "That's where haruspicy comes to play."

One of Signe's perfectly slender brows shot up. "You mean a sacrifice?" She glanced around the room as if she thought she might find the animal stowed away somewhere nearby. "Here? In Caelora? I thought magic was outlawed here."

"It is," Aenwyn said, rising from the bed. Remembering that Ser Darius was still posted outside, she crossed the room toward her sister and lowered her voice. "But I'll be gone before they find out."

"Gone where?" Signe asked, but then she rolled her eyes, recognizing the expression on her sister's face. "Right. The haruspicy will tell you." Aenwyn nodded. Begrudgingly, so did Signe. "Then I guess this is yet another goodbye before one more queen's reign begins."

Turning on her heels, Signe bent to retrieve her corset before marching toward the door.

The knob was in her hand when Aenwyn called out, "Signe, wait."

"Wait? What for?" Her sister threw her arms in the air, somehow managing to maintain her grip on the corset. "You are as stubborn as a glacier. Once your mind is set, there is no convincing you otherwise. I'd merely be wasting my breath."

Before she could twist the doorknob, a desperate plea ripped from Aenwyn's throat. "I could use your help."

Jaw unhinged, Signe spun around to face her eldest sister. She blinked once, twice, before finally calming herself enough to speak, even if her words were clipped and her smile taut. "Help how?"

It was an impressive thing to witness. Aenwyn had never seen Signe rein her emotions in like that before.

Aenwyn wished they had more time to talk about how they'd grown and changed over the last year, and why. She wished they were able to sit around a fire in the middle of the night, sipping mead and sharing stories about how their lives had been the past year without each other. She wished conversations with Signe ever ended in anything other than fuming irritation.

For now, she'd have to do with restrained annoyance.

Aenwyn summoned her away from the door. For a moment, it didn't look like Signe would oblige her, until she reminded her sister with a nod of who was just on the other side. Begrudgingly, Signe came.

Ignoring the roll of her sister's bright eyes, Aenwyn leaned in closer. "I can sacrifice one of the pigeons in the dovecote, learn what I need to about where the dragon is and how to slay it, and then flee the castle."

"And? What part of that am I helping with? And before you even ask, no I will not be helping you practice illegal magic inside your kingdom."

"I wouldn't ask you to," Aenwyn said. "However, I might ask you to create a distraction."

8

THE DISTRACTION

AENWYN

S igne flung the bed chamber door open, screaming over her shoulder, "I don't know why I even bothered coming here! You're a horrible, dreadful person and I never should've thought I could count on you!"

As she whisked past Ser Darius, he staggered to catch his bearings.

"Pardon me," she growled, feet scuffling past him in a blaze. Only once she was halfway down the hall, only once she was within earshot of as many servants as she could be, did she finally turn around, just as they'd planned. Straightening the corset that they'd hastily tied back into place, she glared at Aenwyn, one finger outstretched. "You just became an enemy of Irongate!"

Slowly, Ser Darius' head swiveled toward Aenwyn, accusation brimming in his umber eyes.

Aenwyn ignored him, shouting back, "Go on and leave, Signe. Beg your new king to fight your petulant battles for you."

The plan was simple. Rumors of a potential war befalling the two most powerful nations in Grimtol all due to the petty squabbling of two Skogar sisters would reach King Everard quick enough, and he'd have no choice but to try to smooth things over with Signe, seeing as she was their guest. He'd of course want to speak with Aenwyn as well, but later, only after he'd heroically saved the kingdom from war.

It would give her just enough time to do what she needed to do.

Now, it was just a matter of getting rid of her pesky guard.

Aenwyn stormed toward the door to slam it shut, but Ser Darius caught it with a sturdy arm and pressed his head inside.

"What happened?"

Playing the role of an irate, quarreling sister, Aenwyn paced back into her room and threw her arms up. "You saw her! She's acting like a child."

She plopped on the edge of her bed and folded her arms as Ser Darius took a timid step inside. It was the opposite direction Aenwyn needed him to go, but she hoped she could correct his course.

"I didn't ask what she was acting like," he said, glancing over his shoulder as if the king himself might sneak up on him and find him where he shouldn't be. "I asked what happened."

"Are you a brother, Ser Darius?"

"No." Even beneath the scruff of his beard, Aenwyn noticed the muscle tic along his strong jaw. "Not anymore."

There was so much pain in that statement. So much left for her to wonder. But she couldn't afford to ask.

Sitting straighter, she crossed her legs. "Well, this is just what siblings do. They bicker over foolish things. The only difference is that this time the bickering happens to be between two queens overseeing two kingdoms, and one of them is still a petulant child who hasn't grown up and now has too much power in her hands."

"Bickering. Sisterly bickering." He mulled over the words, unsatisfied. "Your sister just threatened the Caeloran crown."

With a haughty laugh, Aenwyn shrugged. "What do you want me to do about it? If you're so concerned about the safety of the kingdom, you go after her."

It felt heavy-handed, the bait too obvious for someone as keen as him to lap up. And for a long moment, Aenwyn wasn't sure that he would. In silence, he watched her, expression as stoic as ever.

"Wait here," he finally said, spinning and exiting the room, and closing the door tight behind him.

Aenwyn didn't waste a moment. She leapt to her feet the instant she heard him shouting orders to the guards and servants nearby. She couldn't quite hear what he was telling them, but she knew the corridor was quieting, people fleeing to somewhere else in the castle. Good. All she needed was an hour, maybe less, and she thanked fate for bringing her sister here to her today. Hopefully she'd be able to thank Signe someday as well.

With her ear pressed to the door, Aenwyn listened for the commotion to quiet before slinking into the hallway and heading for the dovecote.

9

WHEN QUEENS FEUD

DARIUS

"*You just became an enemy of Irongate!*"

Signe's words kept beating against his skull. The last thing he needed was rumors of a war between Caelora and Irongate breaking out through the castle.

On second thought, it might be exactly the sort of distraction that could serve him well.

It could keep King Everard occupied with something other than the conflict that he now faced with all of Xira; he might even forget that Darius had even been mildly involved.

Unless of course, Darius would be blamed for both wars, one with Xiran rebels, the other with the soon-to-be Queen of Irongate. After all, he had been in charge of supervising both Queen Aenwyn and her sister just before the outburst.

Yeah. He would undoubtedly be blamed for all of it, which meant he desperately needed to fix it. The only way to stay on the king's good side now was to prevent at least one of the wars from happening—and even then, there was no telling how King Everard would deal with him once he had the chance. But Darius had to try.

"Wait here," he told the queen before returning to the corridor outside her bed chamber.

He could've sworn just moments prior it had been nearly empty. Now it seemed flooded with every servant in King Everard's employ. They all gawked, awaiting his instruction, his guidance. Even the knight stationed at the end of the hall who was still standing at attention couldn't seem to pry his gaze away from where Darius stood in the queen's opened doorway.

He wasn't sure what they thought he was going to say? That Irongate was on the attack and for everyone to run and hide?

If Signe were to summon them, it would take weeks for them to arrive. Maybe months depending on the size of their army. If war was truly on the horizon between their powerful kingdoms, they at least had time to prepare.

But truthfully, he doubted it would come to that anyway. It was like Queen Aenwyn said: this seemed more like sisterly bickering than anything. Caelora had a long-standing, positive relationship with Irongate. He hoped it wouldn't be jeopardized so easily by the emotional whims of a young queen.

For now, his real concern was to stop any paranoid rumors from spreading. It didn't mean that no one should take Signe's threat seriously and check in on her, but it did mean that there was nothing to panic over. Not yet anyway.

As Darius made his way toward the knight, he flashed what he hoped would be a comforting smile to every servant he passed, ushering them along and instructing them to return about their duties.

Only once the corridor had cleared did he give the knight instructions.

The knight saluted him. "Ser Graeme."

Darius mimicked the gesture out of respect.

"What's going on? It sounded like—"

"I know what it sounded like," Darius interrupted. "We need to contain this before it gets out of hand."

The knight nodded, eager to fulfill any duty for his kingdom. "Anything."

A sigh worked itself out of Darius. The way he saw it, there were two tasks that needed to be seen to.

"One of us needs to find the Lady Signe and make sure she doesn't do anything rash, while the other one needs to stay here and protect Queen Aenwyn."

"Protect her?" Fear tweaked the young knight's expression. "Is everything okay?"

"It will be. It's no more than...sisters fighting. We just need to get this sorted." He patted the young man's shoulder, hoping it was all he needed to be reassured. Truth be told, he wasn't sure the boy was up for either task, especially speaking with Lady Signe, but he had no other options. King Everard and commanded him to stay with the queen, and so that's what he needed to do. "Can you talk with Lady Signe?"

The boy surprised him then, beaming with the confidence of a bard before a show. "I have seven sisters, sir. I have handled a few squabbles in my short days."

"Good. Then go. If she heads anywhere other than her own chambers, you alert the Guard immediately to secure the perimeter, as well as her."

The boy looked concerned. "S—sir?"

This was a future queen they were talking about after all. But on the off chance that Lady Signe *was* on her way to declare war, either by pigeon or fleeing on horseback, Darius couldn't allow her to leave. Not without speaking with the king first.

"You heard me."

The young knight stood straighter. He saluted again. "Yes sir."

And then he was off. Darius watched him until he disappeared down the hallway, and even for a time after. He kept debating on going with him. Despite the man having experience calming his own sisters after an argument, it was very likely that experience would differ from trying to soothe a Skogar woman after one, let alone a future queen.

In the end, he had to trust that the boy could do.

Darius turned around and made the short walk back to his post outside the queen's door. When he found it ajar, he was only mildly concerned. After all, it was possible that he had left it open in his haste to get everything sorted outside in the hall.

But when he rapped his knuckles against the ornate wood and there came no reply, he knew he was wrong.

"Queen Aenwyn?"

Darius cracked the door open and peeked inside. The room was empty. His first thought was that she'd been taken, his thoughts quick to veer toward the rumor of an attack and knowing just how valuable stealing a queen would be in a war.

But upon closer inspection of the room, Darius knew that wasn't it. The queen hadn't been taken. There were no signs of a struggle; nothing seemed to be out of place or knocked over as if she'd fought her attacker—and he knew she would've. If someone had come for her, there would've been screams or shouts, and even though he'd been down the hall, he would've heard her.

The events of the mid-hours caught up with him. The argument between her and her sister, it almost seemed so obvious now, so fake and staged.

They'd played everyone. Played him.

Anger bubbled up within him and he clenched his jaw. He wouldn't be made a fool of. While the rest of the castle went on believing their rouse, he would turn his attention on finding her.

The only question was, where had she gone? And if Darius was being honest with himself, he hadn't the slightest clue what the answer to that question was. For months, he'd watched her, noting her daily habits and schedule, the people she associated with. But if he was to believe what she'd told him in the halls last night, then none of that was useful intel right now. It would tell him nothing of where she might be, who she might be with.

Instead of focusing on what he didn't know, Darius concentrated on the facts as he saw them.

The queen and her sister had effectively created a distraction. Lady Signe had fled the room, while the queen had convinced Darius to address the situation. This likely meant that she'd been hoping he would chase after Signe, giving the queen an opening to slip from her bed chamber without notice. It also seemed to Darius that if Queen Aenwyn wanted him on Lady Signe's trail, it was unlikely that the two sisters had planned on reconvening.

Signe was the rouse. A cold trail meant to keep Darius preoccupied. Queen Aenwyn was the real concern. She was going somewhere. But where?

Maybe somewhere outside the castle walls? After all, a rumor such as a war with Irongate would send every staff member into a gossiping frenzy. Everyone would be too distracted to notice Aenwyn slipping out of the castle.

But for what? Why?

Darius supposed he didn't need to know that yet. For now, he rushed to her balcony and leaned over the balustrade. From the side of the castle, it offered at least a partial view of the surrounding kingdom.

Down below, the streets were mostly unoccupied—thank the sun. It seemed that most of the citizens were busy with their trades or perhaps at home for lunch.

It made the flash of auburn hair racing past the Drunken Owl that he just barely caught from the corner of his eye stand out.

Though he spotted her, it was still difficult to tell where she was headed. There wasn't much on that side of town—there wasn't much this close to the castle regardless. Most of Caelora resided beyond the keep, beyond the bridges that led across the Unfathomed Waters. The dwellings inside the keep mostly belonged to the Caeloran Guards and their families: homes and lodgings, the tavern, a small market.

There were also the royal stables.

Which were in the exact direction Queen Aenwyn was fleeing.

"What are you up to, Queen of Wildfire?" Darius asked, bolting back into the castle to begin the very indirect route toward the stables. He just hoped he could make it there in time to stop her from doing…whatever it was she had planned.

10

OF FEATHERS AND BLOOD

AENWYN

The pigeons stirred when Aenwyn entered the dark, confined structure; their coos and ruffling of feathers echoed within the circular walls surrounding her.

She'd never been in a dovecote before. In Skogar, they had no use for messenger birds. Few of the kingdoms were on speaking terms with them anyway, and Baug the Bear preferred to communicate important matters in person whenever possible. The only birds Aenwyn had ever seen him interact with were the few ravens that sometimes provided insight on decisions that impacted the kingdom, and the falcons Baug the Bear kept for navigating the tumultuous seas.

So Aenwyn wasn't sure what she had expected when entering the dovecote, but it wasn't this.

Sun shone down from a hole in the topmost point of the ceiling, giving her enough light to see in the dimness. If she had to guess, she would say there were close to two hundred holes carved in every stone wall, shelves upon shelves of small cubbies that led all the way up to the tip of the ceiling. It made her feel like she'd walked into a beehive, an unsettling image at best, and one she quickly forced herself to shake.

Aenwyn removed her ring. At the release of power that surged through her, she sucked in an invigorating breath. It never did cease to astonish her just how freeing it was to have magic flooding through her veins again. How powerful it made her feel. Nowadays, she was so accustomed to feeling useless, helpless, that the surge of magic tingling her skin from head to toe made her panic. For half of a breath, she feared what might happen to her if she couldn't control it, the sheer force of it like hot coals crackling throughout her body.

It was tempting to put the ring back on, to hide behind the binds that she'd been told she needed. But King Everard wasn't here to make her feel small now.

Up until a year ago, Aenwyn had lived her entire life with this magic at her beck and call. She didn't need to fear it. It was a part of her, just as much as the heart pumping beneath her breast.

She almost chucked the ring aside, for she knew there'd be no need to contain her true self during the journey ahead. On the off chance she was caught before she could finish though, she wanted to be able to thrust the ring back into place before her husband could berate her for it—or worse.

Tucking the gaudy thing into her bodice for safekeeping, Aenwyn glanced around the dovecote. It was only then that it dawned on her that she didn't know how to approach a live, wild animal. Not for a sacrifice, anyway. All the other times she'd needed to use this type of magic, the beasts had been brought to her, tamed and some of them even on a leash.

As the pigeons continued their protesting at her intrusion, she knew this was going to be more difficult than she'd anticipated.

Her first thought was to try to knock one out. If she had a slingshot, it might not have been a bad idea. Like many of the children she'd grown up with on the island, it had been her weapon of choice in her youth. They'd spent countless hours on the beach seeing who could knock a coconut from a tree first, or who could hit a crab skittering across the sands. It was a rarity for her to lose those feats.

Even now, all those years later, she was almost certain her aim would be nearly perfect. But there was no slingshot in sight. Not to mention, she feared that if she startled the flock too much, she'd alert someone in the castle.

For now, keeping them docile was a priority.

Aenwyn grabbed the evergreen pouch tied around the crook of her elbow and slid it off from her arm. She had just barely remembered to retrieve it from where it was tucked inside a vase atop the fireplace mantle before fleeing her chambers earlier. Most days she tried to keep it close, hiding it in her bosom, or securing it to her inner thigh. But some of her garments made it too difficult to conceal, including the modest gown she had chosen to wear today for her reunion with her sister—she hadn't wanted to appear too different, too lost to the Caeloran ways. It seemed Signe would've understood though.

Loosening the drawstrings, Aenwyn peered inside and rifled through the contents until she found the sprigs of a dried plant with light purple flowers—an herb called laverdia that possessed calming properties.

She crushed a sprig in her palm, and held it out to one of the pigeons that was perched in a hole nearby.

"Here, birdie." She spoke with sweetness she hadn't heard from anyone in years, not since her own mother had perished and stopped whispering kind sentiments in her ear to help her endure the demon-sleep.

The bird's beady eyes didn't blink, but the frantic, gurgling coo that it made in response caused her to stop in her tracks.

The sound ricocheted around the room, a call to the others who answered in kind. A chorus of danger. A racket of alarm.

Birds leapt from their holes to fly to higher ground, and

Aenwyn tried desperately not to flinch as their wings grazed past her.

This wasn't going well. If all it took was one, cautious step to send the flock in a frenzy of fear, there was no telling what they'd do once she actually began her work.

However, the bird she'd started for, remained where it rested.

Aenwyn dared another step. Sure enough, the pigeon fussed again, and the others grew restless, but she didn't let it deter her. She'd set her marks on this bird, and as long as it remained in its hole before her, she'd attempt to grab it.

Step after step, she crept toward the frightened thing. By the time she was finally within arm's reach, at least a handful of the other pigeons had flown the coup through the small opening at the top. She tried not to worry about someone noticing, and instead kept her focus on the grey-blue bird before her.

When she reached a hand for it, it ruffled its feathers and took a waddling step back, farther into darkness. She didn't know how intelligent they were, but she thought she noticed it glancing up, as if it was trying to gauge whether it could still make it past her, or if it had made a grave mistake retreating farther.

Just as the pigeon ducked down, readying its wings for flight, Aenwyn slapped her hand atop it.

The sharp sound echoed like a crack of thunder. The pigeons grew wild. They startled from their holes, two to three dozen of them gusting around her like a tornado before rising, bolting for the top of the shelter.

As they vacated, Aenwyn was reminded of the bats that would emerge from the caves at dusk on the island where she grew up. Hearts in their throats, Aenwyn and her friends would sit outside the caves, waiting for the sun to drop to the horizon, just to see who would wait the longest before fleeing from the hoard of bats coming for them. Sometimes though, when it had just been her, she would nestle into a cozy patch of grass in the meadow outside and just watch and marvel at them as they took flight, wondering where they would go, and how they always knew to return before the daybreak, even with as irrational as it could be.

There was no time to marvel at the pigeons now though. No time to admire their instincts.

Although Aenwyn had caught one of them, she'd only managed to trap part of its body against the hole. One wing was free, and it flailed about frantically.

All too fast, the bird was jerking from her grip, and before she could close her other hand around it, the pigeon squirmed free enough that it was able to launch itself from the hole. A whoosh of wings, and the bird was in flight. Aenwyn only just barely managed to capture one of its legs before it wildly spun around the cave-like room.

Chaos erupted around her as the rest of the flock erupted. Every bird swarmed the dovecote, their burbling cries as hysterical as their wings.

"Hold still!" Aenwyn grunted, wings beating in her face. The poor creature in her hand twisted, desperate to get away, and she feared the angle that its leg was making. "I don't want to hurt you."

And it wasn't a lie. Although she'd come here with the intent of killing this bird, she didn't wish to bring it pain first. Sacrifice was an honor. It was a sacred event, one that she usually took great lengths to ensure didn't involve so much fear.

The more the pigeon flailed about though, the more fear and pain she'd inflicted until finally she felt its leg snap between her fingers.

She was left with no other choice now.

As the birds fled and chaos dwindled, Aenwyn reached her

other hand up to the captured bird and grasped its head. In one fluid motion, she brought the creature against her chest and gave its neck a swift, merciful twist.

The last of the fluttering died out.

There were no tears in Aenwyn's eyes as she lowered the limp creature to the ground, but the pang in her heart was there, aching, bleeding.

"I'm sorry," she whispered to the dead pigeon. "But you will not die in vain."

Outside, the flapping of wings dwindled as the flock dispersed, and in the wake of the silence that followed, Aenwyn imagined the distant pounding of heavy footsteps. Knights assembling to investigate. She didn't know how much time that gave her, but she knew it wouldn't be long before they arrived and stopped her from completing the ritual.

Time was slipping through her fingers, and she had to act fast.

Aenwyn had no knife. Caeloran women weren't allowed to carry one—it was deemed *unladylike*. If any Caeloran were here to witness what she was about to do next, she bet they would rethink their stance on arming their women.

Barehanded, Aenwyn dug her nails into the bird's chest, felt for the poke of small bones, and tugged.

The poor thing's ribcage cracked open, and she dug inside for the tender organs she needed. The liver. The small intestine. Sometimes she could use the gallbladder too, but she wasn't familiar enough with the anatomy of birds—normally she performed this ritual on livestock—so locating such a small organ would've been too difficult and taken up too much time.

Tossing the organs to the ground, Aenwyn let them land where they might, and drew the jagged shape of a wing around them using her bloodied finger.

"Sky-Blessed guide my sight," the queen said, sitting back on her haunches and letting her voice fill the dovecote. It reverberated in every empty nesting hole, a thousand echoes fluttering around her. "Help me see the dragon I am meant to find."

Aenwyn's gaze rested upon the red sheen of the bird's intestines where they lay sprawled, and the vision overtook her.

Her eyes rolled into her skull, and she was transported. Ocean waves crashing against her eardrums. Saltwater spraying her face. The stifling, humid heat beating down upon her.

Aenwyn found herself deserted on a tropical island with water lapping at her bare feet. In the distance she could just barely make out a graveyard of ships, ones that had been scorched by dragon's fire and abandoned off a distant coastline. She recognized the landmark only because of Baug's teachings: she was looking at the coast of Vallonde, which meant she was opposite it.

As her heart clenched at what that meant, everything darkened. A shadow cast her in a veil of black over her. Slowly, Aenwyn looked up, already knowing what she would find.

A blue dragon glided above her, mighty and majestic.

She watched it fly overhead, circling the island until it finally landed with an earth-quaking thud somewhere in the forest.

Aenwyn blinked and the island disappeared. In an instant, she was back in the dovecote, even though she swore she could still feel sand in-between her toes.

"The Lost Isle," she said to herself, voice fractured and distant. So many of her nightmares took place there already. A place where she had sworn she would never return. Fate could be so mocking that way. "Of course that's where I need to go."

Back to the beginning.

Back to where her life had nearly ended and then began again when Baug the Bear found her.

Back to a place she had long ago called home.

But there was no time to lament. The thudding of footsteps thundering her way was real this time and not just in her head. The Caeloran Guard was coming, and she needed to be long gone by the time they arrived.

Aenwyn leapt to her feet. As she bounded out of the dovecote, Aenwyn realized she'd left the evidence of her haruspicy for anyone to find. The slain animal would soon be discovered, guts spilling from its body, of that she had no doubt. And they'd know for certain who was responsible for such dark, vile magic.

Whatever punishment awaited her; she'd worry about it once she returned.

If she returned.

Rocks crunched in the dirt beneath her scrambling feet. She didn't know where she was running, only that she needed to leave, and fast. If she slowed, she feared whoever had been racing to check on the pigeons would find her, apprehend her, and take her to the king. And she doubted he'd let her out of his sight once he learned what she'd done.

A horse whinnied as she raced past the stables, an idea making her skid to a stop. Aenwyn checked over her shoulder before she approached the barn and when she reached for the doors, the horse cried out again. As if summoning her. As if fate's hand was still at play here.

Aenwyn wasn't one to disobey fate.

She pulled one of the doors open as silently as she could, but the groaning of old hinges still creaked loudly. Once inside though, she turned around and almost laughed.

Standing in the middle of the barn was a horse, one already wearing a saddle and what looked like two plumply-packed travel bags hanging from either hip. She didn't waste any time peeking inside them to see if there were enough rations packed for the journey ahead. She already knew there would be, or at least that there would be enough to get her by until she could procure more.

Cooing to the horse and caressing its muzzle, Aenwyn guided the calm creature back toward the door. She peeked outside first, to verify whether the coast was clear, and finding it so. Fate was in her favor today. She'd awoken the blue dragon and now it was time to lay it to rest.

Aenwyn thrust the double doors of the barn wide, the loud creaking of dry wood and rusty hinges making her cringe, as she climbed atop the horse and gently guided it outside.

Before she could gallop across the outer courtyard and toward the eastern entrance, something clutched her wrist. *Someone.*

"And just what are you up to, Queen of Wildfire?"

11

A QUEEN AND HER KNIGHT

AENWYN

Fear and fate were wicked sisters. Aenwyn had only ever felt their divine intervention once before. The day she'd lost everyone and everything.

For centuries, a noxious fog had kept the Lost Isle shrouded. Until the day it crept over the shorelines and engulfed her entire village. Aenwyn had closed her eyes as it folded over the tree line, tumbled to the edge of her village, and then swallowed building after building, suffocating everyone it touched, and racing toward her to do the same.

She'd buckled, fallen to her knees. And just before the fog could consume her too, Aenwyn screamed.

Power had exuded from her. She couldn't see it. But it was felt and heard. A blanket of silence that muffled the world.

When she'd opened her eyes again, everyone was gone. The veil around their isle had dissipated. And she'd been left all alone.

Until the day Baug the Bear had found her.

When Aenwyn had pushed the magic out of her, she hadn't been thinking about what she was doing; she wasn't even entirely sure it had been *her* doing, at first. She'd reacted on instinct, a reflexive, defensive part of her magic that would always protect her because her fear had beckoned it and fate had answered.

The same thing happened when Ser Darius Graeme caught her wrist.

Aenwyn released the reins, thrust out her arm, and magic blasted from her.

Ser Darius went tumbling like a leaf on the wind. His backside skidded across the dirt until he thudded up against the corral.

For all his surprise, however, it was nothing compared to amount of shock Aenwyn was experiencing. Usually, in order to access magic, she needed a divine intervention. To beseech the Sky-Blessed so that they might provide her aid. For it wasn't that she possessed magic herself, it was that the Sky-Blessed had chosen her as a vessel, a conduit for their power in moments of need.

But she hadn't called for them. She had only felt bleak.

There had been only one other time in her life that she had found her magic on her own, just waiting at her fingertips, ready to erupt.

Aenwyn tried concealing her confusion, her awe, and stood straighter, facing off with the crumbled knight.

"I'm off to save Caelora. Do not try to stop me again." A bout of wooziness made her head loll. The price of using what she could only surmise was considered forbidden magic without the approval of the Sky-Blessed above.

He was still gaping up at her when she spun around and trotted for the gates.

The warning bells rang in the distance, the kind of hollow, resolute sound that shook her chest and made her blood pump. The gates were closing. But not fast enough.

"Wait!" someone shouted behind her, but she wasn't about to heed them.

As swift as a gust of wind, she and her trusted steed thundered out the gate. Even once she knew Caelora Castle was a distant speck on the horizon behind her, she kept a steady pace, her horse seeming to relish the run.

They headed toward the desert kingdom of Vallonde. She wasn't sure if they'd ride across the entire barren wasteland, considering it was such a treacherous place. But for now, it was her only option. The town of Nivernia was maybe a week's ride out, and once she arrived, she could decide if she would be traveling to her homeland by ship or on horse.

The horse's ears twitched, and it let out a disgruntled whinny.

Aenwyn dared to look over her shoulder and saw that someone was following her. Not just anyone. The same knight that she couldn't seem to shake, the one who had seemingly become her shadow since they met last night.

"What did I tell you?" Aenwyn huffed. She tried flicking another gust of magic back at Ser Darius, but the ride was too bumpy. She missed her mark by what felt like a mile. So, she decided to change tactics. "Leave me alone!"

It wasn't a very effective strategy.

In fact, it seemed to have the opposite of her desired effect. Bent low over the horse's neck, Ser Darius actually gained speed.

Not to be outmatched or thwarted, Aenwyn followed suit. With a whip of her horse's reins, she pressed onward, weaving in and out of the pedestrians crossing the magnificent bridges, headed in the opposite direction toward the royal castle.

"Sorry!" she shouted behind her when a young woman carrying a basket of fruit had to jump out of her horse's path.

Aenwyn was grateful to see that someone had caught her before she'd inadvertently thrown herself over the ledge, and less grateful to find that Ser Darius was gaining on her. She didn't like the look in his eyes. It was the same kind of fierce determination she'd seen reflected in Signe's gaze just before she found herself wrapped up in some challenge or feat.

Aenwyn knew from experience that when someone had *that* look in their eyes, they would stop at nothing to claim victory.

If she just kept running, he'd keep chasing, and she couldn't very well think, let alone follow an intuitive path, when she was on the run.

Coming to the end of the bridge, Aenwyn veered right, the desert cities not yet in sight but somewhere beyond the small forest before her. At full speed, she led her horse into the cover of trees, Ser Darius not too far behind.

His presence thickened the closer he became, and she knew it wouldn't be long now before he captured his prize.

She needed the upper hand, so she created one.

Aenwyn jerked the reins to the left, hard. She and her horse took a sharp turn around a particularly massive caelwood tree for which the kingdom was named.

With a cloud of dust at her heels, they disappeared behind the tree, and it took Ser Darius a moment to register what had happened. He couldn't react fast enough. At the speed they were running, and with his delayed reaction, he couldn't hug the tree sharp enough and instead led him and his horse straight for another.

Face-to-face with the other tree, the horse reared on its hind legs, and for the second time that day, Ser Darius was flung through the air until he slammed to the ground.

The scowl on his face as Aenwyn and her horse trotted up to him filled her with satisfying glee. "I did warn you to stop following us."

Picking himself up from where he lay sprawled and defeated in the dirt, Ser Darius sat upright. He leaned forward to rest an arm on either knee as he peered up at her. "Yeah, but I don't take my orders from you."

This caused Aenwyn's chest to tighten. "What do you mean, *orders?*"

She hoped the king hadn't discovered her disappearance yet. She thought she'd have more time before the entire Caeloran Guard was hot on her trail. Now that she thought about it though, if that were the case, she would've never run into one of the king's most trusted knights. Ser Darius would've had no other reason to be down there, unless he'd been instructed to retrieve her.

Although, the king *had* ordered him to guard her room. Maybe once Ser Darius was done checking on Signe, he'd returned to find Aenwyn missing. Maybe she was worrying about the king knowing about her absence for nothing.

"To find you and bring you to the king before you could do anything foolish," he answered.

Not *bring you back to your room*, she noted.

"Why? What does my husband want?"

Rumors could spread quickly among the bored lords, ladies, and servants of the court, but she hadn't thought news of Signe's threat would reach him that fast.

Ser Darius' derisive laugh told her otherwise. She really should've learned by now not to underestimate the tittering of nobles and their servants.

"Why do you think?" he asked. Hands to knees, Ser Darius shoved himself to his feet. He clapped his hands and dirt dusted around them. "Now, I don't know about you, but I'd rather not spend the rest of the day chasing you through the woods. What do you say? You follow me—*calmly*—back to the castle, and we get all this sorted."

Haughtily, Aenwyn's horse stomped its hooves. Together, they backed up a step, putting some distance between them and the knight who seemed like he might be ready to tackle her off her mount, should she give him an answer he didn't like.

And her answer was unlikely to appease him.

"What part of *leave me alone* are you not understanding?"

"The part where I've been given a direct order to do the opposite."

Aenwyn flipped the thickness of her red hair over her shoulder in a show of defiance. "Well, then I'm afraid you're about to spend the rest of your day doing the thing you didn't want to do."

She started to lead her horse away from him, acting as if she might break out in another run, but she could tell by the weariness in his tone that it wouldn't come to that.

He sighed, clearly bored and frustrated by the circumstances he found himself in. "What will convince you not to give chase again?"

"Truthfully?" She glanced back over her shoulder. "Even if I wanted to, fate wouldn't allow it."

"Fate?" He breathed a laugh. But then, noticing how serious she was, he screwed his face back to its seemingly normal state of aggravation and sighed again. "And what path does *fate* have you set on? Becoming another missing queen who fled from her disappointing union?"

Her stomach sunk to consider whether what he was saying could be true.

All day long, she'd convinced herself that she was doing this for Caelora, for all of Grimtol, but could it be possible that there was also a selfish part of her that was doing this for herself? Itching to get away from the confined and torturous life she'd fallen into?

She had to shake the thought aside. Even if it was part of the truth, it wasn't her sole motivator.

Once she was able to refocus her attention on the conversation, it took Aenwyn a moment to realize he wasn't just talking about her. There had been only one other missing queen that she could think of. If it hadn't been for her own sister's involvement, it might've not even piqued her interest. But he'd said it in a way that suggested he knew more, so she couldn't resist asking, "You mean King Ulfaskr's first wife? Queen... Sparrow, or something?"

He made another snorting sound, a pitiful excuse for laughter. "Queen Yui," he corrected. "And, yes. Unless you know of many other disappearing queens in Grimtol's history?"

Considering she'd spent the first sixteen years of her life on a remote island isolated from the rest of the continent, and had only spent a few years on Grimtol, she admittedly didn't know everything about its history, but she didn't like to show it. As far as everyone knew, she was Skogar, and had been since the day she was born. She'd worked hard to study the important histories once Baug had found her, and even harder to learn about Caelora once her betrothal had been declared.

"No, that sounds right," she said, tucking away all previous notions of doubt. "Anyway, to answer your question: no, I am not attempting to become another queen who simply fades out of existence and history. The opposite, actually."

He cocked a brow. "*The opposite?*"

Feeling affronted, Aenwyn sat straighter. "I don't appreciate your tone, sir."

"My tone?" Ser Darius dragged a hand through his thick, brown locks, a condescending smirk on his face. "Well, *Your Majesty*, I don't appreciate being lied to by a girl who stupidly believes she's going to change the realm by sneaking out of the castle on a fool's errand, then having to chase said girl through the courtyard only to discover her stealing a horse—for which I attempt to stop her, as it is my knightly duty to uphold the law—but I'm met with a blow of *illegal* magic that knocks me on my arse and am forced to give chase—yet again—only this time I'm led outside the castle's guarded walls and into an unguarded forest, only to be jerked around and continually disrespected by the same girl whose caused all this ruckus to begin with."

Aenwyn's cheeks puffed. "I've been telling you from the start: you do not have to follow me."

"And I've been telling you—"

She sighed emphatically, cutting him off. "I refuse to keep having this conversation."

Talking with this man was like walking in a circular path without knowing it was just leading you around and around. She was getting nowhere fast with him.

With another huff, Aenwyn examined the forest, making note of the purple hue sinking around them. Dusk—or perhaps even dawn—was coming quickly. That didn't necessarily mean that night would follow though. She hoped it wouldn't. The last thing she wanted was to be wandering the woods in the dark.

"Look," she said at last, returning her gaze to him. She took note of his closer proximity and the slight bend in his knees that suggested he was still ready to pounce. "You're duty-bound to Caelora, correct?"

He tilted his head as if to say *sort of*.

She'd take what agreement she could get from him.

"And one of the dangers that you protect the kingdom from are the dragons, yes?"

That made him flinch. That muscle in his jaw twitched again, catching Aenwyn's eye.

"Yes," he said slowly, lethally.

"Well," she continued, averting her attention from that strong jaw of his. "If you let me go, you're still upholding your honor."

He looked skeptical.

She didn't want to tell him about the prophecy. It was a risk to admit to him, a trusted member of the Caeloran Guard, that she'd had her ring off not only while she was sharing a bed with him, but then again in the dovecote. But the prophecy was beginning to seem like the only way she'd be able to convince this thick-headed man to let her do what she needed to do.

"I...had a vision."

To his credit, he didn't so much as flinch at the mention of magic that sent most Caelorans buckling at the knees or fleeing her presence. Instead, he merely awaited her explanation.

She obliged him and continued—although, in the interest of attempting to cover her own hide, she embellished the story a little. "Last night, my ring fell off while I was sleeping, and I was visited with a vision of a dragon destroying Caelora."

"A vision?" he repeated. "You sure it wasn't just a dream?"

"Yes. I'm sure."

"How?"

There was never an easy answer to that.

When she'd arrived in Skogar, some of their most devoted people had taken an interest in her magic, believing her to be a direct descendant of the Sky-Blessed, even though up until then, no one had believed them capable of reproducing. Some of them had been eager to learn about her powers, how they manifested, what they felt like. However, she was always woefully incapable of explaining them.

It would be no different today, and she was growing impatient with how much time she'd wasted already.

"They're just different."

"And I suppose I just have to take your word for it?"

"For the sake of time, yes."

Stance widening, he folded his burly arms, and considered her. Finally he said, "Fine. I'll bite. Tell me what's so special about this dream—I mean, *vision*."

His mocking tone made her prickle, and Aenwyn suddenly felt compelled to at least try to explain it to him.

"Dreams are something your mind does while you're resting. You fall asleep, your thoughts, feelings, and experiences come together to mimic something you witnessed, or something you're worrying about, or looking forward to. They show you places you've been. They're filled with the people you know or have crossed paths with.

"Visions are vastly different," she said, adding emphasis. "In a vision, I don't recognize the places or the people because I know them, but rather because the events playing out for me tell me what and who they are. Sometimes, in a vision, I'm not even present. But always—*always*—when I awaken from the demon-sleep, I am left impacted. If I was watching the scene while wading in water, my feet might be wet when I awaken. If I am sobbing over someone's dead body, I'll rise from bed with tears streaking my cheeks."

Ser Darius shifted where he stood, seeming uncomfortable with the doubt creeping into him that she might not be lying after all.

"And what happened last night?" he asked. "I saw no water or tears."

She shook her head, both in answer and trying to clear the flames from her thoughts. Flames that still left her skin feeling scorched.

"Dragon's fire," she said, one hand instinctively caressing her cheek where the fire had been closest. It was a miracle it hadn't actually burnt her. "Last night, I watched a Caeloran town go up in flames. I saw the blue dragon flying overhead."

"The *blue* dragon?" he asked, shoulders tensing.

Aenwyn swallowed down the guilt threatening to drown her. She understood what this revelation would mean to him. "Yes."

The blue dragon that had killed his mother after all. Maybe this would give them a common goal? Maybe this was how she got him to stop chasing and fighting her, but to join her instead? It likely wouldn't be bad to have a knight in her company for the road that lay ahead of her.

Returning her hand to the reins, Aenwyn checked their surroundings once more. "I know where it lives."

"The dragon?" he repeated, and when Aenwyn looked back at him, Ser Darius was riddled with doubt. "No one knows where they are. That's why they're still alive."

Aenwyn held her head higher. "Well *I* do. And that's where I'm going now. To slay the blue dragon. It's my duty and you're not stopping me."

"Your *duty*?" He leveled her with a ridiculing look. "Because you saw yourself killing it in this *vision* you had?"

Not exactly, she almost said. But she'd worked so hard to earn his investment and she wasn't about to squander it now. It was for her to know, and her only, that she hadn't actually *seen* anyone slaying the dragon. No one else would be able to understand how intricately her life was connected to it. How inexplicably tethered all her choices were to it.

There could be no one else to kill it because it was her who had given it life. She didn't know why that was the way it was, but she believed it with all her being.

She was also beginning to believe that Ser Darius—for whatever reason—was inexplicably intertwined with all of this, as well. What other reason could there be for why they'd never spoken to each other before last night? Or why their paths kept crossing so much today, the day she was setting out on her mission?

She wondered if he could feel it too. There was only one way to find out.

"So, Ser Darius of Caelora, what do you say? Will you aid me in ending the blue dragon's tyrannical reign over our lands? Will you uphold your most sacred vow to the people to serve and protect them? Or will you try to thwart everything and wind up being knocked on your arse again?"

The smirk he flashed surprised her.

"Is that a smile?" she asked, gloating. "Dare I say, did I crack the gloomy mask of one of the king's most boring knights?"

The smile dropped. "And what about the king? What's he going to think when I return with you?"

She waved him off, already enthralled by victory. "He knows who he married: a daughter of the Skogar Chieftain. I'm a free woman with magic in my blood. He'll understand that you stood no chance at stopping me."

"Ouch," he groused, blithely clutching his chest in mock affront. "Insults at my ability to be a reliable knight aside, do you even know the man you married?" He shook his head, watching her the way someone might watch a fish that said it could fly. "Have you ever known him to *understand* something he didn't like?"

She worried at her lower lip. "Fine. You're right. He'll be displeased if you don't return with me. But it won't be difficult to remind him of how wild and untamed my people are." It hurt to admit it, but she swallowed the bile rising at the back of her throat and continued. "When we return, if he's not over-joyed at the news of the blue dragon having been slain, you'll tell him you had no choice but to follow me. You'll tell him I kept using my magic like the heathen I am, but you kept seeking me anyways, as it was your order to do so. And then you'll boast about how, in the end, you were finally able to slip my ring back onto my finger and drag me back to Caelora, to him."

Ser Darius considered her for a moment, but she wished he'd make his choice by staring somewhere else. Everything she'd said had been such a betrayal of herself and her people. They weren't the heathens that everyone else seemed to think they were, and it ripped her apart to even suggest that they were. It had cost her dearly to suggest such a plan, one that would require her complete obedience and humility upon their return, and most likely cost her lashings or imprisonment, should they convince the king properly.

But she needed him to agree. She couldn't keep fending him

off all across the continent. She needed to conserve her energy for the dragon.

Without a word, Ser Darius rounded his horse and began to climb.

Aenwyn watched him, uncertain of what it meant. Her first instinct was to run, but she wanted to be certain before she began. If he meant to drag her back to the castle, she had just enough of a spark left in her to knock him down one more time to give herself a decent head start.

After a year of not practicing, her reserves were dwindling fast, and she wanted to be sure she didn't waste the last bit of her power unless she really needed to. It would be a while before she could rest and replenish it again.

Reins in hand, Ser Darius nickered to his horse as he spun the black steed around to face her. He quirked an eyebrow when he saw that she was still sitting there, gawking. "Well, Queen of Wildfire, where shall I follow you off to now?"

12

ONLY THE DEAD REST

DARIUS

I t surprised Darius that in just the few short days that they'd been traveling they were already on the outskirts of the forest and beginning to encroach on the deserts of Vallonde.

He wouldn't have expected to make it this far so quickly. Not with a queen for a travel companion. But he was beginning to understand that what Queen Aenwyn had told him had been true: she was unlike any other royalty he had ever known, or likely ever would.

In fact, it had been Darius who had insisted on taking the rest they were having even now—not the queen. She likely would've continued pressing forward until she dropped, if it hadn't been for his recommendation to stop. For all her bluster, the *Queen of Wildfire* was spent. He didn't know for certain, but he suspected it had as much to do with her display of magic as it had their arduous horseback ride.

Regardless, Darius had finally been able to convince Queen Aenwyn to rest for a few hours; all it had taken was him pointing out that the horses seemed weary.

She hadn't argued after that. Neither had her eyes. The

moment she laid her head down, the queen had fallen fast asleep.

Darius took first watch, pacing the perimeter for a time, until he became thirsty, tried taking a drink from their canteen, and discovered that it was empty. He remembered also that just before setting up camp, they had heard the trickling of a stream nearby and although Aenwyn had insisted on checking it out, Darius had convinced her to rest, volunteering for the extra journey himself.

But seeing as he wasn't the only one who'd forgone water that day, Darius untied the horses and followed the trickling sounds of the brook, still within earshot of where Queen Aenwyn was resting.

He filled the canteen, drank the entirety of its contents, and then filled it again.

Darius waited as the horses drank their fill as well, patting their necks and keeping a sharp eye on their surroundings. While they lapped up the water, he busied himself with foraging apples from a nearby tree for their party of four.

Soon, they were making their way back to camp. Even after all these years, Darius still found himself doing his best to stay out of the light that filtered through the canopy. He wouldn't necessarily consider himself the superstitious sort, but his mother was, and her warnings always haunted him:

Never wander into beams of sunlight, for the Sky-Blessed might snatch you away.

It would be the last thing he needed this week.

Darius tied the horses to their trees again and then he was off again, alone and scoping out the area.

It was the first time in days that he'd had a true moment to himself, and although he would've liked to have relished in the peace and quiet of the forest, instead he could do little else but contemplate the consequences of his actions over the past few days.

It seemed every chance he got, Darius was forgoing his vows. He'd sworn an oath to the Caeloran crown, to protect their people, to be loyal to their king. In the past few days, he'd not only managed to knowingly bring rebels to court, but now he was aiding a runaway queen.

He was so far off the path now, but what made it worse was that he hardly felt astray at all.

Something about the way the events were unfolding they just...felt right.

A smirk twitched his face and Darius could've sworn he heard the queen's voice touting about the ethereal power of *fate* and *destiny*.

Darius didn't believe in such things. But he did believe in his gut, the way it could tighten at the first hint of danger, the way it seemed to flip whenever he was on the verge of adventure, or how it could be soothed in moments of serenity and calmness.

Since Emile had found him in the training grounds, not once had Darius felt like he was in danger. Worried at times and skeptical, sure. But nothing that made him think that something awful was on the horizon.

Until now. In this moment of quiet and stillness, when he was finally alone and no longer running.

His stomach wasn't just in knots, the entire middle of his torso seemed to wrench like the heavy, metal chains of a draw bridge as they wrapped tighter and tighter around the churning gears that drew up the gates.

Darius knew what was expected of him. Knew that the king would demand that Darius drag the queen back by her hair if that's what it took.

By any means necessary.

But Darius couldn't. He wouldn't.

Queen Aenwyn's affiliation toward magic aside, this was the closest Darius had ever come to hunting down the dragons and avenging his mother. Even if all their plans revolved around a dream and weren't founded on anything concrete. It was better than nothing. Better than continuing to serve a crown that stood for nothing.

This wild chase—this *plan*, for lack of a better word—was more than just a dream to the queen. Darius knew that. Knew that she believed in it with every ounce of her being.

Truthfully, he envied her for that. Admired the fervor for which she trusted her instincts. Her magic. Her *fate*—if that's what she wanted to call it.

Maybe that was part of it too. The reason he had been so willing to follow her.

Because although he didn't behold the same fervent belief that fate was guiding them, there was something inspiring about the fact that *she* did. Something that made him want to believe in it too.

Or maybe he wasn't. Maybe he was just desperate. Maybe he knew that the final vestige of hope he'd been clinging to would soon be lost forever if he didn't *do* something.

Darius sighed, lowering himself against the wide base of a half-fallen tree that clung to the edge of an eroded slope. He let his feet dangle over the ledge, the wiry roots poking through the crumbling soil and scratching at his armor as he watched their camp below.

Everything was silent.

Everything was at peace.

Every*thing*, but not every*one*.

When Darius's attention fell upon the queen, when he noticed her panicked gaze, the pupils stretched wide like black, ominous caves, his heart lunged. As did he.

Darius jumped into action with such haste that he nearly tumbled down the ravine. He only barely managed to avoid disaster by snatching at one of the branch-like roots that reached for him like a hand and pulled himself upright, narrowly escaping his doom.

He bolted along the ledge, searching for the path back down. All the while, he kept looking back, kept searching for any signs of disturbances: birds fleeing, screams or shouting, movement. He found none.

The whole while he raced down the ravine, tree branches snapping him in the face, Darius scolded himself. He should've never left her alone. No matter the view that the ledge provided of the surrounding area and all the routes that could've led to their camp, it hadn't been enough.

And now he'd doomed her. Doomed the entire kingdom. Maybe even the whole realm.

By the time Darius had made it down the ravine, his skin had gone cold, his flesh tacky with sweat.

Queen Aenwyn's body was still—*too* still. Her skin was as pale as the underbelly of a fish. Was it as white as death? Or had it always been that way? Darius couldn't remember. But it didn't matter. As he drew nearer, all he could think about was how much her motionless body looked like the dead. Not the bodies they had to bury in Rayong; those had been scorched to ashes, many of whom didn't even have enough of a body left to be identifiable, much less buried. No, the queen's body reminded him of the dead in the dungeons, the prisoners who'd been forgotten for too long and left to rot, those who'd been pushed beyond their means, tortured too hastily, their frail bodies shocked into death before they even had a chance to break and tell the king what he wanted to hear.

Darius knelt down beside her, his stomach churning. Queen Aenwyn's eyes were wide and frozen. Death had claimed her, just as it had so many others before her; he was sure of it. But what had done it?

Darius scanned the forest, one hand resting on the hilt of

his dagger, but still he saw nothing. Not the slightest sign of danger.

Perhaps she'd been ill? But that couldn't be it. He would've known. He'd kept such a close eye on her leading up until now that he would've known. The king would've known. Surely, he would've told—

Something cold fluttered against Darius' wrist and he flinched.

With his heart galloping in his chest, he peered down, saw the queen's pale hand, one slender finger straining, reaching for him.

He felt as if a sheet of snow had blanketed his bare flesh. Slowly, and with dread clawing up his throat, Darius dragged his frightened gaze further up, until he found hers. Instead of finding her lifeless and still staring straight into the clouds, now those eyes had shifted, pinning him in place with their sharp, jewel-like gleam.

Darius forced his throat to work. "Queen Aenwyn? Are you alright? Did something happen? Is someone here?"

He started to pull his dagger free, but the queen's protest stopped him. Or at least, he assumed it as a protest. The sound that crept out of her was hardly decipherable, more of a frog's croak than a queen's command. But Darius had worked for the crown long enough now to sense power when it was being wielded.

Thrusting the dagger back in place, his scowl deepened. "What is it? Tell me how to help!"

He was growing impatient, and that made him feel childish.

But it was more than that. It was deeper. For whenever Darius felt helpless around someone he'd sworn to protect, his guilty and perceived failure only worsened.

He thought of his mother and how miserably he had failed to protect her.

The queen's eyes fluttered shut with tremendous effort, but

she didn't speak. She left him there with nothing to go on. No sense of purpose or action. All he could do was wait.

He took the grazing of her fingers as they climbed up his wrist as a sign that whatever had happened was improving. Whenever she opened her eyes and glanced in his direction again, he could've sworn she was trying to tell him as much.

Finally, her lips parted. She struggled for every word as if she were fumbling for slippery worms.

"Soon…I'm well."

It was as good as the incoherent mumblings of a drunkard half-drowned in a barrel of whiskey. But she'd said it to alleviate his worry, and so Darius did his best to abide.

Fortunately, within another few moments, she was blinking normally again. Her breaths steadied. Her limbs, although still limp, seemed to twitch back to life.

With great effort, Queen Aenwyn flung herself onto her side and finally managed to pull herself up. Darius tried aiding her, but any time he touched her, she growled at him. Eventually, he realized she just wanted to do this alone, and so he let her.

"S-sorry. That happens…sometimes."

But as she rose, shielding her face behind a tangle of red that looked more like tree roots than hair, Darius understood. It wasn't that she wanted to do it alone. She felt like she had to. Whether out of pride for her reputation, or fear for it, he didn't know. But what he did know was that she looked embarrassed and somehow even more exhausted than she had been before laying down.

"Hold on," Darius told her before trotting over to the horses and returning with their canteen. "Here. Drink this."

The queen's hand shook as she reached for it, but she managed to hold it up to her lips and drink deeply. She paused to ask, "You found water?"

"You really did need the rest, didn't you?" Darius laughed. "We talked about it, remember? The stream?"

"Right."

She spoke softly, and it wasn't until then that Darius finally met her timid gaze. He felt as if she was waiting for something to happen, something she feared. Not from any potential danger lurking nearby, but from him.

"Are you alright?" he asked with what he hoped was enough gentleness to reassure her that she had nothing to fear from him.

He received a weak smile in return. That would have to be good enough. "Yes."

"What was that?" he asked, well aware that it was not the sort of question someone would usually be allowed to ask of their queen. But these were strange circumstances they found themselves in, so he figured why not play by their own rules.

Queen Aenwyn worried at her lip and looked at him as if to ask if he really wanted to know. He nodded. "My mother called it the demon-sleep," she told him. "It's like...when it happens, something is preventing me from awaking fully."

"Like...a demon?"

Darius came so close to angling his cocky eyebrow at her but thought better of it. This was hardly the time to mock her let alone the beliefs that often seemed so foreign compared to his own. Besides, it was his own naivety that deserved scorn anyways, not her customs. And he was honestly curious to learn more about this secret thing that she'd kept hidden so well, even from him.

In answer, the queen shook her head. "Not exactly. I don't know. It's possible, I suppose, but I've never seen anything like a demon about me when it happens. It's more like...it's more like I'm no longer in control of my own body. I am aware of everything—I can see the world around me, I could hear the leaves rustling, I could feel the cold earth beneath me, but I could not will myself to move."

Darius began nodding again, but it was only once her expression had shifted from one of openness to one of obvious confusion and doubt that he realized he was the source for it.

"Oh. Sorry, I didn't mean that I suffer from the same ailment. But—" Now it was Darius' turn to watch her warily and consider his options. It wasn't like he owed her to share anything personal about himself. But there was something so vulnerable and chilling about what she had endured and what he had just witnessed that he almost felt compelled to. So far everything they'd done together had felt like that, one action after another that he might've otherwise ignored or refused, but in her presence, it seemed compulsive, necessary. This was no different. So, ultimately, he decided he would share. "Sometimes I get the same way, like I can't will myself to do what I want either."

"Like what?" she asked, lips quirked up in challenge.

Too many replies came to mind.

Like how he had desperately wanted to follow his mother's rules, to be more dependable, more honorable. Even before her death, buried somewhere deep inside of him was the desire to make her proud of the young man he was becoming, but no matter how hard he tried, he always lacked the follow through. Every time temptation had reared its ugly head, Darius became lost to it. He wasn't content with himself, so he drowned himself in ale, girls, and as much trouble as he could wind himself into.

Eventually, he stopped trying to fight it.

With the Caeloran Guard, things had been different though. For a time. But that was no indication of his own willpower. Grief had made him collapse inward, not strength. Nothing had been tempting enough to wrangle him out of his darkness. But the thoughts—his temptations—had always been there. It was just that self-pity and self-loathing kept a tight enough grip on him that he could disobey them.

But saying any of that was going too far. He couldn't bring himself to share so deeply. Not with her, someone he barely knew. Not with anyone.

Instead, he tried shifting the focus back onto her. "I imagine it's a very powerless sensation. To feel like you can't wake up or move."

"It is."

When the queen answered, her face angling up to meet his, it was like she was looking at him for the first time.

There was a softness to her gaze that hadn't been there before. A vulnerability. Like the shield she had been trained to wedge between her and the world was falling.

Darius felt himself doing the same—his heart softening to hers as they explored the depth of each other's eyes. For the first time that he could remember, he truly looked at the queen, let himself see her through the eyes that he might've gazed upon anyone. He took in the brutality of her beauty. It wasn't the same as the other ladies of court. There was no gentleness about her. No regal elegance or anything close to resembling compliance; it was likely one of the reasons that most of Caelora loathed her.

But Darius thought he could see the appeal of it. The wild nature that sparked behind her verdant eyes. The fiery hue of her hair that matched the raging spirit tucked within her.

Elegance was an illusion. It was the lie of a predator told to foster trust among their prey.

But splayed on the ground before him, the queen had never seemed more prey-like, yet somehow more powerful than ever. A lioness basking in the sun, recharging for her next hunt. And he found himself admiring her.

And that was a problem. For so many reasons.

Clearing his throat, Darius turned away from her and

anchored his gaze on the towering pine trees, anything to distract himself from the unhelpful thoughts now burning into his mind.

But it was to no avail, for Queen Aenwyn shoved herself onto her feet and the words that came out of her mouth next were far more tantalizing than anything he had been thinking about previously.

"Well, I, for one, am in need of a bath." She was smirking, a wicked gleam in her eyes as he whipped his neck around to study her. "Care to join me?"

Darius was staggering to his feet without a second thought, but if he *had* been thinking, he would've known better than to so much as budge.

"I—my queen, it wouldn't be—" The harder it was for him to gather his thoughts, the hotter he felt his face flushing.

She didn't wait for him or his reply. Spinning on her heels, she was already heading for the horses. She pointed away from the cliff that sheltered their backside. "Was the stream that way?"

She already had one horse untied.

Over the past couple of years, Darius had fought hard to suppress some of his more hedonistic impulses, but dragon's fire, did Queen Aenwyn make it near impossible for him to contain those thoughts now.

"Queen Aenwyn!" he commanded, all but stomping his feet. He was too flustered to say much else, but fortunately she paused long enough to listen, giving him time to collect his racing thoughts. "I think it would be a little unfit for me to accompany you to your bath. Don't you?"

Her unamused expression told him she disagreed. "I think we're well past what's fit and unfit, wouldn't you agree?" Before he could answer, she was leading her horse away. "Besides, you know the first thing I noticed when I woke up, before I could move?"

"What?" he growled, not yet following after her.

"My rank odor, and then yours, Ser Darius Graeme."

The corner of his lips twitched upward despite himself, and as if on instinct, he found himself lifting one arm to test her theory. It was a mistake, of course. They'd been on the road for days now, sweating in the late summer sun for almost the majority of that time since the sun had only bothered to truly set once.

"Alright," he conceded. "So we reek of fish left out in the sun. And?"

"And?" She stammered, her steps faltering as she whipped around to gape at him. "*And* there is a source of water nearby where we can wash away some of the stench before the longer leg of our journey where we will very likely *not* have fresh water."

She was avoiding the obvious issue at hand here, and that made Darius uneasy. He felt like he was being tested. Like perhaps the king had followed them all this way just to examine Darius' loyalties.

"You are a queen," he stated plainly.

"Oh please—" with a flick of her auburn hair, Queen Aenwyn brushed his concerns off and continued walking. "If you're worried for my modesty, don't be. I'm not suggesting we make the beast with two backs. In fact, I'm trusting you to keep your eyes and hands off what isn't yours, and I'll do the same."

The insult caught him by surprise, as did the rage that swept over him. As much as he tried not to take it personally, it was difficult not to. He was many things, but Darius would never lay harm to a woman—

Or at least, that had been a creed he'd lived by before he became a Caeloran Guard and was responsible for torturing the Ashen Princess, among others. Mostly men, thank the clouds, but there had been a few women among them.

At the time, he'd made excuses for his actions—they'd all

done something wrong that deserved punishment and he just so happened to be the man on the job on that given day. But now? So far away from the suffocating castle walls, watching his actions from the outside, it made him sick to think he'd ever been capable of such monstrosity.

The truth was he *had* been capable though. The queen had every right to be wary of him, let alone any man who had followed her out into the forest all alone.

"Of course," came his reply. "You will have nothing but my respect, my queen."

13

A FORGOTTEN OASIS

AENWYN

"I hate to break it to you, but—" Ser Darius said when they reached the top of a sandy dune overlooking an oasis. He scanned the small town below, any signs of possible displeasure shrouded in that condescending smirk of his. "The king's army has searched every inch of Vallonde already. Despite its scorched appearances, there are no dragons here."

Although the small heap of a barren wasteland before them was surrounded by golden sand and a lake as bright as the sky during first-hours, the rest of the lands that could be seen from their vantage point were black and steaming.

Vallonde had always been a repeat target for the dragons.

Now that Aenwyn knew where they lived, she understood why.

With a flick of her reins, Aenwyn trotted forward, not allowing his doubt to get to her. "I didn't say the dragon lived *here*. We're just traveling through. Looking for something."

More specifically, *someone*.

There were some benefits to being the daughter of the Skogar Chieftain. For instance, although she might not possess a boat herself to cross the sea that separated Grimtol from the Lost Isle, at least she knew someone who did. Someone who'd made the voyage before.

"Mind telling me what it is we're looking for?" Ser Darius asked, following after her, down the sandy mountainside. His horse wasn't used to the give of sand. Hers, however, seemed utterly unfazed.

She didn't answer him. Wasn't sure how to. So she let them descend in silence, giving him time to focus on steering his increasingly concerned stallion.

Once they were on flatter grounds and had found the path that led to the town's front entrance, he finally caught up to her, muttering, "Or not. I'll leave the plan to the *fated one* and focus on keeping us safe from Vallondean ruffians."

Aenwyn scowled at him, suddenly overcome with a sense of kinship to the people of Vallonde. Apparently, Skogar wasn't the only nation hated by the rest of Grimtol.

Ever since the dragons rose and laid waste to Vallonde's territories, rumor had it that it had become a treacherous wasteland, in more ways than one. The people who'd chosen to stay—or return—after the great fires had swept across the lands had been left with little to make ends meet. Vallonde had become rife with miscreants, thieves, and other nefarious doers looking for an easy score.

Or at least, that was the way everyone talked about it.

But Aenwyn had seen a different side of the people who lived here.

She'd seen their impressive survival instincts. Their resourcefulness. But most of all, it was their acts of kindness that she remembered most.

Especially from Baug's friend, Hissa.

As an outsider, Hissa hadn't owed Aenwyn anything remotely resembling trust or care. But when Baug had returned to the Vallonde shores with a trembling, nearly-feral sixteen-year-old girl, Hissa had found them shelter and sustenance until Aenwyn could travel north. More than that, she'd reminded Aenwyn what it meant to be part of a community. What it meant to live.

"Don't call them that," she chastised him as they approached the modest gate that marked the entrance of the town, even though the rest of it wasn't wrapped by fencing. A sign just outside read *Nivernia*. "Especially not here. Not aloud, anyway."

"You got it, oh *fated one*."

Aenwyn shot him another scowl to which he held up his hands in mock defense.

"So what *is* the plan here? I hope it's not just to die of starvation and thirst."

Aenwyn could take his sarcastic remarks no more. Before they could enter the dusty, old village, she whirled on him, her horse whinnying.

"What is your problem?"

He feigned confusion. "With dying of starvation? I thought that was pretty obvious, but maybe not for you, Lady Death-Wish."

"I thought I was Queen of Wildfire?"

Darius shrugged. "Titles change."

Aenwyn rolled her eyes. "Whatever. Regardless, it would be *Queen* Death-Wish to you," she growled. "But I'm not talking about that. I meant with me. Why do you keep acting like I'm some simple-minded toad that would jump off a cliff and be none the wiser for it?"

He rolled his eyes. "You're not a simple-minded toad about to jump off a cliff." That made her feel better. But he was quick to shatter that moment. "You're worse."

Aenwyn balked. "Excuse me?"

"I'd rather deal with a lost toad than an untrained, self-indulgent brat who's put herself on a quest to slay a dragon, even though she doesn't have so much as a sword or shield—or armor of any kind, come to think of it."

Exasperated, she flung her arms out at her sides. "If I'm so infuriating, then why are you here?"

"Because you refused to listen to reason."

Swinging one leg over the saddle, Ser Darius climbed down from the stallion and patted the creature's neck.

Aenwyn noted how seemingly effortless the motion was for him. In fact, he'd seemed rather comfortable with their horses the past week. It was endearing to her the way he'd groomed them at the end of their days, or how whenever he foraged food, he was always sure to bring back tasty treats for Rocky and Charmaine—the names they'd bestowed upon their noble steed, Rocky for his seemingly ever-shifting disposition, and Charmaine for her delightful one.

It was more than just endearing; it made the whole journey all the easier, and she appreciated it immensely. It was a relief to be in the company of someone else who wasn't afraid to get their own hands dirty, let alone someone willing to show another living being compassion.

If it had been the king with her, he'd have servants to tend to his horses, basins drawn at every interlude for him to wash away the grime, hunters to fetch and prepared his meals for him.

If only her read on Ser Darius was more consistent. The snide remarks had become so tiresome because they always threw her for a loop. Every time she thought they'd finally reached a better place, he seemed to revert back to insulting her as a way to show his distrust of the plan and her abilities to guide them safely to the dragon.

As he adjusted what remained of his armor—half of it had been discarded a few nights back due to its cumbersome weight—she averted her gaze from the tight fit of his leather trousers and climbed down from her own horse.

"Come on," he said, voice low and gruff. And with the reins still in his grasp, he guided the both of them and their horses through the front gate of Nivernia.

Aenwyn didn't *want* to follow him. She was still a bit peeved at the thought of being compared to something that was *worse than a toad*.

But he was headed in the direction she needed to go, so she had no choice but to follow him.

However, she decided that for the remainder of their walk, there would be no more talking. Not with him, anyway. It seemed whenever she tried to maintain a conversation with him, it always ended poorly. Better to sit in silence than to continue brewing up tension.

The near-deserted village only served to amplify the silence that she let fall around them.

There wasn't a person in sight. Not as they first entered.

At first, it was like all of Nivernia belonged to them, and them alone. The streets, dusted with sand, showed no signs of life. No people. No footprints. The stone buildings seemed ancient and abandoned, their modest walls cracked and threatening to crumble.

Despite still being mad at him, Aenwyn felt herself huddling closer to Ser Darius.

Noticing too, he smirked down at her. "Not part of the plan?"

She bit her lip, refusing to respond. Not only would it mean breaking the pact she'd made with herself, but it also felt like they needed to be quiet. Something didn't seem right here. She'd heard about how deserted Vallonde had become, but it hadn't been this way when she'd been here last. That was a few years ago now though.

Beside her, something bumped into her elbow, and she looked to find Ser Darius watching her, one thick brow raised. "What? Not talking now?"

By way of answering, she swiveled her attention forward again and continued creeping about.

Fortunately, after they passed the first few buildings, the town started to show more signs of life. Brightly colored blankets woven from alpaca fur and likely dyed with wildflowers hung on the railing of one house, their fibers pristine and bright without a speck of sand on them. Someone had clearly hung them up recently, which explained the well-fed horse tied out front as well. And although she couldn't see anyone yet, she heard coughs coming from inside the house, as well as down the road.

"Really?" Ser Darius blurted, seeming increasingly irate about her lack of engaging with him. Truthfully, she hadn't expected it to get under his skin so much. She kind of thought he'd relish the silence. "What are we, twelve?"

The flames of Aenwyn's own ire were being stoked now.

For a moment, she considered continuing with her decision. She still believed it to be the least likely to cause them more strife. But she didn't want to give him any more evidence of the childish nature that he kept accusing her of.

So she settled for brevity.

"It doesn't seem productive, talking with you."

She thought about defending herself about her age, but even she recognized how immature that would make her sound, so she left it at that.

Groaning loudly, Ser Darius dragged a hand over his face. "Look. I'm sorry I said you were more difficult than a toad. And you're not *all* infuriating. I even..." He paused, actually seeming to strain himself to find the words. "I believed you. About the vision."

Confusion and hope swept through her. "You do?"

"Yeah. Not all of it. I'm sorry, but I've seen legions take on one dragon and die, so I have a hard time believing it's going to be you to slay the blue dragon. But I've felt your magic myself, so I know you're not lying about having magic. And I don't pretend to know what all that entails, but I suppose it's possible you could've seen where the dragon lives. At the very least, it's worth finding out if you're right."

"I am right," she said. Feeling for the first time like this exchange hadn't gone completely south, she smirked up at him. "And I can't wait to shove it in your face when we get there."

All mock humility, he bowed. "And I will deserve all the gloating you lay on me. Assuming, of course, that you last that long."

Her smile faded and she found herself shooting him a familiar scowl. "See, there you go again. That smug doubt in my ability to do the most basic thing in human history: survive."

His shoulders bobbed, seemingly uninterested in elaborating further.

But Aenwyn wasn't done. She wasn't about to share her fate with someone who was going to blatantly disrespect her every step of the way. Whatever he was holding against her, they needed to get to the bottom of it, especially the more that the town woke up around them and she became more and more assured that they weren't in immediate danger.

This time, she wasn't letting him off the hook. Even if that did require some vulnerability.

"I'll have you know I wasn't always a useless queen."

That smirk of his reappeared. "Oh, so you do agree that your crown means so little? And just a few days ago, there you were trying to convince me that you gave me my orders."

She rolled her eyes, choosing to ignore the bait. "Do you know what the Skogar are like? Have you ever met one before me?"

"In passing, maybe. They'd pass through Silent Crossing sometimes to do trade in the southern lands." At her wrinkled brow, he answered her unasked question. "Before my mother and I moved to Rayong."

"Okay, but did you ever talk to them? *Know* them?"

His head shook. "Can't say that I did."

"Okay, well, I can promise you that we're a lot more capable than the women you're used to associating with in Caelora." She let herself drift into memory then. Although she'd spent her childhood on the Lost Isle, she knew her upbringing shared similarities to true members of the Skogar. "I was setting traps and cleaning fish by the time I could walk. Once I was strong enough to hold a sword, I was taught how to wield one. I understand why you would doubt a Caeloran lady with the task before us, but do not make the mistake of lumping me in with those sheep."

That earned her one of his infrequent smiles, and a chuckle that actually sounded real.

They continued in silence for a while, passing stray animals, emaciated people sitting in shade, and a few stalls with colorful awnings that looked handwoven, but only a handful of wares on display.

She didn't remember the place seeming so dreary and disheartened the last time she'd been in the desert. But she supposed they could've been elsewhere, in another village that had been a little more prosperous. She wondered how difficult it would be to find someone with only their first name to go off of. Even if she mentioned the ship in the woman's possession, people this far inland might not know of a sailor on the other side of the kingdom. For all she knew, Hissa might be the most common name in Vallonde.

"You're right," Ser Darius said at last, jarring her from her thoughts. "I forget that you're...different than the rest of that stuck-up Caeloran Castle."

Aenwyn couldn't stifle the laughter that burbled out of her.

No one spoke so blatantly disrespectful about the king and his people. No one, in her experience, but Baug.

"Just speaking the truth." He shrugged. "I've never met a more selfish, cruel lot."

"And yet, you still serve the king. I don't understand," she admitted. "Why not return to Rayong? Or go back to Silent Crossing if the people were kinder there?"

He glanced at her sideways, assessing her. "I think you do understand. You just call it something different than I do."

At the same time he said, "Duty," Aenwyn answered, "Fate."

As if she'd thrust a wheel of rotten cheese beneath his nose, his face bunched. "I prefer duty, but yeah. It's about committing yourself to a cause, or in your case a path. The blue dragon destroyed my home, so I joined the largest army in Grimtol and vowed to stop it. You had a vision of the blue dragon destroying Caelora, so you decided to stop it. We've made it our duty."

Aenwyn mulled over his words, ultimately unsatisfied. "But they're different things. They might overlap in some cases, but duty is just blind allegiance to a cause without knowing the outcome. But it is my fate to kill the blue dragon. I've seen it. I know it without a doubt."

He leveled her with a look before finally shaking his head. "Call it whatever you want, but for me, fate sounds—it sounds powerless. I'd rather have a choice in my future, and know that I made decisions to get from where I was to where I am."

Aenwyn's steps faltered.

She'd never really thought about it like that. So much of her life was already devoid of power, of options. Her maids told her what to wear and eat. Her kingdom told her how to act. Her husband told her when to speak and when to give herself to him in bed.

Was her life just one long string of fated events that served as the catalyst for the next? Or did she have a choice in the matter—in any matter?

It was difficult to consider. So much of her life had felt predetermined.

How else but by fate's hand had Baug been able to find her on that abandoned island?

How else had her touch—and hers alone—awoken the dragon from its egg?

How else had she just so happened to cross paths with someone she'd rarely interacted with before who was equally as committed to killing the dragon as she was, just a day before she fled the castle to do that very thing?

Without the concept of fate, the questions surrounding her life would remain unanswered.

She needed fate. As much as it seemingly needed her.

Before she could say as such, Ser Darius continued their previous conversation.

"I've been unfair to you. We knew since the announcement of your wedding that you would be unlike any Caeloran bride the king could've chosen. My apologies if I've caused any offense."

"*If?*" Aenwyn challenged, though she hoped he heard the playfulness in her voice.

Clearing his throat, he glanced to his horse for strength before addressing her again. "My apologies *for* causing offense."

Not wanting to belabor the point or fall back on his bad side, Aenwyn smiled. "Apology accepted. And because I actually believe you, I'll let you in on the plan."

"How kind of you."

She snorted before remembering herself and the tenuous relationship emerging between them. "I need to find someone named Hissa. She has a ship and I believe she'll let us use it."

"A ship?" he asked, and for once he seemed more intrigued than dubious. "Where are we headed?"

Worrying at her bottom lip again, she assured herself it was okay to tell him. He'd find out soon enough anyway. "To the Lost Isle."

The passersby who were close enough to hear her actually gasped at the name.

Baug had told her that the Bay of Lost Souls and anything beyond it was a sort of superstitious nightmare for the people of Grimtol. Untold sailors had lost their ships, crews, and lives to the waters there. As far as he knew, Baug had been the first to ever cross those waters and return safely.

Judging from the look in Ser Darius' face, he held the same fears.

He grabbed the crook of her arm, tugging her close. "Are you out of your mind?"

"Of course not," was all she could say. After all, it wasn't like she was about to tell him that she'd successfully made the journey herself already. But she could fabricate what she knew. "Hissa's made this voyage before. She knows where to cross and how to get back. It's why we need her."

"And you know this how?" There was that furrow she'd grown so accustomed to.

She jerked out of his grasp. "I met her once."

"Once."

"Don't say it like that," she complained. "Yes, once. Baug was doing trade with her. But the shipment wasn't ready, so we waited, and while we waited, she talked in great detail about that voyage. If anyone can make it again, it's her."

Exasperated, he growled his displeasure. She could almost imagine him when he was younger, all scrawny, defiant, and full of eye-rolls. Before puberty and a rough life had turned him into the grizzled man before her.

"And she's here, is she?" He held an arm out to the dismal, filthy town. "In Nivernia?"

Her voice shriveled in her throat. "I don't know."

Laughing, he barked, "Oh, good! Very good. So we're back to a plan of wandering aimlessly until we die of starvation and thirst then."

"No," Aenwyn protested haughtily. "Not exactly. But if she was a trader, someone here might know who she is, or at least be able to steer us in the right direction."

Aenwyn flashed him a smug grin when his laughter died.

Suddenly invested in her not-too-terrible plan, he asked, "What kind of trade did your father do with her?"

Those memories were not so easy to draw upon. At the time Baug found her, Aenwyn had been semi-feral at her worst and catatonic at her best. She didn't remember most of the ship ride inland, and only remembered snippets of the time they'd spent in Vallonde.

However, she remembered the room where she'd stayed. A dark, subterranean hovel that smelled of oak and something akin to bread before it had been baked. At the time, she didn't know what filled the barrels stacked along the wall. She'd learned all about it once she was in Skogar though.

"They traded lots of things, but their biggest shipment was of mead."

"We should start at the tavern then. Anyone who trades mead will have buyers there."

It was the same conclusion she'd come to a few days ago when they first started on this trip, but she didn't feel the need to tell him that. For now, she was just happy to have his cooperation. However, she was more concerned that the plan wasn't as fool-proof as she'd originally thought it to be.

Careful not to insult anyone nearby, Aenwyn covered her mouth and leaned in closer conspiratorially. "Are we sure there's even a tavern here? This place looks…"

"Destitute?" he finished for her.

"Yes."

As if on cue, somewhere down the road they heard a

commotion, men shouting and grunting. She was familiar with the sounds of brawling. Almost daily, the young men and women of Skogar would challenge one another in a battle of bare skin and fists. The entire kingdom would gather to watch their friends break each other's noses, to leave each other bruised and bloodied, barely able to hobble much less fight by the end.

Aenwyn herself had participated a few times. They'd called her the Red Fury for the deafening blows she'd land, and the bursts of blood she'd leave splattered throughout the arena.

As much as she could relish the idea of a fight, today it seemed like the sort of thing they should avoid.

Apparently, Ser Darius thought the opposite.

"In my experience, it's the destitute who frequent taverns the most." He clicked his tongue, ushering his horse forward. "Come on. Let's go find Hissa."

14

RUFFIANS OF VALLONDE

AENWYN

When they walked up, a man with a belly so plump that it looked like it might pop was staggering forward, fist half-cocked.

The sloppy man in front of him had a pint of ale knocked back, although the vast majority of it was spilling down his cheeks and soaking his sweat-stained shirt.

The plump man's fist collided into the sloppy man's cheek and amber liquid spewed everywhere, dousing Aenwyn, Ser Darius, and the other onlookers in a mist of beer, saliva, and probably a little blood—although Aenwyn tried focusing on the beer. It smelled exactly as she remembered it, honeyed and fragrant, and her tongue puckered for a taste, even despite herself.

Both men went tumbling, the sloppy one to the ground and the plump one headfirst into a nearby trough that had fortunately been licked dry.

A collective groan escaped the crowd that had been watching them. Sullen, they turned on their heels and began to amble back into the tavern that Ser Darius had predicted would be there. He hadn't been wrong. So far, this establishment was thrice more populated than any of the others they'd passed.

"Excuse me." Ser Darius' voice boomed over the quiet, slurring murmurs, and all eyes turned to him, including Aenwyn's.

"What are you doing?" she asked, teeth pressed together in a forced smile for the locals.

"What we came here to do," he answered plainly. "To find your sailing trader."

He thrust Rocky's reins into Aenwyn's hands, and she grabbed them before she could think better of it.

"Fellas," he bellowed, arms opening wide as he strode forward. It reminded her more of the shifty salesmen that would travel to Skogar promising that their potions could cure any ailment, rather than the trustworthy neighbor image they were trying to convey. "I wonder if you mind helping us. You see, we're in search of—"

The squint of the drunkards' eyes told her they were skeptical of his showmanship as well. She knew from experience just how unlikely private folk were to share information with strangers.

They'd need to gain their trust first.

And Aenwyn could think of only one way to gain the trust of belligerent drunks.

"A good pint!" she shouted, pumped her fist in the air in cheers, and strode to Ser Darius' side. She ignored the glare he shot her way. She'd catch him up later. Gesturing to her disheveled clothes, she carried on. "As you can probably tell, we've been on the road awhile. We could do with a nice, cold glass of whatever it is that had those two up in arms."

She pointed back to where the plump one still lay face-first in the trough. The sloppy one had started to pick himself up and chortled a delirious chitter when he heard her talking about him, pumping his fist in drunken victory.

Lost in character now, she punched the sky in return.

At the tavern's dark entrance, a man the size of an ape appeared. Arms crossed, he leaned against the doorway and sized Aenwyn and Ser Darius up.

"You're Caeloran," he surmised, likely from the colors of their tattered clothes.

Aenwyn acted offended. She slapped Ser Darius in the chest and a whoosh of air escaped him. "This flower might be, but I'm of Skogar blood. No petals here."

"Yeah, only thorns," Ser Darius grumbled, earning him another smack in the chest.

The man who she suspected was the owner of the tavern examined her, and she felt compelled to examine him in return. If it weren't for his towering height, she would've suspected he came from Galorfin descendance. Maybe he did in some small way. His dark skin tone and the impressively thick, intricately braided beard sure aligned with the Molten living under the volcano.

What he thought of them, she couldn't tell from his stoic expression.

But her heart nearly plummeted to the floor when he finally spoke.

"You're the daughter of the Chieftain," he said, nose twitching. "The one who married the boy-king."

Dragon's fire, she hadn't thought about how obvious it would be to announce her Skogar heritage. How foolish that oversight had been. There weren't many—if any—Skogar in Caelora, let alone ones waltzing around in expensive dresses sewn in Caeloran colors.

The barkeep jutted his jaw at her knight. "Who are you then?"

Somehow, Ser Darius had already placed himself in between Aenwyn and everyone else. She hadn't even noticed him inching forward.

Little did he know, if it came down to a bar fight, she might be better suited than him.

"I am Ser Darius Graeme, a Caeloran knight duty-bound to protect my queen from any harm that might come to pass on this journey."

The drunkards around them grew uneasy. Facing off with a knight likely hadn't been the reason they'd come out for a drink tonight.

"And what journey is that?" the barkeep asked.

His heavy boots thudded in the sand as he approached them. This close, he was even larger than she imagined. But Aenwyn was used to being in the presence of large men. Baug the Bear still had at least an inch or two on him, although he might've had a hair's width on her husband.

Hand readied on his broadsword, Ser Darius looked to Aenwyn, awaiting her lead.

It was so small a gesture, it made her feel ridiculous to appreciate it as much as she did. She couldn't remember the last time someone had allowed her to make a decision, for her voice to be the one that carried the power.

She hoped he wouldn't regret it. But it seemed like they had no choice but to be completely open now.

"My apologies. It was never my intention to deceive you about who I was. I didn't realize I'd be known here." The confession was genuine, albeit naïve. "You are correct though. I am Queen Aenwyn, Red Fury of the Skogar. And from here on out, I promise to be nothing but honest and forthright with you."

He didn't seem like he believed her. Yet.

As the owner of a tavern, he likely heard empty promises constantly. But he did, at least, seem open to being convinced otherwise.

"You know of my magic?" she asked him.

The corners of his mouth tucked downward. "Rumors of it."

Nodding, she thought about how to proceed next. "Well, part of my magic is that I can sometimes see the future, and I had a vision last week about the blue dragon, and I think someone in Vallonde can help me."

Beside her, Ser Darius' fingers twitched over the hilt of his sword. She tried conveying calmness to him with nothing more than a look. If it came down to a fight, so be it. But until then, they needed to remain docile.

The barkeep's dark eyes remained fixed on her, unblinking. "And who's that you're looking for?"

"Her name is Hissa," Aenwyn answered. The moment she did, recognition sparked in his eyes. "She trades mead and ale. Do you know her?"

To her surprise and immense dismay, he shook his head, braided beard waggling. "Can't say that I do. We're part of sea-trade now. We get our supply from Xira."

A few things sparked her intrigue about that statement.

The first was his usage of the word *now*. As in, he'd had a different trader before.

The second—albeit a much smaller spark—was the mention of Xira. The couple who'd sought an audience with the king last week—Carmen and Emile—they'd come all the way from Rayong, a town bordering the Xiran Sea, and they'd proclaimed sovereignty.

If she cared as much about power as her deranged husband, she might keel over at the thought that with or without his permission, alliances were already being forged.

However, the third and most notable thing about what the barkeep had said was that it was an utter lie. And a blatant one at that.

Ser Darius bowed the barest amount. "We're sorry to have bothered you then."

Spinning on his heels, he grabbed Aenwyn's elbow and led

her away from the tavern. She followed him with haste, sensing the danger unfolding around them.

"I warned you," he said when they were out of earshot. "This place is no place for a queen."

She had a million retorts to that, but she couldn't stop her thundering heart long enough to utter a single one of them.

They weaved in and out of the tight alleys, dodging loose chickens and handmade pottery.

Nivernia was a sparse town, but its expanse was wide. By the time they reached the other side, both of them were starting to feel better and Aenwyn finally tugged her arm out of Ser Darius' grasp.

"Sorry," he muttered sheepishly. "I only meant—"

"It's alright. Thank you for leaving with me, and not leaving me."

She meant it as a joke, but it was clear from his dumbstruck expression that he didn't take it for one.

"I'd never leave you," he swore to her.

Something in her chest ached as she replied, "I know."

He stared at her for a long moment. Those rich, ochre eyes nearly consumed her. But it was his scar that called to her most, had her hand itching to reach up and touch it. And they were standing so close that she could. His flesh was just a reach away from hers and her skin ignited at the thought.

When he pulled his gaze away, it felt like someone had tossed her over a cliff.

"I don't think anyone followed us." Despite the assurance, he kept scanning their surroundings. "We should be safe, or as safe as we can be here."

"They knew her," Aenwyn said, recalling the barkeep. She shook her head. "Why would they lie?"

He grunted, itching at the collar of his tunic. They'd washed their clothes in the Inniset Sea a few days ago, and rubbed them with wildflowers for good measure, but nothing could clean away the grime from their travels.

"In my experience—" he said— "People lie when they're scared. I don't know this Hissa woman, but he didn't want to be associated with her."

Worrying at her bottom lip, she wondered what that could mean. Maybe that was why he'd sought different trade routes? She remembered Hissa as such a kind, spirited woman, but perhaps she'd been wrong. Maybe she wasn't the sort of person to associate with?

"What next then, oh fated one?"

Aenwyn glowered at him so fast she feared she would pull a muscle. "Stop calling me that."

"What should I call you then?" The corners of his mouth lifted into something taunting. "Red Fury?"

"I swear, I will end you."

He laughed then, a robust sound that warmed her very center. "Queen Aenwyn, then."

"Just Aenwyn is fine. I'm hardly a *queen* right now. Just look at me." She gestured down to her grimy attire, and his smile broadened.

"If King Everard could see you now. See *us*—" he said, glancing down at himself with mock disgust— "He'd shut us out at the borders, and deny we were ever part of his court."

She snorted, but the laughter wasn't as a bright as the rest had been. Suddenly she found herself longing for that outcome. A reality where she would return to Caelora after all of this and King Everard would turn her away at his gates, freeing her from their union and from her misery.

"Just Aenwyn then," Ser Darius agreed, bowing deeply. "I suppose that makes me just Darius."

Cheeks flushing, she nodded. "Well, Darius, I don't think we'll have much luck at the tavern. And if I'm being honest, all of Nivernia chills me to the bone." There was something about this place that reminded her of her own home, during the years she'd spent there all alone after the fog had taken everyone. Something sinister and lonely and she didn't like it one bit. "There are other towns we can visit, ones closer to the shoreline where maybe their relationships with her won't be so mysterious."

"Agreed. I don't think it wise to ask around here more. And at the very least, we know now to be stealthier with our inquiry in the next town. The sooner we leave, the better."

"True, but—" Hesitating, Aenwyn glanced down at her tattered attire. Although the green velvet was fading beneath a thick layer of dust and grime, it still marked her as Caeloran, and she didn't think there were many Caelorans with hair as red as flames. "Before we go, we should stop for supplies. Find something to wear that's a little less…conspicuous?"

He examined the both of them and shrugged. "You're not wrong. We stick out like thorn bushes."

"I didn't bring any coin though."

With a sigh, he shot her a long look that again chastised her for how woefully unprepared she was when she left the castle.

For once, she agreed.

"Fine. I know. I should've worn trousers and brought a sword and shield and packed my own supplies."

She thought back to the bags that had been ready and packed for her when she'd found Charmaine in the stables. Although there had been enough grain to keep one horse sated, but not two. And much to their dismay when Aenwyn and Darius had taken their first rest, they soon discovered that there wasn't enough food and water for their own bellies either.

Fortunately for the both of them, Aenwyn knew how to ensnare rabbits and Darius had a knife sharp enough to skin them. It hadn't been the royal meals she'd grown accustomed to since her wedding, but it sure beat starving. Still, she should've at least been smart enough to pack her own knife, or to bring anything that might be useful to help her survive in the wild. It wasn't like she had no experience with doing just that.

"I should've taken more time to plan out this journey," she continued. And then begrudgingly added, "And maybe I shouldn't have relied so heavily on fate providing for me. But I was hasty, and we're here now, so we'll have to figure out how to make do—"

Cutting off her rant, Darius jingled a leather pouch before her. "Luckily for the both of us, I don't travel anywhere without enough coin for an unplanned, reckless journey into the desert."

The corner of Aenwyn's lips twitched upward, mimicking his own. "Do my ears deceive me? Or did Ser Darius just make a joke?"

His chest puffed proudly. "He did. You know, despite what you think, I am quite capable of humor."

"Forgive me for ever doubting it." This was possibly the most pleasant exchange they'd had since meeting. Before it could sour, she pointed down the nearest path. "Come on. Let's go find us some clothes."

But before they could take another step, grey folded over Aenwyn's vision.

A scratchy fabric covered her head and she shrieked and at the same time an agonizing cry burst from Darius' lungs. He sounded hurt.

"Darius!"

The only response she got from him was grunting. Struggling with all his might, but against what, she didn't know.

At least he was alive. For now.

The sack formed to her face with the breath of her cry. Against her lips, it tasted like flour and dirt.

Hands clawed at her. They wrapped around her arms and then her legs like iron jaws.

"Unhand her!" The rage in Darius' voice made her chest ache. He was fighting for her. Defending her when she was unable to defend herself.

It was stuffy beneath the confines of the sack, but at least she could still breathe. The rough fabric was too loosely woven to suffocate her, and for that, she was grateful. She was also grateful for the spaces between the fibers that were specked with light.

She squirmed, not only to break free, but to try to catch a glimpse of any of the shadows closing in around her. But it wasn't enough to see anyone's faces. Only shadows.

All she could hear were the strained breaths of men.

Once they lifted her from the ground, she knew there was nothing she could do, but she kept trying anyway. Kept wriggling and kicking.

Their grip held tight though. At least a half dozen of them, judging from how many hands she could feel upon her body.

Behind her, Darius seethed. She could imagine the spit foaming from his mouth when he growled, "I swear by the Hollows, if you don't let her go, I'll—"

"Someone shut him up," a man grumbled.

On command, Darius guffawed as if he'd been punched in the stomach. The series of thumps and pounds that followed made the panic in Aenwyn's chest wrench hold of her until she couldn't breathe.

"And will you get that on her already?" the same man shouted from above.

"I'm trying!" spluttered another.

It was only then that she realized they weren't just holding her. Someone was fidgeting with her wrist like they were trying to shove something onto it.

It made her think of her wedding day. Of King Everard

chaining her magic under the guise of a gift of a beautiful ring. It made her think of Irongate. Of King Ulfaskr and the garment he had made Signe wear.

Aenwyn would rather be burned alive before letting another man shackle her again.

She had no blood to draw her symbols and call upon the Sky-Blessed. But she hoped she didn't need to.

There had been power within her the day she lost her mother. She had found it again the day Darius tried stopping her at the stables.

She could find it once more.

Aenwyn turned her focus inward. To a swirling darkness that crackled somewhere deep in her chest.

With a flick of her hand, Aenwyn unleashed the power from within her.

It whirled from her fingertips, a cyclone of magic meant to destroy.

The might of it slammed into the man at the end of her arm. His ribs cracked, his body sent hurdling backward. The other person holding onto her arm hadn't been in the direct line of power, but even he was sent staggering back, costing him his grip on her.

Suddenly, one of Aenwyn's arms was completely free.

Dangling awkwardly, the sack around her head fell and Aenwyn's fingertips brushed the ground.

Sand.

Something to draw in.

It wouldn't be perfect. Far from it while she was suspended there, upside down, frightened, and with the men struggling to right her. But she hoped it would be enough.

Aenwyn swept her finger across the sand in an arch and scribbled a jagged line connecting the bottom of it.

"Sky-Blessed, save me," she breathed when the crude wing was finished.

Aenwyn didn't know what to expect. She didn't know if her appeal would be heard, let alone answered. She had lost count of the times she had called upon them only to receive no aid in return. Sometimes her offerings weren't enough. This time she had nothing to give them. Just her cry for help. It was unlikely they'd head her at all.

Then the sand began to rumble beneath her.

The men hushed, recognizing the ethereal message in her plea too late, the raw power of her undulating words.

Holes began piercing the ground, like chunks of hail were falling from the sky. The thin chasms speared through the earth, making the land sound like a den of hissing vipers as the sand fell into the holes appearing around them.

Or that's what she thought at first.

Tiny, bug-like heads started to poke through, their long, flaxen bodies following after. They spewed from the holes by the dozens, their thin wings buzzing as they launched into flight.

Aenwyn had never seen such creatures, but judging from the looks on her captors' faces, she knew they were to be feared.

"Locusts!" one of the men shouted.

And with that, Aenwyn was released.

She hit the ground with a thud, but it was softened by the sand and a half dozen locusts that crunched on impact. Nausea would've twisted her belly, except her lungs felt like they had collapsed. She strained to suck in a breath, but none would come. Just a cold, wrenching hand, squeezing her chest.

Around her, chaos erupted.

The men reached for the weapons at their waists, but they were unfamiliar, netted things that were used to trap and crunch the insects. Others stomped on the holes, or plugged them with the wooden shafts of rakes, hoes, and other miscellaneous items found nearby.

"What in the Hollows are they doing down here?" someone bellowed, dumping a bucket of water down one of the locust-infested tunnels. "It's not even nightfall!"

"I don't know!" another shouted—the one who seemed to be giving the orders. "Just kill them!"

Finally, Aenwyn's chest cracked. Her lungs gave, and a burst of air bled into her, warm and sweet. She tucked her hands beneath her, wincing at the carcasses and broken wings that crunched under her fingers, and prepared to shove off the ground.

But her momentary victory was crushed by a man barreling atop her.

"Oh, no you don't."

It was the one in charge, the one with a snarl like one of the bitter snow bears that prowled the peaks of the Skogar Mountains.

Aenwyn struggled beneath the weight of him, not yet having a chance to recover her breath, let alone her strength. Her flailing only enraged him more and tired her out all the same.

She was no match for him. Not in this condition. Not after exerting herself with all the magic she'd already used. She wondered if she had it in her for one more invocation.

"I've got her!" the leader snarled. "Get the hailstone!"

Hailstone? That couldn't have been right. What would the people of Vallonde know of Hailstone? She doubted any of them had been there considering it was a sea in Skogar. A place where she, Signe, and their friends had often passed the time, chasing snow foxes as they darted through the snowy forests and daring one another to cross the ice once it had frozen.

It was also where Baug the Bear had earned his moniker after the giant, snarling grizzly tackled him into the Hailstone Sea and he'd wrestled the creature to its death.

But if they were talking about *that* Hailstone, it wouldn't make sense for the leader to tell someone to get it.

Aenwyn assumed she had misheard them and refocused. She needed to escape. She tried twisting and torquing, her pinched flesh burning where he had her wrenched in his grip, but nothing would give.

She had no other options to try.

"Sky-Blessed, hear me—"

The man slammed his shoulder over her mouth. Heat and pain swelled her lip before she tasted blood. Her teeth ached.

"I don't think so," he growled as someone else fumbled with her limp arm.

Something cold and sharp clasped around it. She didn't need to look to know what it was, but she did anyways. She had expected to find a black band of iron clamped around her wrist, but this was different.

The manacle around her wrist was an iridescent shade of light blue. It looked like stone that had been carved into the shape of a gnarled branch that twisted around her wrist.

It would've been beautiful, elegant, if not for what it represented.

Aenwyn was their captive. There was no chain attached yet. Nothing securing her in place. But she knew this meant she was a prisoner, nonetheless. Just like all the Skogar before her.

Dimly, she became aware of the lack of buzzing around as the sack was thrust over her head again. They dragged her through the sand by her wrists. But they had left her un-gagged, and she wasn't ready to stop fighting yet.

She spoke rapidly, fearful they might intervene. "Sky-Blessed, guide my hands. Channel your power into me so that I may survive and be your conduit again."

Aenwyn waited with bated breath. But nothing happened.

One of the men snorted. "Ain't gonna be using your spells any longer, I'm 'fraid."

The others laughed with him.

Their confidence unsettled her, but before she could think too much about it, as her captors carried her away, she heard Darius grunting behind her, knew he was writhing and contorting with all his might to break free from the hands that were likely restraining him too.

Only, his sounds were growing more distant. And a chilling thought occurred to her then.

What if they were only taking her? What if their plan was just to subdue him and leave him behind?

Or worse, what if they planned on killing him?

"Darius!" she shouted, hoping that he could still hear her. The men dragging her through the sand were moving fast.

"I'm here!" he managed to grit out, still fighting, and closer than he had been before.

The tightness in Aenwyn's chest tried to ease, though it was difficult with impending doom still awaiting them. At least she wouldn't have to endure this alone.

Finally, the men dragging her stopped. No longer could she hear their horses nickering. No longer sense the eerie presence of onlookers.

The sack was lifted.

They were no longer in the town of Nivernia. She could tell because the desert winds that had been blocked by the derelict homes were now billowing at full intensity around her, so much so that a tangle of red hair was quick to sweep over her eyes the moment the burlap sack was lifted.

With a jerk of her head, Aenwyn cleared the mane of hair long enough to catch a glimpse of her surroundings.

A caravan of desert animals.

Darius bound, but still struggling.

And the bearded barkeep standing before her with arms crossed.

"Where are you taking us?" she snarled.

"I'm afraid you're going for a ride," he said. "The Scorpion wants to meet you."

Then, scowling, he nodded to someone behind her, and before Aenwyn knew it, something heavy whacked against the back of her skull, and the desert disappeared into the black.

15

THE MARCH OF DESPAIR

DARIUS

T he barren peaks of the Barga Mountains had been a fixed landscape on one side of the horizon for what Darius was estimating had been days now. He couldn't say for certain. There had been no way for him to keep track of time.

However he had managed to keep track of other things. Like how they'd only stopped in one other village since leaving Nivernia. How, not including himself and Aenwyn, they were traveling with a total of five; two were Animali and mostly stayed in their animal forms—a camel and a hyena—since they were hauling the supplies and Aenwyn on their backs; the third was the burly barkeep who hadn't let Darius out of his sight once; the fourth, a woman as capable at navigating as she was at keeping the others in line; and the last was a man so scrawny that he'd nearly been blown down during the sandstorm they'd been caught in the first night cycle after leaving Nivernia.

Most notably though, Darius had kept track of how many times he had attempted to fight off their captors, and how many times he had failed.

Seventeen. And he had the bruises and torn clothes to prove it.

The stab wound in his leg burned with every step as he limped through the deep, sandy dunes of the desert. By now, the wound was surely festering from their lack of care. But they wouldn't let him stop.

He'd learned to endure it though. By fixating his thoughts on plotting out his next plan of escape, Darius had been able to stop himself from fixating on the burning that throbbed over his thigh.

And it was just about time for him to put another plan into action now.

In an effort to get one of his captor's attentions, Darius moaned over the leather they'd wadded into his mouth. It had been there ever since his first failed escape, which had involved shouting for help at all the onlookers who watched as he and Aenwyn had been dragged out of Nivernia.

Ever since, they had only removed his gag to allow him to eat, drink, and on a rare occasion, when he made it seem urgent that he tell them something.

It took an hour of constant pestering, but Darius finally got the attention of the man who dueled as a barkeep and their abductor.

"What is it?" the rugged man barked, stopping the entire group.

Darius did his best to indicate that he needed to say something, but with his hand bound and his mouth gagged, the best he could do was bulge his eyes at the man until he finally grumbled and tore the leather from his mouth.

Darius worked his jaw, moved his raw tongue.

"Go on with it then," the man urged. "Spit it out. We haven't got all day."

"I need to relieve myself."

A hideous smile slivered into the man's dark face. "Not falling for that one again." He pointed to the dark shadow beneath his eye, the one that Darius assumed matched his own. That one had been well worth it. The tavern keep continued. "We'll be there soon enough."

Before he could shove the leather back into Darius' dry mouth, he jerked his head away. "And where's that?"

They still wouldn't tell him. All anyone ever said was—

"To the Scorpion. Now shut that mouth of yours. No one speaks while we pass the Cursed Prison."

"The Cursed Prison—" Darius began to ask, but he was cut off by the man's growl as he shoved the gag back into place.

"Couldn't even manage that. Now, could you?"

Anger simmered from within Darius' chest. He grumbled and yelled every expletive he could think of, and even though they came out muffled, their intent was not lost.

However, it was ignored.

Darius had learned that the barkeep was an easy target for riling. One smart taunt and the man was ready to throw blows normally.

But today he didn't so much as glance over his shoulder back at him as he led the caravan onward.

The rope around Darius' wrists pulled tight. He thought about making it difficult—digging his heels into the sand and straining against the pull. He thought about forcing the man to come face-to-face with him. It hadn't been his original plan, to provoke another fight, but if it was the only option he had, he'd take it.

Or at least, he thought he might. Until he noticed the casual conversation dying among the others. It was then that Darius remembered what the man had said: *No one speaks while we pass the Cursed Prison*.

Something cold and oily dipped into Darius' stomach, a

sensation he had learned to trust when in battle. And so, though he couldn't bring himself to blindly obey the men responsible for capturing him and Aenwyn, he could obey himself, and Darius quieted with the others.

An eerie silence settled over the group. It dripped around them like grains of sand meant to bury them alive.

It seemed like danger lurked all around them. Darius kept a watchful eye on their surroundings and checked on Aenwyn more frequently than he had been the last few days, after having decided that she was relatively safe where she'd been slung atop the camel's back. He could hardly consider her safe anymore though. None of them were. Especially not her. Their captors had kept her unconscious by blowing some kind of smoke into her face, so it wasn't like she could defend herself if anything were to happen.

As long as they kept quiet, Darius had to believe they would be safe. And if not, he'd find a way to keep her protected.

At the base of the Barga Mountains, a tower came into view. The closer they became, Darius noticed it was more than just a tower; there was an entire fenced sanctuary surrounded by mountains on one side and yellow dunes on the other.

For a moment, Darius thought they might enter. It had been a while since their last stop; he was sure they could use more supplies and the opportunity to rest with a roof over their heads and without the threat of scorpions climbing over them while they slept.

But then he saw the front gate was wide open.

Through it, the sanctuary was dead. Not dead in the sense that Nivernia was—a once thriving town that had become a cesspit of crime and poverty after the dragon attacks started.

This place was different. This place was dead in the way that a battlefield is. There was a haunting energy surrounding it. Even if Darius hadn't been told to keep quiet, something instinctual would've kept him so, the air seeming to suck from his lungs as they tiptoed by the vacant place.

It wasn't exactly vacant though, he noted.

Through the wide gate, Darius could make out figures inside, the shapes of humans that were frighteningly still. Men and women. Some hunched over from old age or ailment. And there were children too.

He wasn't as familiar with Vallondean traditions as he would've liked to be, but he wondered if it was a ritual of honoring death, a way of preserving life.

Only once the mysterious place was far, *far* behind them did the others finally begin talking again. He figured it was a fine time to ask—

"Mmm hmmm mmm hmm?"

The tavern keep cast an irritating look over his shoulder. But he must've been able to tell that Darius wasn't going to let up, because in the end, he removed the gag once more.

"I said, what was that place?"

"That would be the Cursed Prison."

"What were all those..." Darius almost called them statues, but he knew that wasn't right, so he reconsidered. "Who were all those people?"

"Stay on good behavior and you won't have to find out." The man balled the leather into his fist before shoving it into one of his pockets. "We're here."

Considering that they were still nowhere near anything, Darius didn't know what to make of such a statement.

Seeing Darius's confusion, the man stretched out a finger and pointed through the mesas to a dark shadow just on the other side.

"There. The Great City of Vallonde. We'll be there in about an hour."

Worry was vice grip around Darius' heart. That meant he

only had an hour left then to figure out how to get him and Aenwyn out of this mess before they were delivered to the mysterious Scorpion. But he was running out of ideas. Already he had tried fighting them, turning them against each other, and convincing any number of them to let him and his queen go.

The only other choice he had was to attempt to run and find help, but that wasn't an option he would consider. He would not leave Aenwyn alone with them.

Behind him, there was jostling. It wasn't the alarming kind, more like someone feeling around in their pockets for lost coins. But since the group hadn't started their march again yet, Darius allowed his curiosity to get the better of him and he pivoted so that he could find the source of the commotion.

Blood as hot as flames beat into his skull when he found the two other humans rifling through Aenwyn's clothes.

"Unhand her!" Darius roared, peeling away from where he stood.

The tavern keep caught him by the shoulder. "Calm yourself. They're not doing anything nefarious."

Blinking, Darius looked again. It took him a moment to realize that they weren't undressing her. They were searching her. The man plucked the rings from Aenwyn's fingers while the woman searching her satchel and the seams of her garments.

Eyebrow cocked, Darius returned his gaze upon the tavern keep. "Nothing nefarious?"

"Piss off," the man retorted. "This is the only payment we'll get for all the trouble you've put us through. And if you say another word about it, we'll find something worse to shove into your mouth."

The threat was believable enough. Besides, the last thing Darius needed now was more restrictions.

"Fine," he grumbled.

The man seemed surprisingly pleased. "Well alright then." He whistled, drawing the others' attention. "Let's wrap it up. I'd like to make it before the next night cycle if possible. It's been a while since we've had one, and the last thing we need is to be caught out here for it."

Darius didn't like the sound of that, but he knew asking about it would only end poorly for him. He had other matters to figure out right now.

But in the hour that it took them to navigate the large mesas, no new ideas surfaced. And once they reached the Great City of Vallonde, Darius was consumed by its vivacity. People crowded the streets in hordes. So many of them, it was a wonder the other villages had been so vacant. Maybe everyone had come here though. Maybe they'd sought refuge where their numbers would be greatest.

As him, Aenwyn, the camel, the hyena, the tavern keep, and the two other captors weaved through the bustling city, judging eyes followed Darius everywhere. It didn't matter if he were to yell out for help, he realized. As long as he was bound, he looked the part of a criminal, not the knight he was.

The soft sands of the dunes surrounding the city turned to cracked earth as they went deeper into Vallonde. The buildings changed from minimalist huts and stands, to well-constructed buildings with vibrant and decorative stonework.

At every crossroad, in the center of the road itself, stones the color of the oceans, forests, and flames, were arranged in an intricate and unique design to resemble any number of animals. There had been a bird, a fish, a rabbit, and Darius had a feeling there were dozens of others scattered throughout the city.

As beautiful as they were, with any luck, hopefully he wouldn't see any more of them.

The tavern keep left Darius with the others while he went to speak to a vendor. This was his chance.

Without the burly man, Darius thought he might actually stand a fighting chance against the others. If he could incapacitate and de-arm the woman first—she was likely his most formidable foe, assuming that the hyena, wouldn't attack as an animal, for fear of injuring Darius too severely. He would have to shift back into his human form first, and that would give Darius time to turn the woman's dagger onto the scrawny one and threaten to slit his throat if the others didn't release Aenwyn and let them leave.

But Darius wasn't even sure he could carry her. Not with his leg as bad as it was.

Even if he could, where would they go? By now they were weeks away from Caelora or anyone he could trust. They had no money. No weapons. Even the little jewelry the queen had been traveling with had been stolen and was now being bartered with.

With a cart in tow, the tavern keep returned before Darius could commit to anything.

"Get in."

"What?" Darius looked from the cart that looked like it had recently been used to transporting hay back to the man. "Why? I've walked all this way, haven't I?"

"Because I don't like the skittish look in your eyes."

The man gave him a shove. Darius staggered forward, his thigh bumping into the edge of the cart and his vision bursting white from pain.

"I'm not gonna say it again. Get. In."

Begrudgingly, and with the taste of blood and something rancid on his tongue, Darius climbed into the cart.

He hardly had time to settle before one of the others handed the tavern keep a bundle of herbs or sticks, the tips smoking. It took Darius but a fraction of a second to realize what it was, but it was already too late.

His captors blew on the smoke until a plume of it wafted in front of him.

"See you on the other side of bars," was the last thing Darius heard the tavern keep say before he succumbed to the sickening darkness.

16

BOUND

AENWYN

Aenwyn awoke to a metal door clanging shut, and her body being tossed to the ground.

Her knees crashed against the stones, and for once she regretted not wearing the frivolous layers of skirts, underskirts, crinoline, and whatever else her handmaidens had wanted to stuff her with back in Caelora. Today, she'd pay for forgoing such decorum with aching, bruised knees.

When the upper half of her body came crashing down after the rest of her, she expected the same painful landing.

Instead, it wasn't stone that met her face. Her cheek landed atop something warm and firm, some place decidedly pleasant. Especially compared to the rest of the cold, dark room.

At some point since her abduction, someone had put the burlap sack back over her head, so she couldn't see a thing, only could feel around to catch her bearings.

Her fingers traced the soft fabric and the hard plane of muscles beneath. With a jolt, she realized she had landed directly atop someone's broad chest, only a thin undershirt between them. Somehow, she knew exactly who's chest it was.

Darius cleared his throat, voice rumbling beneath her hand as he said, "Are you all right, my queen?"

Any other Caeloran woman would've blush and profusely uttered her apologies.

But Aenwyn had found herself in far more compromising positions with men before, so she felt no such compulsion.

Instead, she used their proximity as an opportunity to ask him for a favor.

"Can you take off my—"

Before she could finish, Darius removed the sack from her head, their dismal surroundings coming into focus soon after.

She half-expected to find them tossed in a pit of scorpions, since that's where their ambushers had said they'd be taking them: to the Scorpion.

Thankfully, there were none.

From where she was resting, head tilted and staring down the length of his legs, Aenwyn could see the entire span of the room—which wasn't much, by any means. The pigeons in the royal dovecote had more space than they did inside their sandstone cell. Not to mention, the amenities were abysmal: a bucket for excrement—she supposed they were just expected to share the same one; a window small enough that even a rat couldn't fit through it; a single cot—again, either they couldn't do the math, or they hadn't anticipated the arrival of more than one prisoner today; and a hole where the wall met the floor with a tray shoved through it, a single serving of food and water awaiting their divvying.

"You're not bound, you know."

Aenwyn twisted to look up at him. She had to suck in a breath at the banged-up sight of his face.

One of his eyes was almost swollen shut, his scar barely visible beneath the purpled skin. His already full lips were engorged and busted. Dried blood speckled his forehead just beneath his hairline.

Ignoring her look of horror, Darius showed her his own hands, covered in just as many cuts, blood, and bruises. No signs of shackles. "See? They took them off before tossing you in here."

Aenwyn decided against making a big deal about his injuries. Men were so rarely keen on women pointing out their weaknesses, and she doubted he needed to be reminded of them. Plus, she could guess as to their whereabouts.

"Maybe they removed yours, but I'm still—"

Aenwyn moved to show him where her arms were still bound together; she could, after all, still feel the bite of stone against her wrist. But when she lifted her arms, she found that they moved freely. Her wrists came apart. Only the light-blue bracelet remained, but nothing was tied to it. No chains. No ropes to keep her bound.

If it wasn't to shackle her, then what purpose did it serve?

Aenwyn examined the shimmering blue with curious disdain. "Yeah, well they left *this*."

Darius inched up to get a better look. The movement made him wince.

It was then that Aenwyn remembered the agonizing bellow that had erupted from his lungs when they had been captured. Now that she knew she wasn't helplessly bound and therefore stuck atop him, she shoved herself up.

"Where is it?" she asked, eyes scanning for injuries as she knelt over him.

"I'm fine," Darius growled.

It didn't matter. His assistance wasn't necessary anyway. The blood was telling enough.

"Clearly you're not." She shot him a look before examining the wound she found on his thigh more closely. The blood had seeped through the leather, but at least it wasn't spurting. That was a good sign. It looked like a clean cut.

"A knife?"

He nodded. "It's already starting to heal. I'll be fine."

She knew that was impossible. Wounds didn't heal that quickly, unless the use of healing magic was involved. And as far as Aenwyn was aware, she was the only person in Grimtol who possessed it.

The Ashen had their touch of death.

The Molten had their resistance to flame.

The Animali had their animal forms.

And Aenwyn had...everything else.

She didn't know why. Neither had her mother. Or even the Skogar, once she'd finally told them.

All she knew was that she possessed a gift that was beyond explanation and came with tremendous responsibility and power.

And in this moment, she could put it to good use.

There was sand all over Darius, including around the hole in his trousers where the knife had pierce him. Chances were there was sand in the wound too, among who knew what other kinds of grime, maybe even rust.

Sitting on her heels, Aenwyn placed her gentle hands around his knee and was about to shift his leg so that she could have a better look when he jerked from her touch.

"What are you doing?" he asked, voice breathy with accusation.

It wasn't the first time someone feared her for the magic she possessed. Nor would it be the last. In fact, this was the treatment she was used to it, people acting as if getting too close to her would give them the plague.

It was how almost everyone in Caelora had treated her since the moment she'd arrived.

Everyone, except for Darius.

Maybe he judged her for her impulsive decision making and undying belief in fate, but she'd never once felt like he was afraid of her or her magic. Before now, he hardly seemed to notice it.

Shoving down the bubble of pain that threatened to rise up her throat, Aenwyn forced his shoulder back.

"Sit still, you." The bite in her voice was unintentional, but unavoidable after the last year of dealing with this kind of judgment and fear. "Or you might end up with feathers instead of skin."

The corner of his mouth twitched, surprising her. "Funny. But if that were the case, I'd be pretty upset to find out that you could've given us wings, but instead chose to keep us trotting around a desert on horseback."

A small, uncertain laugh escaped her. People didn't usually joke with her about her magic. It was such a rare occurrence, that she wasn't even convinced that's what he was doing. But she watched him for a long moment to be sure and found no real evidence of disdain or disgust.

She found herself reassessing him for what felt like the hundredth time, but ultimately knew that now was not the time. She shook her head and resigned to resume her work. But when she reached for his leg, he jerked it away again.

"Will you hold still?" she snapped.

"That depends. Will you tell me what you're doing?"

Aenwyn inhaled deeply. "I'm doing what only I can do. I'm going to heal your wound."

Darius was quiet, his face unreadable. "With…magic?"

Not exactly. Mostly she would just be using regular herbs that could be found anywhere in Grimtol, although in his case she might try to bolster the effects with a divine blessing. However, normally her skills with healing exclusively involved natural elements. She used what the land provided, nothing more. But Caelorans were a suspicious sort. They were unfamiliar with the way she used her materials, and therefore presumed the worse. And she never corrected them about it.

"Yes," she bit out, more haughtily than she meant to. Anger was a comfortable defense against the hatred she was used to enduring.

Deflection was her greatest shield. Impassivity, her sword.

But as she braced herself for the backlash she had heard so many times before, the room fell silent.

Casual as ever, Darius nestled against the wall at his back, arms folding behind his head as he watched her, waiting for her to begin.

"How healed will it be?" he asked, and she almost swore he sounded impressed, if not intrigued.

"Hopefully entirely," she said, lips still pursed into an uncertain but guarded line.

He snorted a breathy laugh. "I didn't realize you could do that. I didn't realize anyone could."

"They can't," she replied hastily. With just the herbs, they couldn't. But if the Sky-Blessed were feeling generous, and if she could find a way to draw some of her own blood to use as an offering, she might be able to bring him a full recovery. Leaning over his leg, she examined the fabric around the wound and elaborated. "Or at least, I've never met anyone else who could."

Despite taking care not to touch the open wound, he still winced when she ripped the hole in his trousers wider. All four times, once in every direction to make sure she could see the place where she needed to work more clearly.

Underneath the dusty trousers, Aenwyn could finally see the angry, oozing slit in his leg. A deep wound that had likely damaged some of his thigh muscle and was visibly infected.

If he thought this was considered *healed*, she worried about his ability to think clearly. Maybe the infection had worked its way into his bloodstream already. But that would've taken weeks.

Slowly, she blinked up at him. "How long was I out for?"

His look was grim. "A couple of weeks."

"Weeks?" Her voice squeaked. That was impossible. It had only felt like her eyes had been closed for a few hours, maybe a day.

"They kept you drugged," he said. Before she could ask with what, he answered her, "I don't know what it was. A dried bundle of something that they'd light, blow out the flame, and then blow the smoke in your face every day after they fed you and gave you some water."

She was familiar with the substance at least. Hollowroot. Found in the dead forest just south of Skogar known as the Hollows.

Baug would use it in certain ceremonies as the Skogar believed that since smoke rises, it would bring them closer to the clouds and therefore closer to the Sky-Blessed. Aenwyn couldn't say whether that were true, but on the few occasions she had whiffed smoke from the hollowroot, she had felt herself opening up to the world, the colors and shapes shifting around her.

If someone indulged too much though, they were fast to fall asleep and painstakingly slow to awake. She knew that because she'd had to help carry some of the Skogar into their huts whenever that had happened.

"Do you remember any of it?" Darius asked her, pulling her out of her memories of home. "Any of it at all? The smoke? The desert? Eating?"

Aenwyn couldn't move her mouth enough to speak, but reflexively she felt for her stomach. She still wasn't thin by Caeloran standards, but she could feel the difference, the loss in pound. The loss of self.

She swallowed, forcing the word out. "No. Do you?"

I shrugged, looking a little sheepish. "I was awake. For most of it, anyway. I guess they figured they didn't need to drug me. I wasn't making it far if I had run."

As much as she disliked being the only one subjected to hollowroot, she supposed she preferred it to both of them being unconscious. At least he would've been able to keep an eye on her.

"Did they—"

"No," he said, apparently understanding the worry building in the back of her throat. "No one touched you. I would've died to defend you from that."

The feral protectiveness in his tone stirred something deep within her.

With a grateful pang in her chest, she nodded, and it took everything in her to tear her gaze away from those dark, alluring eyes.

Fortunately, there was work to be done.

Aenwyn returned her attention to the inflamed wound. Though a scab of sorts had tried to form, the skin beneath it was purple.

"Well—" Aenwyn said, tucking thick strands of hair behind her ears before reaching for her pouch— "Let's make sure that the next time you have an opening to run, you can actually take it."

He quirked a brow. "You think we're getting out of here?"

"Of course we are," she said, hand clasping empty air where she thought her pouch would be around her thigh. "I had a vision, remember?"

"How could I forget."

Even despite the crack in his lip, when his smirk broadened, he was still ruggedly handsome. A different kind of appeal than her husband. King Everard was beautiful in the way that freshly manicured rose bushes were beautiful. Pretty to look at, but there were deadly thorns concealed behind that flawless exterior.

But Darius was turning out to be the opposite. He carried

himself with his thorns first, a shield to guard his kinder, lighter, funnier center.

Eager to avoid him catching her staring, she returned her attention on finding her dratted pouch. It wasn't tied around her elbow either. She went to search their bag and realized—

"Our stuff! It's gone?"

He fixed her with a sympathetic wince. "You thought they'd leave our things in here with us? That they'd lock us away, but give us our weapons?"

"No, but—" Aenwyn twisted to get a better look of the cell, even though she knew she wouldn't find anything. "I just...I needed my things. I have caelwood bark and blacknettle and—."

"I have no idea what any of that means."

She rolled her eyes. "They have healing properties, you oaf. I won't be able to mend your leg without them." An idea was beginning to take form and she chewed on her bottom lip. "Not easily anyway."

Before it could form more completely, Darius placed his large hand closed atop hers. She hadn't realized she was still holding onto his leg.

"It's alright," he said. "You don't have to do this."

The tenderness in his voice, in his touch, sent shivers through her.

She hadn't noticed their close proximity until now. Until she felt the intensity of his gaze pressing into her own. Felt the warmth of his breath across her face.

The way she was sitting beside him, her leg pressed up against his, made the ache in her chest tug low. It plunged even deeper when she realized that her hand was wrapped around his upper thigh, dangerously close to a part of him that she hadn't dared let herself think about.

She couldn't remember the last time she touched a man like this. With slow intimacy that made her breaths quicken with

equal parts dread and anticipation. With the king, there had
been no touching. No affection. No tenderness. They simply
removed their clothes, pressed their bodies together, and when
the deed was done, they went their separate ways.

Now she couldn't help but wonder how things might be
different with Darius. A man whose tenderness was beginning
to peak through the thorny bramble exterior.

She couldn't stop her gaze from drifting to the thick bulge
in his trousers. Just above her fingertips. She could practically
imagine him lying there, naked and gleaming in a thin layer of
sweat as the desert heat pressed down around them, the
impressive length of him just within reach.

A deep, delicious ache swelled between her legs at the
thought that if she dared, all it would take was a subtle shift of
placement of her hand, and she could graze the thick tip of
him. She could slide her hand up and grasp his girth. She
could—

The groin of his trousers twitched, the fabric beginning to
pull taut where he was expanding. Was he thinking the same
as her?

On impulse, she snapped her hand back. They couldn't do
this. *She* couldn't. There were too many lives at stake for her to
give into her temptations now. She had promised Baug an
alliance with the most powerful kingdom in Grimtol. If she
squandered it now, she would not only be letting him down,
but all of Skogar. All of Caelora. They had both sworn their
lives to protect Caelora, not dismantle it from the inside.

There was too much at stake.

Before she could regret losing the warmth of his touch,
Aenwyn decided she needed a distraction, and magic was as
good as any.

She might not be able to heal him herself, but she could still
ask the Sky-Blessed to do it for her. To channel their power
into her so that she could fix his leg. They had been supportive

of her on her quest thus far. She was starting to wonder if they were invested in the outcome and were willing to do anything to aid her.

If that were the case, maybe they could even free them from their cell. It was at least worth a shot to ask.

Aenwyn began frantically look around.

"What are you doing?" he asked. She was grateful he wasn't asking why she had so suddenly pulled away. But then again, he already knew, considering the stakes were just as high for him.

"Looking for something sharp," she replied, walking over to the iron bars. She examined them thoroughly, took note of their sharp, jagged edges.

"And why is that? I thought we were talking about healing my leg, not stabbing it again."

Somehow, despite her embarrassment, or her fervently trying to tell herself that she needed to stop finding him so charming, he still managed to coax a smile out of her. "I'm not going to stab you. I need something to cut myself—" when she felt the tension in the room thickening, she added— "I need blood for an offering."

Darius was quiet for a moment as he considered. "Does it need to be your blood? Or could it be mine?"

She looked down at his festering leg. "I don't think we should draw from that."

"Definitely not." He grimaced, as if even just imagining her dragging her finger across it brought him immense pain. He shook it away and pointed to his busted lip. "I meant this. It's fresh. Earned it before we arrived, and it hasn't stopped bleeding yet."

Aenwyn came closer. Took a look. Sure enough, the split in his lip was bright red.

"That could work," she agreed before fully realizing what this would mean.

She would have to stick her finger into his mouth.

A part of her thrilled at the thought of getting to be close to him again. And another part of her cursed her for putting herself in this position. But they needed the blood if she wanted to give this a true try.

Biting down on her cheek, Aenwyn scooted closer. She felt her leg bump up against his again and her heart began to race. It took every ounce of willpower within her to keep her hand from trembling as she extended it.

Darius licked his lips before they parted. The slickness of them brought a rush to her stomach as she started wondering how they would taste.

But it was just a moment of distraction. One moment of weakness before Aenwyn regained her focus, brought her finger to the inside of his bottom lip, and stroked.

Seeing the red droplets made it a little easier to stop thinking about how it would feel if he clamped his mouth shut around her finger and started sucking.

"Will it be enough?" he asked as she pulled her hand away. "Or do you need more?"

She swore he sounded hopeful that her answer might be yes.

"We'll see," she said, not daring to take her eyes away from the blood streaked on his finger. "It depends on how much I use."

The answer was a lot.

Aenwyn found a flat stone beside them and began to draw the wing symbol, but it had taken her five different strokes to finish it. Five different times she had to go back for more. Five times she had to lean in close to Darius, and refrain from leaning closer. Five times she had to slide her delicate finger into his mouth and try not thinking about the way he tasted. Five times she had to squeeze her legs shut for fear that she might straddle him the next time that delicious ache in her twisted harder.

When the symbol was done, Aenwyn splayed her fingers above his wound and spoke to the sky somewhere above.

"Sky-Blessed, hear me. Lend me your power to mend this man's leg. Lend me your strength to gain us our freedom from this prison."

They waited a moment.

Darius tried peering around her hands, but they were blocking his view. "Is it done?"

Without looking, she already knew the answer. "No."

His wound remained as miserable as ever and Aenwyn sunk back onto her heels, examining the symbol beside her, and then her inept hands.

"Why?" Darius sat up from where he was reclined, as if trying to see what she was seeing.

She shook her head, eyes narrowing at the thing they had called hailstone clasped around her wrist. Their abductors had fought hard to get it onto her. Now she knew why.

Shaking her arm at him, she stood. "It's this. This thing is preventing me from accessing my power. Just like my ring!"

"Your ring?"

Reaching into her bosom, Aenwyn searched for the ring she'd stashed there, grateful to find it. She held it out for him, the light-blue stone still gleaming despite the darkness of their cell.

"This was a gift from my husband. He gave it to me on our wedding day and told me to wear it always."

Darius squinted at the ring before answering "That's typical for Caeloran weddings." He sounded unsure, cautious.

She flashed him her other hand, the one without the hailstone bracelet where she usually wore her wedding ring. But to her surprise, it was gone.

When she looked back at him, he looked remorseful. "I forgot to tell you about that."

"What happened to my wedding ring?" Noticing the rest of

her missing jewelry, her voice grew louder. "What happened while I was unconscious?"

Darius shrugged. "You're the Caeloran queen, traveling through thief-territory wearing rings with gemstones bigger than the scraps most of these people have eaten in days. They did what any struggling peasant would've: they took your valuables to trade for something they could use."

She supposed she couldn't blame them for that. Most of those things weren't even hers; they belonged to the Caeloran crown. Besides, the king would forgive her for losing her wedding ring. But the other ring? She imagined the taut lines of his face as his quiet rage settled in.

She would not lose the ring that bound her magic.

Seeing as they weren't out of this situation yet, she tucked it back in the bosom of her undergarment.

A muscle in Darius' jaw ticked and he averted his gaze when he added, "They took Rocky and Charmaine too."

Now that was taking it too far.

She felt her skin crawling with the urge to act. But what was there to do? They were trapped in this small cell until someone would come to retrieve them.

"I need to get this off," she shrieked, the stony bracelet suddenly chaffing at her wrist so much she couldn't stand it. She struggled against the hailstone, pulling and twisting it. She raised her arm to smash the thing on the ground.

"Don't!" Darius grabbed her arm before she could.

"What else am I supposed to do? They bound my magic—everyone always wants to bind my magic!"

She tore away from his grasp and paced the small, confined space in great, powerful strides.

She hadn't noticed Darius stand himself upright, hadn't seen him hobbling toward her until his large hands folded over her shoulders and steadied her. His presence was firm and grounding. His caressing touch, soothing.

Whenever King Everard took her into his arms, she felt like a burden he didn't want to deal with. Unlike a Skogar heir, who would've been raised to rule a battlefield, King Everard had the scrawny arms of a young boy raised to rule from a throne. He was weak, in physique and character. When they shared a bed, he insisted on Aenwyn being beneath him, and she knew it was because the one time she wasn't, he complained of discomfort and being unable to breathe. Whenever his hand would graze the voluptuous curves of her side, he'd grimace and withdraw his touch.

He made her feel unwanted. Undesirable.

But in Darius' grasp, it was the opposite.

In his powerful clutches, she wasn't a stubborn ox to be routinely fought against and prodded into submission. She was a wild mare trotting through a blooming field in spring, and he was just grateful to be allowed near her.

"We will figure this out," he said, steadying her with the warmth of his voice, the closeness of his body. "They didn't capture us just to bring us here for nothing."

He was right, she realized.

For weeks they'd been traveling. If they wanted them dead, it would've been much easier to do so in Nivernia where she had no doubt that dead bodies disappeared without a trace easily enough.

"They said they were taking us to the Scorpion. Do we know who that is?"

Darius shook his head. "They wouldn't tell me a thing."

She worried at her bottom lip. "They must want something. If we can figure out what, we might be able to bargain with this Scorpion person."

Darius nodded, and Aenwyn noted he hadn't released her yet. She hoped he never would.

"Any idea where we are?" she asked him, hoping to drag the conversation on forever, or at least as long as she could.

But the moment was brought to an abrupt end when from down the hall they heard a heavy, wooden door creak open. The two of them startled, Darius spinning around and shoving her behind him. Aenwyn swatted his arm away, glancing pointedly to his wounded leg, and thankfully, he didn't try stopping her from taking her place at his side.

Someone approached from the darkness. Their sandals clacked, the delicate echoes bouncing from one stone wall to the next. Before that sound, Aenwyn would've thought it was the barkeep coming to make their lives miserable.

But as the person drew closer, she noted the flowing silks, sheer scarves, and strings of coins and beads draped over a womanly frame.

The woman stopped before their door, but with her head dipped as she fumbled with the cell key, Aenwyn could see nothing of the face that was hidden behind her bulging waves of dark hair.

Only once the lock clicked open did her violet eyes finally look up.

"Well, if it isn't the Red Fury of Skogar. I heard you were looking for me."

A SCORPION'S RULE

AENWYN

The woman smiled, and the pit of dread that had piled into Aenwyn's stomach vanished.

A grin bloomed across Aenwyn's face. "Hissa? Is that you?"

As the cell door sprung open, Aenwyn shoved past Darius and leapt into the arms of her old friend—at least, she'd thought she was a friend. Hissa had been the one who'd smuggled her into Grimtol after Baug had found her. She'd housed and fed them. Sung to her as she rested. Helped her bathe. Brushed the knots from her hair.

"You're the Scorpion?" Aenwyn asked, incredulous.

But then she remembered where she was standing. This was no happy reunion amongst friends, for friends didn't abduct and imprison one another.

Releasing Hissa's shoulders, Aenwyn took slow strides backward until she was beside Darius once more.

"What are we doing here?" she demanded. Holding out her arm, she shook the hailstone around her wrist. "Why have you bound my magic?"

With a humorless laugh, Hissa planted a manicured hand

on either hip. "That's the thanks I get for releasing you from this cesspit?"

Aenwyn didn't think that question deserved an answer.

Patiently, Hissa's sharp nails tapped, their deep plum shade complimented her eyes, just like the rest of her ensemble. Everything she wore was purple. Lavender scarves, a mauve choker, and layers of skirts that alternated between wine, lilac, and berries. Only her jewelry wasn't purple, all the necklaces, rings, chains, and earrings were as golden as the desert sands of Vallonde.

Hissa was the embodiment of beauty and power, just as Aenwyn remembered her. When she entered a room, she commandeered it. Even a room with a queen.

It made Aenwyn realize, although Hissa seemed similar in the most memorable respects, there were differences about her as well. Namely her apparent command over a jail.

It was clear to Aenwyn that Hissa no longer ran some simple backwater trade system. She had obtained a new sort of power. Maybe even wealth, judging from the gold that glinted from every piece of her garments.

But if she already had money, then what did she need to abduct a queen for?

Silence settled in the dingy cell, until Hissa snapped her fingers. A guard came to her side.

"Take that thing off our guest."

"But—" Her warning glare was enough to make him obey without any protest. "Yes, Sultana Hissa."

As the lumbering oaf sauntered toward them, Aenwyn exchanged a glance with Darius that she hoped told him to get ready. He didn't look like he'd hesitate, but the way he was leaning, favoring one side, reminded her that he was in no condition to fight. Not yet. Not until she was able to heal his leg.

Soon, the guard detached the light-blue bracelet from

Aenwyn's wrist. Her skin ached from where the hailstone had bit into her flesh, trapping sand beneath and chafing it raw. She wanted to rub at the tender flesh. But her attention was solely fixed on Hissa.

"What's to stop me from killing you now that I'm unbound?" Aenwyn glared. There had been powerful, dark magic inside her before; she could muster it again if needed.

But Hissa looked at her like she was a pesky gnat buzzing around her head.

It wasn't the way Aenwyn normally liked to be looked at. But for some reason, in this moment, Aenwyn found it slightly reassuring. Hissa wasn't looking for a fight. In fact, the shimmer in her violet eyes seemed to suggest the opposite, like she was awaiting a joyous reunion.

Aenwyn stared beseechingly at the woman she hardly knew and yet felt like she'd known forever. "What are we doing here, Hissa?"

She examined her quietly. Then, flipping a long rope of hair over her shoulder, she spun on her heels and glided for the door. Through the sheer fabric draped behind her, Aenwyn could just barely make out the scorpion tattoo on her lower back. "Actually, I was hoping you might be able to shed some light on that, as I was told that it was *you* who was asking for *me*."

Aenwyn's jaw popped open, but it was Darius who barked a response.

"We didn't ask to be captured and hauled across Vallonde, half-starved."

"And drugged!" Aenwyn added pointedly.

With the speed of a striking snake, Hissa snapped her gaze to her guard. The gold beads adorning her hair smacked against each other, reminding Aenwyn of a rattlesnake's warning.

When the man looked as if he was about to start splut-
tering some pathetic apology, Hissa held up a hand before he
could.

"That was never supposed to happen," she said to them over
her shoulder. "But let's not have this conversation down here in
the trenches. Please, come. There is beauty in the Great City of
Vallonde. We will speak more there."

* * *

Hissa was not doing it justice.

The view that stretched out from the pavilion
they stood upon was of beautiful red and orange
and purple mountains. The lake at the base of the Barga
Mountain Range was like liquid crystal, and it dazzled in the
early dawn light, but not as much as the desert sands
surrounding it. They were so golden, they sparkled. And
Aenwyn had to avert her gaze to the city below them.

This was the Vallonde she remembered. A bustling city of
white spires and dome rooftops adorned with thousands of
gemstones that dazzled in sunlight as much as they did in
moonlight. This place was a work of art. Aenwyn could see that
even from their high vantage point, in the open-air lounge that
overlooked it all.

"Please, take a seat. You'll find your belongings intact, I
hope."

Hissa's smoky, sultry voice summoned Aenwyn from the
balustrade where she leaned. It took more willpower than she
knew she possessed to turn her back to the impressive empire
below them. But with a comforting nudge from Darius,
Aenwyn managed eventually.

Hissa was holding out an arm, the gauzy fabric of her sleeve
fluttering in the subtle breeze. She gestured to the lush beds of

pillows on the floor in the center of the room and to the saddle bags in the center.

Aenwyn was so focused on reaching them and finding her pouch of herbs that she almost didn't notice the child already seated. She bore strong resemblance to the Sultana, but Aenwyn didn't know if she was her sister, daughter, or niece; there had been no mention of her the last time Aenwyn had been in Vallonde. She was maybe a few years older than Katla and her face lit up at the sight of them. But Hissa silenced her the same way she had silenced the guard.

There was no denying the authority Hissa held here in Vallonde. She'd come a long way from hiding in abandoned dens and smuggling illegal goods with the outcasts of Grimtol.

Aenwyn took a seat on one of the pillows across from the girl and made quick work of going through their bags. Not much of value was left—she supposed her jewelry had long been pawned off—but she found the green velvet pouch and hastily fastened it to a belt she tied around her trousers.

Darius limped behind her, his grimace worsening with every step. Since they had left their cell, he hadn't veered farther than he could reach her. He'd kept one hand on her lower back at all times, guiding her as they were lead through the palace, as if he was the one protecting her, when in reality it was the opposite way around. At least until she could heal his leg.

Now that she had her supplies back, there was no better time to heal him.

Aenwyn opened the pouch and grabbed the caelwood bark first. She was fully aware of Hissa's intense gaze watching her every move, and even more aware that she was making the Sultana of Vallonde wait on her, but in that moment she didn't care. They had already been imprisoned once. What more could the Scorpion do to them?

"Chew on this," Aenwyn told Darius as she shoved a few

chunks of the dried bark into his mouth. "It will clear the toxins in your bloodstream that have been preventing you from healing."

His face soured at the bitterness, but he chewed. Gesturing to the leafless vine she retrieved next, he asked, "And what's that?"

"Blacknettle."

He choked on a piece of bark, brown saliva splattering one of Hissa's vibrantly yellow pillows. "Blacknettle? As in—"

"Yes, as in blacknettle bushes." Aenwyn rolled her eyes. "Despite the nettles being poisonous, the vines actually have many healing properties."

Darius looked uncertain as she hung the green vine over his leg. Before he could protest though, she twisted the length of it, wringing it until a clear droplet beaded at the bottom end and dripped onto the angry wound. She let a few more drip before rubbing the liquid in with her thumb, making sure the whole cut was coated.

That was just basic use of natural herbs though. It would take weeks for a wound like his to heal. Unless she had help.

With her wet thumb, she drew a wing around the wound, and then hovered her hands above his leg. She called upon the Sky-Blessed, told them of her quest and how instrumental Darius had been in it, and asked them to heal him sooner so that he might still prove useful.

Warmth swelled between them and when it was done, Aenwyn withdrew her hands. It had only taken mere moments and the wound had knitted itself together, the infection gone.

The bruises on his face had cleared too, and she was reminded of how roguishly handsome he was.

Darius flashed her a grateful smile and the pit of Aenwyn's stomach did a strange little flip. It made her buoyant and dizzy, like the world was spinning around them and they were just feathers caught in the current.

. . .

I t didn't help that by the time he settled onto the pillows beside her, his knee was grazing hers.

She couldn't afford to be distracted right now though. They needed to focus on gaining Hissa's trust. On convincing her that she *wanted* to aid them in their quest.

Before Aenwyn could demand answers and recompence, Hissa sat across from them, and Aenwyn saw the woman in daylight for the first time. For a moment, all fight went out of her.

Now that they were no longer in the dark bowels of the palace, with light sifting through the gossamer canopy like spun silk above them and illuminating their host, Aenwyn could finally see that she *had* changed. Even more than Aenwyn had previously realized.

When their paths had crossed all those years ago, Hissa's coppery complexion was the kind of flawless that would've made the Caeloran ladies gab over for hours. They would've swooned over her, begging her to tell them how she maintained such a natural golden glow, how she kept the blemishes at bay, and how she remained looking so youthful, even into her thirties.

That wouldn't be the case anymore.

Now they would run in fear.

Burn scars covered most of Hissa's body, as far as Aenwyn could see. From the left side of her forehead all the way down under her cropped blouse and peeking through the exposed flesh of her stomach, her skin was mottled and raised, and it looked as if it even continued beneath the hem of her billowing skirts.

Delicate patterns of crimson had been painted in thin lines over every single one of her scars. It didn't conceal the mutilation. But perhaps, Aenwyn thought, it made her feel power over it. As if she refused to allow anything to mark her as damaged.

Hissa took a seat on a plump, velvet pillow beside the small child. One of her people ran over to her, a large branch with thin leaves cradled in their arms, but Hissa shooed them away.

Only once they were alone did she finally speak.

"How is your father these days?"

It was not the question Aenwyn had anticipated. Talking about her father was the farthest thing from her priority. She and Darius had been abducted, drugged, and held prisoner. What Aenwyn wanted to know was why. It was the question that she and Darius needed answered before they could proceed. They needed to know if Hissa and her people could be trusted, if she would let them go or if Aenwyn would have to make her.

But it also just seemed uncharacteristic of Hissa to ask about Baug. As a woman of trade and business, Aenwyn hadn't thought that Hissa would start off with something so personal, so trivial. It hadn't seemed in her nature before to casually converse with friends when there was a deal to be struck—and they both knew there was.

But it had been a long time since they'd last met.

People changed. Adapted.

Aenwyn knew better than most the way that responsibility and expectation could creep up on someone once they possessed the right amount of social status. How it could suffocate their personhood, their own identity, until all that was left was what everyone else told them they should be.

Sultana, the guard had called her.

It wasn't the title she'd had when they'd first met, nor one Aenwyn was familiar with now. But she had sensed the esteem with which the guard had spoken it. She'd noticed the reverence with which the people had watched Hissa as she walked past them, leading Aenwyn and Darius through the city and onto the pavilion for this meeting.

Hissa had become the leader to these people.

Unfortunately for her, Aenwyn wasn't too keen on trusting leaders blindly anymore. Not after spending a year in marital torture with her husband.

However, this leader did know her father. And that had to count for something.

"Don't you speak to him?" Aenwyn replied, neither seeming too interested or disinterested in Hissa's response. Even though she was.

The two of them—Baug and Hissa—had seemed as thick as thieves the last time they had been in Vallonde. As far as Aenwyn could tell and remember, Hissa had been the primary supplier of Skogar's mead. She had heard Baug mention her many times in the years that followed.

It seemed unlikely that the woman would need to ask her how he'd been faring.

Besides, Aenwyn hardly knew herself.

Baug hadn't spoken to her since he left Caelora the day after her wedding. Not a single response to any of her letters. The only reason she even knew he was still alive was because Signe had told her so once in her own message.

Hissa sighed, reaching around the small child and retrieving a golden tray filled with plums, dried apricots, flat breads and round breads, kebabs of roasted meat, and a delicious pudding-like dessert that smelled of cinnamon, saffron, and cardamom.

Without thought, Aenwyn and Darius shook their heads, despite the protesting of their watering mouths.

"Just as stubborn as your father." Hissa sighed. "If I had meant you harm, you would still be in that cell. Come. Eat. Your bodies need it after your long journey, and what you endured."

The two of them exchanged a look, but ultimately hunger

won over them, and Aenwyn and Darius greedily plucked one food after another, until their mouths were so full, they could hardly breathe.

Looking pleased about her hosting duties, Hissa finally took the opportunity to answer Aenwyn.

"I don't speak to Baug as much these days. Not after the fires. Not after..." She trailed off, lost in a horrific past that Aenwyn knew many others had lived as well.

Not her though. She'd only been the catalyst for their misery, for the dragon's destruction, a guilt for which stung her every day.

"It's not often these words leave my lips, but I fear I owe you two an apology."

Aenwyn stopped chewing. She wanted to make sure she heard every word, every inflection of tone.

Plucking a quince from the tray to examine, Hissa continued. "My claim to these lands is new and not yet accepted by everyone, especially along our border. My men are instructed to be cautious. If they suspect someone means me harm, they intervene."

"All we did was mention your name," Darius growled, fists clenched in his lap. "We said nothing about meaning you harm."

She eyed him the way a mentor might watch a pupil, challenging them to complete one final lesson to prove their competence. "And do you suppose all of my enemies go around blatantly stating their murderous intent?"

An acquiescing grumble was the best response she was going to get.

Hissa took a bite of the yellow fruit. "They did what they always do. They bring the suspects to me so I can decide what to do with them. It wasn't until your arrival that I learned of who you were. Aenwyn, my dear child, you are no enemy of mine. I came down to set you free the moment I learned. Can you accept this apology?"

She didn't like being called a child, but fortunately pride was King Everard's downfall, not hers.

Despite Darius and his insistent glare ramming against the side of her face and beseeching her to not be so hasty with this, Aenwyn knew she had to be.

Trust was a fickle thing. Hissa was offering them hers, but it came at a price.

They had trusted each other once before and could again, but only if both sides were willing to make a show of good faith.

"You're forgiven."

Hissa inclined her head slightly.

The little girl whined, glaring up at Hissa. "Does that mean I don't get to drink from the goblet?"

"Hush!"

If Hissa had been trying to silence her before they could arouse suspicion, she'd woefully failed. Her actions had done the opposite. Aenwyn wouldn't have thought anything of the goblet mentioned, but now it was of great interest, if only because it seemed to have something to do with the possible outcome of Aenwyn and Hissa not being able to make peace.

"What is she talking about?" Aenwyn asked, deciding that being blunt would save them time and heartache in the end.

"And who is she?" Darius added.

With an exaggerating groan, Hissa flipped the length of her hair over her shoulder and began combing through it with her sharp nails. "This is Nariah. You weren't able to meet last time, but she is my sister—and she is far too young and still doesn't quite yet grasp the idea that there is a time to speak, and a time to not."

Aenwyn bristled. Suddenly she was back in the Caeloran

palace, sitting in her throne beside the king, as silent as a mouse because he'd told her to be.

The girl was about Katla's age, maybe a couple of years younger. And if Aenwyn's growing disdain for her husband and anything remotely resembling him or his dominance hadn't been enough, it was the familiarity of being in the presence of a younger sister that sparked Aenwyn's fierce protectiveness.

"I disagree with the idea that there are correct and incorrect times for someone to speak their mind." Aenwyn snapped with the vicious precision of a queen. She turned her attention to Nariah, softening at the girl's shocked expression. "What did you mean about drinking from a goblet? And why won't you be able to now that your sister and I have made up?"

It was like the girl had been waiting for this moment to thwart her older sister all her life. Her lips were an unhinged floodgate.

"You know? The wishing goblet." Nariah pointed to a golden chalice on a circular stand beside them. It was inconspicuous beside a bottle of wine and a tall vase with red flowers in it. "You drink from it, and you're granted three wishes. But you can only drink from it once and she's already had her drink. That's why her eyes are all weird—" she added the last part conspiratorially, then resumed her excited tenor. "It was supposed to be my turn this time. If you were bad, I was going to drink from the goblet and wish that you and everyone you knew would never be able to find their way into Vallonde again. And if I did that, she was going to let me use my other wishes to wish for my own palace and to have green hair."

Hissa's laugh was harsh and scornful. "That is precisely why you are still not allowed to drink from the goblet. You're too young and naïve to know what would be worth requesting."

Nariah grew red in the face.

Aenwyn heard her own voice before she knew she was speaking. "And what did you wish for, Sultana Hissa?"

The Scorpion shifted where she sat as she considered the question. "The wrong things. For I was too young, as well."

Aenwyn couldn't imagine what someone who lived in Vallonde had thought was more important than wishing for the death of the dragons that had laid waste to their lands. If Aenwyn had drank from the goblet…

The idea struck her like a brick to the skull.

The goblet! She could drink from the goblet; she wouldn't even have to go fight a dragon.

Eyes wide, she looked to Darius to find that he was staring at her with the same hopeful expression.

"It would save us the rest of a brutal journey," he said, reading her mind. With a teasing tone, he added, "As well as an impossible fight."

Aenwyn didn't need any other confirmation.

"You didn't ask for the dragons to die," she said. "But I could."

A pained expression folded over Hissa. "You cannot use the wishes to kill. It only kills the wisher instead."

Aenwyn shuddered at how they'd discovered that fun fact. She didn't know why her next question was, "And your scars? Could you wish those away?"

"No." Solemnly, Hissa reached for the goblet, swirling the empty bowl of it in her dainty grasp. "One cannot bring life back to the dead either. And those parts of me are very dead."

Darius' curious gaze drifted back to Aenwyn, full of awe and questions, but she ignored it. The moment they'd been waiting for was finally arriving and she needed to be prepared to do whatever it took to convince Hissa to help them.

But the Sultana spoke first.

"I think it fair that I ask some questions of you now."

She leaned behind Nariah again and pulled the bottle of wine from the table. She poured herself a glass, and for a moment Aenwyn was surprised to see her drinking the wishing goblet itself. Then she realized who was before her: a woman, lavish in riches and power. Of course she'd keep a powerful goblet close at hand, and of course she'd drink from it in front of her guests. A show of dominance and strength.

"Why have you come looking for me?" Hissa asked.

It didn't take long for Aenwyn to supply her with the details of her vision and their journey thus far.

"We came here seeking your aid," she said when she was done. "I remembered that it was your ship that brought Baug across the Bay of Lost Souls. I was hoping you might make the journey once more."

Coolly, Hissa took another sip from her chalice, a gold bracelet jingling around her wrist.

"But—" Aenwyn said slowly, testing the weight of the syllable the same way she was testing Hissa, gauging her every reaction, every subtle and minute change of behavior. When she saw none, she shared the rest of her still-forming idea. "Maybe we don't need a ship at all."

The violet auras around Hissa's pupils sparked. It was the first spell of fury she'd seen from her that wasn't directed at her younger sister. The bout of laughter that followed it was sharp and caustic, making Aenwyn recoil into the softness of the pillows surrounding her, and the comforting presence of Darius.

"You wish to drink from the goblet?" Hissa spat. "Foolish girl. You do not know what you ask."

Aenwyn was tired of people treating her like an impulsive, imprudent child.

Baug had doubted her choice to marry King Everard. He'd

even made her question it herself on more than one occasion, even though she knew in her gut that this was the path that she was meant to take, even if she didn't want to.

Darius had not been quiet about his own judgments of her plans, and although he'd finally agreed to see her through it and support her in the ways that he could, sometimes he still acted like she wasn't thinking things through. Like with trusting Hissa. As if she wasn't mulling over every possible outcome and danger before making the best decision that she could.

And then there was Hissa. A woman who hardly knew her. Sitting before her on her proverbial throne, dining like a queen, and having the audacity to insult another queen's intelligence.

Their affronts to her sense of judgment would be suffered no longer.

"You're wrong. I know that I, alone, am responsible for that dragon. Baug gave *me* the egg. It hatched because of my touch. *My* magic. People have died because it was born, because of me. They've been scarred, they've lost loved ones…"

Pausing, she turned toward Darius, hoping that the look in her eyes might convey to him just how sorry she was. She wasn't sure if he'd be able to receive it though. There were endless nights of hurt and grief warring behind his expression now. She couldn't expect anything less, not after he'd only just learned that it was her fault that he'd lost his mother.

He would need time. But Aenwyn could feel herself rapidly running out of it. She couldn't be distracted by his heartache right now, not when every day cost the people of Grimtol more misery. More destruction. More death.

She returned her attention to Hissa who was deeply engaged in watching them, analyzing their interactions, and awaiting more.

Steeling herself, Aenwyn took a heavy, shuddering breath.

"I'd first throw myself into the Maw of Death before abandoning my duty to kill that dragon. The question is, Sultana Hissa, will you help me? Or am I wasting my time assuming that you want to put an end to your people's suffering as well?"

By the time she finished, Aenwyn's chest was heaving.

It had felt like such a long time since she'd truly believed in herself and her abilities, much less spoken them aloud to people who'd routinely doubted her.

She was invigorated by it and vowed to never allow herself to be silenced again.

Quiet stretched over the room, punctuated only by Nariah's munching on a handful of nuts and seeds.

Finally Hissa sighed. "The options you've presented me are not choices I'd like to make. I try not making a habit out of condemning friends to their deaths."

Calling them *friends* seemed like they were on the right path.

"You won't," Aenwyn promised, shaking her head. "I told you. I saw—"

"I know what you claim to have seen," Hissa said, cutting her off. "But you do not remember the horrific voyage across those dark waters. Nor do you understand the sacrifice required of drinking from the goblet."

Aenwyn was growing impatient with Hissa's elusiveness around the goblet. And she wasn't the only one.

Darius rose abruptly, pillows tumbling at his feet. "Then tell us! Tell us what sacrifice is required so that we can make an informed decision."

There was a glare in her violet eyes as Hissa finished chewing another bite of her quince. She took her time wiping the juice from her jaw, letting Aenwyn and Darius sit in their anticipation. But Aenwyn could tell that they'd gotten to her.

Placing the devoured core of the fruit back onto the tray,

she finally spoke. "The goblet grants whoever drinks from it three wishes, but they do not come freely and there are rules."

"Like not killing someone," Aenwyn answered.

"Or bringing someone back from the dead," Darius added.

Their answers seemed to only half-appease her. Hissa coiled a finger around one of the numerous golden chains dangling from her neck. "You have the right idea, but the rule stretches further. Anything involving life is off limits. Death, resurrection, conception, birth, immortality. Should you make a wish involving your life or the life of another, there will be dire consequences."

Aenwyn was afraid to ask. Instead she focused on soothing Hissa's concerns. Regardless of how they decided to proceed, all of their options required gaining her approval.

"Done," Aenwyn agreed. "We won't wish for any of that. All I want is a faster, safer way to get to and from the Lost Isle."

The vast majority of the time, Hissa had one of those countenances that left her mouth permanently downturned. Now, that same mouth twitched into a humorless smirk.

"That is the problem. All you're thinking about is what you *want*, not what you are willing to give up." Her gaze went distant, hollow as it traveled to the pavilion and looked out across the vast wasteland. "There is a price for drinking from the goblet and having your wishes answered. What are you prepared to pay?"

"Anything," Aenwyn answered without hesitation. She'd been preparing for this battle for all of her young adult life. "I am willing to pay anything. Just tell me the price."

Finally, Hissa was done delaying.

"The price is a life."

18

A STEEP PRICE TO PAY

AENWYN

"Or at least, the potential of one," Hissa continued after a long enough dramatic pause that had Aenwyn's chest in binds.

"A p-potential one?" she heard herself stammering, trying and failing to make sense of it.

Exasperated as ever, Darius flapped his arms. "And what does that even mean?"

"It means that those who drink from the goblet are asking for the world to provide for them, to bend around them, to bow down to them. And for whatever reason—unknown to even me—the price for having your every whim granted is that your legacy ends with you. You will not be allowed to pass your riches onto your heirs, for there will be none. Not for you or any of your siblings, your cousins, your entire familial generation. Should you have children already, they will perish, as will your nieces and nephews. Your line will end with you."

Aenwyn's mind reeled.

Of course, that was the price. Of course it would be the one thing she had desperately hoped for but hadn't been able to provide.

All year she had wondered, but of course she had known. No matter how many men she had bed in Skogar, no matter how careless some of them had been in the heat of the moment with their seed—and sometimes at her imploring—no life had bloomed in her belly.

Her mother had struggled with her fertility as well, but she had finally been able to conceive a child after years of trying. Some small part of Aenwyn had hoped that it would eventually be possible for her too. That she could someday create a life, build a family to surround herself with after spending so many years without one.

After drinking from the goblet, that hope would be gone forever.

Despite not wanting to, Aenwyn would become the barren queen who ended the Highmore legacy for Caelora once and for all. There would be no heirs for King Everard. Or, more likely, there would be, but they'd be the bastard children of peasant women who were paid off and stripped of their child.

"That is the price," Hissa said, drawing Aenwyn out of her fog. "Do you still wish to pay it?"

No words could find their way to the top of her lips though. They were lodged in her throat along with a sea of despair.

Aenwyn was thankful when Darius' face appeared before hers. He'd taken a knee and was now reaching for her hands. He held them in his own like they were precious gemstones, even though they were the hands of magic, the same hands that rose the dragon and killed his mother.

"You don't have to do this," he said to her. She was trying so hard to hear him, but that despair kept pulling her down. "We can take a ship, like we originally planned."

A week of travel to Nivernia.

Another week or longer to Vallonde.

Aenwyn guessed that it would take another month or more

to reach the eastern coast, and who knew how much time after to cross the ocean to the Isle of Lost Souls.

They didn't have that kind of time. She couldn't explain how she knew it, but she did. The wishing goblet had been presented to them and now it was part of the path she needed to take.

Still stuck in her trance, Aenwyn shook her head. "No."

"No?" Darius asked gently. He looked as if he wanted to reach up and tuck a strand of hair behind her ears, but refrained.

"It's alright," she said, blinking back into the room and out of her head.

She would do this. It was the way it had to be.

"My line is already destined to end with me," Aenwyn confessed. "I was an only child to a mother whose siblings died before my birth, and—" She took a deep, quaking breath, the familiar, nagging knife of shame twisting into her— "And I am already barren and unable to produce an heir."

Hissa's head bowed, the amethyst in her head necklace falling forward. "My condolences. It is a heavy burden to be a queen without an heir."

The sympathy in her tone gave Aenwyn pause. She found herself wishing she knew more about Hissa, how she'd come to be in this place, and just how intimately she might know the woes of a barren queen.

Instead, Aenwyn sucked in another breath, the stinging in her lungs almost unbearable now.

"But you are wrong about your family, Red Fury," Hissa continued. "You are no longer an only child and haven't been for a few years."

Confusion and worry creased Aenwyn's brow. She thought about it for a moment and then asked, "Signe and Katla are not my sisters by blood though."

"I do not think it matters," Hissa told her. "They are sisters to you regardless. Are they not?"

They were. And there was that torsion in her chest again. That building ache. Something ominous lingered at the end of this road. Something Aenwyn wanted to avoid.

But already she could feel that she was stuck in its gravitational pull.

"Correct," she answered in a voice so low even she almost couldn't hear herself. "You're saying if I drink from the goblet, that it will also make my sisters barren?"

Hissa didn't reply. It wasn't a question that needed to be answered. Aenwyn already understood.

What she didn't understand was whether she could condemn her family to such a fate.

Signe was about to marry a king. She'd be expected to produce an heir, just as Aenwyn was. If neither of them could, they'd mark Skogar as a kingdom unworthy of marital alliances for the foreseeable future.

Then there was Katla. Sweet, innocent, little Katla who had yet to have many dreams of what her own future might hold.

How could Aenwyn make such a choice for her? For either of them?

Then again, when the fate of Caelora and possibly all of Grimtol rested upon her shoulders, how could she not?

It wasn't until she heard liquid pouring that Aenwyn realized Darius was no longer beside her.

Across the seating area, Darius stood with the golden goblet in one hand and the bottle of wine in the other.

His name might've left her lips, as he poured himself a drink, or it might've been an exhale. All she knew was that her knees suddenly felt too weak, her head too light and spinny.

Everything was moving in slow motion.

Darius lifted the goblet to his mouth.

His lips parted, the wine sloshing at the edge of the chalice.

It was a mistake. Darius was making a huge mistake. He thought he was being helpful and protecting her from having to make a difficult choice, but he was wrong. It wasn't either of their choices to make. This wasn't his debt to pay, it was hers.

It was all unfolding before she could do anything to stop it. To fix it. But there wasn't enough time to reach him. Not physically, anyway.

Before he could knock the goblet back any farther, his name tore from her lungs.

It was a shrill, horrendous sound that stretched out of her like a black hand of death. Agony ripped her apart, the power unbearable after already having so little to give. Magic answered her. Not a blessing from the Sky-Blessed. Not their power or will. But the pool of dark forces buried deep within her.

But she didn't care. She didn't need to know where it came from or why. All she knew was she was learning to use it.

Power erupted from the palms of her hands. Frenetic and compact. She barely felt in control of it as it burst from her fingertips and whacked the goblet out of Darius' hand.

It did more than just that.

Not only did her blast throw him to the ground, but also Hissa and Nariah who'd been sitting close by. They were flung like ragdolls, crashing to the ground in heaps. Thankfully the floor was covered in pillows, so Aenwyn didn't have to worry about them being too injured. But she did still feel a slight twinge of guilt that any of them had been impacted.

"Dragon's fire, Aenwyn!" Darius groaned from where he landed on floor, a bed of pillows around him. "What in the Hollows is wrong with you?"

The impact from the fall might not have hurt him, but judging by how delicately he massaged his chin, it was clear her magic had. He was sluggish in movement, dazed in speech.

That wouldn't last long though.

If she allowed him to regain his bearings, there would be no stopping him from trying to volunteer himself again. Only next time, she wouldn't have enough magic to stop him.

This needed to end.

Exhausted and weak, Aenwyn staggered forward. Some of the disheveled pillows caught her feet and she stumbled more than once, but the goblet wasn't far, nor difficult to reach.

The bottle of wine, however, was another story.

It lay shattered on the floor in the space between two previously white now stained burgundy pillows. It was either her magic or the tile floor that caused the damage. She wasn't sure. What she did know was that she could only drink from the goblet if she had something to drink.

Fortunately, Aenwyn didn't need a bottle of wine.

She didn't even need her magic.

The tears she shed earlier were still fresh and beaded on her cheeks. She lifted the goblet to them and collected the few that remained.

When she pulled the goblet down and peered inside, she saw the single tear glinting up at her. She had cried enough in the past year to fill the cup tenfold, but hopefully this one tear would be enough.

Aenwyn tilted the goblet back and licked the salty droplet that hung from the golden edge of the cup.

19

GONE

DARIUS

The queen was gone. Evaporated into nothing. And Darius felt the cold, clawing grip of terror seize his heart and give it a yank.

Then came the molten rage.

He charged for the sultana, a murderous glint in his eyes. "Where is she?

Hissa was unfazed, and thoroughly not intimidated by the likes of him. With a calm wave to her guards who had readied their weapons to intervene, she gathered herself from where she had landed and gracefully made her way back to her seat.

"She has gone to make her wishes," she said as the servants brought her a new tray of treats. She plucked a grape from the bundle and plopped it into her mouth.

"Where?"

There was fire in his veins, blazing and wild. Nothing would soothe it until he had his answers. Until his queen was back with him, safe and unharmed.

"If you care to know so badly," she said, licking her lips after she swallowed the small fruit. "Why not drink from it yourself and find out?"

The thought hadn't occurred to him yet.

Darius didn't think twice. He lunged for the goblet.

He was already raising it to his lips when a bitter laugh broke out under the pavilion. He was intent on ignoring it, until not a single drop wetted his lips.

Fingers biting down on the warm, golden stem, he angled his displeasure at her.

"Right," she chuckled. "I suppose it is still empty. Perhaps you should refill it?"

In her grasp was a pitcher covered in jewels the color of seafoam and rose buds. Darius marched back over to take it from her, but she jerked it away before he could.

"Of course, should you drink from it now, you won't be here when she returns."

"What do you mean?" he asked, even though what she was saying already made sense.

"I mean that she is in the sky now, speaking to the powers that be."

Darius stiffened. His throat became drier than it had been all those days they trekked through the deserts of Vallonde. "She's with the Sky-Blessed?"

The knowing look Hissa gave him was answer enough.

Stunned by such a revelation, Darius plopped down where he stood, grateful for the plush pillows that caught his fall. It was unthinkable to imagine speaking to a Sky-Blessed. At least to him it was. For him, they'd been no more than legends and lore. He knew the histories, of course. Knew that long ago the Sky-Blessed had fallen from the clouds and reigned over humankind for centuries—or maybe it had been millennium. He knew that some still remained, tucked away in Arrin, the City in the Clouds.

But in all his years, he'd never once met one. Nor had anyone he'd known.

Since the war that had nearly obliterated them into extinction, the Sky-Blessed had kept themselves secluded beyond the Clouded Mountains. But not even seclusion could wipe the terrifying memory of them away.

They were all-powerful, bewitching beings worthy of fear who had ruled with violence and greed. Misery and pain.

Since birth, Darius had been raised to fear them. His mother had dozens of cautionary tales and warnings that rattled through his mind even now:

Don't stare into the clouds too long, lest you risk the wrath of the Sky-Blessed.

Never wander into beams of sunlight, for the Sky-Blessed might snatch you away.

Storm's a brewing. The Sky-Blessed must be angered and out for blood.

All his life, Darius had been taught to fear them.

And yet...

And yet the Skogar had stood by them during the war, fought alongside them. And it had not been the hands of the Sky-Blessed that the Skogar had suffered by, but those of Irongate.

Though the people of Grimtol had been taught to hate the Sky-Blessed and fear their magic, it seemed to Darius that those without had been far more dangerous and brutal.

The Skogar had been enslaved.

The Ashen Princess captured, imprisoned, and tortured—by his own hands.

And now Carmen was bringing to him stories of the Animali being executed for nothing more than their nature.

Perhaps drinking from the goblet and meeting the Sky-Blessed wouldn't be such an awful thing.

But the sultana was right; he needed to be here when Queen Aenwyn returned.

"When will she be back?" he asked, glaring over at Hissa as

if this was all her fault, even though he knew better. Nothing could've stopped this from happening. Even if Hissa hadn't mentioned the goblet, one way or another, Aenwyn would've found out about it and drank from it. "How long does it take for the Sky-Blessed to finish granting her wishes?"

Hissa snorted and leaned back against the propped pillows behind her that formed a sort of throne. She dangled another grape into her mouth. "It depends on what she asks. If they are simple requests, I imagine she won't be much longer."

That was a relief. Darius didn't like the idea of waiting for an uncertain amount of time, but he could manage a few more moments.

"If she is greedy—" the sultana continued, making a face that skirted the border of thoughtful and disgusted— "Then she will not return here to you and I."

That grip around his heart tightened. "What does that mean? Where would she go?"

Hissa set the bundle of grapes down on the golden tray before examining her long, pointed nails. "When you came to Vallonde, you traveled from the south of Caelora, yes? You passed the Cursed Prison to get here?"

Nodding was compulsory; he just wanted her to get to the point. But right before she made it, he understood what she was hinting at.

"You saw the stone statues then," she said, her voice ethereal and foreboding. "If she attempts to break their rules, that is where they will leave her, like they have left so many others."

Darius remembered the stone statue graveyard more vividly than even his mother's warnings about the Sky-Blessed. A prison of hundreds of people, frozen in the sands of time. When his and Aenwyn's captors had dragged them past that awful place, he swore he'd felt every eye of the statues upon them.

Now he knew why.

People were trapped inside.

Part of him wondered about those lost souls, but he was becoming increasingly more concerned about Aenwyn and therefore unable to think about anyone else.

The time between her disappearance and now had already felt like it had stretched on too long. He couldn't just sit there. He couldn't do nothing while her life was potentially on the line.

Darius shot to his feet again, paced the room for what felt like a century, and sat once more among the pillows.

"So we wait, and they bring her back here?" he clarified after so much time had passed that he'd convinced himself he must've heard her wrong.

"Yes."

"Then where is she? Why isn't she back yet?"

One of Hissa's sharp brows rose up like a dagger. "Do I look like a Sky-Blessed to you?"

He was done with her taunts. He was done with her flippancy. Darius shot to his feet again, chest all a bluster with the wind he held inside, ready to burst.

"Cursed sky! I don't care what you look like! Animali, Sky-Blessed—you could be a headless specter raised from the Hollows itself for all I care. But you know how this works. You've seen, what? A dozen people fail before her? A hundred? You know how long this takes. So tell me, should she be here, or did something go wrong?"

The guards standing watch along the perimeter of the pavilion tensed, their muscles bulging beneath their robes, ready for action. Hissa settled them all with a simple, swift show of her hand.

She stood from her nest of pillows, her scrawny sister scrambling to follow suit. The sultana and the knight glared each other down.

Finally, she summoned her guard. "Take the knight back to the Cursed Prison. Let him search for his queen there. And let us pray to the Sky-Blessed that he does not find her among the stone ruins."

20

THREE WISHES

AENWYN

The pavilion blinked away behind a white light so fierce that Aenwyn had to shield her eyes.

"Hello?" she called, voice echoing in the nothingness around her. Even the warmth of the desert sun had been sucked away until all that was left was emptiness. "Darius? Hissa?" As a last-ditch effort, she even found herself hollering for Nariah as well. "Is anyone there?"

But no one answered.

No one she knew, anyway.

A feminine voice as mighty as a sea storm shook through her. "I am here, Aenwyn Red Fury of Skogar. Welcome to my domain."

Aenwyn startled. She spun around, searching for the source of the alluring yet ominous voice. But there was no one. She was alone in the white abyss.

"Who are you?" Aenwyn demanded. "Where—what is this place?"

The voice didn't answer her, but the shift in the air did. A crackle that Aenwyn took to be a warning not to venture too closely to matters deemed unsuitable for someone like her to ask.

After a long, uncomfortable bout of silence, the female voice finally spoke again, only this time it came clipped. "Speak your three wishes, and they will be my bidding."

Aenwyn waited for her to say something more, for the rules of the game to be laid out and explained, even though she already knew them. Nothing regarding life; it was a simple enough rule to follow.

But when the being made no mention of the rules that Hissa had shared with her, Aenwyn was filled with an inconsolable rage. How many people had died making a wish to this creature without knowing what they had been getting themselves into? How many had wished for the wrong thing without knowing and been punished for it? Or for the right things and lost something they didn't know they were giving up?

It was an unfair disadvantage, but Aenwyn supposed that was maybe to be expected. The way the voice spoke to her, there was a vexation about her. As if she disliked this arrangement more than anyone else who found themselves in it.

Perhaps that was why she didn't want to share who she was, or even where they were.

Unlike Aenwyn, maybe it wasn't by choice that she had been brought here at all.

Or maybe it was. Maybe Aenwyn was thinking too much into something that she knew nothing about.

Regardless of what brought the being here, it didn't make it right for her to take her displeasures or frustrations out on the unsuspecting people who found themselves in dire need of her services. They deserved to know what they were getting themselves into.

Whenever Aenwyn was reunited with Hissa again, she'd be sure to thank her for warning them ahead of time.

For now, she just needed to think of three wishes.

The first one was simple: safe passage to complete her task.

But what of the other two? She had a feeling that she needed to ask all three before a single one could be granted because she didn't think she'd be able to leave this place until all three wishes were fulfilled.

But what did she need three wishes for? What did she truly want?

To go back in time and undo her marriage with a man she felt more alone with than when she was by herself?

To save her mother from whatever dark force had taken her?

To refuse to touch the dragon egg, thereby preventing it from ever hatching and laying waste to Grimtol?

As much as she wanted all of those things, Aenwyn was far too superstitious to ever allow herself to wish for them. Fate was a fickle creature. One alteration could change the entire course of her life, as well as others, and it wasn't guaranteed that it would be for the better. Who's to say that if she hadn't married King Everard that she wouldn't have died that day in Skogar instead. Or if she'd never touched the dragon egg, sure maybe it would've saved Darius' mother, but someone else might've died in her place. Maybe Signe or Katla. Maybe even Darius.

Tampering with the present by meddling with the past was not something she was willing to do. Not to mention, she wasn't confident that those wishes wouldn't fall under the category of matters that alter life: marriage is said to be the onset of a couples' life together, she wasn't sure if her mother hadn't died or merely vanished, and her touch had hatched the dragon egg, thereby bringing life to it.

It left her with few options. So Aenwyn chose to be practical and safe.

Before she could start, the being instructed her, "You must state your wish with the words *I wish*."

"Okay," Aenwyn agreed, the formality of it making her shift uncomfortably. "I wish for armor for myself and my...travel companion, Darius. Something suitable to our needs."

The disembodied voice didn't make any sort of verbal acknowledgment, and after a long wait, Aenwyn finally spoke her second wish.

"I wish for us to have weapons, as well. Dual axes for myself, and I think Darius is most comfortable wielding a broadsword." A second too late, Aenwyn realized she was limiting herself. Here she was, speaking with a being powerful enough to grant wishes, and she was making simple requests that could be made at any blacksmith. She hoped it wasn't too late to amend. "The weapons need to be capable of piercing dragon skin as well. Better yet, weapons *made* for fighting dragons, if you can do it."

"I can do many things," the voice cooed, and Aenwyn could've sworn she detected pride in that mysterious undertone. "Weapons and armor. You shall have both. And for your final wish?"

Steeling herself with the courage and bravery that the Skogar had instilled in her, Aenwyn took a deep breath and answered, "For my final wish, I want—"

"*I wish*," the being hissed, sounding slightly annoyed that she had to remind her already.

"I wish—" Aenwyn amended— "for safe passage for Darius and me, to and from the Lost Isle."

There was another stretch of silence before the female voice finally repeated, "The Lost Isle. What a perilous place full of death and turmoil." She made an irritated sound. "What you ask of me is not possible."

"Not possible?" Aenwyn's laugh was sharp and disbelieving. But more than anything, her rage was beginning to rise. She hadn't come all the way here, hadn't sacrificed everything she'd sacrificed, just to be told that it was impossible. "How? I was told you could grant any wish that didn't involve life or death."

"And tell me, Aenwyn Red Fury, what does that island represent if not death? How does one ensure safe passage and departure to a place so wrought with danger?"

On some level, Aenwyn knew what she was saying made sense. She had lived there herself, after all, long after there was no one left but her. She knew firsthand the ominous nature of the island, how many lives it had swallowed.

But Aenwyn was beyond seeing reason. Not when it came to this

"Are you saying that you can't do it?"

By way of answer, the entity changed topics. "Tell me, what else is it that you wish for?"

"Nothing," Aenwyn proclaimed. "This is the only reason I've come to you, to save myself time on a trip I had already planned on taking. If you're unable to fulfill your end of the bargain, then I demand you rescind my first wishes and send me back to Vallonde."

The faceless being clucked her tongue. "I'm afraid that is not how this works."

"I don't care how it works!" The darkness in Aenwyn's core rumbled to awakening. She felt the charge of her magic sparking at her fingertips, stronger than ever. It was this place. It had replenished her. Fortified her. And she knew the being noticed it too. "If you can't take me to the Lost Isle, then give me nothing and return me to my people, or I promise I will make you regret ever meeting me."

The silence that surrounded her was deafening.

Trapped in the white nothingness, Aenwyn wasn't even sure if the being was still with her.

"Is that your wish? To be returned to Sultana Hissa?"

Outraged, Aenwyn sounded like a steaming kettle. "No it is

not my wish! You aren't able to give me what I came here for and therefore I am not willing to pay your price for nothing."

"Mmm."

Only because the entity sounded like she was considering did Aenwyn stop screaming. Otherwise, she had a charge of magic just waiting to be unleashed, should she need it. She'd rather throw herself into the dragon's fiery flames than leave here having condemned her entire family to barren lives without receiving what she came for.

"There might be a way," the female said at last. Her voice drifted around Aenwyn like wisps of smoke, heady and treacherous. "There are strange forces on the Lost Isle. Dark magic. Dragons. I cannot make all that simply go away. But…"

Aenwyn leaned forward, still not entirely sure where the being was. "But what?"

"There might be a way to time it so that you may enter safely. But I cannot provide you safe passage in return. That would require a separate wish, and you have already used all of yours."

Aenwyn could work with that. Once the dragon was slain, it would be easier to leave anyway. The only problem was that she would have no way of getting off the island.

Maybe that wouldn't be such a bad thing. It would mean she would never have to return to Caelora. She would never have to bed the king again. She could live out her life on the island in isolation.

It wouldn't be the first time. And perhaps it was only fitting that she would find herself stranded there again.

At least this time she would have Darius for company.

"I understand," Aenwyn said at last, chest aching with tortuous hope. "At least get us there, and it'll be up to us to survive."

The nothing whispered back, "It is done."

A chill dragged its claw up Aenwyn's spine.

The blinding white began to shimmer, the opposite of stars blinking asleep all around her.

Her time in this domain was ending, but there were so many things she wanted to know, wanted to say. But only one seemed to matter.

"Can I please know your name?"

If her suspicions were correct about the woman being here against her will, she owed her the courtesy of knowing her name at least.

Already her voice was beginning to fade though. Aenwyn was being pulled out of whatever realm they'd been suspended in.

The being sounded alarmed by the time she answered, "My name does not matter to anyone anymore."

Something about the morose way she made that confession struck Aenwyn like an axe to firewood, cleaving her in two. It was one of her fears as well. Especially while she had been trapped on that island for all those years. She had worried that she would die, and no one would remember her. Even now, as the Queen of Caelora, sometimes she worried about the legacy she'd leave behind, if she was able to leave one at all. The history books mostly chronicled the conquests and accomplishments of the great kings, while the queens and their contributions were omitted and lost to people who had died long ago.

Aenwyn didn't want to be unmemorable. It saddened her to think that anyone could be.

"Your name matters to me," she told the faceless woman. "Tell me who you are so that when I make history, I can be sure to credit you for your contribution in aiding me."

The white was fading to grey fast now. Even as her eyes adjusted to the less offensive glow, she could see no one. Sense nothing.

What a lonely existence to be stuck here, unable to see a

thing. Only to be called upon when someone needed something.

Aenwyn didn't know how to help her, but once the dragon was dealt with, she knew that would be her next task. She couldn't stomach the idea of someone being so utterly alone. Not after her own experience with prolonged isolation.

Everything was blooming into color around her now, the specks of white winking out of existence. Soon, she and Darius would be on an island that Aenwyn hadn't set foot on in years. A place she never thought she'd return.

She had almost convinced herself that she was out of the being's grasp when she finally spoke. A melodic string of syllables that Aenwyn knew she would remember forever.

"I am Melinae," her velvety voice replied. But then her tone turned dark, her words dipped in black ink. "But I fear, Aenwyn Red Fury, that my story will end with you."

HE WOULD WAIT

DARIUS

Darius scoured the Cursed Prison for hours. Of the hundreds of unfortunate souls he found trapped and sculpted in sand there, he searched every face twice—just to make sure.

Their frozen, horrified faces would be carved into his skull for the rest of his days.

But at least Queen Aenwyn's face wasn't among them.

By the time Darius made it back to the pavilion atop Hissa's palace, he was certain that Aenwyn would be there waiting for them. He'd convinced himself that they'd been too hasty, him and the sultana, declaring Aenwyn lost far too prematurely. She had needed more time is all—it could be difficult to determine a worthy second and third wish on the spot. But surely, by the time he returned hours later, she'd had plenty of time to figure it out.

Finding nothing but Hissa's long face was another blow to the guy. Aenwyn was still gone, going on a full day by then.

Darius refused to leave as the moon rose high, ignoring the numerous warnings Hissa and her younger sister gave him about the creatures that would rise with it. He'd seen the locusts in Nivernia; they were nothing compared to the crocodiles he grew up with in Rayong, the ones that lurked in the waters where his and Carmen's homes floated. Their village was wrought with deadly inkspill flowers that could kill with a single prick of a thorn, with spiders and snakes that could kill with a single drop of venom. He, himself, had been bitten on more than one occasion, and had to seek immediate care from a healer who'd had to extract the venom with leeches.

Darius wasn't worried about whether or not he would be able to survive a single moon's passing in Vallonde with their locusts.

That was until darkness claimed the lands.

Darius had never experienced anything like these creatures before and it was near impossible not to wonder what Vallonde had done to personally piss off the Sky-Blessed above.

Below the pavilion, it sounded as if monsters were taking over the streets. Wings droned as swarms of locusts and bats washed over the Great City of Vallonde. In Nivernia, it had only been a few dozen. But judging by the cacophony of buzzing that cascaded like a storm around him, he guessed that there were hundreds here tonight. He hadn't seen anything like it, not the entire time they trekked across the desert. They might've been a regional pest, which would've explained why their captors had been so shocked to see them bursting from the sand in Nivernia.

But they weren't even the worst of it.

There were other beasts that snarled down below. Fortunately, they kept to the streets, but Darius could imagine their sharp, glistening fangs all the same. A shiver ran through him when he heard those same teeth shredding into a poor, unfortunate soul who had been caught outside the safety of their home.

Darius had to fight off a scorpion or three, and occasionally shield himself with the serving trays that had been abandoned to the night, but he didn't care. He wasn't leaving. If Aenwyn were to return, he wouldn't forsake her to face this horrific land alone; he wouldn't leave her up here to wonder where he had gone.

But daybreak crashed around him, hard and fast, and Aenwyn never came.

Another day came and went. Then another.

Darius was growing impatient. Restless.

"Where is she?" he growled by way of greeting as the sultana and her sister returned from a few hours' rest.

"Pleasant day to you as well, good knight." There was a bite in her voice that—although it might've been warranted—rubbed Darius the wrong way. The way he saw it, this was still all largely her fault. And he would continue blaming her until he had his queen back. "I see you are your usual, cheerful self today. Still refusing to rest?"

His glare followed Hissa as she strode passed him, but she either didn't notice the frustration he had aimed at her like a dagger to her spine, or she was exceptional at the art of ignoring the frustrations of men.

Instead, Hissa made it look effortless the way she glided across the pavilion, heedless of the pressure he hoped to put on her, or the blistering sun beaming down on them. Her sister Nariah, on the other hand, frolicked like an injured bird, all bumbling limbs and staccato rhythm. Next to her sister, he supposed she could hardly compare.

With more grace than he'd seen anyone else muster, Hissa floated down like a flower petal atop a maroon pillow that matched her current attire for the day. Nariah dropped like a rock onto her blue pillow.

Darius snorted as he followed, her floral perfume leaving a

fragrant trail behind her that stung his nostrils and made his eyes water.

As Darius sat across from her, a servant came to Hissa's side and offered her a tray of jams and breads and legumes. She waved her away before anyone could grab anything, and Nariah watched with a watering tongue as the servant and the food disappeared down the stairs.

"I think it's time we consider that your queen is not returning to us," Hissa stated without emotion.

Darius felt every muscle in his broad frame tighten. He crammed a hand in between the pillows to brace himself, the cool, sand-scattered tiles beneath biting into his flesh.

"We considered that already," he reminded her. "I checked your cruel prison. She wasn't there."

Hissa held up a slender finger, freshly painted in red ink. "It is not *my* prison, Ser Graeme. Remember that. Those people would be exposed to the dangers of Vallonde—without food, without water, and without any idea as to where they found themselves—if I had not had the prison constructed so that they would be kept safe, should they ever return to us." She averted her gaze then, voice growing distant. "I will spare you the details of what the locusts did to the poor souls who'd arrived there before the prison's creation."

Darius swallowed, a lump in his throat that felt an awful lot like a fistful of sand. By now he knew full-well the kind of damage those pests were capable of. In the few days he'd been waiting for Aenwyn's return, he'd survived five run-ins with the moon, one of which had been so devastating that the lower neighborhoods of the Great City of Vallonde had shut down for an entire day afterwards just to repair the damage done to the market and their wares.

Even now, if he stretched his gaze far enough, he would likely still see some of the citizens who dwelled there rebuilding carts, awnings, and food stands.

"Fine," Darius growled. "Not *your* prison, but *the* prison. We checked there already. Twice now. She's not there and she's not going to be."

"How can you be so sure?" Hissa raised a slender brow, the delicate brushstrokes of red above rising with it. Darius almost couldn't see the scars beneath the thin, swirling lines of paint. He guessed that many wouldn't. But his eyes were deftly attuned to the taut tug of skin he saw there in a way that many people weren't. "You'd be surprised what people will ask for when they are desperate—and in my experience, most are."

He knew that to be true as well. He'd dealt with more desperate people than not.

But he also knew that Aenwyn wasn't among them. Not in the sickeningly greedy way that so many could be.

"Not our queen," he defended her.

And Hissa merely shrugged. It wasn't that she was convinced, but she would concede. At least for now.

Darius considered taking a cue from the sultana and dropping the conversation entirely. Arguing just for the sake of arguing wouldn't get them anywhere. But it had been a long few days, and they would just be sitting there in silence otherwise. Darius wasn't sure how much more silence he could take, and there was still something about her that he'd wanted to know.

"If everyone is so desperate," he asked after a short while. "Then what did you ask for?"

Like piercing, twin daggers, her gaze was upon him. "We do not speak of such things." She collected herself, straightening as if she were finally remembering her diplomacy, and said softly, a warning edged in her tone, "What occurs in that strange, ethereal place is for those who have braved the goblet, and no one else."

"I thought it wasn't about bravery, but desperation?"

Her nostrils flared almost imperceptibly. Darius only

noticed because the golden ring hooked in one of hers twitched ever so slightly. "It is impolite to ask someone what they wished for."

"Why?"

"Because—" came her answer, sharp and final. For a long moment, neither of them said a thing. Darius was certain he'd gotten as much out of her on the topic as he would and his appetite for conversation had been sated, at least for the moment. But then, Hissa looked to the sky and sighed as if she were responsible for putting wind in the clouds. "Because, Ser Graeme, to know such a thing is to know someone's soul. Their deepest, darkest desires. And to know what they're willing to pay to reach them. And *that* knowledge is a dangerous thing for another to possess."

Darius understood that sentiment all too well. He had been an expert in hiding his true self from others, locking away his most prized pieces of himself so deep within him that no one else could even glimpse them.

Before these past few weeks, he'd have called it survival.

Now he understood it for what it really was.

Fear and cowardice.

But he couldn't blame her—couldn't blame anyone. It was only natural for her to want to protect herself from anyone or anything who might cause her harm. But he was beginning to wonder...

"What if the true danger—" he pondered aloud, not really thinking about who was listening "—is in keeping yourself locked away and never allowing anyone in. Not even those who might want it. Who might deserve it."

The thought soured in the pit of his stomach, and thoughts of Aenwyn flooded him again, as they often had these past few days whenever he thought on his regrets.

If he could just see her again, then maybe...

Maybe nothing.

Because the truth of the matter was that nothing would be different. She would still be the queen of the country he had sworn to protect. And he would still be a knight. Someone to watch her back when she found herself in danger.

And he wasn't even doing a good job at doing that.

Across from him, Nariah elbowed Hissa in the ribs. Darius watched curiously as the two shared a brief, hushed conversation, where each of them were growing more aggravated by the word.

Finally he overheard Nariah argue, "If she trusts him, shouldn't you?"

Hissa huffed, pouring herself a glass of wine. But after she drank deeply, she turned to Darius and said, "I asked for shelter, safety, and prosperity."

"For me," Nariah added with verve.

"For *us*," Hissa amended. "And for the people. They needed a leader after everything they'd endured. Who better than someone many of them already trusted."

"Do you regret it?" Darius heard himself asking and he wasn't sure why. Morbid curiosity, he guessed? Or maybe he was just trying to understand what Aenwyn might experience whenever she returned.

Hissa was thoughtful before answer, "No. I do not regret my choices. They have served our people well and will continue to do so for years to come."

Darius nodded, and he could finally understand what had bonded Aenwyn and Hissa all those years ago. Their fierce sense of loyalty. Their valor.

He could think of no better woman to be their queen.

. . .

hinking of Aenwyn again brought a pang to his chest and Darius buried his face in his hands.

He didn't know what else to do. They'd searched the prison twice already. He couldn't imagine that after days of being wherever she was that Aenwyn would wish for something contrary to the rules that had been shared with them. If she was taking this long to make her demands, it was because she was being cautious. Deliberate. Clever.

No, he was certain. She would not wind up in the Cursed Prison.

But then where in the Hollows was she? Where else could she have possibly been taken—

And with aching embarrassment, Darius realized the answer. Realized he should've known all along.

He sprang to his feet and Hissa startled. "What is it?"

"Foolish," Darius muttered, wading through the pillows. He had eyes only for the stairs, ready to abandon Vallonde behind him and never look back. "I've been an utter fool. Of course she's not here."

He had become so fixated on his exit that he hadn't noticed Hissa rising until her fingers were wrapped around his wrist. She jerked him to a stop.

"Where then? Where is Aenwyn?"

Those unnaturally bright eyes of hers searched his. Darius shrugged out of her grip and was grateful that she didn't attempt to keep him restrained. At this point, he'd fight every last guard in the Great City of Vallonde if he had to. Nothing would stop him from reaching his queen. He'd already made her wait so long...how much longer would it be now until he reached her?

He began his stride again.

"Will you not tell me?" Hissa's voice cracked. It was the first sign of weakness he'd seen from her in the long days he'd been there. For that reason alone, he paused, turning to face her. She was worrying with one of her golden chains, had it wrapped around her finger. "She is my friend too. If I can help in any way, I—"

"She's exactly where she said she'd be."

It took Hissa a moment. Then understanding crossed her. "The Lost Isle?"

Darius gave a somber nod before turning his back to the sultana again. He didn't know how he was going to cross the cursed waters between here and the island, but first he just needed to reach the coast. Surely someone there would know something about the cursed fog that he didn't.

"Ser Graeme," Hissa called again. "Take this."

He was loathed to halt in his tracks yet again. Every second he wasted was another second he left Aenwyn alone on an island with a dragon so fierce and deadly that it had laid waste to a quarter of the continent. But the intrigue was too much to ignore.

Begrudgingly, Darius turned toward Hissa who was extended a decorated hand. He almost didn't see it at first, tucked between her fingers and blending in with the many rings she wore. But then he saw it. Something gold and round. It fit perfectly in the palm of her hand.

He jerked his head toward it. "What's that?"

Hissa dangled it further, perhaps expecting him to retrieve it. When he made no such movement, she stifled a sigh and crossed the threshold, hips swaying, and slamming it into his hand when she was near enough that he finally reached out.

"What is it?" he asked again.

"It is a talisman," she answered hastily. Darius looked up in time to notice the nervous look she gave her guards. She wasn't sure if she should be doing this. "Bestowed upon only those deemed worthy of trust."

He cocked an eyebrow at her. "And I've been deemed worthy?"

She smirked. "Sometimes my sister is wise beyond her short years. She has reminded me that if you have earned the trust of the queen, then you have earned my trust as well."

Force of habit had him bowing at the waist. "I will wear the honor proudly. I wasn't even aware such talismans were granted from Vallonde."

"It's not a token of Vallonde," Nariah corrected in her excited manner. "It's from the Veiled Bane."

His face contorted. "The Veiled what now?"

"The Veiled Bane," Hissa replied with a wave of her hand. "And it is not given lightly."

Darius examined the medallion more closely, as if the answers he sought would be etched in the gold coating. Not coating, he realized, but real, actual gold; he could tell by the weight.

He turned the coin over in his hand. On one side, a bear's mighty maw stretched wide, its teeth hungry and savage. Darius ran his thumb over the point of one of its fangs and flinched away, the skin pricked and beading with the tiniest droplet of blood.

On the other side, he found a scorpion.

A bear and a scorpion. It couldn't be more obvious.

"What is this?" Darius pressed the sisters harder, the protective knight in him who'd sworn allegiance to Caelora now rearing its head. "Some kind of secret alliance between Vallonde and Skogar? For what?"

He felt ridiculous to ask what seemed like such an obvious question, but he was too flustered not to. He needed to hear her say it. Because she knew what he represented. Who he worked for.

For Hissa to have shown him this medallion was a slap in the face of his loyalties. A test of his allegiance. And the unfortunate truth was, though his loyalties had been teetering since the day he joined the Caeloran Guard, he wasn't ready to admit it yet. Wasn't ready to commit to overt coups with Rayong or the underground Veiled Bane society that Hissa was part of.

Not until he had a better reason.

"For the sake of my people," she said simply, matter-of-fact. As if no other explanation was needed.

It wasn't good enough, but it was, perhaps, a start.

Darius pocketed the medallion. "Thanks."

Hissa bowed her head, something that Darius knew someone of her status did very seldom, making it seem all the more meaningful. "Head to Ilandor. Find The Night's Rose— she's one of my best ships. Show her captain that talisman, and she'll help you find your way to the Lost Isle."

It was more than enough help. Darius knew without the offer he would've had no other way of making the voyage. So it would've been enough, but before he could leave, Hissa tossed something golden and jeweled at him. He barely caught it.

"Take the wishing goblet as well. Just in case."

Darius gaped down at the ominous chalice in his hands as if it were a decaying skull. "I can't take this?"

"You can, and you will." She held up a painted hand before he could protest. "In case you find yourself in desperate need of a wish. And I hate to be the one to tell you this, but where you're heading, you most certainly will.

He considered her for a moment, but ultimately, he knew she was right.

Darius stuffed the goblet into his satchel, declined Hissa's following offer to send a few guards along with him, but did accept the map she provided as he set out for Ilandor. As it were, it would take two or three weeks to reach the tropical village nestled in the jungle on the eastern shores of Vallonde, and he didn't want to be slowed down by additional travelers.

It was best to do this alone. That's how he and Aenwyn had begun this mission, and that's how they'd end it.

Or at least, that was how he'd hoped things would play out.

But as he exited the lower levels of the Great City of Vallonde, the rocky spires in the distance jutting from the cracked soil like skeletal fingers clawing their way to the surface, Darius laid eyes upon something so terrifying, it made his knees buckle.

The Caeloran Guard was approaching the city, King Everard himself at the helm.

2 2

LOYALTY

DARIUS

In the torture chambers, Darius had witnessed the many responses that people had when facing fear. When he'd unsheathed his most terrifying utensils—blades and pinchers meant to draw out the pain rather than bring them to death's knees—oh, how some prisoners would struggle against their restraints, snap their jaws, spit, and act like wild animals in an attempt to fend off their soon-to-be-attacker. Other times, their eyes would flit to the door or a window, searching for a way to escape as they struggled to unbind themselves. Then there were those who wouldn't do a thing; their bodies immobilized in fear, as if they had died already.

Confront the problem head on, run away, or to freeze.

As his king marched forward, Darius felt himself warring with all of his options.

As much as he wanted to run and hide, it would do him no good. Once the king spoke with Hissa, he would know Darius had been there anyway. He couldn't very well fight the entire Caeloran Guard either. Even if he did think himself that skilled on the battlefield—which he didn't—he had trained most of the men and women in the king's guard; he knew their families;

they were good people. He wouldn't bring about their blood-shed just to avoid facing the consequences of his own actions.

And so, Darius chose to remain in place as the king and his army drew nearer.

The sour scowl that permanently contorted King Everard's face deepened once he recognized the man awaiting them. He climbed down from his horse who seemed grateful for the reprieve. The sandy dunes of outer Vallonde were not meant for horseback riding.

"Darius Graeme," the king snarled.

It was not lost on the knight that his title had been omitted, but it was also not unexpected. The king knew how to wield his power, how to cut to the bone. He knew what Darius' position meant to him, what he'd worked so hard to achieve, and he would use that against him. After all, Darius had been gone for weeks without word. For all the king knew, his knight had abducted the queen and fled.

There was no telling what other horrific punishments he had in store for Darius.

But the king was not an impulsive man. Methodical, yes. And in the weeks it had taken them to travel all the way here, he had surely thought of a plan for every scenario that awaited him. But still, he would at least hear Darius out first.

"We've been looking for you." The king's voice quaked with uncontrolled rage. "You and my beloved."

Something twisted in Darius' chest at the sound of that word on the king's lips. There was no true emotion behind it. No passion or love. And that somehow made it better and worse.

Darius bowed deeply, trying to show some modicum of respect for the man who had already lost it all. "My king. I should've sent word to you sooner."

"You should have," King Everard replied, heady with arrogance. "But you failed to do even that. And now we are here, and I am forced to determine what to do with an absconded knight—one of my best."

This wasn't about what Darius had been up to. It was about how it made the king look that one of his best guards was nowhere to be found, and he was none the wiser.

Darius realized he wouldn't have time to explain. There was no remedy for the king's bruised ego.

If he wanted himself to be spared, Darius would need to choose his words wisely. Be convincing. Intriguing. He'd need to play to his audience, and right now that consisted of what looked like the majority of the Caeloran Guard and their egotistical, megalomaniac king who, fortunately, Darius knew exactly how to appease.

In all the time they'd worked together, there had only been one thing on the king's mind.

"I know where to find the dragon responsible for the death of your parents."

The desert fell impossibly silent, as if even the subtle winds ceased their breezing in order to hear what came from Darius' lips next.

"How did you come across this intel?" the king asked, his jaw tightening as he stood straighter, though the effort it took to do so was profound. He wasn't used to wearing such constricting armor, especially not in a place like Vallonde where the heat would bake a man from the inside out.

Then it dawned on Darius: the king hadn't been traveling for comfort, but for war.

Maybe Darius could still give him one.

So he told the king everything. Or at least, a version of it.

In order for the king to find the story acceptable, Darius would have to omit that he and Aenwyn had ever agreed to work with each other.

"I've been chasing her since she left Caelora," he began, and fortunately, the lies came easy. He knew what was at stake. If the king found one detail out of place or unsatisfactory, Darius could be locked away—or worse—and then he wouldn't be able to go to Aenwyn. "I found her near the stables that day, which was odd, but I didn't think anything of it at first. She said she missed being around the horses and sometimes liked to visit them. I let my guard down. But once the alarms started ringing, I knew. I didn't want to take her by force—she's the queen—so I tried convincing her to come back with me. But she told me that she'd had a vision of the dragon and where it lived, and that nothing would stop her from finding and killing it."

The king cocked his head. "Killing it? Why in the cursed sky would she think it her duty to do that?"

A pang ached in Darius' heart. For a while, he'd wondered much the same. But now he understood.

Duty, as it turns out, was closely akin to guilt.

Aenwyn blamed herself for the damage the blue dragon had caused. At one point in time, Darius had been so swallowed up in self-loathing and wanting someone else to blame that it would've been easy for him to blame her as well.

But he couldn't bring himself to now. When she had confessed about freeing the dragon from its egg, he'd understood the magnitude of her blame. He'd done it to himself too. If only he had been there for his mother; if only he'd been more focused on his profession, they might've been able to afford a different farm, one of the ones that hadn't been struck during the attack.

They couldn't keep blaming themselves for the events that were outside of their control.

"Well?" the king pressed, impatience building and pressing upon him just like the sun's unrelenting heat.

"I'm not sure," Darius replied, dragging himself back from his thoughts. "I assumed because she knew how much it would mean to you, my king."

It was a heavy-handed attempt at flattery, but it seemed to

do the trick because the king switched from suspicious to irritated. "Then she is a fool, leaving the castle on her own to hunt down a dragon. Does she not understand how many thousands of lives it has claimed already? How many armies have faced it and been obliterated?"

If there hadn't been an army at his back, Darius would've ripped the king's head from his shoulders for speaking about Aenwyn in such a way.

"I tried telling her the same," Darius managed to say with some modicum of control over his rage. "She was stubborn against reason."

King Everard rolled his eyes upward, only to blinded by the sun. "Yes, well, that's the Skogar for you. No brains to guide their brawns." It took everything in Darius not to argue the opposite, to stand up for Aenwyn who, although at times could be hasty and reckless, was no mere fool. But the king spoke instead, saving him from himself. "But I suppose that's to be expected when your people reside somewhere immune to the dragon's wrath. She doesn't understand what she's up against."

Though Darius disagreed that Aenwyn would be so naive, today was about appeasing the king, so he said, "I couldn't agree more."

He found it profoundly sad just how little the king knew about his wife after a year of marriage though, compared to how well Darius understood her after just a few short weeks. Granted, he'd spied on her before all they'd been through. But still. He'd learned more about her in these past few weeks than he ever had in Caelora.

"So," the king prompted. "You failed to convince her to stay. I'm guessing this is the part where you make excuses for why you've let her get this far?"

Playing the part of the ashamed knight who'd let down his king, Darius let his head fall. "It is, although I make no excuses for what happened in Caelora. I should've never let my guard down around her."

"No, you shouldn't have." The king's teeth were clenched; Darius could hear it in the way he talked. But his tone softened. "However, the Skogar are crafty, my wife more than most. There aren't many a man who could've tamed her."

The king spoke about his wife like she was cattle; he spoke about everyone in that way. Like they were all beneath him. Like he was their divine shepherd, and them his herd of fools.

The longer they stood there talking, the harder it became for Darius to believe that he had ever tried to serve this man with honor.

"How did my wife evade you, Ser Graeme?"

There was intrigue in the king's voice, but not the innocent kind. This was a trap, one that Darius would need to navigate carefully.

He couldn't tell the king about Aenwyn's use of illegal magic; she had already broken too many rules, and Darius wasn't about to draw the king's attention to yet another. But he also couldn't make himself sound more incompetent than he was, not when the king knew him to be otherwise.

"By being one step ahead of us," Darius replied, unsure how well he was concealing the tremble in his voice. He played to the king's view of the Skogar being crafty and cunning, used it to his advantage. "When she took off on her horse, I raced for the barn to grab one for myself but found the doors had been tied together with rope. I was able to cut through them, but it cost me precious time."

The king's flaxen eyebrow rose, bunching beneath his golden crown. "We found no rope outside the barn."

"I took it with me." The lie came to his swiftly; he almost didn't know what to do with it. "I thought maybe I could use it; tie her up, if I had to."

"You would tie up your queen?"

"If it meant returning her to the castle, then yes." Darius' heart thundered in his chest for fear of providing the wrong answer. But he knew his king. Knew the directive by which he commanded his guards whenever there was danger afoot, whenever he wanted intel from a prisoner, and whenever he needed Darius to spy on his wife. "By any means necessary."

A cold smile crept from the corners of the king's mouth like black poison streaking veins.

"Very good," the king crooned. "Smart of you to bring the rope. I don't see it among your...possessions." He made a point of examining the lack of belongings on Darius, who had not thought to demand them back from Hissa or the men who'd captured him and Aenwyn and brought them to Vallonde. "Does that mean you used it?"

"I was robbed." It was the first thing that came to mind, but he needed something more convincing. He was one of the best knights in the Caeloran Guard, after all. "And Aenwyn was on the move, so I sacrificed my goods to stay on her trail."

It sounded reasonable enough in his head. But he'd made one crucial error.

"*Aenwyn?*" The king perked up, amusement thick and dangerous in his singsong voice. He took a step closer, hands folding behind his back as he peered down the tip of his nose at Darius. "I see the two of you have become quite well-acquainted."

Cursed sky! Of all the mistakes Darius could've made, this was by far the most perilous.

The last thing he needed was to draw the suspicions of the king, especially when it came to his relationship with Aenwyn.

He had to fix this. He *would* fix this.

"Not entirely," Darius argued, but not too forcefully. He didn't want to appear defensive and guilty. "We've barely seen each other; she's kept a steady pace and I've had difficulty catching up with her. I lost her a few times and took to asking the locals if they'd seen her, but none knew her as a queen. Simply as Aenwyn. So that is what I've taken to calling her when I ask about her."

The king looked pensive, his skepticism just within reach.

Darius bowed again. "My apologies, my king. It was a slip of habit. One that should've never left my lips but that I will correct immediately."

Darius took mental note to remember his place in this world, alongside this kind, and reminded himself to forget that he'd ever been on a first-name basis with the queen. The second part was more difficult when even the mere thought of her set his face aflame. Darius couldn't help but think about how she had fought for them when they'd been captured in Nivernia. How brave she'd been when she'd taken the goblet from him and drank its contents without a second thought for herself.

In Aenwyn's presence, Darius had begun to make sense of the world and his place in it.

For her, everything was connected. It wasn't about one person or another. It was about doing her part in the grander scheme of things—or as she would call it, fate.

Darius had never felt that calling before. He'd been a wanderer in his own life, bumbling around from one thing to the next without any real tether. Serving under the Caeloran Guard had given him a sense of direction, for a time, but even that hadn't been enough. It hadn't satiated him. Hadn't inspired him.

Aenwyn though? She was someone worth fighting for. Worth fighting alongside.

And if Darius had to return to the Caeloran Guard, he would at least use the king and his army to find and protect the woman he had fallen for.

"Let's get on with this, shall we?" the king groaned, pulling Darius back from his thoughts. "Where is my wife now?"

251

"We were separated," Darius answered. He almost made mention of the Sultana Hissa, but thankfully he remembered just in time that the king was not privy to her rise in power just yet, and Darius didn't want to distract him. He jerked his head back, indicating to the Great City of Vallonde behind him. "Some of the locals saw her leave the city a couple of days ago."

The king's upper lip twitched with what looked like a restrained snarl. "Where was she headed?"

"It took me awhile to find out, but I finally tracked down a merchant she'd purchased some supplies from. He said she was heading for Ilandor."

The lies were flowing now like the mighty Tristfall River, twisting and forking of its own accord, so much so that even locals sometimes got lost following it. But Darius would not be lost in his storytelling. His and—more importantly—Aenwyn's lives depended on it.

"Ilandor?" The king grimaced as if someone had slapped his tongue with rotten fish. "Nothing is in Ilandor except destitute mongrels. It's hardly a large enough village for a dragon to be hiding."

Darius just shrugged. "That's what the merchant said."

He needed the king to believe him. It was the only way he was making it out of this alive, let alone making it to Ilandor to find Aenwyn before it was too late. But Darius had been so focused on forming one lie after the other and not getting caught in any, that he'd almost forgotten who he was talking to, or more importantly, how to appeal to a man like King Everard.

"I don't think he was lying, my king. When I told him who I was—who *she* was—he'd been more than forthright with information."

And right on cue, the king's ego snapped.

"You told him who she was?"

Darius nodded, but he kept his expression uncertain and

apprehensive. "I did. It's how I've gotten intel from everyone I've talked to."

"Who's *everyone*?"

Darius shrugged and began counting on his rough fingers. "A few stable hands, a barkeep, some merchants—anyone who seemed to have seen or encountered her."

The king fell silent, the kind of pensive irritation that made most who found themselves in his company quake with fear. Not Darius though. The king was exactly where he wanted him. Right now, King Everard was realizing that people throughout Vallonde already knew about Queen Aenwyn's disappearance. It wouldn't take long for the rumors to abound: a runaway queen, an alliance shattered.

He wouldn't be able to leave her now.

"Come then," the king said through his irritation. "Saddle up. We ride for Ilandor now."

* * *

It was the hardest ride of Darius' life.

By their tracker's calculations, they rode across the desert for nearly three weeks. In that time, they were fortunate enough to only encounter seven true nights, but when the moon brought with it carnivorous creatures that outnumbered them easily, even seven nights was too many.

They lost about a hundred men on their journey. Darius would bear the guilt of their deaths, of their families' grief, until the end of his days. And he would bear the deaths of more to come, as well.

Before they arrived in Ilandor, Darius scouted ahead. The king didn't want Aenwyn to see his army and get spooked. Darius was eager to oblige; he used it as an opportunity to fabricate another lie, this time about how he'd come into possession of Hissa's medallion and what to do with it. It was easy enough to fabricate a story about joining the local fisherman at the pub for a few pints, drunkenly singing into the night until he'd gained their trust and they'd told him about the queen seeking passage to the Lost Isle. He also took the opportunity to find the captain of the Night's Rose first and ask for her aid. He explained the situation and asked her to lie to a king.

"You want me to tell him what?" she asked, so Darius repeated himself.

"Tell him that you just returned from your last voyage. If he asks about his wife—and he will—make it seem like she just left on the same voyage we're requesting of you."

"But that wouldn't make sense. The fog only clears every few months. I haven't made that trip in even longer still."

"It doesn't matter," Darius assured he. "He doesn't know that."

When Darius returned to their camp, King Everard was none too pleased with hearing that the queen had crossed the sea, and he was even less enthused about following after her. But he also wasn't turning back now.

They found their way to the docks the next day. Darius pretended to search for the Night's Rose, even though he knew exactly where she'd be. With sails as dark as a starless night, pricked with petals and roses as red as blood, it was easy enough to find.

When he found it, he made show of flashing the captain his golden medallion.

"Sure, I can take you to the Lost Isle," she said, her accent thick and rolling. "But it'll have to wait until the fog clears."

"And when might that be?"

She frowned, calculating something that Darius wasn't privy to, something not part of their rouse. This was an honest answer. "Another month or so. Maybe longer."

The king was far from pleased. He threatened to lay siege to the quiet, humble town of Ilandor.

But the captain was unfazed by his threats. She marched right up to him, stuck her face into his, and planted her hands upon her waist.

"Go ahead, your Highness. Won't be anyone here to take you across the sea then, now would there? And then what would your poor wife do?"

The king regained his composure then, if only barely. After a few more sad attempts at haggling for an earlier departure, King Everard finally caved in and agreed to the captain's terms.

"Choose your best men—I want no more than ten of them on my ship—and meet me at the Bay of Lost Souls in two weeks. Then, we wait for the nightingales to take to the sky. That's how we'll know that the fog has cleared, and only then can we navigate safely to the Lost Isle."

Darius thought the weeks it had taken to cross the open desert had been long. Not a moment had passed that he hadn't been worrying about Aenwyn, where she was, what she was facing, what she was thinking. He didn't know why he wasn't with her, but he hoped she knew that he was coming.

Although those weeks had been torture, waiting in Ilandor for another month was excruciating. At least before he'd been walking, moving, slicing through scorpions as large as boulders and battling serpents who might as well be the rulers of the desolate expanse that encompassed most of Vallonde.

Here in Ilandor, they just waited.

A week ticked by like grains passing through an hourglass.

The second came even slower. But at least when it was over, they were moving again.

Only for two days though. Then they were waiting again, this time at the Bay of Lost Souls, which made time move even slower. By the end of the week, everyone was restless. But the day finally came when the nightingales flocked into the clouds like a swarm of locusts, and it was time for the king's men to set sail on the Night's Rose.

Only, Darius never made it aboard that ship.

The moment the first bird took flight, something cold and unseen wrapped around his chest. It ripped him from where he sat in the sand, staring out across the horizon. Wind rushed around him, everything a complete blur as he was hurled across the blue sea.

It happened so swiftly, he barely had time to panic. But soon, the motion stopped. Darius found himself on yet another coastline, but this one unfamiliar, foreign in its foliage and citrusy scent.

As he scanned the coastline to see if he could figure out where he was, there was only one thing he recognized.

His heart splintered at the sight of Aenwyn's red hair.

NOT A QUEEN

AENWYN

" **A**enwyn!"

Her eyes blinked open, but all she could see was white sand and tall blades of grass.

"Aenwyn!"

Someone was calling to her. Blearily, she tried making her mind figure out who it was, but she simply couldn't. Every bone in her body was weary and throbbing. Her skull felt as if it might crack open from the pounding coming from inside it.

"Aenwyn!"

They called again, each time sounding closer than they had before. It was a man's voice. Of that much she could finally tell.

She mustered enough strength to push herself upright, and on wobbling, trembling legs finally came to stand. Everything was spinning. Bright colors that her eyes couldn't adjust to fast enough.

Something solid was running toward her though. Something human-shaped. And plated in gold that dazzled in the low sunlight.

"Aenwyn!"

At long last, she recognized Ser Darius Graeme's voice. He was charging toward her at full speed.

The sound of her name on his lips split her clean down the middle.

"Darius?" she groaned, his name like gravel in her pained throat.

It took her a moment to realize why, but now that she was standing, she recalled her encounter with the wishing goblet and then with Melinae. She wasn't sure how long she had been unconscious, but she expected a few hours at least considering how much her throat ached, how parched her lips were.

Darius was just starting to come into focus when his arms engulfed her.

Aenwyn blinked in surprise. For a moment, she didn't know how to react, whether or not to hug him or to shove him away. Given her role as queen, this sort of contact with any man other than her husband and perhaps her father wasn't permitted.

But Darius held nothing back. All caution and restraint had been tossed to the wind.

And so she allowed herself this moment. To feel wanted. To relish the passion.

She gave into his embrace and pretended, for at least this one moment, that they were just two people with no other responsibilities in the world.

They clung to each other so tightly she wondered if they'd ever be broken apart again.

"Where have you been?" he asked, breathless and trembling. "I wasn't sure you'd—I didn't think I'd ever—"

The unsteadiness of him unsettled her.

Sure, she had missed his presence while she'd been talking to Melinae. Of course she had. But she'd only been gone a few moments.

Then again, she tried seeing it from his perspective. She

didn't know what had happened to her, whether she'd disappeared or simply fallen unconscious. Had time continued on without her or had it paused during her visit? The way he was acting made her think it had not, and that he'd been distraught while he waited for her to return to him. She would've been much the same, near inconsolable if he'd disappeared, even with Hissa there to walk her through the process of the wishes with her while they waited.

Head buried against Darius' shoulder, it was then that Aenwyn also realized with great surprise that she was cold.

There was a cool breeze pelting against her back and the only source of warmth she had was in Darius' arms.

Stranger still, she could hear the crashing of waves.

Aenwyn glanced up to find that she was on a shoreline. In his arms, she felt the strong plates of his armor as she breathed in the salty sea air.

Her wishes had worked.

She and Darius were no longer in the middle of the desert, but on a tropical beach off the coast of the Lost Isle.

"It worked!" she exclaimed, but her attention caught on the look of concern weighing down Darius' eyes.

She stared up at him, and him down at her.

"Your eyes," he whispered. Darius exhaled, both of his hands coming up to cup her cheeks. A spark dancing through her body at his touch. "They're beautiful."

She didn't know what he meant at first, she was too distracted by the flames that whipped across her face until she was certain she was as scarlet as her hair. Then she remembered the goblet and what Melinae's bargain had done to Hissa's eyes.

But none of that seemed to matter. Not with Darius's face so close to hers, his touch so gentle.

She should tell him to stop. To let go of his queen and to never touch her again in such an intimate manner.

But Aenwyn didn't want to do that.

She wanted him to keep going.

To lean into her and brush his lips across hers.

For his hands to explore the many curves of her body.

She wanted to be close to him, for this moment to last forever.

But confusion prevented her from succumbing to it fully. She didn't understand. What had changed for him? Just earlier that day they'd been strictly friends, maybe even less than that. A knight accompanying a queen on a quest. He followed her to keep her protected. Nothing more.

Although she'd *felt* more. Aenwyn knew men, and she knew he'd felt it too.

But why was he acting upon it now when there had been dozens of other opportunities to do so before?

"I'm so glad I found you," he said, his words like a whip cracking against her bare heart.

"Found me?" Aenwyn swallowed, beginning to understand.

It was the same reason he was running so desperately toward her. The same reason he stared with bewilderment at her now-changed eyes. The same reason that the entity in the goblet had said she couldn't take Aenwyn to the Lost Isle unless she timed it perfectly.

"How long was I gone?"

Darius' brow wrinkled. His hands dropped from her face, and she felt the sting of the sharp sea breeze smacking against her cheeks where they'd rested.

"You disappeared almost three months ago."

Again, she was spinning. Falling. Lost in a dizzying spell of reality and perception.

Three months she'd been trapped in that other domain, that hidden place.

For three months, she'd been unable to complete her mission. She kept losing time. First to the hollowroot imposed on her by Hissa's henchmen. Now this? She was growing tired of the hours being stolen from her.

But worst of all was that she had kept Darius worrying all that time.

Her mouth hung open. "I-I'm so sorry. I didn't know—"

The warmth of his hands cupped her face. "Of course you didn't. None of us did. Not even Hissa."

"What happened?" She found herself wondering. It was a missing part of her life and she wanted it back.

His breathing deepened as Darius bit his lip. "We waited at first. For the night. Then a full day. Hissa said it could take a while sometimes, especially if the wisher didn't know what to wish for."

Aenwyn could relate to that, although she thought she'd managed to think of two other wishes fairly quick.

"But nothing happened," he continued. "I stayed on that pavilion for three full days before realizing that you weren't coming back. Of course you weren't because you had made your wishes, one of which was to come to the Lost Isle." He smirked then, a touch of sadness behind his tender eyes. "When Hissa told me how specific the wishes had to be, I thought maybe you had forgotten to ask that I come with you."

Aenwyn blanched. She tried recalling the memory, searching her mind for the exact words she'd spoken, but it wasn't clear. She couldn't remember if she'd only asked that *she* be brought to the Isle or both of them. She supposed the answer was right in front of her though. She wouldn't have been missing for three months if she had asked for safe passage for both of them.

"I'm so foolish," she lamented, but Darius shook his head.

"No you're not," he said softly. "Your wish worked. I was brought here with you…in time. There was just…a delay."

She remembered what Melinae had said then, about timing

the travel correctly. "So it did work? You were brought here like I was?"

He nodded. Then, glancing down to his gear, he added with an amused grin, "And with new armor and weapons. I imagine that was also your quick thinking?"

She blushed again, but not the demure way a Caeloran woman would tuck her chin in and bat her lashes when complimented on her needlework. Aenwyn beamed with pride the way a hunter would stand over a felled caribou, admiring their accomplishments.

"I'm a practical lady. What can I say?"

Tapping one of the axes on her belt, his smirk widened. "No lady I know would've asked for this."

She boasted further, "No lady you know would've knocked you to the ground, taken that goblet for herself, and…"

Her pride flickered out like a candle flame caught in a draft.

The sacrifice she'd made to be here wasn't just hers to make. She thought about her sisters. She wondered if they knew the change that had happened to their own bodies, or if they'd simply have to find out some other day. She wouldn't want it to be sprung on them. To find out years from now, all on their own, with no idea as to why? She wouldn't allow it. Once this was over, she'd tell Signe and Katla both what she'd done, and beg for their forgiveness.

Darius was looking down at her hands, as if contemplating on taking them into his own. A shuddering breath shook him instead. "You didn't have to do this."

Aenwyn laughed. "I couldn't just let you do it. This wasn't your sacrifice to make. You've already lost too much."

Exasperated, Darius dragged a hand over his face and through his short beard. He looked like he was struggling with finding the words he wanted to say to her.

"It's not your fault, you know," he finally blurted. "You didn't hatch the dragons—"

"*Dragon*," she corrected. "Just the one."

"Fine, *dragon*. It doesn't matter. What I'm saying is you didn't send them—or it—to Grimtol to wreak havoc. It's no more your fault than it is Baug's for giving you that egg. But you don't blame him, do you?"

No, she didn't.

When Baug had given her that egg, he hadn't known what it was. He was just trying to give a frightened girl something pretty and unique to help ease her woes.

"You need to stop blaming yourself," he said. "I know I don't."

His forgiveness was a sword piercing her heart. She didn't deserve it. She didn't deserve anything from anyone who'd suffered because of the dragon.

At least not until she made this right.

Worrying at her lip, she turned away from him. "I'm afraid I disagree."

He grabbed her shoulders and spun her back around. "And I disagree with you disagreeing."

The ridiculousness of that statement made a laugh squeak out of her. A smile eased its way into his rugged features as well, and now it was her turn to reach out and touch him. Her hand was trembling as her fingers traced the strong line of his jaw. Something deep in her center tightened as her touch trailed to his chin and then to his mouth.

He licked his lips and her breath caught.

"I thought I'd lost you," he said, voice low and tight with emotion. He reached up, tucked the thickness of her hair behind her ear. "For three months, I thought you'd been sent here to fight the dragon on your own. And I didn't know if you'd survived. I didn't know if the dragon had killed you or if you'd found some place to hide and were just stranded here alone, and the thought ate me up inside."

Guilt inched its way into her then.

She hadn't been forthright with him about her past. He didn't know it wouldn't have been the first time she'd been stranded on that island all alone.

Later. Later she'd tell him everything. He'd earned her trust by now.

"I had to come for you."

She figured it out before he could finish explaining. For whatever reason, the entity in the goblet had held onto her until the time was right for them to travel to the Isle, but since Darius hadn't been in that other domain with her, his life had continued on. Only a few minutes might've passed for her, but like he said, for him it had been three months. Three months he'd been left here without her, wondering where she was and if she was alright. And what a panic he must've been in that entire time.

Until today.

Today Melinae had found an opportune moment to fulfill Aenwyn's third and final wish. She'd brought them to the Lost Isle together. She had reunited them.

Up until that moment though, Darius had been roaming. Searching for her.

He wasn't going to let her be alone and abandoned.

He had been coming for her.

And it was that understanding that was her undoing.

Here on this island, here with Darius, she wasn't a queen. She wasn't even a wife, as far as she was concerned.

This was her motherland. Her home. And here she would always and only ever be Aenwyn. A girl who'd learned how to fend for herself and keep the monsters at bay. A girl who'd learned how to build her own strength, inside and out. A girl who discovered who she was by losing everything first.

And in this moment, Aenwyn was a young woman who was tired of doing everything for everyone else but herself. She was tired of giving her body to a husband who didn't love her.

Tired of holding her tongue during court, even when she had decent ideas—*good* ideas about how to solve the problems of their people. She was tired of keeping her magic concealed so that she wouldn't scare everyone else in the kingdom. Tired of trying to fit in with the Caeloran woman. Tired of holding herself back.

Aenwyn had wants and needs and desires of her own.

She was done curbing them.

Standing up on her tiptoes, Aenwyn inched forward.

His heavy-lidded eyes slid to her parted lips. "Aenwyn, we shouldn't."

"Shouldn't can burn in a fiery inferno for all I care."

"But—"

"Shh," she hushed him and traced a finger along his bottom lip. "I don't want to hear about what we shouldn't do. Right now, I only care about what we *want* to do. And I...I want to kiss you."

A low growl rumbled in his throat.

She wetted her lips as they curved upward. "Is that what you want too?"

Another untamed sound escaped him, and his eyes flashed molten.

She brought her lips closer. So close she could feel the heat of his ragged breaths on them. But she stopped just out of reach.

"Say it," she told him. Commanded him. It had been so long since she'd been the one in power when it came to her love life, and she wasn't about to give it up now. "I want to hear you say it."

It wasn't even so much a want as it was a need. She craved to hear him tell her that he was feeling the same way, and that this wasn't all just in her head. That the electric pull between them was as strong for him as it was for her. That they could do this because they both wanted to.

His broad chest rose and fell beneath the golden armor. He looked as if he was about to lunge for her, but she stopped him with a hand to his chest. She shook her head.

"Say it." It was a dare, one that she hoped would be the primal release of him. And it was.

His hand climbed up her spine and wove itself into the thickness of her hair. He tugged her head back, gentle enough not to hurt her neck, but firm enough to let her know that he was capable of giving her the exact kind of satisfaction she'd been craving since her marriage. Something fierce. Something passionate.

Looking deep into her eyes, he held his restraint but did as he was told. "I've wanted you since the day we crashed into each other in those castle halls. You were unlike any lady I've ever met and if you had been anyone but the queen, I would've charmed my way into your bed chamber, pinned you up against the wall, and ravaged you until you couldn't stop yourself from screaming my name."

The delicious thing that had coiled itself deep inside her unraveled.

As her stomach dipped low, Aenwyn sprang high and kissed Ser Darius Graeme for the first time.

She'd almost forgotten the magic that came alive when two people came together in such a way. So full of desire and curiosity. So undone by the spell they had placed on each other.

The coastline shattered behind them, lost to some distant place that no longer mattered.

With his hand still tangled in her hair and the other splayed against her lower back, Darius gripped her tighter, pulling her against him. Their lips parted and the kiss deepened; they explored the way each other tasted.

He devoured her every moan as his hand found the way down her backside. In King Everard's grasp, there had been too much for him to hold onto, his small hands grasping but never quite being able to seize all of her.

Darius had no such problem. His firm grip around her rear was grounding. There was a comfort to knowing that he could take her on, that she could trust him with every inch or pound of her.

She leapt into his arms, and he caught her without hesitation. Without struggle.

With both of his hands now firmly placed on either of her haunches, Aenwyn wrapped her legs around him, pulling herself against him. She could feel the heat of his groin against the apex between her legs

She wanted to feel more.

There was too much armor between them. Too many clothes and belts and satchels.

She'd never wanted to be naked so badly in her life.

Breaking their lip lock, Aenwyn leaned back and began fumbling—gripping at the golden plates of his armor, trying to peel it off of him. But she was unfamiliar with how to take it off. There were so many pieces; it was nothing like the Skogar armor she'd torn off her occasional lover back at home.

Breathless, she asked, "How do I—"

He set her down and lifted his arms. "There are straps."

Her hands moved quickly, freeing his arms first before moving back to his body. Under her breath, she muttered something about wishing she'd been more specific about armor that wasn't so cumbersome to take off, to which Darius chuckled. He went to work on kissing and nibbling the shell of her ear.

"You're not making this any easier," she moaned, eyes rolling back as his lips trailed down to her neck.

He stopped abruptly and looked at her. "Oh, I'm sorry. I didn't realize you didn't like it."

Playfully, she glowered and gripped his shoulders tighter to thrust him back into her neck. She stopped trying to undress him as his kisses continued down to her bosom.

It was Darius' turn to start unthreading her leather laces now. With each loop he pulled them through, he'd kiss a different spot on her—first the top of her forehead, then her chin, her neck, her cheek, and the tip of her nose.

Aenwyn beamed at every one of them. She relished every pleasurable, playful moment of it, and forced all acknowledgement of infidelity out of her mind. This couldn't be wrong when it felt so blissfully right.

When he finally had her laces loosened, he tugged the leather chest piece until it was wide enough to fall down to her feet, leaving nothing behind but a white undershirt.

Darius traced a finger around the loose neckline, and with delicate precision pulled it down until he could see the swell of her breasts.

An ache built between her legs as he examined her. She wanted his touch. She craved to have his lips upon her.

But he took his time with her. His bottom lip brushed against the soft, tender flesh of her breasts, his tongue flicking out. Tasting. Teasing.

Slowly, he continued to pull the neckline of her shirt down until the light brassiere was exposed. His lips traced a path, tickling and licking and kissing all the way to the place where her breasts bulged against the hem of the stiff fabric.

She tilted her head back, already prepared for the ecstasy of his mouth wrapping around her nipple.

But it never came. Instead, he stood upright, something shiny between his teeth.

He pulled it out and examined it, and Aenwyn recognized the flash of blue.

"Oh," she said, embarrassment punching her in the gut. "I forgot I'd put that there."

She reached out to take the ring from him, but he jerked it back. "No."

"No?"

Darius brushed back the waves of her hair. "You don't need this ring when you're with me. I would never make you lock a part of yourself away. I want you as you are. Every part of you."

Her heart swelled. But as much as she wanted to agree with him, worry overcame her. "I can't lose it though. When we go back, I'll have to—"

Darius crammed the ring over the tip of his pinky. "There. Safe for now if we ever decide to go back."

Her heart was sent a flutter again. *If* they went back. Oh, how she had hoped for it too. To run away from Caelora and never return, especially now that she had him.

Could they really do that though? Could they abandon their duty for the sake of their budding love? What about the alliance with the Skogar?

She blinked away the tears, letting them fall as a way of cleansing herself from such worries. She would face reality later. Nothing would soil this moment.

Worry had worked its way into Darius' features, and it was her fault. She had foolishly mentioned the lives they'd left behind, the ones they would need to return to.

"Aenwyn, I—"

She barreled into him, engulfing his mouth with her own. He kissed her back, but it wasn't the same. They were the short, rapid kisses of someone trying to end an embrace, someone trying to say something. And it was her fault.

She pulled back, shaking her head. "I'm sorry. I've ruined it."

"*You've* ruined it?" His eyes bulged and he cupped her cheek in the palm of his hand. "No. Nothing's been ruined." Relief flooded her and she leaned forward to resume her sampling of him. But he stopped her. "It's me who's about to ruin this perfect moment."

Never before had her heart been so torn. Where there had once been relief, now worry soured into the mix. "How do you mean?"

"I need to tell you something."

A nervous laugh twitched through her. "Tell me what?"

When he inhaled deeply, she knew she didn't want to know. Knew that there would be no returning to this moment afterwards. A moment that they deserved after everything they'd been through.

"Don't." Aenwyn pressed a finger to his lips. She held his gaze. "Tell me, does this have to do with our responsibilities back at home." He made a face that said she was close but not close enough. So she amended, "Does this have anything to do with my husband?"

Darius winced. "Yes."

"Then I don't want to hear it." Aenwyn pressed her body closer, stretched onto the tips of her toes, and folded her arms around his strong neck. The back of his armor bit into her forearms and she couldn't wait to finish tearing it off of him. "I know what I want, Darius. Do you want the same?"

He seemed nervous to respond, but his gaze kept drifting to her cleavage, his chest rising and falling in short, rapid bursts said it all. "I know what I want. But I—"

"But nothing! I want this. I want *you*."

His next breath came sharp, and she knew she had him. But that didn't mean she was going to stop there. She wanted to see him sweat, to make his knees weak, and hear the crack in his voice as he begged to take her.

Her voice became heady with seduction as she twirled a finger in his hair. "We're about to go into battle, Ser Darius Graeme. I wouldn't want my knight distracted while he was fighting."

The start of a smirk emerged. "No, we wouldn't want that."

"Not at all," she purred, and it was so silly how wonderful it felt to do something so simple like flirt with a man who actually seemed interested in her. "Fortunately for you, I know just the thing that will clear your head."

He swallowed hard, the ball of his throat bobbing as she reached for one of his hands and smacked them into place on her backside. The growl that escaped him was guttural and just as intoxicating as she had imagined it would be.

Darius had been as straight as a column until then. Now he leaned into his grasp, clutching at her hefty haunches as if his singular goal was to hold onto as much of her as he could and never let go again.

When he was thoroughly distracted by the curving expanse of her backside, Aenwyn tore at the leather straps keeping his chest and belly armor in place. They hit the sand with a soft thud, and she turned her attention to his legs.

After untying the chainmail skirt, Aenwyn brought her hands to the plates of armor tied over his legs and delicately began pulling at the laces. She was slow and teasing at first, pausing occasionally to grind her hips against his groin, relishing the grooves of the gold plates against the tender apex between her thighs.

It wasn't long before her need outgrew her desire for play though. Her hunger deepened, as did his, and soon she was tearing at the strings.

Their movements hastened with every tug of clothing, her words pressing down around them like the suffocating sands of time. Because, the truth was, they didn't know if they'd ever get the chance to be with each other again. One or both of them could die facing the dragon. One or both of them could die facing King Everard. The only time they were assured was the time they had now. In this moment. Here. On the coast of her motherland. And Aenwyn could think of no better place to share their first—and quite possibly their last—time.

When the last article of armor and clothing had been torn

from their bodies and haphazardly discarded in the sand, the two of them stood there, panting and wild-eyed as their ravenous gazes took in one another.

Aenwyn knew Darius would be fit. She knew that the knights in the Caeloran Guard had regimented routines that involved sparring multiple times a day, among other various trainings designed to keep them in fighting shape.

But she hadn't imagined he would be quite as perfect as he was. All bulging muscles and chiseled abs. And that was to say nothing of the impressively long broadsword erect at his hips.

He reminded her of a bull, the way he stood there, primed, and ready to charge. She'd let him penetrate her any day.

Something tugged low in her stomach. She wanted to drag her tongue from the top of his decadent chest, all the way down the front of him, to the tip of his glistening head. From the look in his eyes, he was thinking the same thing.

Not another moment was wasted.

Darius scooped her into his arms like she was nothing more than a cloud, making Aenwyn's stomach dipped.

He carried her to a spot of grass, his voice gruff when he asked, "How would you have me?"

Aenwyn's cheeks went aflame. "Hmm?"

She couldn't think, let alone speak coherently. Not after that kiss. All she needed—all she craved—was more like it. More caresses. More tastes. What need did they have of words right now anyway?

He chuckled and clarified, "On top or bottom, my queen?"

It cleaved her in two to hear him ask, to have him leave the choice up to her. The king had never asked. He hated when she was on top. Complained about being crushed beneath the weight of her. Really, he just hated letting her be in control.

This would be nothing like the passionless trysts she'd had with him though. Of that much, she was certain.

"A queen keeps her subjects beneath her," she purred, her hungry gaze promising to devour him.

Primal need flashed molten in his eyes. "There's no place I'd rather be, Your Majesty."

He lowered her down gently, but Aenwyn was determined to let that be the last bit of tenderness they shared. She didn't want tender. She wanted animalistic. To feel something other raw and untamed.

Darius got down to his knees and Aenwyn shoved him backward. The hunger in his eyes flashed molten as he crashed into the bed of grass, egging her on.

Climbing atop him, Aenwyn straddled his hips. She felt the heat of him against her slickness.

They looked at each other one final time before she sheathed him into herself. Pleasure lanced through her, hot and urgent. It skittered from her head to her toes, making her dizzy with desire and ecstasy.

And that was just the first thrust.

With a shuddering breath, Aenwyn pulled her hips away enough to plunge his velvet hardness back into her, and another rippling wave of heat set her body aflame.

Darius groaned, their pace quickening as he rolled his hips in time with hers, feeling the depth of her, drawing out the ache that was building deep inside her.

She needed more of him. Needed him to keep stroking that internal flame.

Aenwyn leaned over as her hips bucked beneath her. At the sight of her breasts rocking in time with their bodies, Darius' eyes bulged with that unsatiated hunger again. She let him stare; practically begged him for it. She wanted to be revered, for him to worship her body like she wanted to worship his. This moment was meant for their deepest darkest desires. It was meant to fulfill all the shameful curiosities they kept hidden inside, all the hopeful cravings. She wanted to give it all to him.

But as the pounding pleasure built inside her, nearing crescendo, as she felt the hardness of him pulsing with restraint, she knew their time would end soon.

Aenwyn pried one of his hands from where it had made a home on her rear. He almost looked as if he was about to protest, but then she dipped his fingers into her mouth, wetting the tips, before placing his hand between her legs.

She could worship that hand for the rest of her days for how attuned it was to her need. The small circles stroking her core, building her pleasure until her body was abuzz. At the peak of rapture, he pushed her over the edge with a final pounding thrust, and Aenwyn shattered into oblivion just moments before he did.

The queen collapsed atop her knight, spent but in utter bliss. She had never experience sex quite like that. Before marriage, it had been a meaningless, playful romp in the woods occasionally. After marriage, it had been dull and painful and numbing.

Thinking of her husband now and how he would all but shove her away after their time together, she almost started to roll off Darius. To give him the space that she was starting to convince herself he wanted.

But Darius folded his arms around her naked body, collapsing her doubts and fears as he held her in place against the hard plains of his chest. Voice weary, his words were a dreamy sigh. "So that's what being close to wildfire is like."

Aenwyn smirked where she rested. "It beats being a mindless, obedient puppet any day."

He snorted. "I'll say."

Those were among some of the very first words they'd shared together that night in the dark halls of the castle. It was a fond memory to look back on now and to see just how far they had come. But it was also a disheartening reminder of the lives they still had to return to, about the duty they shared to their kingdoms.

Aenwyn felt the tension pull on Darius' body and knew he was thinking about it too. Perhaps he was thinking about more. There had been something on his mind before. Something she had forced him to wait to tell her.

Rather than postpone the inevitable pain that she was sure would come from whatever confession he had waiting, Aenwyn chose to face it head on.

Begrudgingly, she pulled her body away from the heat of his and made her way across the beach to where their clothes and armor lay discarded. Darius was right beside her the whole time, quiet as the two of them helped each other back into their garments and prepared for what was to come.

Only once they were both wrapped in the safety of their clothes and armor did Aenwyn dare ask, "So, Ser Darius Graeme, what was it you wanted to tell me earlier?"

There was a look in his eyes that she didn't like. Something dark and foreboding. Something that looked a lot like guilt.

Averting his gaze, Darius stared out over the crashing waves. The scar over his eye caught in the dim sunlight. "There's something I need to tell you. Something I did."

"What is it?" she asked, her heart in a frenzy.

He opened his mouth to answer, but in place of his voice, a mighty roar boomed overhead like thunder.

A dragon was nearby.

HOME

AENWYN

"Do you think it saw us?" Aenwyn huffed as they tore across the sand, her eyes trained on the pile of armor they'd left discarded.

"No." Darius panted beside her. If their lives hadn't been in danger, Aenwyn would've taken the time to admire his rippling muscles as he sprinted. "We would've seen it."

Maybe they'd have time for ogling after. First, there was a dragon to deal with.

Aenwyn supposed Darius was right. A beast of that size wouldn't remain hidden so easily.

They scrambled to redress themselves. Aenwyn's traditional Skogar armor, complete with leather bracers to match, was far easier to get on than the cumbersome ensemble that Darius was wearing. They both cursed as Aenwyn struggled to retie the dozens of belts and fastenings it took to secure every gold-plated piece of his suit back into place.

She almost joked about wishing they would've left it on him, but that would've been a lie. Now more than ever, she was grateful for what little time they'd had together.

Once they were fully dressed and the only signs of them

being on the beach were the dips in the sand from their feet that would soon be washed away by the incoming tide, Aenwyn looked out over the forested island.

She was back home. A truth that proved difficult to grasp considering how long she'd been away, and how little she'd ever thought to return.

The hilts of her axes were wrapped in thin strips of leather. Aenwyn rolled them in her hands, familiarizing herself with the weight of the weapons that Melinae had procured for her. They were much lighter than Darius' broadsword, but that suited her perfectly. It had been a while since she'd wielded anything heavier than a hairbrush.

Darius' sword must've weighed a ton, though he hardly made it look it. He swung the blade in sweeping arcs, also getting acquainted with how it felt, how it moved.

She noted it wasn't a typical sword. Not one made from steel anyway, but pure gold. The length of it gleamed in the dimming sunlight.

Aenwyn didn't know how practical his sword would be. In her experience, gold was a rather fragile metal, something more commonly used to make delicate jewelry, not blades for evisceration. But she'd asked Melinae for weapons built to slay dragons, so she had to assume that's what they'd been given.

Seeing the confidence with which Darius wielded it, the way he tested its movements, the precision with which he struck, it put Aenwyn at ease. And for the first time she realized she was grateful that she wouldn't be facing the dragon alone. She'd spent far too many of her days doing things alone.

A bout of homesickness punched Aenwyn in the gut as they entered the dense woods.

She wasn't sure when she had felt lonelier: the year she'd spent in Caelora or the untold years she'd spent here, alone on this island.

Being here now was stirring far too many memories. Some

pleasant. Some painful. Simple moments like washing clothes in the stream with her mother and the other women on days when it was too hot to do anything but wade in the cool waters. Singing songs and telling stories about the ways of the world while they weaved baskets made from tall blades of grass or made bowls out of dirt and crushed seashells. Netting her first fish in the inlet just south from here, and seeing pride illuminate her mother's face when she carried it back to their village.

And then having to do all of it on her own.

No one to sing with.

No one to tell stories to.

No one to beam at her accomplishments.

It was so strange returning to a place she had known so intimately at one point in her life but now felt foreign. It was as if the island had no problem moving on without her. She wondered if it would be the same with Skogar. If she ever had a chance to return, would it feel as lonely and wrong as it did here?

When she and Darius came upon a path that she knew from experience would lead them to her former village, a broken part of her was tempted to follow it. No one but ghosts would be there, of course. Their living memories ambling around her aimlessly.

Aenwyn tried shaking away the dark cloud pressing down upon her and pressed onward, trekking deeper into the humid, misty forest, hacking away at the vines that blocked them.

"Do you know where we're going?" Darius called from behind.

Guilt swept through her at the hint of suspicion in his tone. Guilt for everything left unspoken. And even though she owed him no explanation, there was a hungry part of her that longed to give it.

The story of the fall of her people had only been shared once with one other person.

Baug had been the one to coax the words out of her, and then he'd been the one to tell his crew, Hissa, and even Signe. He'd saved Aenwyn from the horror of having to recount those painful memories ever again.

And then, when she had become betrothed, they'd agreed never to share that story, ever again. No one in Grimtol needed to know she wasn't Baug's natural-born heir. And since the Skogar kept to themselves, no one dared question when he proposed the alliance between his eldest daughter and King Everard.

But that promise seemed so trivial now.

Now Aenwyn wanted to share her story. Here. With Darius.

"I do," Aenwyn finally answered.

It was hardly the perfect moment to bare herself to him, but she needed him to believe her. Needed him to understand her and this quest they found themselves wrapped up in, how much it meant to her—all of it.

This was the most secretive and vulnerable part of herself, and she wanted to share it with him. And if she didn't do it now, they might not get another chance.

Aenwyn swallowed the dryness in the back of her throat. "I've...I've been here before."

"What?"

She couldn't tell if he didn't believe her, or if he just hadn't been able to hear over his grunting as he hacked away at unkempt bushes. She chose to believe it was the latter.

"It's how I knew that Hissa had a ship that could get us here. I've sailed on it before. It had black sails that looked like they'd been splattered in blood."

His heavy trudging halted. The insects buzzed in her ears as Aenwyn spun around, meeting his uneasy gaze.

"The Night's Rose? That's the ship I sailed to get here."

Before she could respond or continue the confession she was trying to get out, a look of confusion overcame him. "What are you saying? That Baug the Bear brought *you*—his eldest heir— on a voyage to the Lost Isle? For what? Some kind of coming of age, rite of passage?"

"No." Aenwyn shook her head. "He didn't bring me *to* the island. He rescued me from it."

All Darius could do was blink. "H-he did what? How is that…"

And as he trailed off, understanding beginning to sink into his expression, Aenwyn felt the shame creeping up her chest, the blotches of red staining her neck and cheeks.

As one of the Skogar, she had grown accustomed to the constant judgment, the ridicule, even the fear.

But it had been easier to ignore the cruelty considering she hadn't truly been Skogar.

This would be different. This would be far more personal. More painful.

"Aenwyn?" Darius ventured, cautious and hesitant. She didn't like how tight his grip remained on the hilt of his sword. "What are you trying to tell me?"

Aenwyn sucked in a deep breath and prepared to tell him her story. To tell him everything.

"I grew up here, on this island."

Aenwyn kept it as brief as she could. As much as she wanted to tell him about her mother's fondness of orchids and how their garden was always full of them, or how she'd taught Aenwyn how to thatch rooftops, forage for truffles, and— perhaps most importantly—hone her haruspicy, Aenwyn focused mostly on when her life began among the Skogar.

"For as long as anyone could remember, a fog kept the island shrouded. We couldn't see anything past it, and any time anyone would try to leave, they would just wind up back on our shores.

"But then one day, the fog lifted. It was the first time we had ever been able to see the distant shores of Grimtol—not that we knew that's what it was called—and for the rest of the day, all anyone could talk about was attempting to travel across.

"They never got the chance though."

Her hands trembled at the memory. Darius must've noticed because he came closer, his mere presence a comforting reminder that she was no longer alone. She had survived, and therefore she could find the strength to continue.

"But when the fog came crashing back, it swept over everything. I watched it consume everyone I'd ever known, including my mother." Aenwyn stared down at the hands that had saved her that day. "It would've taken me, too, if it hadn't been for—"

"You're magic?"

Darius slipped his free hand into one of hers and she nodded.

"The fog was intermittent after that day," she said, her resolve strengthening now that she was done sharing the most painful of the memories. "Every few months it would clear again. The first few times, I feared for my life. I couldn't help but think that the fog had made a mistake in leaving me behind, and that it would come back and do to me what it had done to the others."

Darius sheathed his own sword and for that she was grateful. It was just the two of them now. Not two warriors marching into battle. Not a queen and a knight. Just two, ordinary people, one baring her soul to the other.

He watched her with gentle eyes, and Aenwyn felt his acceptance. His love. And she knew she had been right to share this part of herself with him.

But she wasn't done just yet.

"Instead of the fog that came for me," she continued. "It was Baug the Bear. Him and his men arrived on a ship so large that

I thought it was another monster risen from the sea to drag me to its salty depths.

"I'd never seen a ship before then. Only the small canoes we used to navigate the streams when the fish were spawning. But I was curious and so I stayed on the shoreline to watch as the ship docked. Twenty or so men disembarked, weapons of every kind in hand. They wore skulls of dead animals as masks and head pieces. Their skin was painted with thick black ink. Their armor sparse. They were a terrifying sight to behold."

Darius snorted. "I can imagine. They're not known for being the most civilized bunch—"

She bristled at that.

"Sorry," he said hastily, apparently noticing. With a bow of his head, he urged her on. "Please continue."

Aenwyn swallowed, the memory of what happened next still frightening to recall, even though she knew it ended well enough.

"They spotted me." Her voice cracked, and for a moment, she was sixteen again. Frightened and alone. "My red hair against a backdrop of white sand made it easy, I guess. And they gave chase."

His hand drifted to the hilt of his sword as if they were there now and he was prepared to defend her to the death.

"I don't remember much of what happened next," she continued. "But Baug has recounted that day many a times. The way he tells it, those men had to fight off a feral warrior trapped in the body of a frightened, mangey, skeleton-of-a-child. I nearly killed half a dozen of them with my first blast of magic. I knocked a few more unconscious with the next. By the time I tried to summon a third, I was spent, and they finally managed to restrain me. Baug himself was among those who dragged me back to the ship, kicking and screaming the whole way."

She smiled at the memory, even though she knew she

shouldn't. Not with the way it sounded. By basic definition of the word, Baug had abducted her. In fact, the entire purpose of his voyage had been to find new land, invade it, and take their resources to strengthen Skogar.

But she could hardly hold that against the man who saved her from her isolation. Besides, his motives changed the moment he found her.

"I lucked out that the Skogar are different from the rest of Grimtol," she said, a hand floating to rest over her heart. It was aching so fiercely at the memories now. At all she had lost. All she had gained. "If it had been someone from Caelora or Irongate to cross that sea? If it had been King Everard himself who had witnessed me wielding such powerful magic? I would've been killed on the spot."

Rage simmered behind Darius' expression.

This was the man he had chosen to serve. The man he'd sworn his life to protect.

Not anymore. He didn't serve a king anymore. She knew it as well as he did.

Darius had found a queen to honor and protect instead.

She held his gaze, all of her fears dissipating at the look of sheer devotion reflected in his dark eyes. He was someone she could trust. Someone she could show her true self to, now and forever.

"But Baug was different," she said. "The Skogar are different. They wouldn't harm an innocent child, and they didn't fear magic; they revered it."

Whenever she thought back to that day, she knew Baug had never meant her any harm. If anything, he had only wanted to remove her from the gruesome conquest he'd been preparing for.

Little did he know—little did any of them know—that there was no one left to fight them.

No one but her.

"When Baug's crew returned after finding my village abandoned, he gave me a choice: I could stay here if I wanted to, or I could come with them. But before I chose, first he wanted me to understand his people. He told me how the Skogar had recently escaped slavery. How before then, they had fought in a war alongside the Sky-Blessed—the same deities that I'd been raised to worship—and how his people had defended them and their magic against the rest of Grimtol. He told me that if I were to leave with him, there would be no safer place for me than with him and his people. But more importantly, he promised that I would never be alone again."

The memory made her throat tight.

For who knew how long, she had been stranded on that island. Alone and afraid.

When she first met Baug the Bear, she'd been terrified of what they might do to her if she left with them, but even then, she'd been far more frightened of being left on that island all alone again. She would've chosen death over returning to that cold and endless solitude.

There had been only one choice for her. And after that day, Baug became her family. Him and Signe and Katla. Maybe not immediately, but she learned to trust and love them all like they were her own kin.

She missed that feeling. Missed having them around.

A tear came to her eye, and she was too late to blink it back. It fell freely, but Darius caught it with his thumb. He stroked her pale cheek before weaving his fingers into her hair.

When he drew her into him, her breath hitched.

Every part of her ached for him. Only this time, it wasn't just a longing for touch. This story had been held inside of her for so long, it was like breaking down a castle barricade just to let it out.

It left a gaping hole inside her.

The kiss they shared was gentle and brief, but it was everything she needed in that moment. Reassurance that none of it changed how he felt about her. That he still remained loyal to her.

When their lips parted ways, he pulled her against his chest, and it was perhaps even more comforting than a kiss. In his grasp, she felt safe. Steady. Secure. He wouldn't ever let he go. He wouldn't ever leave her alone.

Darius nestled his face into her auburn hair. His lips brushed the shell of her ear. "It's not easy surviving on your own after your parents are gone. It's not the way it's meant to be."

Her heart squeezed and she hugged him tighter, remembering his own loss of his mother.

"But I am not surprised to hear that you survived it."

Aenwyn pulled back to get a better look at him and found him beaming down at her.

"I doubt it's easy being back here. For me, when I return to Rayong? Even the mention of it sometimes can take me to the darkest of places." His eyes threatened to hollow, but he clung on tight to stay with her instead, to not give in to the darkness now. Cupping her chin, he tilted her head up, imploring her to do the same. "But you are stronger than this place. You've survived it once before and you'll do it again, Aenwyn Red Fury."

This conjured up a smile from her, one that he mirrored in kind.

And it was that smile, the ease with which he put her in, that convinced her to press her lips against his again. One more time before she faced the fate that awaited her. She wanted this one to last.

Before she could deepen the kiss though, Darius gave her a gentle nudge and shoved her back.

With a lopsided smile, he cleared his throat. "As much as I wish I could do that all day, we should maybe—"

"Right. The dragon. We should probably—"

"Yeah." He rolled his eyes, but she could tell it was just in good jest.

Her heart was warm, the smile on her face still bright, when the dragon's roar rumbled through the earth again.

"Are you ready?"

It took her a moment to realize the question was directed at her because she still wasn't used to being someone's equal. The king had never treated her as such. Honestly, Baug hadn't either. Maybe for the small things, but not when it came to strategies and decisions that would affect all of Skogar.

It would take some time getting used to. But she could get used to it.

And this was *her* quest, after all. They had both fought hard to get where they were.

And the fight had only just begun.

Tightening her grip on her axes, Aenwyn nodded. "Let's go."

Weapons raised, they raced into the dense woods, a place that had long ago been Aenwyn's home. Even though the trees had grown taller, the foliage thicker, the insects more insatiable, Aenwyn recognized where they were within just a few strides. This side of the island had been where they would hunt wild boar.

Or at least it had been.

As she and Darius darted between the moss-covered tree trunks and leapt over their wide-reaching roots, Aenwyn spotted no signs of the boars, nor the truffles they coveted. No upturned earth. No tracks.

She wondered if that was because the dragons had claimed this island as their own. Perhaps they had depleted the boar supply first before turning their eyes to Grimtol for their hunts. It might be why she also hadn't heard a single bird call since their arrival.

Or perhaps that was just the way the world worked: places

changed over time, as did the people who once frequented them.

She saw it then. Through the dense undergrowth. Movement up ahead.

The treetops shook as the dragon's behemoth body knocked and bumped against the trunks, the beast tramping through the forest on all fours like a clumsy mutt who had lost its way. Fortunately for them, instead of heading straight toward them, it was heading in what Aenwyn was considering west.

She held out an arm, the blades of her axe clinking against Darius' armor as he walked into and halted. The sound carried, a tinny chime that rang like a dinner bell, announcing their arrival.

They crouched, afraid to of being spotted. But the dragon paid them no mind. It might not have heard them over the clamor it was causing.

When Aenwyn glanced beside her, she found Darius's brow furrowed, his attention trained on his broadsword, as gold as his armor.

She gave him a nudge. "You're not getting cold feet on me now, are you?"

He huffed a laugh, but fell back into his thoughtfulness before replying, "I just hope we succeed where so many others have failed."

Aenwyn thought she understood then what was causing him to doubt himself. She shifted her axes into the same hand and reached out to pat his shoulder.

"Others failed because they didn't have these—" With a mischievous glint in her eyes, she gave her axes a wiggle. Then she nodded to his sword— "And that. I asked Melinae for weapons that could slay a dragon. If this is what we were given, then these will work."

"Melinae?"

"The woman I met when I drank from the goblet."

"I can't wait to hear more about that," he said, before turning his scrutiny to the sharp edge of his blade. He inspected it with different eyes now, ones full of approval. Then he leveled her with a crooked smile. "Let's see how well they work then, yeah?"

Aenwyn grinned back with feral glee.

She hadn't felt this alive since she was in Skogar, preparing for a hunt. The hunters would spend the entire day prior fasting to keep their minds alert; they would sharpen their blades to ensure swift kills; and they'd perform a variety of rituals that would bring them good fortune once they were in the wild.

They didn't have time to dance around a fire or to forage for the mushrooms Aenwyn would sometimes see Baug ingest before becoming frenzied. But she did have time to draw one of her—

Taking her grin as agreement, Darius charged from where they'd been hiding, sword at the ready.

Dragon's fire! She wasn't ready for him to be so brazen. Then again, she supposed she should've been, given everything he'd told her about Rayong and how his mother had died. He'd been waiting for this moment for years.

Before Aenwyn raced after him, she hastily drew her lines in the dirt, and called up to the Sky-Blessed. "If you can hear me, please protect us."

And then, she too was dashing out from her cover. Darius was a healthy distance away, but with the protection of the Sky-Blessed, and the mysterious power of Melinae on their side, she knew they were unstoppable.

As she sprinted forward, Aenwyn threw the second axe back into her empty hand, relishing the balanced feel once more. Up ahead, Darius was veering left, trying to round the dragon off at the front. The beast hadn't seemed to noticed them yet. They could use the element of surprise to their advantage, she thought.

So Aenywn kept sprinting forward, aiming to flank the dragon's other side.

Before she could make it further than its thick, swishing tail, she heard Darius bellow. His menacing war cry stopped the dragon in its tracks.

Aenwyn ducked beneath the swing of its mighty tail, tumbling underneath it as the dragon trained its attention on the knight charging it.

A thud carried across the way, the hollow sound reminding her of when she and some of the other Skogar would hack away at the trees, chopping them down for firewood in preparation of the brutal winters that would freeze over the kingdom in the mountains.

When the dragon roared, Aenwyn understood. No one was felling trees here. Darius's blow had struck.

They had lost the element of surprise though and would not be so lucky again.

The blue dragon kicked back onto its hind legs—legs that were just a few strides away from her. This was her moment, her time to shine. Fate had brought her all this way and she would not disappoint.

Aenwyn's legs pumped. Her grip tightened on either axe, and she charged forward like a ravenous bear.

But just as she swung her blades, the dragon shot into the sky.

In its wake, Aenwyn spotted Darius, his sword glittered with blue scales. They raced toward one another.

"You got it?" Aenwyn asked, glancing from the sky to his sword once the dragon had disappeared above the canopy.

"Not good enough," Darius grumbled. "I barely nicked the beast's ankle."

"But it worked? Your sword?"

Finally meeting her gaze, he let pride and hope stir and he nodded. "It did."

Aenwyn looked down at the axes in her hands. The blades had dragons etched into the metal, as if they were meant for this fight.

"Then let's hunt this wretched creature down and—"

Fire rained down from the sky.

Darius shielded her behind him, but it was no use. The downpour of flames encircled them, the heat trapping them inside. Over the roaring flames, Aenwyn almost didn't hear the dragon's wings as it descended from the sky, but its heavy landing shook the earth and commanded their full attention.

The blue dragon stared her down, a challenge in its serpentine gaze.

But Aenwyn wouldn't be intimidated. Not ever again. She was the Queen of Wildfire. She was the Red Fury of Skogar. Flames wouldn't hold her back now.

Battle axes raised, determination ripping through her lungs, Aenwyn charged the dragon.

But fate was a fickle creature.

Because before she could attack, the dragon's snake-like mouth opened, and words hissed from its lips. "We meet again, Aenwyn Red Fury."

Aenwyn staggered to a stop, her axes hanging limp. She hadn't expected to hear it speak. And...she swore it had addressed her by name.

But that was impossible. Dragons couldn't speak. They had no reason to. They were vile, feral creatures that knew nothing but bloodshed and violence.

Darius ran up beside her. "What's wrong?"

She was too numb to answer. Too stunned to move. But somehow she managed to force herself to look up at him and became even more shocked to find that he was entirely unchanged. His expression was still wrought with vengeance and resolve. There were no signs of the utter dumbfounded confusion that she was experiencing herself.

"Did you hear that?" she asked.

"How could I not? The entire island shook."

Eyeing him warily, she realized they weren't talking about the same thing.

"Not the roar," Aenwyn argued, taking. A cautious peek at the dragon that towered over them beyond the flames. "My name. It said my name."

"*Aenwyn,*" the velvety voice roared again.

This time, there was no mistaking it. No convincing herself of anything but the truth:

The dragon was speaking to her. It knew her by name. And, of course, the most chilling realization of all: it recognized her, the woman whose touch gave it life.

2 5

FURY

AENWYN

" I t's some kind of trick," Darius reasoned. "I've seen warriors driven to madness in the presence of their kind."

Aenwyn had never heard of such a thing though. Nor had she ever felt more level-minded.

The heat of the inferno blazing around them was oppressive. They were both squinting away from the flames.

But Darius mustered the strength to level a glare up at the blue dragon as he yelled, "You won't deter us! We came here to fight. Are you so much of a coward that you won't face us like warriors?"

The beast before them grunted, smoke billowing from its nostrils with pointed tedium. "That one is no warrior. He is but a man."

What did that say about its opinion of Aenwyn then? She was about to ask it, when Darius bellow again.

"Bring down your walls of fire and let us fight!" His grip tightened on his sword, the blade seeming molten surrounded by so much heat.

"I do not take orders from the likes of mere men," came the dragon's reply.

Aenwyn stepped forward. "Then will you take orders from me?"

"What?" Darius asked, finally sounding as confused as she was.

But Aenwyn didn't respond. She let the dragon considered her in silence, holding her breath that it wouldn't decide to simply eat them.

"Not all your orders," it finally said, and Aenwyn realized for the first time that the voice was decidedly feminine. Sultry and smooth. Rife with mockery and scorn. "But some, perhaps."

Judging from the way Darius clutched his ears, he understood none of it. Only the booming of a dragon's roar.

Aenwyn exhaled her relief but doubt quickly crept in again. None of this was going as planned. They had come all this way, endured so much, all with the goal of finding the dragon and slaying it swiftly, bringing about a dawn of peace for Grimtol.

But she couldn't very well kill a creature that had enough sentience to talk, let alone one that knew her by name and recognized her on sight. Could she?

She wasn't sure, but Aenwyn knew she had no clue how to talk to the creature, what to say, how to approach it. As far as she was aware, no one had done this before.

But if the dragon was willing to answer her questions, perhaps Aenwyn owed her to hear her out.

Slowly, reluctantly, Aenwyn lowered her axes. "If we promise not to strike you again, will you put out the flames so that we can talk?"

"Talk?" Darius snapped around to face her. "You're bargaining with it now?"

She knew what this meant to him. Understood his reluctance for she had her own reservations about it. But she wasn't sure what other choice they had.

"It's either that or let her incinerate us."

Darius balked. "*Her?*"

"Her," the dragon confirmed, drawing Aenwyn's gaze upward once more. The dragon was so close now, all she would have to do is reach her long neck through the fire to gobble them whole.

Yet, she wasn't. She hadn't.

Then again, she didn't need to. She had them surrounded by a ringlet of fire that was burning closer and closer. They were at her mercy.

Taking a leap of faith and trusting in the fate that had brought here to this moment, Aenwyn shoved the hilts of her axes into their holsters, aware of Darius' seething glare as she clasped them in tight.

"I don't want to burn alive, Darius. I don't think you want to, either." Her suppliant gaze fell upon him. "Trust me? Please?"

Where he clutched his sword, his grip might as well have been welded shut. But with quaking hands, Darius finally sheathed his sword.

The intensity of his gaze as it collided into hers, nearly knocked Aenwyn from where she stood. "I trust *you*, my queen. It's the dragon that I have little faith in."

"And the feeling is mutual," the dragon taunted.

Considering what little ground Aenwyn had been able to gain with Darius, she was grateful that he, for whatever reason, was unable to hear what the dragon was saying.

Ignoring her, Aenwyn replied to Darius, "I'm not asking you to. I'm only asking that you believe in me."

He nodded, the last sign of approval that she needed before she would begin. They were in this together now, after all.

With his approval, Aenwyn turned her attention back on

the dragon and screamed over the roaring flames, "There. The weapons are away. Douse the fire, would you?"

The dragon's tail whipped around them, the mighty weight of it crashing atop the cyclone of flames. Sparks scattered and Aenwyn shielded her face against Darius' chest.

She felt the whoosh of air around her, and when she pulled away from him, she saw that the dragon had lifted its tail away to reveal the black, singed circle in the grass surrounding them. Ashes drifted down from the sky. Darius shuddered as they landed on the brim of his nose, likely reliving the traumatic events of the last time he'd been this close to dragon fire.

"Well then?" the dragon purred. "You have come all this way, Aenwyn, Red Fury. Let us speak."

The creature was too familiar with her name. Too at-home on *her* island. She wanted to know why.

But Aenwyn knew better than to allow herself to be distracted by her personal concerns. This wasn't about her, her island, or her people. This was about the vision that had brought *her* here. That had chosen *her* to find the blue dragon and gave *her* the ability to speak with it.

Aenwyn hadn't prepared for any of this conversation, but she knew where she needed to start.

"Why can't he understand you?"

"Because he and I do not share a connection."

Aenwyn nodded, comforted to have her suspicions validated. "This is because I was the one who hatched you from your egg then, right?"

The dragon thought for a moment, its bright blue scales dazzling in the twilight. "It is more than that."

Curious. Mysterious.

Aenwyn wanted to press her further, but considering the cryptic nature of that answer, she knew it wouldn't get her anywhere.

Her neck craned as she considered the imposing creature

before them. Her gargantuan body filled the clearing and then some, the trees bowing from the robust curve of her shoulders and hips.

If the dragon wasn't as massive as the Caeloran Castle, she was at least as large as Baug's stronghold in the northernmost corner of Grimtol.

Aenwyn still remembered how small it had been. When Baug first handed her the egg, she'd cradled it between her hands, curious and enthralled with the idea of discovering what kind of creature dwelled inside.

When it had hatched, the blue dragon had curled into the center of her palm, rested there for a few hours, before bolting into the sky, and disappearing.

Aenwyn hadn't seen her again until today.

But others had. Hundreds, if not thousands, of people across Vallonde and Caelora had met their demises thanks to the dragon's reign of terror. Aenwyn had dragged their deaths around with her like a wagon full of boulders. She had always blamed herself, even though the rational part of her knew that there was nothing she could've done differently. No one could've known what had been inside that strange-looking egg.

"Why do you kill our people?" was her next question.

Beside her, Darius nodded his approval once more. Something dark churned behind his watery gaze that made her want to squeeze his hand. To tell him his mother had not died in vain and that she would have her justice.

But the longer this conversation continued, the less Aenwyn was certain.

The dragon cocked her head. "Why do you hunt? Is it not for sustenance? To survive?"

"Yes, but you've destroyed our lands. Laid waste to entire kingdoms." Aenwyn snuck a cautionary glance to her knight. "You've killed innocents. You call that survival?"

"Yes."

"Why?"

The dragon's tail flicked, and Aenwyn had to wonder if she needed to tread more carefully.

"We do what we must to keep your kind at bay," the dragon replied, irritation edging her tone.

Protection? That's what this was about? All they wanted was protection? It couldn't be that simple. The island was already safeguarded—hardly anyone from Grimtol dared approach it, for fear of the fog taking them.

Before Aenwyn could challenge the dragon's response, Darius whispered into her ear. "Ask her about the Ashen."

Confused, Aenwyn looked at him. "The Ashen? What about them?"

He mirrored her own perplexity. "What do you mean what about them? That's how they were created; I know it is. King Everard has been trying to get proof for years, but it's the only logical explanation considering they surfaced right after the Ashen came—"

The dragon sounded bored when she interrupted, "The Ashen have nothing to do with us. We are here because of the Sky-Blessed."

Aenwyn's heart lodged itself in her throat. Fear pricked her skin. The people of Grimtol hated Skogar enough for supporting the skyborn immortals. She didn't know what they would do once they found out that the Sky-Blessed were not only responsible for magic, but also the creation of dragons.

That was a lie though. She knew exactly what would happen.

War would ensue. Once more, the Skogar would find themselves caught in the middle.

Aenwyn felt her lips working before she was aware of the words coming out of her mouth. "How is that possible—"

"What is it saying?" Darius asked, interrupting her and

cutting off any opportunity for the dragon to reply. He corrected himself after a moment. "What is *she* saying?"

Aenwyn shook her head though. As if she could clear the information from her mind.

She didn't want to be the one to tell him. Didn't want to tell anyone. There had been enough suffering. Enough blame.

"*She* has a name," the dragon purred in that dangerously alluring way of hers. Like a poisonous flower begging to be plucked. "Do you care to know it? Or would you prefer to slaughter a nameless beast once our conversation has ended?"

"That's not what…"

Glancing from Darius to the dragon, Aenwyn lost conviction in her argument and trailed off. Truthfully, where this conversation would end remained to be seen. And learning of the dragon's name felt simultaneously like a trap and a missing piece of the puzzle.

"Tell us then," Aenwyn said. "What is your name?"

Beside her, Darius rolled his eyes, but Aenwyn ignored it. She kept her focus on the dragon, waiting.

Something far too clever tugged at the edges of her blood-stained, serpentine mouth. "My name is Fury."

It was Aenwyn's unraveling.

Her resolve faltered. Darius noticed because he started asking, "What is it? What did she say?"

Aenwyn could hardly hear him. The name just kept replaying in her mind and she kept telling herself that it couldn't be true. She'd heard her wrong. Or the dragon had been lying.

Fury couldn't be her name. It would be too much of a coincidence. Too alike to Aenwyn's own moniker.

"You're lying," she blurted, voice shaking.

That had to be it. It was just a trick. The dragon was using the information she had about Aenwyn's Skogar name to try to make her feel some sort of kinship toward her, to save her own hide.

"What did she say?" Darius pleaded, but the dragon replied faster than Aenwyn could.

"I am not lying." There wasn't a hint of defensiveness in her tone, nor was she taking the offense. She spoke as if it were a mere fact. "Lies are the downfall of men. I have no need of them."

A disturbing chill settled over Aenwyn's bones. She tried forcing a smile to reach her lips, but it was brittle and weak. "I don't believe in coincidences."

"I never said it was." Fury's long neck stretched up, gaze veering across the canopy, searching. "The others are named after their masters, as well."

"The others?"

Fury's golden eyes met hers. "My brother and sister."

The air caught in Aenwyn's lungs. She hadn't thought about the other dragons, one pink and one purple. Not in a very long time.

When she had first learned of the dragons and their attacks on the southern regions of Grimtol, Aenwyn had been determined to learn everything she could about them: how many there were, where they came from, how they came into being, and whether or not she was responsible for them as well. But answers were impossible to come by. And at Baug's insistence, her obsession was short-lived.

"Everyone has regrets," he'd told her once, expression unreadable as he gazed out over the frozen tundra. "But if we kept living in the past, there would be no one to build a better future."

In time, Aenwyn learned not to think about the others. Harboring the responsibility of one dragon's evil-doing was more than enough. She had convinced herself it was just the blue dragon she needed to worry about.

And so, when she found herself on the island, Fury now towering over her, she hadn't even remembered the others existed. That they and the people who hatched them might be connected like she and Fury seemed to be.

A distant part of her wondered if they were like her. If they had received visions and were on their way to the island as they spoke. She wondered if she knew them already.

Then she realized with sinking dread that the only reason they would have to come to the island would be to find their dragons, and that was assuming their dragons were here too.

"Are they—"

"Here?" Fury finished for her. Apparently, they were connected in more ways than one. "No. I sent Ink and Song away for the day."

She wanted more time to sit with their names. To rack her brain for anyone who shared a similar nickname or related hobby. But something ominous had shadowed Fury's tone at mention of her sending her siblings away.

"Why?" Aenwyn dared ask, heart thundering in her ears.

"Aenwyn?" Darius was growing impatient beside her, the unknown becoming uncomfortable for him to stand in. But he'd need to wait just a little longer.

"Hold on," she told him. Then asked the dragon again, "Why did you tell them to leave?"

"Because I knew what was coming today. I couldn't risk them being here."

Aenwyn's first thought was that Fury meant her and Darius. But then she heard it. The shouts of men in the distance.

"What was that?" she asked, neck snapping to look to Darius for an answer. It wasn't that she expected him to have one, she had just grown accustomed to turning to him in times of need. He'd proven that he was easy to rely on.

She hadn't expected to find guilt reflected in the dark gaze that met hers.

Each syllable was a shard of glass slicing her throat as Aenwyn asked again, "What's going on? What do you know?"

Never before had anyone looked so wounded and frightened. But as he reached for her, Aenwyn jerked out of his grasp.

"Please, let me explain."

Her whole world tipped sideways, her legs threatening to buckle beneath her and throw her off the world's edge.

Let him explain? She would do no such thing. She had trusted him. Shared her darkest secret with *him*. Torn her chest apart just to let him inside, and he'd been harboring...something. This. Whatever it was, he had kept it from her. Abused her trust.

There wasn't a thing he could say that would make this better because no matter the words he chose, she would never believe him again.

Aenwyn stumbled backward, putting as much distance between her and him as she could. And in so doing, she was stumbling toward the dragon.

"Wait! Aenwyn, don't!" Darius scrambled after her, his sheathed sword clanging against the armor around his thighs. "The dragon!"

"I don't care about the dragon!"

It caught even her by surprise to say it, but it was true. In that moment, she didn't care about Fury, or fate, or saving Grimtol. The only thing that mattered was the throbbing pain of her chest. The raw ache of betrayal.

She was a fool. In so many ways.

A fool who had willingly volunteered for a loveless marriage.

A fool who had bowed down to an egomaniac of a husband.

A fool who had stupidly believed she would be the one to save Grimtol—as if that would somehow give her life any meaning at all.

A fool who had been falling for a clever liar with dark eyes and dark hair and an even darker heart.

Aenwyn was well into the dragon's clearing by now.

Darius stopped advancing, hands held high in surrender. He was out of moves.

"Look, I was going to tell you—I tried telling you," he said, and Aenwyn cursed the forest, the dragon, and the men's shouting for not being loud enough to drown him out. She didn't want to hear any more of his lies. Didn't trust herself not to fall for them again.

The dragon's cool voice purred in her ears. "Listen to him now, Aenwyn Red Fury. See if he supplies the truth you deserve."

"What?"

Slowly, Aenwyn glanced over her shoulder at the large beast. Fury cocked her head, as if in challenge. As if to suggest she owed him that much.

And perhaps she did. After all, on the beach it had been Aenwyn who had shushed him when Darius said he needed to tell her something. It had been Aenwyn who insisted he wait until later, and then didn't bring it back up.

Begrudgingly, the queen shifted her glare back to the knight, and waited.

Dragging a shaky hand through his brown locks, Darius gathered his thoughts.

"I guess I'll start at the beginning?" He looked to her for confirmation, but she was unmoving. "Alright then. You were gone, remember? Three months. I didn't know where you were or if you were alive, but I knew if you'd been able to make your wishes, that one of them would lead you to this island. I just needed a way to get here."

Darius reached into his pocket and pulled out a gold coin.

"Hissa gave me this—" he said, holding it out to her. But still, Aenwyn was motionless. She wouldn't move from her spot until he convinced her otherwise, and she didn't have high hopes that he would be able to do that. "She told me to find her crew in Ilandor and that they could get me to the Lost Isle. But when I left Vallonde, King Everard and his men were waiting for me.

"They had heard of our capture. They came to settle a war."

A cold laugh shattered Aenwyn's lungs and her eyes rolled back. "Like I'd believe that. The king wouldn't care if I was taken any more than he would care if you were."

Darius shook his head. "Maybe not, but the man doesn't like being slighted. And for Vallonde, a kingdom in ruin, to steal *his* wife? *And* his personal guard? That wasn't something he was going to allow."

Aenwyn supposed not. Her husband didn't take too kindly to losing control of his things.

But she wasn't ready to admit the logic in his words yet. Not to herself, and definitely not to him.

Aenwyn folded her arms and tried not to sound as interested in his story as she was beginning to be. "And? What next?"

Darius sighed. "Will you just come here, please? We can finish talking about this once you're farther away from *that*."

Aenwyn followed Darius' watchful eye to find the blue dragon's long neck hovering just above her head. The creature could lean down and swallow her whole at this distance. Only, Fury's eyes were fixed on him. Almost as if she was on guard, defending Aenwyn from the man she now deemed a threat.

But she didn't need Fury's protection, nor did she need Darius'. Magic was crackling at her fingertips. It was violent beneath her skin. She'd never felt more charged, more ready for battle, and it remained to be seen if she would launch her magic at Fury, Darius, or whoever was on their shores.

"I'm not moving," Aenwyn ground out. Darius looked equal

parts aghast and offended. "Finish telling me what's going on here. Be quick about it."

Wiping a hand over his face, Darius started again. To his credit, he did talk faster. "In short, I had to convince your mad husband out of beheading me and instead steer him toward rescuing you."

"That couldn't have been easy."

He snorted. "That's an understatement. But I figured once I told him about your vision and your quest to kill the dragon—"

And there it was. The wrong she had been awaiting.

Red burned Aenwyn's vision. "You told him about my vision?"

But instead of looking like a boy in trouble, Darius's expression soured. It took on a pinched quality, looking grim and sorrowful.

"I'm afraid I wasn't the first," he said.

And the knot in Aenwyn's chest bound tighter. A slow heat crept from her heart up into her throat.

She tried making sense of it, but the logical side of her was being stubborn. Refusing to listen. Blocking the truth because she knew how much it was going to hurt.

"I don't understand. That's not possible. Nobody knew about the vision except you and…"

Signe's name lodged in her aching throat and her lips trembled.

Aenwyn gasped. Her hands clutched her mouth as if to prevent herself from uttering such an atrocious possibility into the world. But it didn't need to be spoken for the magnitude of it to hit her. The damage had already been done.

Signe, who had always had an aptitude for meddling and stirring up drama.

Signe who had believed competition and winning were akin to breathing and eating, the basic necessities of life.

It was all beginning to make a certain kind of unthinkable

sense. Before Aenwyn arrived in Skogar with Baug, Signe had been his eldest natural-born heir. Now she was being traded off to a horrid, ancient king who'd kept her people enslaved up until the day they freed themselves during the Rebellion.

Now that Aenwyn thought about it, she was surprised she hadn't seen it sooner. Her knees threatened to give out beneath her. But to her surprise, something thick and scaly curled around her waist, catching her before she could fall.

"Let go of her!" Darius bellowed, sword shrieking as it became unsheathed.

But Fury ignored him, her golden gaze pinned on Aenwyn. "There are more truths being kept from you. Parts of you they've stolen. Should I return them?"

A broken part of her wasn't sure how many more revelations she could handle. But she heard herself answer with unwavering certainty anyway, "Yes."

The dragon's lips twisted with cynical pleasure before she blew a cloud of smoke into Aenwyn's face, and everything faded grey.

26

WHERE ALLEGIANCE LAY

DARIUS

Even as his eyes burned, Darius refused to close them. He coughed into the crook of his elbow and swatted at the smoke with his other arm, trying to get a better view of what was happening through the sulfuric haze before him.

But part of him already knew. Part of him could sense the very same magic sizzling in the air that had taken Aenwyn after she had drunk from the wishing goblet.

The smoke cleared. Aenwyn was gone.

But somehow even more alarming was that the dragon was gone too.

Darius kicked at the earth and strode forward. He paced along the matted grass where the dragon had once been. Right here—it had been right here! Right in front of him. He'd been so close to fulfilling his goal; all it would've taken was a few more steps and Darius could've landed a killing blow and laid his poor mother's soul to rest.

Instead, he had hesitated.

For Aenwyn.

For the woman he had come to love.

And it wasn't that he regretted it—Darius was certain by

now that he would do anything for her, anything to make her happy, anything that involved standing by her side—but he didn't understand why they hadn't just killed it. Why she had wasted time talking with it instead of attacking. He didn't understand what the dragon could've possibly been saying that would've made her change her mind about slaying it. He couldn't for the life of him imagine what could redeem it after all the carnage and destruction it had caused.

It didn't matter now though.

Not only was his chance at slaying the dragon gone, but Aenwyn was too. Again.

The breeze was a cool caress against Darius' neck, and it helped to calm him down before true despair could settle in.

He turned his thoughts away from regret and panic, and toward action. Toward doing something. That would make him feel better, that would help him be useful while he waited...

Waited for what though? For Aenwyn to return?

Memories of the last time she disappeared sent his heart into an erratic staccato. Three months she'd been missing. How long would it be this time? And where would she return? She could resurface anywhere. And if she did, how would Darius go about finding her? He had no leads. No inkling of where she might've gone or would wind up next.

The only other thing he'd come to this island to do was kill a dragon that wasn't even there. How else could he pass his time? How else could he find Aenwyn, or figure out where to meet her? He didn't know, and he wasn't sure he'd find his answers any time soon.

Darius plopped to the ground, golden armor clanking against itself with sharp severity. It should've disturbed the forest, but as he sat there in the clearing, Darius didn't see a single bird flee from the trees. He hardly heard a sound outside of the armor plates grating together with his every breath.

But as he focused on the silence, Darius became aware of the men shouting in the distance again.

The Caeloran Guard. He'd almost forgotten them.

Darius sprang to his feet. He drew his sword as he raced to the edge of the clearing, pushed through the dense trees—careful to keep track of how to get back just in case he needed to—and found himself at the edge of a cliff overlooking the beach below.

Over the canopy, he could just barely make out the familiar black sails on the ship, and though he was too far away to say with certainty what the red splotches on them were, he knew all the same.

The Night's Rose was here. That meant the king and his men were, as well.

Only, Darius couldn't see a single one of them among the people he saw on and surrounding the ship. Not that he could discern anyone's face from this distance, but he could tell by the lack of Caeloran garb, the colors of the sailors matching the ship's sails instead of the earthen shades of Caelora, that the king's men had already dispersed.

He heard shouting again and realized that the commands were coming from far closer than the shoreline.

The king and his men were coming.

For a brief moment, force of habit had Darius thinking he should run toward them and share everything he'd learned about the queen, this island, and the dragon on it. For two years, he'd shoved every instinct aside and forced himself into blind obedience to a king he didn't even respect, let alone trust.

That wasn't who he was anymore.

Darius had never been sure of his place in this world. He'd never had a true calling. But now he knew where he belonged. Even if he still had a thousand questions. Even if he wasn't sure he would agree with the answers. None of that changed the fact that his allegiance, his devotion was now with Aenwyn.

Whenever he found her again, he would make sure she knew that too. Whatever path they needed to take, he would be right there beside her, even if it meant letting the blue dragon live.

That realization alone made his body light and airy. If this was what moving on felt like, what letting go of grief and sorrow could do to a man, then maybe he could get used to this.

But he would only get the chance if Aenwyn returned safely, and if the two of them could...

Darius shook his head. He didn't want to veer down that path of wishful thinking right now, but the possibility had consumed him since he ran into the king outside Vallonde: what if after all of this, they didn't have to go back to their lives.

But he was getting ahead of himself. That outcome wouldn't be possible if the king's men came rushing into battle because Darius knew that once Aenwyn and the dragon returned—and they had to return—that it would be his queen standing between a king, his army, and their goal.

Darius had to intercede them.

With the weight of his sword in hand, the knight grinned a crooked smile and said to himself before darting back into the woods, towards the shouting, "Finally, something I'm good at."

THE LIES THEY TOLD

AENWYN

Coughing away the smoky burn, Aenwyn swatted the grey plume until it cleared, and she found that she wasn't in the forest any longer.

The white landscape was an exact replica of the time she'd spent in Melinae's domain. The blinding pristineness stretched for as far as her eyes could see, in every direction she dared look.

"Not again."

Aenwyn kicked her boot at the ground in frustration, and a tuft of something fluffy and buoyant drifted up into the air. Aenwyn took a knee to investigate the strange substance she was walking on. She pulled some off with her hands. Between her fingertips it was airy and moist, but it dissipated the moment it made contact with her skin, the only evidence of its physical form was the damp residue it left behind.

"Which path will you take first?"

Aenwyn jumped upright, the booming voice catching her off guard. Her thumping heart relaxed once she realized it was only Fury.

In this never-ending emptiness, the echo of Fury's voice

boomed, sounding like an avalanche falling from all directions. But similar to the last time she was in this strange, ethereal place, Aenwyn couldn't see anyone. She could only hear and sense the presence of a being there with her.

This time, that being was Fury.

When the dragon moved, the floor moved with her. Clouds bloomed in the wake of the dragon's monstrous feet, giving the room a magical swirl.

Once Fury was completely behind Aenwyn, two paths revealed themselves to the young queen. One doorway showed a series of flashing images, many with Baug's face and the Skogar Mountains upon them.

The other door held a warm sort of darkness. Of flesh and blood. The beating of a heart pounded from its eerie, blood-red frame.

"What's in there?" Aenwyn pointed to the dark door, a sense of allure and fear guiding her curiosity. She couldn't tell if the door represented something horrible or wonderous.

"Through that way?" rang Fury's alluring voice. "The thing that was stolen from you."

"Stolen from me?" Aenwyn blinked, recalling what the dragon had said before about uncovering truths. "I thought you just meant that I'd be uncovering all the lies that had been told to me."

Though she couldn't see the dragon, she sensed its sage nodding.

"It is one in the same," Fury explained. "What has been stolen is shrouded in lies. But be warned, your fate will be changed forever should you go through that door."

It wasn't exactly the reassuring answer she'd hoped for. Let alone an illuminating one.

Glancing between the two paths, Aenwyn worried at her lip. "I can only go through one?"

"Both are presented to you. Both are choices only you can

make." The dragon shifted, coming in closer behind her. Only then did Aenwyn realize that she couldn't feel the warmth of the fire that was buried deep within it. Not even the warmth of her breath against her ear as she whispered, "Fate is not a fixed thing. There are forks in the road. Caves of darkness, as much as there are starbursts of light, that conceal all that occurs within their reaches. No one can presume to know the future, though some pretend."

Aenwyn's cheeks flushed. She had been one of those pretenders. Still was. But she had the sneaking suspicion that once she walked through one of those doors, all of that would change.

"Your fate is for you to decide," the dragon purred. "But I do believe that you are destined for greatness."

If she was being honest, Aenwyn did too.

Ever since she'd touched that dragon egg—and maybe even before. Maybe when her village had been swallowed by whatever dark force had taken them, leaving only her behind, some small part of her that wasn't consumed by grief and loneliness had known.

She *was* destined for greatness.

And today was the day the world would learn it too.

Aenwyn examined her options one last time. The unknown seemed far more terrifying than getting to see Baug's friendly-albeit-rugged face again.

Seeing as she wasn't quite ready yet to embrace whatever had been stolen from her, along with all the ways it would alter her life, she opted to go for his door first.

Without a word to her dragon host, Aenwyn made the short walk down the path toward familiarity.

The path grew colder the closer she became. With each step, she could smell the crisp Skogar Mountain air better, hear their falcons screeching as they dove for prey.

Aenwyn stared into Baug's doorway. A shiny, viscous

substance formed the outmost layer. It warbled like trickling water, but somehow didn't distort the image being reflected back to her: flashes of snowy mountain peaks, a village of wooden longhouses, familiar faces of friends she hadn't seen in over a year.

And at the center of every scene was the Skogar Chieftain himself, her father, Baug the Bear.

Tentatively, Aenwyn pressed a finger to the face of the door. Her touch disrupted the image, making the door splash around her hand as if she was putting it through a waterfall instead.

Before she could second-guess herself, she submerged the rest of her body through the opening.

On the other side, Aenwyn stepped into a wooden lodge. A dim fire crackled beneath the vaulted ceiling, the only thing that stood between her and the howling winds outside.

Even without a quick glance around, she knew exactly where she was.

The great hall in Baug's remote fortress in the north.

Only a few people knew of its exact location, and even fewer had been invited inside, Aenwyn among those on the short list. It was where he went when he needed guidance on matters that stretched beyond his capabilities, or when he feared he wouldn't be able to make an unbiased choice.

It never boded well when he needed to spend time up there.

It especially didn't bode well when he insisted on the company of all of the clan leaders.

As far as Aenwyn could tell, they were all here. Surrounding the fire, each of Baug's officials and most respected advisors had gathered for the assembly. There was Erik, the father of one of Signe's closest friends, who oversaw Dynskogar, the largest region in the mountains. Beside him sat a fearless woman named Astrid and her best seaman and trader, Torsten, who resided in Oskogar in the east and oversaw most of the kingdom's trade. The quiet and reserved Yrsa, a representative from one of the more remote villages off the Nofaskr Sea, was present as well, and eyed everyone suspiciously.

And then there was Aenwyn's uncle.

Skarde was a near spitting image of Baug—minus the bear claw scar that mangled half of his face. Skarde was responsible for keeping Reyskogar in line, their rowdiest, most rebellious territory in the south.

It was not by accident that he was given reign over their southernmost region, farthest away from his brother. And it was more than concerning to see both of them in the same room together.

Seeing as no one startled at her arrival, Aenwyn surmised that none of them could see her. It still felt strange to linger in the shadows though, so Aenwyn made her way to the place where she felt most comfortable.

She was planning on taking her usual place in the chair beside Baug, but tonight there was none. The chair was gone. There wasn't even space for one.

His throne, carved from the thickest oak tree and fashioned in one of his numerous bear pelts, was fixed at the head of their circle.

Baug had only built a new chair to fit beside his in the great hall after he'd deemed her and Signe old enough to learn about what it took to govern their people. It had usually been Aenwyn sitting in it beside him, studying all of their customs, learning about the conflicts that arose between their people, absorbing every nuance of the way that Baug led them. Signe had never seemed interested. Although in hindsight, maybe she had just been wounded that Aenwyn had received the invitation as well.

Without a chair, Aenwyn merely stood beside him. Even with him seated, they still almost saw eye-to-eye.

When Baug's hand lifted, the room quieted.

"It is an honor to host each of you in my hall tonight. Your dedication to Skogar does not go unnoticed. What we have been building here, what we aspire to keep building, wouldn't come to pass without you."

The others uttered their agreement, steins raising high overhead before they drank deeply.

All except for one.

Uncle Skarde folded his arms across his broad chest and interrupted everyone before they could finish drinking.

"I can't speak for these swine—" his smile was a crooked thing when he elbowed Erik—the scrawny man with a blond beard—making him spew his drink into the fire— "but I for one didn't come here to have flowers shoved up my arse. Are you planning on telling us what this is about?"

The others peered up from their steins, the room fraught with silence.

Aenwyn prepared for Baug to assert his dominance. He'd once told her that sometimes a leader had no choice but to exert their power to keep people in line, though a good leader knew how to rule with patience and kindness most of all.

Her father chose the latter now, wiping a hand over his weary face as he tried ignoring the bait from his unscrupulous younger brother.

Even though this memory was years old, somehow Baug seemed even older than the last time she'd seen him. Untold sleepless nights had left his scarred, peppered face weathered and tired beyond his years. And the flickering shadows of flames from the fire weren't helping.

"Fair enough, brother," Baug said at last, voice as tired as he looked. There was no fight left in him. Which only meant that whatever was ailing him had to be dire. "I've made you trek this far out. Might as well get on with it then. Eh?"

Baug guzzled down the contents from his own stein before glancing out at the group of people sitting around the fire.

315

"One of the seers had a vision," he said at long last. "About the fate of a girl."

No one uttered a word. The room hung on his every breath, waiting for Baug the Bear to tell them more.

Aenwyn, however, felt as if her skin were screaming. She could already guess what *girl* he was speaking of, and she didn't like what that meant for what she was about to hear regarding their supposed chance encounter all those years ago.

"There's an island," he continued, tortured gaze pinned to the fire. "The people who live there will soon be taken. All except a girl. The seer said she saw us saving the girl. She said if we did, she would bring about the rise of Skogar."

Their pleased faces answered him, only one among them seeming wise enough to question what sounded too good to be true.

Skarde leaned forward, an elbow planted on either knee. "Tell us why that's been keeping you up at night."

Baug loosed a shaky sigh. "Many reasons, brother. The first being because this island is tucked away beyond the Bay of Lost Souls."

Murmurs erupted.

The Skogar people were a suspicious lot, so it was unsurprising that so many of them would be outraged by the idea of sending anyone across the doomed sea. Too many ships had tried and failed to see what was beyond the Bay of Lost Souls already, the fog too dense, a curse lingering there that swallowed every vessel that had ever attempted the journey.

As far as Aenwyn knew, Baug's voyage had been the first to make the trip successfully. But even after his return, few dared to make it again. Some superstitions, especially ones rooted in truth, never died.

But that voyage hadn't happened yet. Of that, she was sure.

What he was suggesting, was for them to willingly, blindly go on a suicide mission.

Baug commanded silence with his rough hand again. He didn't answer them quickly enough though and his brother was becoming impatient.

"And the other reason?" Skarde demanded, fingers weaving together. They pressed into each other so firmly that his skin was paling around his black tattoos.

Baug's expression darkened, the torment visible in every crease and shadow of his face.

"The other reason is because before Skogar can rise, this girl's magic will bring about a dawn of darkness."

Aenwyn felt something sharp snap inside her.

This couldn't be true.

She didn't want darkness. She wanted liberation.

But the possibility of her dooming the people wasn't even the most unsettling part of this experience.

Baug hadn't known she was on that island. That's what he'd told her. He'd said that they'd found her by chance. By some dumb stroke of luck, the fog had lifted on the exact same day that they'd been fishing out at sea, and when they'd seen it rise, they seized the opportunity to explore the unknown. It hadn't been a planned expedition. In fact, he'd told her that when they'd left Skogar, he hadn't been anticipating returning back with one more mouth to feed, a new daughter to raise as his own.

But if this vision—this memory—was to be believed, all of that had been a lie.

Everything had been a lie. Everything she thought she knew about him, about her life in Skogar, it was all wrong. All of the people in that room—many of whom she'd come to know and trust, had considered family—they'd known about this prophecy as well, they knew it was what had led him to find her, and yet no one had bothered to tell her.

They'd treated her like any other Skogar. And that made their betrayal hurt all the more.

Before she could hear another word, Baug's great hall faded, giving way to another familiar room of power and prestige.

Now Aenwyn was standing in the king's dining hall in Caelora Castle. At the end of the long table, backlit by a beautiful sunrise that could be seen through the opened window, sat King Everard.

The table was set for two, but there was a feast befitting an entire kingdom splayed out before him.

Yet he sat alone.

His slender finger tapped on the varnished wood.

A door cranked open behind her, making Aenwyn jump.

"You're late," King Everard grit out at the man who entered.

Baug's heavy footsteps thundered, the silverware quivering on the porcelain plates as he strode across the long room.

"You're just as cheerful as I remember you," Baug said before sliding his chair out. The legs scraped along the floor as much as the horrid sound did against Aenwyn's spine, and he took his seat beside the king.

He didn't wait for an invitation to begin. Baug simply dug into the feast.

Before long, his plate was piled high with charred ribs, steamed potatoes, stewed carrots, and anything else within reach.

The king was embarrassingly small next to Baug the Bear, the great Skogar Chieftain. Aenwyn remembered how she had once gazed upon him like a god. Now she could hardly stomach to look at him. Either of them.

King Everard seemed to be struggling as well, but he managed to fix a death glare on the man across from him.

Baug minded him none. There was only one trained, ruthless warrior in the room—as far as either of them were concerned—and it most certainly was not the young king, freshly crowned and deeply drowning in his own grief and sorrow.

"So—" Ferocious as his moniker, Baug bit into a lamb leg. Aenwyn could hear the creature's flesh tear from bone even from across the room. "You agreed to meet. That's a start."

Blood dripped down Baug's beard, and she was surprised to see him wipe it away, even if it was on the back of his arm.

King Everard's lips pursed to keep his likely cruel thoughts to himself. However long ago this moment was, he had already learned how to play the game, how to pretend to be an expert in civility whenever he was in the room with other people.

The king dragged his glare away from Baug and began serving himself. "It was my father's goal to make peace with all the kingdoms of Grimtol, as it shall be mine."

"Oh yeah?" Baug sunk his teeth into another bite and ripped at the juicy meat. "Is that what you tell the Ashen when they plead for the release of their princess?"

Now this was information that was new to Aenwyn.

She didn't know much about the Ashen Princess. Come to think of it, she didn't know much about the Ashen. It seemed like no one did. They were the arisen Sky-Blessed who had fallen brutally in battle during the War of Destruction, as Baug had called it, and the Battle for Freedom, as the Caelorans revered it.

Their touch created death. That was all Aenwyn knew. She certainly wasn't aware of an Ashen Princess being kept in the Caelora dungeons.

Baug wasn't bluffing though. King Everard's face said it all.

He had gone so pale that if he'd been thrown into a plague pile, he'd have easily been mistaken for one of the dead.

The effect didn't last long. His ire was quick to burn his cheeks the color of hatred. His fingers started tapping again.

"How did you know about the Princess Elora?"

"Before he died, your father was spotted making deals in Vallonde, asking around for substances that could negate magic." Baug looked up with a rather smug gin, lips smacking as he chewed on a decadent piece of meat. "There isn't much I don't know, little king. Remember that when I tell you the rest of what I've come here to say."

The king leaned back in his seat, hands gripping the armrests. "Very well. I vowed to hear what you have to say, so let us get on with it."

The now-bare lamb leg thudded on Baug's plate when he discarded it. With his mouth grotesquely full, he haphazardly pawed his filthy fingers onto the even filthier leather armor covering his thighs before reaching for the goblet in front of him. It was empty, having already drained the lush wine, but he made quick work of refilling it. He chugged the entire draft, smacking his lips when he was finished.

To King Everard's credit, he mostly hid away his disgust.

Baug finally said, "I come offering a proposal of marriage."

It was not the direction she'd seen this conversation going. As far as she knew, the proposal for her hand had all occurred through letter.

The depths of his duplicity just kept sinking deeper, and she was at the risk of being buried in the sands.

Aenwyn had to force air into her lungs. She had to drag herself out of the quicksand threatening to pull her under.

This time, the king's attempts to restrain the truth of his revulsion were futile. Aenwyn knew better than anyone how much this man loathed her people. What Baug was suggesting, a union between the civil Caelorans and the heathen Skogar, was likely the most abhorrent idea for his future that King Everard had ever fathomed.

"I—appreciate the offer," he stammered, slowly regaining his poise and control. "But I'm afraid it is still early in my reign. My people and I are still in grief over what happened to my mother and father—"

"No better time for a wedding. In my experience, a joyous

celebration is exactly what a kingdom needs after suffering so much. A reminder that life isn't always as glum as it can be."

The king looked as if it made at least a modicum of sense to him, though Aenwyn wasn't sure if he was convinced quite yet.

King Everard kept a wary eye on his visitor. "And you're offering the hand of one of your daughters?"

"Aye."

Dragging a hand through his golden hair, King Everard made a face that suggested he was considering the offer. "Do I get to choose?"

Baug shook his head. "I'm afraid not. There's only one daughter I'm offering. But I promise, she's the one you want."

"Pray tell, Baug the Bear, what makes you so certain you're familiar with my desires of women?"

The Skogar Chieftain leaned all the way back in his chair, the width of him squeezing between the armrests. His expression was arrogant as he folded his arms over his full belly, as if they were playing a game that he'd already won.

"Because, King Everard, I'm not talking about what you desire in women. I'm talking about what you desire for your legacy as king."

Aenwyn couldn't believe what she was witnessing. Baug the Bear, the man she'd called Father for the last few years, orchestrating her entire betrothal after making her believe that it was of her own doing.

How had he fooled her so thoroughly?

King Everard's piqued interest outweighed his healthy suspicion. "Go on."

The eyes tucked in Baug's weathered face twinkled. "My seers witnessed the future. They saw my daughter, Aenwyn, not only with your child, but also leading you to the dragon responsible for the death of your family. They saw you kill it."

Her skin went cold. Baug knew what she'd been destined

for? He'd known all along, and he had sent her to Caelora anyways?

She hardly had enough time to process though, for what he said next was far more heartbreaking.

King Everard shifted in his seat again. Maybe he was trying to appear taller, larger, more imposing, considering the power in the room was clearly imbalanced. "And this...Aenwyn. Is she pretty?"

Baug's cordial nature disappeared in the blink of an eye. His elbows slammed against the table as he leaned across it. "Are you suggesting I would have anything but beautiful daughters?"

"No, no." The king paled. "It's not that. Our people—we live by different conventions and standards—What I mean is, the ladies of Caelora share a certain...civility."

Now Baug rose from the table, towering over the small king like a shoe about to squash a pathetic ant.

"Are you calling us uncivilized? After everything I'm offering you."

The king closed his eyes, collected himself. When he opened them again, he rose like someone knew, like he had been reborn.

"My apologies, Baug the Bear. I meant no offense. I merely meant to indicate the cultural differences between our people. I am wary of accepting a bride who would feel out of place in my kingdom."

The Skogar chieftain eyed him for a moment before sitting back down and continuing his feast. "Aenwyn is good at adapting."

The king nodded. "And what about...magic. I know your people treat it differently, but here in Caelora it is still illegal."

Baug finished chewing before reaching into his pocket. From where she stood, she couldn't see what he pulled out and slid across the table. Not until the king held the dainty thing up in his hand.

322

"That ring is made from hailstone. The same substance your father purchased to build his prison cells. It'll keep Aenwyn's magic contained."

With no warning, the two men were swallowed in a whirl of grey and black.

"No!"

Aenwyn shouted, a hand reaching for her husband and her father as if to anchor herself in that moment. She wanted to hear more. Wanted to listen in on their scheming just a little longer to hear just how much instruction Baug had given him. She wanted to know just how much of the last year they'd orchestrated.

Not that she needed to see it. She already had her answers. She knew where that story led.

An unfulfilling marriage.

A childless home—which served them both right.

And a reckless quest to slay a dragon.

A dragon, who, Baug was trying to get King Everard to slay because... Because that would be the cataclysm to Skogar's rise and the downfall of the rest of the continent. That was the reason he'd wanted to arrange their marriage. He was playing his part, trying to aid fate in the ways that would suit him and his people best.

Aenwyn wasn't sure she could allow it. She didn't like her life being played with by the likes of men.

The darkness faded, giving way to light once more, until Aenwyn found herself standing in the white realm again.

This time, she felt more alone than usual, the hollowness in her heart feeling as if it were a void that had cracked open inside of her. She fell to her knees and sobbed. Hot streams of tears and shuddering breaths. She hadn't cried so hard since the day she lost her whole village.

"Betrayal is a heavy price for uncovering truths." Fury's voice brushed up against her, gentle and kind. "But I have found that life is less about the act of learning, and more about what one does with the knowledge they uncover."

Aenwyn could hardly hear her over her ragged breaths.

First Signe's betrayal. Now Baug's. Even King Everard was in on it.

Was there no one on her side? No one she could count on *not* to betray her?

Aenwyn wasn't sure how much more she could take. Pressure built inside of her, and it needed a release. But there was none. There was no way to relieve the agony that was tearing her up inside.

She'd always wondered why the majority of Grimtol had deemed him a brutal savage incapable of any amount of human decency.

Now she understood.

Now she saw the truth.

Baug, like all men, just wanted control. They only wanted to use her in whatever ways they could to amass their power.

King Everard only saw her as a means to an end. Their marriage had forged an alliance between Caelora and Skogar, created new trade in the kingdoms, and completed the image he'd been trying to uphold of a peaceful, kind king that the people could trust. All that was left was for her to produce an heir. If she could see him now, the first thing she'd tell him would be how she bargained away her chance of ever continuing his line, and she'd tell him with a smile.

Baug had been no better than her husband. In some ways, he'd been worse.

At least King Everard had never tricked her into believing that he loved her. That she was an important part of his family.

"When you are ready." Fury's voice was like the crackle of fire against her back. "One more door awaits you, should you choose to step inside."

Aenwyn's fists clenched at her sides.

The time of men withholding from her what she was rightfully owed was over. She was tired of them making all of her decisions for her. Tired of them taking away her power. Keeping her in the dark.

Today was the day she stopped blindly listening to them all.

Today she forged her own path. Never minding fate. Never minding the desires of small men like King Everard and Baug the Bear, and any others who might otherwise try to hold her back.

Today, Aenwyn chose for herself what path lay ahead of her. And although she'd come to this island prepared to fight and slay the blue dragon, that path no longer appealed to her.

Fury had shown her honesty when so many others had lied to her.

Fury had given her choice and power through knowledge.

There was something more to Fury's story that Aenwyn didn't yet understand. But first, she needed to complete her own.

And with her head held high, in defiance and in glory, Aenwyn stepped through the second door.

28

FURY AND FLAMES

AENWYN

This time when Aenwyn emerged, she wasn't in some distant, faraway land. Not hidden in the great hall of Baug's remote fortress, nor surrounded by a decadent feast behind the ornate castle walls of Caelora.

The hazy film that had distorted her surroundings earlier was gone.

Now she was surrounded by woods as familiar as her favorite wooden toy as a child.

She was back on the island. Aenwyn was home. The only true home that she'd ever had, and likely ever would.

The sting of Baug's betrayal was still raw, but she had bigger problems at the moment.

The dragon and Darius were gone.

Or at least, she was no longer with them in the clearing.

Aenwyn twisted around to get a better sense of where she might have reappeared. She'd spent so many hours exploring this island in her childhood and foraging in her youth that she knew all the landmarks. But it was still dark, night pressing down upon the forest as thick as smoke.

She tried to catch her bearings anyway, straining to catch a glimpse of anything that might be helpful: moonlight reflecting off the calm lake on the southern side of the island, the white bark of the birch trees that were common on the western side, the scent of truffles and manure where the boars liked to forage.

But her efforts were to no avail, and only served to exhaust her.

Moving at all felt far more strenuous than it should've been. Aenwyn's lower back screamed as if she had been trying to lift a boulder as heavy as a castle. Exhaustion pulled on her, making the heels of her feet throb and her knees beg for relief.

There was an oddness to her lethargy. A strangeness to the sensation that made her own body feel foreign. Different. Like her movements weren't her own. Like something about her had changed.

With dread creeping into her bones, Aenwyn mustered up the courage to finally glance down at herself.

A gasp tore from her lungs at what she found.

The leather armor she was wearing had split up the middle, her belly bursting through the tattered opening. She could no longer see her toes from over the robust curve of her extended stomach. And though she knew what it meant for her body to look as it did, there wasn't a single part of her that could make sense out of what she was staring at.

Aenwyn placed a trembling hand over her pregnant belly. The firm skin beneath moved. Something inside reached out to her, and with the dragon's mocking words inside her mind, she knew what it was.

The thing that was stolen from you.

Something told her this wasn't about the wishing goblet. After all, the being she'd met in that place hadn't *stolen* anything from her. They had made a willing trade. One that, given the extensive challenges Aenwyn had faced with her own fertility, she was fairly certain the consequences of which hadn't pertained to her, just to her sisters.

No, this wasn't about the wishing goblet.

This was something that had happened before. She was sure of it. In fact, the more Aenwyn thought about it, the surer she became. Everything about her life started to make sense when she looked at herself through the lens of someone who'd been cursed—not just having her ability to create life taken, but in having a family at all. Aenwyn's own mother had been taken from her. Her father, long before that. And now Baug, and Signe, and Katla as well, their love but a façade until they had been able to get rid of her.

But why? Why would anyone have cursed her to live such a bleak existence without a family of her own?

Aenwyn supposed it didn't matter now. The dragon had given it back. Whatever *it* was. The baby, sure. But perhaps if she had been cursed, if the notion of family had been taken from her, maybe now she was to receive it back. Maybe if she took the time to explore, she'd find her mother somewhere here on the island. Or maybe the next time she saw Baug and her sisters, everything would be righted and restored to the way she had remembered it.

But Aenwyn knew better than to let hope build into the treacherous thing that it could become.

For now, she would stay focused on what she knew to be true: there was a baby in her belly. And from the looks of it, it would soon be making its way out into the world.

She feared what that meant, if her time with the dragon had been yet another account of her disappearing for months on end without any awareness of doing so.

She feared what it meant for Darius. If he was still on the island, waiting somewhere for her. If the dragon had put an end to him. Or if he'd completed the task that they'd come there to finish.

She feared what it meant for herself to be stranded on an island, perhaps only days away from labor.

Before she could form a plan of action, a man spoke behind her.

"There you are my queen. I've been looking all over for you."

An icy claw of fear dragged along her spine.

Aenwyn spun around, eyes wide as she slid her gaze to where King Everard stood a few paces away. There was a lethality to his regal presence, an elegance to him that promised bloodshed. As much of a vision as he was, there was nothing beautiful in the hateful depths of his eyes. Eyes that promptly noticed the belly she was clutching.

King Everard's irritation soared. Aenwyn knew then that if it weren't for the baby, he might've killed her on sight. And somehow, that made her sadder and more terrified for their unborn child than it did for herself.

Her husband shoved his sword at one of his knights who fumbled to grab it as King Everard marched forward, demolishing the space between them. He seized her wrist, opening her arms to get a better look at her like she was livestock ready to be purchased at the market.

The hand he placed over her belly was possessive. His inquisition of her body, of what lay beneath her skin, was assessing.

Then his malicious glare climbed ever so slowly to meet hers. "You're with child? My own heir?" Even with his teeth clenched, his voice shook with rage. "You knew you had *my* heir in your belly, and you went on this foolish quest anyway?"

A year of marriage had trained her to cower. It had taught her to bow and obey him for fear of ever angering him to the point that he might hurt her.

But that year had been almost entirely erased by the time since she'd left the castle.

Aenwyn wasn't the same person anymore. She was no longer bound to him in her eyes. She was bound to Grimtol, to her baby, and to protecting the dragon that have given her back her life.

He thought he knew fury? Aenwyn had been named after hers. Baug had once joked that her fiery temper was why her hair blazed like dragon's fire.

Aenwyn tore out of the king's grasp. Unfortunately, she was so unaccustomed to her new figure that the effort almost toppled her over. But she regained herself, and never lost her fire.

"Don't act so surprised," she snapped, recalling everything she had witnessed behind the door of truth. Everything the dragon had shown her. "This is what you signed up for, isn't it? A bride in exchange for an heir and a dragon."

Something like surprise flickered across his face. It had been so long since she'd outwardly shown her disdain for him, perhaps he had forgotten what it was like to be on the receiving end of her sharp tongue. Or perhaps more likely, he hadn't expected her to figure out his secrets.

But King Everard was a master of masks when needed. And right now the two of them had an audience of loyal subjects who he couldn't afford to ruin his image in front of. After all, he was expected to play the role of the worried husband who'd dragged his men across the continent and to the edge of the realm just to find her. And so that was the role he would play.

"I'm just so grateful to have found you," he said with a voice so sweet, she might've believed him if she didn't know any better. Before she knew it, Aenwyn could hardly breathe from being squeezed so tightly in his embrace. But that cold, unfeeling voice of his slithered into her ear, so quiet that no one else could hear. "An outburst like that again will cost you gravely, dear wife."

For an entire year, that threat had kept her silent and frightened.

She'd stayed in line, terrified that one wrong move could cost her more than just her own marriage, but the entire alliance between Caelora and Skogar.

Let them all burn, for all she cared.

"What in the Hollows happened to your eyes?" he spat, jaw clenched as he started to pull back. His grip tightened, jerking her nearer again. "Is this your magic?"

Aenwyn bared her teeth and jerked out of reach. "Let go of me!"

The men with the king were easily as shocked as he was to witness such a blatant sign of disrespect, to see anything but blind obedience and affection from her.

No more.

She stood her ground. With or without him, she was a queen. She was as grounded as a mountain, as fierce as wildfire, and as powerful as the sea. There was nothing he could do to stop her.

And though his lips were a taut line of violent, quiet rage, she could tell he knew it too. He could no more control her than a sailor could control a storm. She was only sorry it had taken her this long to figure it out.

But of course, it would be at that very same moment that fate would so cruelly intervene.

Aenwyn's belly tightened. A pulse of pain tightening around her spine.

She didn't scream—not yet anyway. That would come later.

But she did whimper, her hands cradling her aching back and belly.

And though she would always remember King Everard as a heartless, egotistical, child-of-a-man, at least in that moment he did the noble thing and rushed to her side.

"Somebody help her!"

The order was obviously not for her benefit, but instead was said for the benefit of their soon-to-be-born child who would be his heir. But she was grateful for it anyway. She didn't want to do this alone. She'd already spent so much of her life doing things alone.

However, she was less grateful when three knights snatched her out of the king's grasp.

"Take her somewhere safe while I see to the dragon."

As they carried her away, Aenwyn craned her neck to watch which direction he was headed. She waited until he had disappeared behind a thicket of trees.

"Let go of me!" Once the contraction subsided, Aenwyn wrenched within their hold, but it was of no use. Only one thing would make them relent. "Unhand me now or I will use my magic and force you."

All it took was a raise of her hand, a flurry of wind twisting in her palm. The guards practically dropped her. Fortunately she'd been ready for that and caught herself before she could fall.

"Well? Don't just stand there gawking. Go protect your king!" When they didn't appear to be moving, she added, "He's about to face a dragon that has killed thousands. I'm only giving birth. Which one of us do you think needs the protection of trained knights right now?"

If she hadn't convinced them enough, the screeching roar of the dragon in the distance did the trick.

The three knights scrambled toward it, after their king.

In between worsening contractions, Aenwyn staggered after them. She wasn't entirely sure why. The king and his men would most certainly reach Fury first and they'd either kill her or be killed before she would make it to them, neither of which Aenwyn wanted to witness.

More than anything, she wanted to find Darius.

She was still furious with him for having led King Everard

to these shores and not telling her sooner, but it seemed to pale in comparison to the other betrayals and lies she had uncovered.

Besides, she didn't want him worrying. The last time she had disappeared, it had agonized him. She could see it on his face as clear as day when he had finally found her after all those months. She didn't want him to suffer like that again.

Another wave of pain rocked her, this one bringing Aenwyn to her knees.

The contractions were becoming fiercer. They were closing in on each other, as well.

It wouldn't be too much longer now.

Aenwyn had already torn off her leather armor, discarding it in her wake as she hobbled through the deserted woods. She had liberated herself from her trousers as well, leaving nothing but the long undershirt to contain what little modesty she cared to hold onto.

For what felt like hours, Aenwyn dazedly ambled and crawled her way through the dark forest. Before dusk had come, she'd felt her way by hand and moonlight alone, but there was at least some light to help guide her.

Every once and awhile, she'd hear Fury's cry again. No words accompanied it, but at least she knew the dragon was still alive. There was still time to find her, to get her to explain what she had done and why.

Not to mention, Aenwyn needed to warn her about the Caeloran force on her shoreline.

As if in answer to either her wishful hoping or her latest agonizing cries as another contraction assaulted her, the whooshing of air sounded above.

Fury's powerful wings flapped, massive gusts of wind rolling over Aenwyn where she squatted in the dirt.

The mighty dragon landed with a thud that could be heard across the island.

Aenwyn glanced up in greeting, teeth clenched, but it was about all she could muster. She rode the wave of pain until it subsided enough for her to finally speak, but she was so weary, she collapsed instead. Exhaustion was a blissfully alluring creature. And she wanted nothing more than to give into its temptation, to close her eyes and rest before the next bout of agony would come. Surely, nothing was more important than a quick nap.

"It has to be you." Fury's serene and wise voice dragged Aenwyn from the outskirts of slumber.

"Hmm?"

"It needs to be you to take my life. No one else."

Aenwyn wasn't sure if she was in a dream or not, but she responded anyway. "Why?"

"Only you can end this. Break the cycle. Restore truth upon the lands."

Even in her haze, drenched in sweat and her body aching from head to toe, Aenwyn wanted to be the hero. She wanted to be the savior of Grimtol. The person who broke whatever cycle Fury spoke of and restored truth to the lands—whatever that meant. After her own encounter with learning hidden truths today, that was a destiny she could get behind.

If only she could rise.

"I can't kill you," she groaned, eyes fluttering, begging to go back to that quiet place in her mind. "I don't even have a sword." Her weapons had been the first things she'd discarded in her undressing.

"You don't need one. Ancient magic flows within you. Use it."

At that, Aenwyn barked a delirious laugh. "I can barely sit up, let alone summon magic right now."

The dragon paused for a moment. "I can speed up the process."

As tempting as that sounded, Aenwyn wondered again at the allure of things that sounded too good to be true.

"Won't that hurt the baby?"

Fury stepped closer, her large head leaning down. The heat that radiated off her was oppressive. Aenwyn would've rather her been made from ice in that moment. But she lifted her head to give her the courtesy of looking at her.

"That babe is strong. She will live on to do great things."

But Aenwyn only heard one thing, her eyes brimming with joyous tears. "*She?*"

Happiness bloomed around her heart unlike anything she'd ever known. Though Aenwyn had only been pregnant for a matter of moments, she'd had plenty of time to consider what it would be like to raise a child, to have a family of her own. And though her duty as a wife was to provide the king with a male heir, she'd always feared the possibility. How easy it was for men to mold their sons into men who resembled them. Cruel. Selfish. As charming as vipers.

But a girl? A girl he'd have no interest in. He wouldn't need to groom her for the throne. She would be all Aenwyn's to love and cherish and nurture.

Tears burned her eyes as she stared deeply into the dragon's. "Do it. Make this labor quick, and I'll do anything. I'll be the one to slay you, if that is what you wish."

It was only then that Aenwyn heard herself. Heard the conversation they were having. Labor had blurred her mind. She hadn't realized what the dragon was asking until she had already agreed to it.

There was no time to interrogate Fury further.

The dragon blew her smoke. Aenwyn inhaled it. And soon the worst contraction of all hit her.

Aenwyn was flung back against the dirt, spine arching. She tried containing the scream behind her clenched teeth—she didn't want to alert the army of where she was—but this time she could do no such thing.

Her pain had a mind of its own. It rammed itself through her clenched jaw and breeched the dusk sky.

Aenwyn pushed with everything in her, but she knew this was only the beginning.

There had been many a night she had been kept awake while the women in her village and in Skogar had endured their labors. It was not a quick endeavor. Sometimes, they would scream for hours. Days even. Aenwyn could only hope that hers would be one of the quick ones.

The contraction ended, and Aenwyn fell still, utterly spent.

She would have drifted off to sleep then, if it weren't for the battle-cry that erupted across the field.

"Where is she!"

Sword raised high above his head, Darius charged for the dragon. His roar was a curse of death. A vow of vengeance.

Fury screeched, a sound that was both a warning and a plea. Then her mighty wings carried her up and into the sky, and she said to Aenwyn, "I will find you when the babe is born."

Without Fury standing between them, Darius laid eyes upon Aenwyn, and his rage deflated. He finally saw her then, half-dressed and sprawled in the dirt floor.

When he sheathed his sword, he was already racing to her side. His worried gaze took every inch of her in.

"What in the Hollows happened?" Though horror edged his words, only concern reflected back in those dark eyes as he skidded to his knees beside her. He slid a gentle hand behind her head and lifted her, supported her. "You disappeared again. I thought I asked you to stop doing that."

The smile that started to grow soured into a wince as she forced herself to sit up.

"Careful—" he started, and her scowl at his protectiveness

ruffled his feathers. "You can't expect me not to be concerned right now. Look at you. You're—"

"With child?"

He balked at the venom in her tone. "Yes, with child. But you don't have to say it like that."

"Like what?"

The muscles in her stomach were tightening again, another contraction on the horizon. Arguing with him was the last thing she wanted right now, but she needed to hear him say it. She needed to know where he stood.

The storm in his eyes settled and he reached up to cup her cheek. "Like I'm some bad guy who would be upset at you for this. I'm just worried, Aenwyn. And rightfully so, given the circumstances."

Aenwyn felt herself softening to his touch. Leaning into it. Savoring his presence and warmth.

Just in time for another battle to wage war inside her.

The contraction came on quickly, her entire stomach becoming so tight she felt as if a boulder had been thrust inside of her. A boulder that she wanted out. Now.

Aenwyn clenched every part of her. Toes. Teeth. Hands. When she realized Darius' fingers were wrapped around her own, she worried she might snap them off. But he wouldn't let her shake them free. He clung to her, and she to him.

When it finally ended, he caught her in his arms and held her close.

He brushed the hair off her sweat-slicked forehead. "So, the dragon gave you a baby."

Panting, she did her best to answer. "No. Said it was stolen. She gave it back."

"*Gave it back*," he quoted to her. "Cursed sky, what does that mean?"

"I don't know."

Silence surrounded them. The comforting kind that made

her feel as if she was floating in a calm lake, sunlight basking down atop her. With Darius to watch over her, to take care of her, perhaps Aenwyn could finally get the sleep she so desperately craved.

Despite the heaviness of her eyelids and the weariness of her bones though, she knew that wasn't happening. They had too much to catch up on. They had a realm to save.

"My father—" she started, but the word tasted too bitter. She corrected herself. "Baug the Bear, he used me."

Something primal flickered from the darkest depths of his eyes, the only indication that he caught her correction as well. He didn't ask her about it though. His hands just kept working, one brushing the hair atop the crown of her head while the other held her upright.

"Used how?" he asked.

"A seer told him where to find me," she told him, and she had to fight against the urge to close her eyes as she sank into the bliss that was being cradled in his lap. If she had to rake a hot iron poker over this freshly torn wound, then there was no other place she'd rather be than right here in his strong and capable arms. "She told him that I would be the demise of the continent but help Skogar rise in power."

The hand in her hair faltered, but only for a moment. "That might have motivated him to come for you. But it doesn't mean he still didn't—"

She knew what he was trying to do for her. And as gentle and as kind as it was for him to want to salvage her image of the man who'd been her father for the past few years, she couldn't allow him to do that. There was more to the story. Unforgivable parts that he didn't know yet.

"Baug told the king about the seer's vision—at least the parts that would entice him enough to want to stoop low enough to marry me."

"No one would be stooping to marry you."

Her face flushed and her stomach tied itself into knots. Or perhaps that was just the next contraction barreling into her.

She squeezed his hand and screamed. Aenwyn torqued herself up, hoping the pressure from her top half would magically force the baby out. It didn't, but she did think she felt the first signs of tearing, the crown of the baby's head beginning to poke through.

This time when the latest contraction subsided, a new pain replaced it. Something sharp and almost more unbearable than the actual contraction itself.

Forehead slick with sweat—and maybe with blood from the blood vessels she was sure had popped along the crease of her brow as she'd screamed for the baby to vacate her broken body —Aenwyn collapsed back into Darius' lap.

There was little reprieve between the contractions now though, and comfort was not in her near future.

She wanted a distraction. Needed something to bring her out of her body for just a moment.

"We can't let them kill the dragon."

Darius swallowed. "We can talk about it later—"

"No!" Aenwyn huffed. "Now."

He exhaled deeply, looking like he already regretted arguing with a woman in labor. "That dragon has killed a lot of people. It wouldn't be such a bad thing if it died."

She blinked up at him, forced him to hold her strained gaze. "Except that if the dragon dies, it will mean the downfall of the continent."

"What?"

"The seer," Aenwyn said, wincing and clutching her belly. She tried not fearing what it meant for the baby that this pain had hit her now. "It was part of her vision. I lead the king to the dragon. The dragon dies. The kingdoms fall."

He stammered, searching for the right words. "Then don't?"

The only response she'd give him was a lingering glare.

Surely by now, after spending so much time with her, he had more than a basic understanding of how visions worked. She saw glimpses of the future. So did Baug's seer. It was unlikely that anyone could change what she had seen come to pass. Not now that all the players were on the island.

The way she could see it, albeit through hazy thoughts addled by searing pain, they only had one choice.

The next contraction attacked. Aenwyn bared down, pushing with all her might.

Amid the pain and screams that tore from her, Aenwyn hardly felt the ground quake as Fury landed before them.

"The baby will come soon," the dragon said to no one but her. "Then I will share with you what I know of everything."

If she wasn't motivated to birth this child before, that was enough to push her over the edge.

With Darius supporting her back, Aenwyn was able to rock to her feet. She felt more powerful, more capable, to be squatting rather than lying flat on her back like a dead fish out of water, and something instinctual told her that this position would aid in her delivery as well.

Aenwyn bore down on the pain lancing through her middle. She imagined herself opening to it. Working with it rather than against it. She felt herself tear as the babe's head breached air. Never before had she felt such excruciating agony, like she was being split open from the tender place between her legs.

She stopped pushing. Gathered more strength.

Panting, Aenwyn placed her hands between her thighs, and with one more impossible show of strength and resilience and sheer determination, she screamed and birthed her daughter into the realm.

The baby wasn't crying. Not at first. But there was also a web of mucous and viscera covering her mouth and nostrils.

Aenwyn wiped it all away. She cradled her newborn to her

chest, gently patting its back until a surprised cry finally burst from her tiny lungs.

"And another Daughter of Daybreak was born."

Aenwyn had almost forgotten about the dragon's presence until Fury had spoken. Aenwyn didn't like her cryptic tone. It reminded her too much of the dreamy, hazy quality that belonged to visions, memories, and fate.

"*Another?*" Aenwyn tried asking, but her voice was ragged and mauled by exhaustion.

"Here—" Distracting her from her climbing sense of dread, Darius handed Aenwyn a black piece of cloth. It was only once she had the babe fully wrapped inside it and was beaming up at Darius with a mixture of pride and awe that she realized he'd given her his cape.

"Thank you."

Exhaustion caught up with her and Aenwyn laid herself down on the ground.

The weight of the world was lifting from her shoulders. She'd done it. Dragon's fire, she had birthed a child—a child whom she didn't even know was in her belly until just a few hours ago.

And as strange as all of that was, Aenwyn couldn't bring herself to question it. To wonder or fear. Because the truth was that this baby couldn't have come at a better time. On the same night that had Aenwyn lost everything—her father figure, her sisters, her sense of autonomy—she had at least regained some semblance of family in her daughter. Never had she loved anyone more, nor would she ever again.

"She's beautiful," Darius said, and despite the girl's continued wailing, he sank down beside her. He cradled the two of them into his arms as if this was the most peaceful of moments he'd ever been a part of. In the last few months, she supposed it likely was. "What will you call her?"

Aenwyn snorted, but she could muster no smile, nor could

she tear her eyes away from her beautiful newborn child. "What makes you think I have any say in that?"

"You're her mother?" he said, voice twisted in confusion. "Why wouldn't you have a say?"

"Because I am also the queen, and she is the firstborn heir to the Caeloran throne." Dragging a thumb over the babe's head, Aenwyn noted the small patch of fuzz atop her crown, red just like her own. "King Everard will surely want to name her something of significance to the Caeloran people. Something I know nothing about. Maybe he'll name her after his great, great grandmother, or the first queen of Caelora."

Darius gave a derisive scoff. "As far as we know, he is not her father."

Taking her chin between his fingers, he tried lifting her face to look at him. But that statement alone had already done enough to summon her wide eyes and they pressed upon him in an instant.

Her heart fluttered with the thought that he might be right. Though she and the king had bed each other before her departure from Caelora, he wasn't the only man who's seed she had carried inside her.

The thought hadn't even crossed her mind that Darius might be the babe's father. Could it even be possible? They had only just had each other. Then again, she supposed anything could be possible considering she had only just become pregnant a few hours ago.

But it seemed that wasn't what Darius was saying either.

"Your child was given to you by a dragon—" he tried explaining. "Or by magic, or—I won't pretend to know. But I do know that *you* are her mother. You, and you alone, have earned the honor of naming her."

Warmth bloomed inside her. At the kindness he was showing her. At his helpfulness. And most of all, at the thought of having a daughter who was all her own. Not Skogar. Not Caeloran. Just a babe with her whole life ahead of her.

Aenwyn couldn't remember the last time she had felt so happy, so whole.

But it was all just a fleeting moment.

What she was envisioning was just wishful thinking. And she knew it.

Something bittersweet twisted her heart, and Aenwyn brought her gaze back to the squirming babe. Her daughter quieted almost instantly, as if all she ever needed was her mother's loving gaze and attention. She hoped it would always be that way. That her child would always know that her mother would be there to soothe her pains, no matter what they were.

As beautiful of a sentiment as it was to pretend like the girl was all hers, Aenwyn knew that King Everard would view things differently. Even if no one could prove him as the father, he already believed himself to be. And what King Everard believed true, became revered as the truth.

The girl in her arms would be heir to the Caeloran throne.

If Aenwyn allowed it.

If Aenwyn returned to Caelora.

But what was left for her there anyway? A king who made her miserable? A union forged through trickery and deceit? A lifetime of watching her child grow up under the cruel supervision of her unkind father?

Aenwyn owed Baug the Bear and King Everard nothing. And she'd rather be burned alive than ever return to the Caeloran throne, let alone see her daughter there.

She smiled down at the nameless babe. So new to the world. So unknowing of the dangers that lurked out there, waiting for her. But Aenwyn would be there to protect her from them all.

"I always thought I'd give my firstborn a Skogar name. But

now?" She brushed the top of her daughter's soft head and cradled her closer. "I think I will name her after my mother."

Darius nestled closer, his warmth a force of its own that kept Aenwyn grounded and all the more assured of her choices. "I don't think you've ever told me your mother's name."

"I haven't," she said. "No one who wasn't on this island has ever heard me utter her name."

"Why is that?" he asked, sincerity in his tone.

Aenwyn shrugged and tried not to disturb the babe from settling into slumber in her arms. "Because my people were superstitious. It was believed that if someone unknown to the dead in their life were to learn their name after their death, that they'd steal their soul, and destroy it. We were raised to believe a name was sacred and should be guarded from all. So after death, we protected it. Never spoke it aloud again, in case someone unknown could be listening."

Darius inched forward, a serious look about him. "You don't have to tell me, you know. You can keep her name for you and herself."

His dark eyes gleamed in the early dawn light that shifted over them, and Aenwyn felt compelled to kiss him. She would've if the realization hadn't struck her that she didn't know when daybreak had come, and daybreak, of course, reminded her of the dragon waiting quietly in their presence.

Aenwyn glared across the field and up to the dragon. She was surprised that flames didn't ignite in the wake of her gaze.

"What did you mean, *another Daughter of Daybreak was born?*"

Beside her, Darius' confusion only lasted a moment until he saw where her attention had gone.

Smoke filtered from Fury's nostrils. "That is who she is. That is who you are."

"But what does that mean?" Aenwyn demanded.

"What is she saying?" Darius whispered, but she had no choice but to ignore him. She'd have to fill him in later.

The dragon's neck twisted, its serpentine eyes searching for danger behind it. "We have run out of time, Aenwyn Red Fury. If you would like to name your daughter, now is your chance."

Aenwyn's heart flickered like a dying flame. "What?"

Frantic, she peered down upon the sweet babe, so peaceful in her arms.

But she heard it. The thundering of marching feet in metal boots.

King Everard's army was coming to slay the dragon.

"Go!" Aenwyn ushered, hoping that Fury understood the urgency in her tone.

But the dragon only turned her back to them, as if she was standing guard, protecting her.

"What are you doing? They'll kill you! You have to go!"

The dragon glanced over her shoulder, eyes flashing like molten gold. "If I go, they'll kill you and your knight. They'll take your child, and when she shows her first signs of magic, they'll kill her too."

Reflexively, Aenwyn drew her daughter nearer.

And though Darius couldn't understand the dragon's tongue, he must've sensed the danger as well, because he wrapped one arm around his queen and her newborn child and drew his sword with the other.

"But the seer—" Aenwyn tried to protest, but she was cut off by her own grimacing when Darius helped lift her to her unsteady feet.

"We have to go," he said. "They're close and I'm guessing your dragon friend is telling you the same thing. That is...if you want to go?"

Of course she did. She had never wanted anything more in her whole life. To go back to her former life now, to allow the king to capture her and her daughter and return them to Caelora against her will was unthinkable.

But she wanted more time with Fury. She wanted answers.

"But the seer said—" she tried again, calling over her shoulder to the dragon standing guard.

"Cursed sky, Aenwyn! I don't care about what the seer said. I don't care about the fate of the realm. I care about you and this little girl."

Aenwyn was aflame from head to toe. The kind of burning that reminded her what it was like to be alive. To be loved. To be seen and cherished. Not some pawn to be exchanged for power. Not some bride to be domesticated. He valued her. More than the entire sum of Grimtol.

Fury roared, a sound that rumbled in Aenwyn's core.

Darius nodded to the dragon, mistaking it for a show of agreement. But there had been no words in that cry. No agreement uttered.

That was a call for war.

They were coming. And Fury was sacrificing herself. For them.

Darius dragged Aenwyn away and she knew she shouldn't fight him. They had to go, if not for her, then for her daughter. But there was so much she wanted to know. So much left she had to say.

All of it was too much. All she could muster was a mournful, "Why?"

She resisted Darius' prodding for one moment, convincing him to stay while she awaited a simple answer. The dragon took her time, but finally looked back at her.

"Because the seer was blind to some possibilities. There is one spark of hope amidst all the darkness coming for Grimtol now. And that spark is your daughter. She cannot fail." The dragon paused, sadness pooling in her all-knowing gaze as if considering whether or not to share what else she knew. "Tell your knight to keep her safe, to hide her magic, for it will not be you who protects her for much longer."

Aenwyn's blood-streaked legs weakened and buckled where she stood.

Not who protects her for much longer...

The worst part was she believed her. She could feel it. Time slipping through her grasp like grains of sand.

Darius finally pulled her away to escape. But it wasn't long before pain pierced her again and they stumbled between the trees. Aenwyn fell to her knees. The baby, jarred by the fall but still tucked safely against her chest, woke with a precious cry.

Aenwyn wanted to rock her, but she could no longer take in air. The pain in her core felt like a lance spearing her center.

"Take her," she managed to force out through gritted teeth.

Darius followed her orders, despite the confusion and worry overcoming him.

A contraction, or something like it, twisted her insides and Aenwyn had no choice but to start pushing again. She knew there was no baby inside her though. Her belly was too small now—still larger than it had been, but far floppier than a belly with a babe inside.

She squeezed her stomach, both internally and externally, her shaking hands wanting to wrench the agony from inside her.

Something heavy, wet, and warm slipped between her legs.

Just like that, the pain was gone.

"The placenta," Darius said. Then, seeing the crinkle in her brow, he added, "My mother had three children after me. They brought me in after all of them were born."

No wonder he'd been so calm during all of this.

Chagrined, he dragged a hand through his medium-length hair. "I'd forgotten that part comes...after. Are you alright?"

Disbelieving, delirious laughter hiccuped from her throat.

Aenwyn had feared the worst. Fury's omen had haunted

her, made her think that her time had already come to an abrupt and tragic end. For that to not be true, Aenwyn would consider herself more than alright.

The question still remained though: when. How long did she truly have?

Aenwyn's legs were trembling, but she thought she could stand if she tried.

The clang of steel rang in the air as the king's army unsheathed their swords and launched into their attack. Darius and she had managed to get far enough into the woods that they couldn't be seen now, but they still needed to keep moving. She needed to stand up. So she did.

And just as she had righted herself, the sky cracked open with the fury of the dragon's roar.

The first blow had been delivered. Not that Aenwyn needed the roar to tell her that. She knew the moment it happened because she *felt* it. A sharp, piercing force that punctured her gut. Right where her contractions had been.

Only this was worse. Far worse.

At least that pain had been focused. It had stayed within one area.

This agony burned through her, first igniting her core before engulfing the rest of her abdomen, chest, and legs.

Aenwyn couldn't take it anymore. She doubled over again, knees crashing into the dirt once more.

"Aenwyn?" Darius rushed forward, and he was just in time to catch her arm before her face could plummet next. "What's happening?"

Another bolt of agony speared her thigh in time with Fury's mournful bellow.

She should've seen this coming. Fury and her both should've. Their fates had seemed to be intertwined since either of them were born, maybe before.

If King Everard and his men succeeded in slaying the dragon now, they would also kill Aenwyn.

The fallen queen brought her tearful gaze up to stare at the man holding her daughter. A man who had proven himself worthy of the role of protector just by his own loyalty and devotion to her alone. If it wasn't going to be her to raise the babe, then at least it would be him. She could think of no better person.

"You have to go." Her voice wavered, a sob threatening to wrench away her strength in her final moments. She wouldn't allow it. "Take her and get yourselves far away from here. Some place hidden, where no one will ever find you."

His head shook slowly, as if he had already pieced together the horrible truth himself. "I can get you both to safety."

Something else struck Fury, this time in the shoulder. Aenwyn gasped as her body was flung to the ground.

Panic warred on Darius' expression as he fell to the ground beside her. Frantic, he brushed the hair away from her face. Checked her eyes. Her pulse.

She was still alive, but she knew it wouldn't be for long.

"They're killing her," she managed, voice brittle and raw. "Killing me."

Understanding and dread widened his eyes. "No."

"Yes. You—" she winced at the pain consuming her like fire — "Please, for me. Take her and go. Keep her safe."

His rough hand cupped her cheek and she leaned into it, into the small comfort it could provide.

Now it was his voice that trembled. "I won't just leave you here for the slaughter." Dipping his chin, he tried to hide the sorrow drowning in his gaze. But it didn't matter. It pressed down upon him like a dark shadow. "I just went three months without you. I don't want to lose you again."

She placed her own hand upon his face. "You're not losing

me," she said, thumb brushing along his stubble. "You'll have a part of me now."

They both glanced to the resting babe in his arms, still sleeping despite all the commotion.

It wasn't the same. She knew that. More than most, she understood the sacrifice being forced upon all three of them.

A mother taken away far earlier than seemed fair.

A daughter forced to figure out the world without her mother's guidance.

And an unexpected parent suddenly thrown into a lifelong commitment of responsibility, protection, and love—not that she'd known this role for long.

None of this was what they wanted though. But it was the way things were playing out for them now.

"It's all my fault." Darius slammed his face onto Aenwyn's shoulder, face buried in her thick hair. "I shouldn't have brought them here—"

"Hush," she said, wrapping an arm around him tight. The other she used to brush the softness of her daughter's cheek. She didn't blame him. Wanted to tell him as much. But she knew there was nothing she could say to alleviate him from his guilt. And they didn't have the time anyway. "The dragon said they'd kill us all if they found us. Including her."

He drew back, disgust and horror evident in his expression.

The dragon's cries were growing weaker with each new piercing blaze that tore through Aenwyn.

Her own breaths were ragged now. Blood coated the back of her throat. Tears swelling in her eyes until she could no longer see through their bulging pools.

"Go. Keep her safe. Don't let them find her."

Darius nodded slowly, as if it took great effort for him to get his head to cooperate. After all, agreement meant leaving the love of his life—and Aenwyn knew that's what she was to him—to die.

His armor clattered as he raised a hand to his chest, careful not to bang it too hard, so as not to disturb the child who was still somehow asleep.

"The king and his men will never find her. No harm shall ever come to your daughter. This I vow to you, Aenwyn Red Fury, Queen of Caelora, Sole Survivor of the Lost Isle, I will protect her with my life."

Before the tears could stream any harder, Aenwyn nodded resolutely. "And her magic. Don't let them see her magic."

"How do you know she has—" he started to ask but stopped himself. They had run out of time, and it didn't matter how she knew, it was a request that he would carry out regardless.

Steadfast to reaffirm his commitment to uphold her wishes, Darius reached into his pocket and plucked something small and blue from it. A question in his eyes, he held up her engagement present, the ring from King Everard that had been her prison for all those months.

Darius wanted her permission.

Before today, she might have slapped him across the face for even suggesting it. But now? Now she'd do anything to keep her daughter safe.

Throat tight, Aenwyn nodded.

Darius put the ring back into his pouch for safe keeping.

Their eyes found each other, one last time. She heard every mournful word he couldn't utter, and she nodded because she felt the same way. About all of it. How she wanted more time. How it wasn't fair. How she had so much left to say to them both.

Darius pressed a lingering kiss upon her forehead. Aenwyn savored every inch of its warmth, every ounce of affection.

She leaned in and kissed the top of her daughter's head.

"Before I go," he said when she was finally able to break the contact. "What name shall I call her by?"

Aenwyn's laughter spluttered in the pool of blood that clogged her throat.

"Her name—my mother's name—is—"

The final blow struck Fury—and Aenwyn—in the throat.

This time, the pain was ice crackling in her veins. It was aching isolation and fear. The hollow darkness of death and the unknown.

Aenwyn tried blinking through it, tried speaking, but her vision blurred until there was nothing. And she was falling. Falling into the nothingness. Falling into despair. Fury's final agonizing roar echoing all around her.

And in that dark expanse, trapped between life and death, lurked the rage that, in her exhaustion, Aenwyn had forgotten she possessed.

Rage toward Baug the Bear for lying to her, all in the name of glory and power.

Rage toward Signe for ratting her out for her own selfish gains.

Rage toward King Everard for being such a pathetic, worthless husband who had taken not only the past year from her, but now her future with her daughter as well.

These were the rulers and future rulers of Grimtol, a continent that seemed destined to live out its days in greed and bloodshed. Unless someone stopped it.

Fury's bellow stopped and power surged through Aenwyn. Familiar and warm. Powerful and fierce.

They were bound. In this life and in death. Aenwyn, a part of Fury, and she a part of Aenwyn. Only now that connection was stronger.

Flames scorched Aenwyn's skin. Molten the blood coursing through her veins.

And her magic?

No longer did she need to call upon the Sky-Blessed to guide her because her magic had never been more potent. It pulsed throughout her entire being. The crackling darkness in her core breaking, power consuming her from the inside out like a cyclone of fury and flames.

She had never been stronger. Her rage, never wilder.

She was power.

And they would pay for what they had done.

They feared her magic and called her wicked. So she would turn them into monsters and make them fear themselves.

When Aenwyn screamed, every part of her body feeling as if it were shattering from her very core, black magic pulsed across the lands. Only then did darkness cradle her like a babe.

29

THE CURSED DAWN

DARIUS

When Darius saw the vibrant green of Aenwyn's eyes disappear to the back of her skull, he knew something was wrong. Dread as slick as lantern oil pooled in his belly. Of all the other times he'd seen her use her magic, he had never seen that happen before.

Danger was thick in the air, pressing down around him. He was already running away from her and the power building inside her by the time the blast of magic erupted. It smacked against his back, throwing him headfirst into a tree.

When Darius lifted his eyes open again, it was to a world painted in black.

Ashes rained down from the sky.

Laying on his back, vision blurred as he gazed up through the canopy of mangled branches, Darius wasn't sure where he was at first. A forest, of some sort, but one that seemed vastly different than the one he'd been racing through before.

There was no sound. No wind rustling the leaves—there were no more leaves to be rustled anyway. There were no signs of life. Except for him and...

A soft whimper broke him from his spell.

Turning his head toward the raspy cough, Darius found the baby resting atop the crook of his elbow. Soot and tears streaked her cheeks. No blood though. Her skin remained miraculously intact. Somehow, unlike the rest of the forest, she and Darius had not been brutally destroyed.

Not physically anyway. There were no words, however, for the torture strangling his chest, his throat. Although Aenwyn had still been alive before the blast, he knew she would be gone now. Her last-ditch effort to save them, maybe?

He couldn't think about it. Not now. For he had made a vow and he intended on keeping it.

Rolling over, Darius picked the baby up and stood. He cradled her against his chest as he glanced at the decimation around them.

"Aenwyn?" he called tentatively, though he already knew he would find no answer. If the power that had burst from her had caused this kind of destruction, it was not difficult to imagine what it might've done to her own body.

Hope drove him to spin around anyway, searching the area for any signs of his strong queen. A strand of her vibrant, red hair. A glimpse of her cheerful freckles. The scent of her. The feel of her. Anything.

But there was nothing but cursed landscape. Not even her body could be found, and that was perhaps most unsettling of all.

"Aenwyn!"

The baby's soft cries broke into distraught sobs. Darius did what he could to soothe the newborn, rocking and hushing her as he had done with his siblings when he was younger, but he knew it would be of little effect when what she really wanted was the comfort of her mother, and something to curb her growing hunger. Neither of which he could help with.

He needed to find her mother.

He needed to get her nourishment.

He needed to figure out what in the Hollows had happened to this cursed island, and how they were getting off it.

Fortunately, he knew of one way to address all three of his needs.

Shifting the babe to one arm, Darius swung the satchel from around his back and retrieved the wishing goblet from inside. It had been a parting gift when he'd left the Sultana's. She had been wise enough to suggest its usefulness and he hadn't been prepared to turn it down, not after having witnessed Aenwyn vanish from thin air before him. He thought he might need it, though not like this.

He had meant to tell Aenwyn about it. The moment they found each other, he had meant to tell her everything.

But their moments together had been so fleeting, and the number of important things they had needed to discuss so numerous and pressing.

He hoped, at least, that the goblet would serve him now.

Remembering the creek they had passed, Darius retraced his steps until they were at its bank.

There wasn't much left of the once-burbling waters now. Almost all of them had evaporated, swallowed up by the singing charge of the blast.

But there was still a small trickle amid some of the rocks. It would be enough. All he needed was a drop.

Darius thrust his hand into the spring and wondered if it was heated because of Aenwyn's magic, or something else.

When the goblet was full enough for a sip, Darius brought it to his lips, but paused.

Aenwyn's daughter continued to sob in his arms, and he wondered what would happen to her once he drank from the chalice. Would he disappear as Aenwyn had? If so, what would happen to the baby? Would she fall to the ground? Would she disappear with him? He couldn't risk setting her down on the off chance that he'd be gone as long as Aenwyn had been.

Her daughter would die if she was left that long.

He wouldn't allow it. No harm would ever befall her. Not as long as he was around. That was his vow.

Instead, Darius sat cross-legged on the ground to create a cradle for the baby in his lap. Once she was nestled between his legs, he finally took his drink.

The instant the liquid slid across his tongue, Darius was knocked back again. Once all of this was over, he was thoroughly done being knocked on his arse by magical forces.

He tried opening his eyes but was blinded by a colorless opaqueness that just kept brightening and brightening. He tried sitting up, but he couldn't figure out which way that was. His head and feet felt like they were being pulled in opposite directions, his body spinning in an endless loop of emptiness.

Somehow, he managed to right himself, and as his eyes grew accustomed to the brightness, he discovered that his legs were still crossed, the babe squirming fitfully inside his lap. Once more he took her into his arms and shielded her from the light, a profound sense of duty and protectiveness urging him. She was all he had of Aenwyn now.

"Well, well, if it isn't the knight." The voice came from all directions.

When Darius' neck tired of whipping around in search of the source, he finally shouted into the bright void, "I came for my three wishes."

"Then three wishes I shall grant you, in exchange for—"

"My fertility. Yes. Fine. You can have it."

Suddenly, the voice hissed. At first, he thought he'd said the wrong thing and angered the creature, but then he felt it racing toward them, felt it halt just before slamming his back. Its perfumed breath smothered the air as it twisted around him. It seemed like it was getting a better look. Not at him though.

"This child should not be here," the being whispered, her silky voice a touch reverent. "She was already bargained with."

A fierce kind of anger rippled through him. Something primal and instinctual and protecting.

Darius shielded the baby away from the being. "You will not touch her. She is not my child and therefore has no part in our bargain."

"Not *our* bargain," the being said, and Darius swore he could hear her roll her eyes. But that irritation quickly turned to curiosity. Here was an ancient being, bored because she had seen everything in her time. Everything, but this apparently. "She is not part of any bargain. She was not meant to exist."

He didn't know what that meant exactly. But he also didn't care. The girl was with him now. That's what mattered.

Darius shook his head, trying to stay focused. "No harm will come to her by me being here. Are we agreed?"

The voice slithered around him like a coiling snake. "You know the price for being here, do you not?"

Oh, he remembered alright. The steep price for three wishes was not so easily forgotten. Wishes in exchange for fertility. Children.

But then Darius remembered something that Hissa had said about Aenwyn's sisters, how the bargain would impact them as well, even though they were not family by blood.

With dread, he realized what the being was saying.

"She is not my daughter. You have no right to—"

"Perhaps not by blood. But look at how you protect her. Just as a father would his own daughter."

Darius' knuckles were going white where he gripped the babe, and he had to push his ire back just to prevent himself from hurting the poor thing. Dragon's fire, he wasn't fit to parent a child. He had barely been able to care for himself. And now here he was, almost injuring her already.

A vow was a vow though. There would be time to worry about inadequacies later, he supposed.

"I am a knight," Darius replied, mustering courage and

confidence from some place he didn't even know existed. "I vowed to protect an innocent who needed protection. It is no different than when I said my oath to the Caeloran kingdom."

The voice considered him a moment. He swore he felt her brush up against his chest and pause there a moment, listening. It made a chill run down his spine. He wasn't used to not being able to see his enemy.

The feminine voice sounded disappointed as she backed away. "Perhaps your heart has not decided to love her yet, so this time she will not be bargained. But you will not be able to create your own."

"I know."

She sighed, giving him the impression of a cat lazing out in the sun. "Then make your requests of me so that I may return to my peace."

Darius didn't need to think it over. He already knew exactly what he would ask.

"I wish to know where the baby's mother is."

"She is gone," the being hissed, and his heart plummeted so hard Darius thought it would buckle him at the knees until she added— "For now."

He sucked in a sharp breath like steel slicing his lungs. *"For now?"*

"Next wish."

He didn't want to test her impatience, nor waste what precious resources he had. He could accept *for now*. *For now* meant hope. *For now* meant that he could maybe be reunited with Aenwyn again, in time.

Until then, he would uphold his vow. And he would use his remaining wishes to aid him in doing so.

"I wish for something that will feed the baby."

The being didn't answer him with words, but a goat's bleat carried around them and Darius understood.

"She will be with you when you return to your land," she

purred. "And for your final wish?"

Now, this one made him pause.

In the time since he arrived in whatever this place was, Darius had realized something that changed everything. He had come here ready to ask for a way off the island, for he was no longer sure he would have safe passage otherwise.

But once he had drunk from that goblet, something else struck him.

It shattered his heart to even think it.

Darius realized that Aenwyn never got to tell him her daughter's name.

He wanted so badly now to ask this being to tell him. He knew it would be a worthy request. A way to give the child a small part of her mother until they could all be reunited again.

But after seeing the state of the island, with everything scorched, drained, and obliterated, Darius doubted the two of them would be able to survive there on their own. Not even with a goat at their side.

They couldn't go back to Caelora.

He didn't think they would be able to go to Rayong either; it would be among the first places the king would go searching for him. And he wouldn't want to implicate Carmen and Emile anyways. They were already on King Everard's bad side.

He could think of only one ally, only one wish to make. And it broke his heart to do it.

"Take us to the Great City of Vallonde, to the Sultana Hissa's palace."

There was a sneer in her tone when she replied, "You ask for more and give less than what I would normally consider a fair exchange."

He didn't know what to say to that. And so he said nothing and let the being judge for herself whether she was willing to make the trade.

She was unnervingly silent. Darius didn't trust it. Every

warrior instinct that had been trained into him screamed at his muscles to be ready to strike.

But then her lulling voice crept up on him, a whisper caressing him like a warm summer breeze to say, "However, I admit that I would like to see where this child's destiny will take her. I will grant you your wishes, Ser Darius Graeme. Protect her well."

Thank you for reading
A Delicate Betrayal!

To be continued in:

A Reign of Ashes
Book 1 of The Cursed Kingdoms of Grimtol

PREORDER NOW:
https://amazon.com/author/jessacawillis

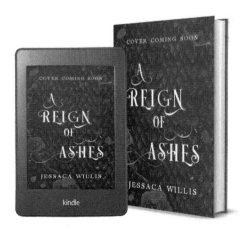

Leave a Review

Help other readers find this dark saga by leaving a review on Amazon, Goodreads, Bookbub, or any other reading website. Even a simple "I loved it!" can really help!

ARC Team

If you're someone who loves leaving reviews and you're excited by the idea of having early access to all of my books, check out my website for more information on how to join my ARC Team: www.jessacawillis.com/ARC

Social Media

And last but not least, if you'd like to stay connected, you can find my social media links here: https://linktr.ee/jessaca_with_an_a

PRIMORDIALS OF SHADOWTHORN
Epic Dark Fantasy Romance

Ruled by tyrants. Hunted by demons.
This vengeful huntress is ready to fight back.

When Halira's parents are slaughtered by the horrifying demons that plague her lands, she joins the Shadow Crusade, a legion of warriors determined to slay the last living Primordial, end its reign of darkness, and destroy demon-kind once and for all.

But as her training begins, Halira soon discovers a secret about the forgotten magic that once thrived throughout the lands, one that could threaten her very survival.

Will Halira be the savior her country needs, or will her own dark secret force her to hide in the shadows?

*Check out the Primordials of Shadowthorn series—the prelude to
Blood & Magic Eternal—on Amazon*

REAPERS OF VELTUUR
YA Epic Dark Fantasy

*In a realm where murderers are taken by
the Councilspirits and forced into becoming Reapers,
one girl is on a path to redemption...*

Sinisa is a Reaper of Veltuur, an assassin born from the underrealm, with fatal magic coursing through their veins.

For three years, she's slain her targets dutifully. Now she just needs one more kill to ascend as a Shade, a coveted status of power. And when the King of Oakfall requests a Reaper to execute his daughter for an unforgivable crime, Sinisa is first to volunteer for the job.

It *should* be easy.

But when the Prince discovers his sister is in danger, he flees the palace with her, leaving Sinisa with only two options: journey through the mortal realm to find and slay her mark, or face the consequences of returning to the underrealm empty-handed.

It's no choice at all. She has come too far to stop now.

Besides, no one can outrun a Reaper... Or can they?

~Check out the Reapers of Veltuur Trilogy on Amazon~

THE AWAKENED SERIES
NA/YA Supernatural Apocalyptic

Supernatural powers destroyed the world...
Now four unlikely heroes have to save it.

The world ended two years ago. They called it the Awakening: the supernatural event that gave some people powers and left others normal. Nations went to war and millions died.

Sean was one of the first to Awaken, but it wasn't until he walked in on his brother's brutal murder that he learned of the darker nature of his power: blood calls to him, and he to it. And in that moment, he showed his brother's murderers no mercy.

Now Sean must fight to keep his inner demons in check, and his path to redemption begins with the establishment of a sanctuary for people like him, people with powers: the Awakened.

But not even in the apocalypse are the Awakened safe...

Can Sean and three strangers unite the remnants of mankind when everything else has fallen apart? Can they face the darkest horror this new world has yet to offer?

~Check out The Awakened Quadrilogy on Amazon~

NOTE FROM THE AUTHOR

When I became a mom, I had no idea just how much it would change me (cliché, I know). But more surprisingly, I had no idea how much it would shed light onto the healing I still had left to do.

To be transparent, I've been numb and disconnected from my work since I started writing *Fate of the Vulture* in June of 2020. The female characters I've written since—Sinisa of that same series, Halira from *Shadow Crusade*, and Charlotte from *Blood & Magic Eternal*—they were all strong women who I admired immensely, but I couldn't relate to them. They overcame every challenge they faced. By the end of all of their storylines, they'd found their place in the dark worlds they inhabited, and they'd surrounded themselves with strong, loyal chosen families.

As much as I strive for strength, belonging, and family, it is a constant battle for me, one that I often feel myself losing.

I wanted Aenwyn's story to be different.

I wanted to write a female main character who was strong, yes, but one who was also irreparably damaged and still searching for her place in this world, her sense of belonging.

One who would sacrifice everything for her chosen family even when they wouldn't do the same. One who remained dissatisfied and unfulfilled, even as she came face-to-face with the destiny she thought she'd been chasing.

I decided to write Aenwyn in a way that showed just how cruel the world could be. How sometimes it can abuse our greatest hopes and dreams, only to deepen our wells of fear.

And I realize that is not the story that everyone wants to read—it can be extremely disheartening when you pick up a book to escape, but instead, find the misery of your world reflected back at you.

But I felt like I *needed* to tell this story. I needed Aenwyn. And I can pretend I did it for all the other women out there who might've felt similar to her—who might've lost children, lost family, found themselves in loveless and manipulative relationships, and felt the world falling into darkness around them —but truthfully, I wrote her for me. I wrote so much of *A Delicate Betrayal* for myself and my healing.

It was how I worked through recovering from a toxic, narcissistic relationship that had done far more damage to my confidence and sanity than I ever realized until I was out of it.

It was an ode to my own journey into motherhood, a grieving process of my own miscarriages and feared infertility; the shock of becoming pregnant and trauma of birthing my child; the utter joy and fulfillment I found in the role of motherhood, only to then have to come to terms with the idea of not being involved in his life full-time, as his father and I now share joint custody.

It was my way of working through the disappointment of always feeling like I'm not where I'm meant to be, not doing enough, not good enough, and always feeling like there was something waiting for me on the horizon, just out of reach.

And it was also how I rekindled my passion for writing and helped me rediscover a part of myself that I worried had died a while ago. It turns out, my love of storytelling, of creating these flawed characters and watching them transform, of building these worlds full of magic and hardship and beauty—all of it was still in me somewhere. It just took a couple of years of self-work and spiritual healing to unbury it.

And so, although I did write this story for me and found it cathartic in so many ways, I truly do hope that you found something in it that spoke to you as well. Something that made you feel seen or reminded you that you're not all alone. Because sometimes, when we've hit rock bottom, we discover just how strong, resilient, and worthy we are.

Thank you for being here. And thank you for reading *A Delicate Betrayal.*

Here seems as good of a time as any to acknowledge the many other individuals who played an instrumental role in helping bring this book to life:

My Platypi writing coven: Erica, Dani, Colby, Chani, Dee, Tiff, & Cass. So many of these pages wouldn't have been written without you cheering me on from the sidelines, or accompanying me on late-night writing sprints—I'm talking to you Dani & Erica! I am so very grateful that our paths crossed, and I cherish every moment we spend together.

A heartfelt thank you to Fay Lane and the work she did for me on this cover. When I realized I needed to change our original one—and include dragons because…this is, after all, a dragon book—she didn't hesitate to make it happen. Fay, I couldn't be happier with the way it turned out!

To my editors and critique partners Kate, Colby, and Dani. Even when I was groaning about the chore of editing to incorporate your feedback, please know that I appreciated your insight. You made this book better than I could've imagined, and I am eternally grateful.

A special appreciation has to also go to my son, Kieran, who even at the young age of four is already teaching me so much about the art of storytelling. He tells me harrowing adventures of monsters stalking the innocent, of superheroes saving the day, and I am always awed by his ability to captivate and entice. I look forward to continuing to listen to and tell stories with you as you grow up.

And last but not least, thank you to all of my readers. I treasure every email, every chat message, and every Christmas card you send my way. Your kindness and support is appreciated and means more to me than you'll ever know.

Thank you all for being on this journey with me. Here is to ten more novels.

ABOUT THE AUTHOR

Jessaca is a fantasy writer with an inclination toward the dark, epic, and romantic sub-genres. She draws inspiration from books like Nevernight & ACOTAR, videogames like Dark Souls III, and television shows like Game of Thrones and The Witcher. She is a self-proclaimed nerd who loves cosplay, video games, and comics, and if you live in the PNW, you just might see her at one of the local comic conventions dressed in one of her favorite RWBY cosplays!

Made in the USA
Las Vegas, NV
19 December 2022